Two sizzling,
stories. An
bestselling au
the first nove
stars, Maisey Yates!

POSSESSION

"Lynne Graham gives readers an exciting
reading experience filled with explosive
tension and a strong emotional premise."
—*RT Book Reviews*

"Yates' smooth dialogue and clever
narrative will pull readers in. These
delightfully spirited, vulnerable characters
will feel like friends by the story's end."
—*RT Book Reviews* on *The Petrov Proposal*

Hand in Hand Collection

May 2012

June 2012

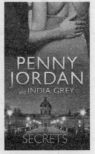

July 2012

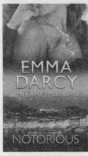

August 2012

September 2012

October 2012

LYNNE GRAHAM

and MAISEY YATES

POSSESSION

MILLS & BOON

Mills & Boon, an imprint of Harlequin (UK) Limited,
Eton House, 18-24 Paradise Road, Richmond, Surrey TW9 1SR

POSSESSION © Harlequin Enterprises II B.V./S.à.r.l. 2012

The Greek Tycoon's Blackmailed Mistress © Lynne Graham 2009
His Virgin Acquisition © Maisey Yates 2010

ISBN: 978 0 263 90182 5

010-0912

Harlequin (UK) policy is to use papers that are natural, renewable and recyclable products and made from wood grown in sustainable forests. The logging and manufacturing processes conform to the legal environmental regulations of the country of origin.

Printed and bound in Spain
by Blackprint CPI, Barcelona

THE GREEK TYCOON'S
BLACKMAILED MISTRESS

LYNNE GRAHAM

Lynne Graham was born in Northern Ireland and has been a keen Mills & Boon® reader since her teens. She is very happily married, with an understanding husband who has learned to cook since she started to write! Her five children keep her on her toes. She has a very large dog, which knocks everything over, a very small terrier, which barks a lot, and two cats. When time allows, Lynne is a keen gardener.

Dear Reader,

Like many of you, I look forward every month to receiving my delivery of Modern™ romance from Mills & Boon's subscription service. I know that in my parcel I'll find books by authors whose work I've long admired and always look out for, and it's also nice to discover stories by new writers.

One author who caught my eye when she debuted in 2010 is Maisey Yates. Her biography in the front pages appealed to me: she's an energetic young mum with three small children who has been writing for herself since childhood. When she discovered a Modern romance in a charity shop book box, she was hooked and realised what she'd been born to do. That drive, intensity and passion is very apparent in her stories and characters, which draw you right in and carry you along at a rate of knots.

So I am delighted that my novel *The Greek Tycoon's Blackmailed Mistress* has been paired with Maisey's first ever book, *His Virgin Acquisition,* in this special edition. I hope you'll enjoy as much as I did the tale of brave Elaine who takes a huge leap in the dark when she proposes a marriage of convenience to gorgeous playboy tycoon Marco de Luca in order to keep her share in her family's company, forgetting to explain that she's totally inexperienced in the ways of love and relationships...

With warm regards,

Lynne Graham

PROLOGUE

'AN ENCHANTING child,' Drakon Xenakis remarked as he stood at a window, watching the little girl playing in the lush gardens of his grandson's villa. 'She reminds me of someone. I can't think who…'

Aristandros veiled his brilliant dark eyes, his lean, darkly handsome face unrevealing. He said nothing, although he had made a genetic connection at first glance. In his opinion it was impossible not to: that blonde hair, so pale that it was somewhere between white and silver, and those hyacinth-blue eyes and pouting pink mouth were like miniature identity-tags. Yes, fate had placed an immensely potent weapon in his hands and he would have no qualms about using it to get what he wanted. Aristandros always kept his conscience well under wraps. Neither failure nor consolation prizes were acceptable to him. Without a doubt he would triumph—and winning most often meant breaking the rules.

'But little girls need mothers,' Drakon continued, his proud carriage impressively upright in spite of his eighty-two years. 'And you specialise in—'

'Beautiful models,' Aristandros slotted in swiftly, conscious that the older man was likely to take a moralistic viewpoint and employ a more judgemental term for the women who entertained his grandson in the bedroom. 'Timon, however, left me his daughter to raise, and I have every intention of meeting that challenge.'

'Timon was a childhood playmate and a cousin, not your brother,' his grandfather countered in a troubled voice. 'Are you willing to give up the strings of gorgeous women and the endless parties for the sake of a child who isn't your own?'

'I have a large, well-trained and reliable staff. I don't think Calliope's impact on my life will be that catastrophic.' Aristandros had never sacrificed anything for anyone, nor could he imagine doing so. But, even if he did not agree with his grandfather's views, he respected him and he would allow the older man to have his say.

In any case, few men had more right to talk frankly on the score of family responsibility than Drakon Xenakis. The family name had long been synonymous with dysfunction and explosive scandals. Drakon blamed himself that all his children had messed up spectacularly as adults with their car-crash marriages, addictions and affairs. Aristandros's father had proved the worst offender of all, and his mother, the heiress daughter of another shipping family, had matched her husband in her appetite for self-indulgence and irresponsibility.

'If you think that, you're underestimating the responsibility you're taking on. A child who has already lost both parents will need a lot of your attention to feel secure. You're a workaholic, just as I was, Aristandros. We're brilliant at making money, but we're not good parents,' Drakon pronounced, his concern patent. 'You need to find a wife willing to be Callie's mother.'

'Marriage really isn't my style,' Aristandros countered coolly.

'The incident you are referring to took place when you were twenty-five years old,' Drakon dared to remark, watching the younger man's bronzed features shutter and chill at that less-than-tactful reminder.

Aristandros shrugged a broad shoulder. 'It was merely a brief infatuation from which I soon recovered.'

Aristandros was, however, pierced by a familiar tide of bitter anger. *Ella*. He only had to think her name to feel that anger. Seven years ago, he had put a price on the head of the one woman he'd wanted, and the one woman he still couldn't forget. He had sworn then that, one day, he would take revenge for what she had done to him. The engagement that never was—an unthinkable rejection. Yet, in some ways, hadn't Ella done him a favour? The early unanticipated disappointment and the sense of humiliation which she'd inflicted had ensured that Ari had never dropped his guard with a woman again. Instead he had concentrated on enjoying the fruits of his fabulous wealth while he'd steadily grown tougher, harder and more ambitious.

His meteoric success had made him a billionaire and the focus of much fear and envy in the business world. Drakon's plain speaking was a rare experience for Aristandros, whose aggressive instincts had brought him astonishing ascendancy and influence over others. Soon Ella too would have to make a bonfire of all her fine, noble principles and prejudices and dance to his chosen tune. He was looking forward to it. Indeed, he could hardly wait for the moment when she realised that he had what she most wanted. That first taste of revenge promised to be sweeter than heavenly ambrosia.

CHAPTER ONE

ELLA sat as still as a statue in the smart waiting area.

Locked deep in her stressful thoughts, she didn't notice the admiring glances she received from the men walking past. In any case, she was accustomed to screening out the unwelcome notice that her physical beauty attracted. Her white-blonde hair, that rare shade most often seen only on children, turned heads as much as her bright blue eyes and slender, shapely figure. Her hands were tightly laced together on her lap, betraying her tension.

'Dr Smithson?' the receptionist said. 'Mr Barnes would like you to go in now.'

Ella got up. Beneath her outward show of calm, a burning sense of injustice was churning in her stomach. Her prayers had gone unanswered and common sense was still being ignored. She could only marvel that her own flesh and blood could have placed her in such a cruel position. When would enough be enough? When would her family decide that she had paid a steep enough price for the decision she had made seven years earlier? She was beginning to think that only her death would settle that outstanding account.

Mr Barnes, the lawyer she had first consulted two weeks earlier—a tall, thin man in his forties reputed to be at the very top of the tree when it came to complex child-custody issues—shook hands with her and invited her to take a seat.

'I've taken advice from the specialists in this area of the law, and I'm afraid I can't give you the answer that you want,' he told her with precision. 'When you donated eggs to your sister to enable her to have a child, you signed a contract in which you relinquished all claim to parental rights over any baby born subsequently—'

'Yes, I accept that, but as my sister and her husband are now dead surely the situation has changed?' Ella broke in with the urgency she was trying hard to keep under control.

'But not necessarily in your favour,' Simon Barnes responded wryly. 'As I mentioned before, the woman who carries the baby to birth is deemed to be its legal mother. So, although you are a biological parent, you cannot claim to be the child's mother. Furthermore, you have had no contact at all with the little girl since she was born, which doesn't help your case.'

'I know.' Ella was pale with strain and a curious feeling of shame, for she still found it hard to handle the fact that her sister, Susie, had pretty much cut her out of her life as soon as her infant daughter had entered the world. Ella had not even been allowed a photo, never mind a visit and a face-to-face encounter. 'But I'm still legally Callie's aunt.'

'Yes, but the fact that you were not named as a guardian in your sister and brother-in-law's wills does harm your case,' the lawyer reminded her tautly. 'Their solicitor will testify that the only party Callie's late parents were prepared to nominate was Aristandros Xenakis. Don't forget that he too has a blood tie with the child—'

'For goodness' sake, Aristandros was only her father's cousin, not an uncle or anything!' Ella proclaimed with helpless heat.

'A cousin and lifelong friend, who putatively accepted responsibility for the child in writing well before the accident that killed your sister and her husband. I need hardly add that you cannot reasonably hope to fight his claim to custody. He is an extremely wealthy and powerful man. The child is also a Greek citizen, as is he.'

'But he's also a single man with an appalling reputation as a hellraiser!' Ella protested fiercely. 'Scarcely an ideal father-figure for a little girl!'

'You are in dangerous territory with that argument, Dr Smithson. You too are single, and any court would question why your own family are not prepared to back you in your claim.'

Ella reddened at the humbling reminder that she stood alone and unsupported. 'I'm afraid that my relatives will not take a single step that might risk offending Aristandros Xenakis. My stepfather and my two half-brothers rely on his connections to do business.'

The lawyer released his breath in a slow hiss of finality. 'My advice is to accept that the law is unlikely to get you any closer to seeing the child, and that any attempt to challenge her current custodial arrangements will destroy any goodwill you might hope to create.'

Tears were burning like drops of fire behind Ella's

unflinching gaze as she fought to retain her self-discipline in the face of that bad news. 'You're telling me that there's *nothing* I can do?'

'I believe that the wisest move in your circumstances would be to make a personal approach to Aristandros Xenakis. Explain the situation and, on that basis, ask him if he will allow you to have contact with the child,' Simon Barnes advised ruefully.

Ella shivered at that piece of advice; it was like a sudden, bitingly cold wind blowing against her bare, shrinking flesh. Aristandros had Callie. Aristandros, who despised Ella. What possible hope did she have of gaining a sympathetic hearing from him?

'Some day you will pay for this,' Aristandros had sworn seven years earlier when she was only twenty-one and in the middle of her medical studies.

'Don't take it that way,' she had begged him painfully. 'Try to understand.'

'No. *You* understand what you have done to me,' Aristandros had urged, diamond-bright dark eyes hard as granite and cold as winter ice. 'I treated you with honour and respect. And in return you have insulted and embarrassed me and my family.'

Gooseflesh pebbling her skin beneath her clothes, Ella left the solicitor's office and headed home to the spacious loft apartment she had purchased jointly with her friend, Lily. The other woman, who was training as a surgeon, was still at work when she got back. Ella and Lily had met at medical school and had been friends ever since, initially pooling and sharing resources, like the apartment and a car, while offering each other support during stressful times.

In common with many young doctors, Ella worked long hours and had little energy left with which to stamp her own personality on her surroundings. She had still not got round to choosing a colour scheme for her bedroom. A pile of books by the bed and a piano in one corner of the airy living-area testified to how she liked to spend her free time.

Before she could lose her nerve, she rang the UK headquarters of Xenakis Shipping to request an appointment with Aristandros. A member of his staff promised to call her back, and she knew she would be checked out since she was not a business client. She wondered if he would even agree to see her. Maybe out of curiosity? Her tummy flipped at the prospect of seeing him again.

She could hardly remember the girl she had been seven years earlier when she'd broken her heart over Aristandros Xenakis. Young, inexperienced and naïve, she had been much more vulnerable than she had appreciated. Her strong sense of self-belief had ensured that she'd stood up for what she believed in, but living with that decision had proved much more difficult than she had expected. Moreover, she had not met another man, as she had dimly assumed she would back then. She had recently begun to believe that she would never meet anyone she wanted to marry.

Was that another reason why she had agreed to donate eggs to her infertile sister? Susie, two years her senior, had suffered a premature menopause in her twenties, and her only hope of motherhood had been through donated eggs. Susie had flown over from Greece to London where Ella had been working as a junior doctor in a busy A&E department to ask for her sibling's help.

Ella had been touched when Susie had approached her with her request. In truth, prior to that meeting, Susie had been as distant and critical of her outcast sister as the rest of the family. It had felt good to be needed, even better to be told that a baby born from her eggs would be much more precious to Susie than a baby born with the help of an anonymous donor. Of course, there had also been the greater likelihood of the child inheriting a closer physical resemblance to Susie through the use of her sibling's eggs.

Ella had not hesitated to agree to her sister's appeal. It would have been unimaginable for her to refuse. Susie had married Ari's cousin, Timon, and they'd had a good marriage. Ella had believed that a child born to the young couple would enjoy a happy, secure life. While Ella had undergone the screening tests and treatment for egg donation, she had also attended counselling and signed an agreement to make no future claim on any child born.

'You're not thinking this through,' Lily had argued at the time. 'This process is not as straightforward as you seem to think it is. What about the emotional repercussions? How will you feel when a child is actually born? You'll be the biological mother but you'll have no rights at all over the child. Will you envy your sister— feel that her child is more yours?'

Ella had refused to accept that there could be anything other than a positive outcome to the gift of her eggs. While she'd been undergoing the donation process, Susie had often talked about what a wonderful aunt Ella would be for her child. But, shockingly, Susie had rejected Ella from the day that Callie was born.

Indeed she had phoned Ella to ask her *not* to visit her in hospital, while also demanding that Ella leave her and her new family alone.

Ella had been horribly hurt, but she had tried to understand that Susie had felt threatened by her sibling's genetic input to her newborn baby. She had written to her sister in an effort to reassure her, but her letters had gone unacknowledged. In despair at the rift that had opened up, she had gone to see Timon when he was in London on business. Timon had admitted ruefully that his wife was eaten up with insecurity over Ella's role in the conception of their daughter. Ella had prayed that the passage of time would soothe Susie's concerns but, seventeen months after Callie's birth, Timon and Susie had died in a horrific car crash. And, as a final footnote, the young couple had been dead almost two weeks before anyone had thought to let Ella know, so that she hadn't even got to attend the funeral.

When Ella had finally found out that her only sister was dead, she'd felt terrifyingly alone—and not for the first time in recent years. Her father had died shortly after she was born, so she had never known him, and Jane, her mother, had married Theo Sardelos six years later. Ella had never got on with her stepfather, who was a Greek businessman. Theo liked women to be seen rather than heard, and he had turned his back on Ella in angry disgust when she'd refused to marry Aristandros Xenakis. The emotionally fragile Jane had never been known to oppose her dictatorial husband, so there had been no point appealing to her for support. Ella's twin half-brothers had sided with their father, and Susie had refused to get involved.

Ella sat down at the piano and lifted the lid. She often took refuge in music when she was at the mercy of her emotions, and had just embarked on playing an *étude* by Liszt when the phone rang. She got up to answer the call and froze in the middle of the room once she realised that she was talking to a member of Aristandros's personal staff. She made no attempt to protest when she was asked to travel to Southampton the following week to meet him on board his new yacht, *Hellenic Lady*; she was simply overwhelmingly relieved that he was actually willing to see her.

Yet Ella could not imagine seeing Aristandros Xenakis again, and when Lily returned from work her friend was quick to tackle her once she realised what she was planning to do.

'What is the point of you upsetting yourself like this?' Lily asked bluntly, her vivacious face unusually serious beneath her curly brown hair

'I would just like to see Callie,' Ella breathed tightly.

'Stop lying to yourself. You want much more than that. You want to be her parent, and what are your chances of Aristandros Xenakis agreeing to that?'

A stony expression stamped Ella's delicate features. 'Well, why not? How is he planning to continue partying with a baby of eighteen months?'

'He'll just pay people to look after her. He's as rich as that fabled king who touched things and turned them to solid gold,' Lily reminded her doggedly. 'And the first thing he's likely to ask you is what has *his* business to do with you?'

Ella paled; a streak of determined optimism had persuaded her to overlook certain realities, like Ari's hardline attitudes and probable hostility towards her. 'Someone needs to look out for Callie's interests.'

'Who had more right than her parents? But you're questioning their decision that the child should go to him. Sorry, I'm playing devil's advocate here,' Lily explained ruefully.

'Susie was hopelessly impressed by the Xenakis wealth,' Ella confided. 'But money shouldn't be the only bottom line when it comes to bringing up a child.'

'It's the size of a cruise ship!' Ella's taxi driver exclaimed while he leant out at his vehicle's window to scan the immense, sleek length and the towering decks of the white mega-yacht *Hellenic Lady*.

'Absolutely huge,' Ella agreed breathlessly, paying him and climbing out on to the quay. She smoothed damp palms down over the trousers of the elegant brown trouser-suit which she usually wore for interviews.

A young man in a smart suit advanced on her. 'Dr Smithson?' he queried, a good deal of curiosity in his measuring gaze. 'I'm Philip. I work for Mr Xenakis. Please, come this way.'

Philip was as informative as a travel rep escorting tourists. *Hellenic Lady*, he told her, was brand-new, built in Germany to Aristandros's exact specifications and about to make her maiden voyage to the Caribbean. As they boarded, various members of the crew greeted them. Philip ushered her into a lift while telling her about the on-board submarine and helicopters. Ella remained defiantly unimpressed until the doors slid back on the upstairs lounge, and her jaw almost dropped at the space, the opulence and the breathtaking panoramic views through the windows.

'Mr Xenakis will be with you in a few minutes,' Philip informed her, ushering her out onto a shaded upper deck furnished with beautifully upholstered seats.

At that announcement, Ella's rigid tension eased a little and she took a seat. A steward offered her refreshment and she asked for a cup of tea, because she thought that if she had something to occupy her hands she would be less likely to fidget. Her mind was rebellious, throwing up sudden memories of the most unwelcome kind. Just then, the last thing she wanted to recall was falling head over heels in love with Aristandros when she'd first met him. She had spent Christmas in Greece with her mother and stepfather, and in the space of one frantic month had lost her heart.

But was that so surprising? she asked herself now, striving to divest that event of any dangerous mystique. After all, Aristandros had it all: spectacular good looks, keen intelligence and all the trappings of wealth. And, in a nutshell, Ella had long been a swot, hunched over her books, while other girls had enjoyed a social life and experienced the highs and lows of consorting with the opposite sex. For the space of a month Ella had thrown her good sense out at the window and had just lived for the sound of Ari's voice, and every heart-stopping glimpse of him. Nothing else had mattered: not the warnings her family had given her about his ghastly reputation for loving and leaving women, nor even her studies or the career for which she had slaved and existed up until that point. And then, at the worst possible moment, her brain had finally kicked into gear again, and she had seen how crazy it was to envisage a fantasy future with a guy who expected her world to revolve entirely around him.

As her tea was served, she glanced up and saw Aristandros poised twenty feet away. Her throat closed over, her tummy executing a somersault. Her tea cup rattled its betrayal on the saucer as her hand shook. She couldn't swallow; she couldn't breathe. In a black designer-suit that was faultlessly tailored to his lean, powerful physique, ebony hair ruffling in the breeze and dark eyes glinting gold in the sun, Aristandros was an arrestingly handsome man. As he strode across the deck towards her—the epitome of lithe, masculine grace teamed with the high-voltage buzz of raw sexual energy—she was immediately conscious of a rather more shameful reaction. Heat pulsed low in her pelvis, and her face warmed.

'Ella…' Aristandros murmured as she got up to greet him, his attention welded to the delicate perfection of her features—the bluest of blue eyes, and the ripe, pink invitation of her mouth. Even wearing only a hint of make-up, and with her spectacular pale hair sternly clipped back, she looked utterly stunning, she was a naturally beautiful woman who walked past mirrors and reflections without a single glance. Her lack of vanity was the very first thing he had noticed about her and admired.

He caught her slim hand in his, long, brown fingers resting against the soft skin of her narrow wrist. Her hand felt hot, his felt cool. That sudden physical contact took Ella by surprise and she glanced up at him, bemused blue eyes connecting with the penetrating dark challenge of his. Suddenly her heart was beating very, very fast and interfering with her desire to show him a confident, composed exterior. She was close enough to catch the faint, musky scent of his skin overlaid with a spicy tang of cologne. That aroma was familiar enough to send a powerful and primitive message to her nerve endings and leave her senses spinning. Her breasts stirred inside her bra, her nipples lengthening as a dart of rampant responsiveness spread tingling needles of sensual awareness through her taut frame. Shame and dismay at her weakness clawed at her.

'I appreciate your agreeing to see me,' Ella told him hurriedly.

'Humility doesn't become you, Ella,' Aristandros drawled.

'I was only trying to be polite!' Ella snapped back at him before she could think better of it.

'You're very tense,' Aristandros husked, sibilant in tone as silk sliding on silk. His attention roamed from her normally glorious full mouth—currently compressed by the extent of her stress level—down to the full, sweet curve of her firm breasts screened by innocuous white cotton. He would dress her in the finest satin and lace; his groin tightened at the imagery roused by that thought.

Clashing with the perceptive glint in his brilliant dark-golden eyes, something trembled inside Ella. In a desperate attempt to distract him, she reclaimed her hand and said brightly, 'I like your yacht.'

Aristandros flung her a sardonic smile. 'No, you don't. You believe it's yet another example of my habits of conspicuous consumption, and you think I should have spent the money having wells dug somewhere in Africa.'

Colour washed as high as the roots of Ella's hair. 'I was a terrible prig at twenty-one, wasn't I? These days I'm not quite so narrow-minded.'

'The Xenakis Trust, which I set up, contributes a great deal to the most deserving charities,' Aristandros confirmed. 'You should find me worthy of approval now.'

Ella paled, because the meeting was not progressing in the way she had hoped. Every word he spoke seemed to allude in some way to the past she was keen to leave buried. 'We're neither of us the same people we were then.'

Aristandros inclined his arrogant dark head, neither agreeing nor disagreeing, and invited her to sit down again. Coffee was served for his benefit. 'I was surprised that you weren't at your sister's funeral,' he admitted.

Ella set down her tea with a sharp little snap. 'I'm afraid I didn't know about the accident until some time after it took place.'

His ebony brows pleated in surprise. 'Nobody in your family contacted you?'

'Not in the immediate family, no. It was my aunt, my mother's sister, who told me after the event. It was quite awkward, because she had assumed I already knew,' Ella explained reluctantly. 'Obviously the news came as a huge shock to me. Timon and Susie were so young. It's a devastating loss for their daughter.'

His lean, strong face was grave. 'And you're concerned about Calliope?'

'I'm sure that everyone in both families is equally concerned about her,' Ella countered.

Aristandros surveyed her with hard, dark eyes and bit out an appreciative laugh. 'Did dealing with patients finally teach you the art of tact?' he mocked. 'I doubt that anyone is quite as concerned as you appear to be—'

'There's something I need to explain about Callie…'

'You think I don't know that you're her biological mother?' The tall, powerful Greek's dark, deep drawl was laced with honeyed derision. *'Of course* I know that.'

Jolted by his assurance, Ella tilted her chin. 'I assume Timon told you?'

'Yes. Naturally, I was surprised. After all, you once told me that you didn't want children.'

'At twenty-one years old I didn't, and when my sole input to the process was donated eggs I didn't consider Callie to be *my* child when she was born. She was Susie and Timon's daughter.'

'How very selfless of you,' Aristandros murmured flatly. 'Yet in spite of that statement you are here.'

'Yes,' Ella acknowledged. 'I would very much like to see my niece.'

'Is that really what you came all this way to ask of me? One single visit with her, and then you walk away again never to look back?' Aristandros outlined with a look of disbelief.

Ella didn't know quite how to answer that. She was afraid to be too honest and reveal the depth of her longing to become a more important part of Callie's life. 'If that is all you're prepared to allow me. Something is better than nothing.'

Brilliant dark eyes rested on her. 'You want so little?'

Colour warmed her cheeks for dissemblance was not her style. She was entrapped by the power of his gaze, awesomely aware of the unyielding strength and shrewd intelligence of the man behind it. She did not dare lie to him, and knew that any form of evasion would be held against her. 'I think you know that I would like more.'

'But would more be in Callie's best interests? And

how badly do you want that access to the child?' Aristandros enquired huskily.

Ella snatched in a charged breath. '*Very* badly,' she admitted. 'I don't believe I've ever wanted anything so much.'

Aristandros loosed a sudden, grating laugh that took her aback. 'Yet she could have been *our* child. Instead, you made it possible for my cousin and best friend to become a father, and let your sister give birth to a little girl who was genetically half yours. Did it ever occur to you that I might find that particular arrangement offensive?'

The colour in Ella's cheeks slowly drained away, and her face took on the pinched quality of constraint. 'No, I'm afraid that possibility didn't occur to me, and I can only hope that you don't still feel that way now that you're Callie's guardian.'

'I got over it. I'm not the sentimental type, and I would *never* hold a child's parentage against her,' Aristandros fielded with a harsh edge of emphasis on that point. 'What I need to know now is how far are you prepared to go to get what you want? How much will you sacrifice?'

'Are you saying that it might be possible for me to establish an ongoing relationship with my niece?' Ella pressed, wondering why he was talking about sacrifices.

A slow, steady smile curved his handsome, chiselled mouth. 'If you please me, the sky's the limit, *glikia mou*.'

CHAPTER TWO

ELLA was thoroughly chilled by the smile on Aristandros's lean, darkly handsome face and his casual term of endearment jarred on her. She had not forgotten what she was dealing with: a very rich and powerful male whose ego she had once dented. Quite accidentally dented, though, she affixed ruefully to that recollection. Their dialogue, however, had taken a sudden step into unknown territory and she genuinely didn't know what he was getting at.

'I'm not sure that I appreciate your meaning,' Ella said carefully, her hyacinth-blue eyes level and enquiring.

'You're far from being stupid,' Aristandros countered in his measured accented drawl. 'If you want to see Callie, you can only do so on *my* terms.'

Ella slid out of her comfortable seat and walked with quick harried steps over to the rails farthest away, eager for the breeze coming in off the sea to cool her anxious face. 'I know that—if I didn't accept that, I wouldn't be here.'

'My terms are tough,' Aristandros spelt out bluntly. 'You want Callie. I want you, and Callie needs a female carer. If we put those needs together we can come to an arrangement that suits all three of us.'

I want you. That was almost the only phrase she initially picked out of that speech. She was shocked. He still found her attractive—seven years on? Even in her sensible brown trouser-suit, when she was stressed out of her mind? In that first instant of astonishment, she almost turned round to tell him that he was the answer to an overworked doctor's prayers. That side of her life had not just taken a back seat while she'd studied and worked her steady path through all the medical hoops she had had to traverse to qualify, it had vanished.

She reminded herself that being wanted by Aristandros did not, by any stretch of the imagination, make her one of a select group. As a woman, she was clued up enough to go on a TV quiz show and answer virtually any question about Aristandros's highly volatile and energetic love-life. She knew that while his sexual skill and stamina in bed might be legendary according to the tabloid press, his staying power outside the bedroom was of exceptionally short duration. Since they had last met, a constant procession of gorgeous supermodels, starlets and socialites had briefly shared his fast-lane, champagne lifestyle before being ditched and replaced. He got bored *very* easily.

Indeed, Aristandros had gone on to fulfil every worst expectation that Ella had had of him seven years earlier. His relationships appeared to be short-lived, shallow, self-serving, and not infrequently featured infidelity. He had closely followed in the footsteps of his notorious father as a womaniser. Nothing Ella read about Aristandros had ever given her cause to regret refusing to marry him. He could no more have adapted to the restrictions of matrimony than a tiger could adjust to being a domestic pet. He would have broken her heart and destroyed her, just as her faithless stepfather had destroyed her mother with his extra-marital diversions. After twenty-odd years of marriage, Jane Sardelos had neither backbone nor self-esteem left.

'You're suggesting that, if I have sex with you, you'll let me see Callie?' Ella queried in a polite tone of incredulity.

'I'm not quite that crude, *glikia mou*,' Aristandros fielded. 'Nor so easily satisfied. I'm even prepared to offer you something I've never offered a woman before. I want you to move in with me—'

'To *live* with you?' Ella echoed in astonishment, a powerful wave of disbelief winging through her taut length.

'Live and travel with me as my mistress. How else could you look after your niece? Of course, there would be conditions,' Aristandros continued smoothly. 'You couldn't hope to work and still meet my expectations. Living with me and taking care of Callie would be a full-time occupation.'

'You haven't changed one little bit,' Ella framed shakily, even as her heart jumped in anticipation at the idea of having the freedom to take care of her niece. 'You still expect to take priority over everything else.'

Aristandros angled back his arrogant dark head, stubborn eyes hurling an unashamed challenge. 'Why not? I have known many women who would be delighted to make me and my interests their main priority in life. Why would I even consider accepting a lesser commitment from you?'

'But you can't make a child part of a deal like that!' Ella condemned fiercely. 'It would be immoral and horribly unscrupulous!'

'I don't suffer from moral scruples. I'm a practical guy who has no plans to get married to give Callie a mother. So, if you want to be her replacement mother, you have to play this as I want it played.'

He was offering her everything she longed for in return for surrendering everything she had worked so hard to achieve. It was blackmail and it was revenge in one cruelly potent weapon. 'After seven years, how can we go from having no relationship at all into living together? And me a *mistress*?' she questioned unevenly, the unfamiliar word thick and unwieldy on her tongue. 'It's crazy.'

Aristandros slowly unfolded his big powerful frame, from his seat and strolled towards her like a sleek panther on the prowl. His narrowed gaze blazed golden and welded to her, homing in on the soft pink of her mouth. 'It's not a problem for me. I find you amazingly attractive.'

'And that's *all* that it takes for you—lust?' Ella slung between gritted teeth with a look of distaste.

'Lust is all that we need concern ourselves with, *glikia mou*.' He lifted a hand and let confident finger-tips trace the proud curve of her cheekbone. Blue eyes spitting angry flame, she jerked her head away in a violent rejection of his touch. 'Let's keep it simple. I want you in my bed every night.'

'No *way*!' Ella launched back at him furiously.

'Of course, I can't force you into agreement,' Aristandros conceded, trapping her by the rails with his size and proximity, while staring down at her with burning resolve. 'But I'm a stubborn and tenacious man. I have waited a long time for this day. Many women would be flattered by my continuing interest.'

'Lust is not an interest!' Ella practically spat at him, her scorn unconcealed. 'This is all because I said no to you seven years ago, all because you never got me into bed!'

Towering over her slighter, smaller figure, Aristandros went very still at that charge. His dark eyes gleamed, diamond-bright and hard as granite. 'I let you say no because I was prepared to wait for you. This time around I'm not prepared to wait for anything.'

Butterflies danced in her tummy while rage preoccupied her thoughts and clenched her hands into fists. 'I can't believe you have the nerve to try this on me!'

He closed his hands over her fists to hold her entrapped. He bent his proud, dark head, his breath skimming her temples as he murmured thickly, 'But I always have the nerve in a fight, *koukla mou*. Fighting for what I want comes naturally to me and, if the stakes are high enough, I will risk *everything* to win. I wouldn't be a true Xenakis if I didn't occasionally sail too close to the sun.'

He was so close she couldn't breath, and she was trembling while her heart pounded as if she was running a marathon. He lowered his head to claim her lips and he kissed her slowly with an irresistible passion. Extraordinary, achingly familiar, that kiss was everything she had steeled herself to forget. For a timeless moment she was lost in the heat and pressure of his hungry urgency, shivering violently at the deeply erotic thrust and flick of his tongue into the tender interior of her mouth. Suddenly her body was flaring wildly out of her control, her nipples pinching into stiff, painful buds, moisture surging between her thighs. Memory took her back and she froze, shutting out and denying those shameful sensations while she shifted away from him in an abrupt, defensive movement that caught him by surprise.

'No,' she told him flatly, throwing her head back, little strands of silvery-pale hair breaking free of the clip to brush her cheekbones.

A wolfish smile slashed Aristandros's lean face. He made no attempt to hide his triumph. '"No" is very close to becoming a blatant invitation on your lips,' he derided softly.

'You can't buy me with Callie. I'm not up for sale, and I can't be tempted,' Ella swore, praying even as she spoke that she had the strength of character to make those statements true.

'Then we will all be losers, and perhaps the child most of all. I doubt if any other woman would be prepared to offer her the honest and genuine affection that you could give her,' Aristandros pronounced. 'Although many women will no doubt try to convince me otherwise.'

That final assurance was like a knife finding a gap in her armour to pierce her skin, penetrate deep and draw blood. The very thought of ambitious gold-diggers auditioning to be Callie's mother-substitute simply to impress her billionaire guardian hurt Ella immeasurably and threatened her composure.

'You're being so cruel,' she muttered tightly. 'I wouldn't have believed that you could be so cruel.'

Unmoved, Aristandros surveyed her with hard eyes. 'It's your choice—'

'There *isn't* a choice!' Ella gasped strickenly

'It's a choice you don't like. But be grateful there is a choice to make,' Aristandros urged harshly. 'I could have said no, you can't see Callie, and slammed the door shut in your face!'

Gooseflesh gave Ella's skin a clammy feel. It felt like the cold breath of reality making its presence felt, for of course what he said was true. In the circumstances, even a choice was a luxury, for he might have turned her request down flat. Furthermore, what happened next was entirely her decision. She glanced up at him from below her lashes. He was on some sort of power kick. With the options and offers that came his way every single day, how could he still be interested in her? Was it just the fact that she was one of the precious few to have turned him down? Wasn't that the real secret of her enduring attraction—her one-time refusal, her apparent unavailability? And wouldn't her pulling power wane fast once she was freely available?

'Just suppose I said yes,' Ella suggested in a driven undertone. 'Your interest in me wouldn't last longer than five minutes. What happens to Callie then? I'm there for about a week and then I vanish again?'

His lean, strong face had clenched hard. 'It won't be like that.'

Ella had to gnaw at the soft underside of her lower lip to prevent herself from screaming back at him in disagreement. It was always like that for him with women, wild, hot affairs that burnt out at supersonic speed. 'What would I know about being a mistress? I'm hardly the decorative type.'

Aristandros rested his attention on her, his golden-brown eyes smouldering below the luxuriant black fringe of his lashes, amusement curling his handsome mouth. 'Is there a type? I'm flexible and very open to new experiences.'

Unamused by this suggestive sally, Ella walked back to her seat and sank down as rigid-backed as if she had a fence post attached to her spine. 'If I did agree,' she said very stiffly, 'What would the ground rules be?'

'Your main objective would primarily be pleasing me,' Aristandros drawled, watching her grit her teeth as if he had said something unspeakably rude. 'Of course, there would be no other men in your life. You would always be available for me.'

'The any-time, any-place, anywhere girl? That's a male fantasy, Aristandros, not an achievable objective for a normal woman in today's world,' Ella countered drily.

'You're clever enough to live that fantasy for me. Focus all that career-orientated zeal on me, and you won't find me ungrateful. Give me what I want, and you will have everything that you want,' he traded in a powerful promise of intent.

'Callie.' She framed the name weakly because it encompassed so much and stirred such deep emotion in her. The child she had never seen but whom she longed to love as a daughter rather than a niece. Aristandros might enjoy almost unlimited power over them both, but Ella was quick to remind herself that she also had the power to make a huge difference in Callie's life. And she badly wanted the chance to be there to love and care for the little girl, who had already lost both mother and father at such a tragically young age.

Her rushing thoughts were so frantic and intense, she was beginning to develop a tension headache across her brow. She pressed the heel of her hand there and snatched in a steadying breath. 'How long have I got to decide?'

Aristandros flashed her a punitive appraisal. 'It's now or never. A today-only deal.'

'But that's outrageous! I mean, you're asking me to give up my career in medicine. Have you any idea what being a doctor means to me?'

'A very good idea. After all, you once chose your career over me,' Aristandros skimmed back, keen eyes dangerous.

'That wasn't the only reason I turned you down. I did that for the both of us—we would have made each other miserable!' Ella flung back at him a little wildly, her emotions finally outrunning her self-discipline. 'And let me warn you of one thing that isn't negotiable under any circumstances—if I agree, I will not tolerate infidelity in any guise.'

Strong emotion animated her features, brightening her eyes and flushing her cheeks with colour. It was a welcome glimpse of the passionate young woman he remembered, who had invested so much emotion in everything that mattered to her, but who had tellingly walked away from him without a backward glance.

'I'm not asking you to marry me this time. I won't be making any promises either,' Aristandros delivered in direct challenge. 'I should also warn you that, regardless of what happens between us, I will not give up custody of Callie. Timon trusted me to raise his daughter, and I hold that sacrosanct.'

A half-dozen fire-starting responses were ready to

tumble off Ella's tongue but she held them back, deeming the momentary pleasure of challenging him to be unwise at that point. She was willing to bet that he knew next to nothing about children or their needs, for he was an only child, raised as a mini-adult by parents who had had no time and even less interest in him. Even so, she could not believe that he would do anything that might harm the child in his charge. For her own peace of mind, she had to believe that if she succeeded in forging close ties with Callie he would recognise the damage that the sudden severance of those bonds would cause and make allowances.

'Ella…' Aristandros growled, impatience etched in every angular line of his lean, bronzed features. 'It's decision time, *glikia mou.*'

Ella pictured the imaginary child in her head and studied Aristandros with determined cool. Regardless of how she might feel about him and his methods, she still thought he was drop-dead gorgeous, and that was a plus, wasn't it? But how would it feel to engage in an unemotional sexual relationship with him, particularly when she was totally inexperienced in that line? She suppressed the critical part of her brain because she saw no point borrowing trouble in advance of the event. She forced herself to concentrate on Callie and shut out all the personal, selfish stuff like the injured pride, the fury and the sense of humiliation threatening her. If she gained the right to take care of Callie, couldn't she learn to cope with the rest?

'Okay.' Ella threw her head back and lifted her chin. 'But you'll have to give me time to work out my notice at work.'

* * *

'Are you finished?' Dr Alister Marlow queried from the doorway of Ella's surgery as she lifted a cardboard box from the desk. The room looked bare.

'Yes. I took the bulk of my stuff yesterday.' As her colleague helpfully extended his arms, Ella relinquished the box and then took the opportunity to perform a last-minute check through the drawers. Finally she straightened. 'Will you ask the cleaning lady to keep her eyes peeled for a small photograph? It was of my father and I was attached to it,' she admitted ruefully ' I broke the photoframe last month and took out the photo, and now it seems to have vanished.'

'We'll keep an eye out for it.' The tall, broadly built blond man promised, concerned blue eyes resting on her. 'You look exhausted.'

'There's been so much to organise.' Ella said nothing about the considerable emotional fallout of having to resign from the job she loved. All her years of hard work had been nullified and all her goals had been wrenched from her. She would miss her work and her colleagues a great deal. She would not play any further part in what happened to her patients, nor would she see the benefits brought by the breast-care clinic she had helped to set up. Already she felt lost without the structure of her busy, demanding routine. It had all happened so fast, as by the time her unused holiday entitlement had been added in she'd had only had a couple of weeks' notice left to work.

'I can't say I approve of what you're doing, because you were too valuable a part of our team,' Alister remarked as they walked towards her car. 'But I do admire your commitment to your niece, and know that our loss will be her gain. Stay in touch, Ella.'

Ella drove home while reminding herself that the spacious loft would soon no longer be her home. Lily was buying Ella's share of the apartment. Ella would have preferred to retain her stake in the property, but had felt it would be unfair to impose that on Lily, who was reluctant to take a chance on a new flatmate. Of course she knew Lily would be quick to offer her a bed if she was in need, but it wouldn't be the same as owning her own place.

Just how long would it be before Aristandros tired of her? Her shadowed blue eyes gleamed with resentment, for she was convinced that their affair would be over within weeks. Her novelty value wouldn't last long. Then where would she be without a job and with no home to return to? The proceeds from her share of the apartment would not be enough to buy another property, and she would have to go back to renting again. But, when Aristandros did throw her out, her main concern would be Callie and whether or not she would be allowed to maintain a relationship with the little girl, Ella acknowledged worriedly. She had told nobody the truth about her impending intimate relationship with the Greek tycoon. She had simply said that she was going to help to take care of her orphaned niece whose life was currently based in Greece.

Lily, however, remained suspicious of that explanation. 'I'm trying so hard to understand all this. Do you really want Callie so much that you're happily giving up everything that matters to you?' She demanded that night over the restaurant meal they had organised for their last evening together. 'If it's just that you're getting broody, you could easily have a child of your own.'

'But I want to be with Callie—'

'*And* the oversexed billionaire?'

Reddening, Ella pushed her plate away. 'Aristandros happens to be Callie's guardian and a non-negotiable part of her life.'

'But you do have a thing for him, don't you?' the brunette said suddenly.

'I don't know where you got that idea,' Ella countered with a laugh that sounded more brittle than amused.

'Oh, maybe it was when I noticed you only bought tacky newspapers and magazines so that you could read about him and his exploits.'

'Why not? I was curious because I met him years ago and Susie was married to his cousin!' Ella protested.

Her friend was still watching her closely. 'That last Christmas you spent in Greece before your family started treating you like a pariah—that was when you met Aristandros Xenakis, wasn't it?'

More defensive than ever, for she preferred to hold on tight to her secrets, Ella shrugged a slim shoulder. 'My stepfather made sure we never missed a chance to rub shoulders with the super-rich Xenakis family. I suspect we first met as kids but I don't remember it. Aristandros is four years older than I am.'

'I just feel there's a history there that you're not telling me about,' Lily confessed. 'At the time, I thought you'd had your heart broken.'

Ella rolled her eyes while trying to suppress the memory of the nights she had cried herself to sleep and the days when only work had got her through the intense sense of loneliness and loss. But she had chosen and accepted those consequences when she'd realised that she couldn't marry the man she had fallen in love with. In any case, he had not made the smallest effort to change her mind on that score, had he? In truth her heart had got broken over a much longer term than most. A chip had been gouged out of her heart with every woman that had followed her in Ari's life. But all that was water under the bridge now, Ella reminded herself thankfully. She had lived to see her worst misgivings about Aristandros vindicated; she had made the right decision and had never doubted the fact.

Tomorrow morning, however, she would be picked up at nine, and she had no idea what happened next for Aristandros had not deigned to inform her. Would they be staying in London for long? Would she meet Callie tomorrow? Lying sleepless in bed that night, watching shadows fall on the bare walls, she recalled that Christmas vacation in Athens midway through her medical studies. Time rolled back and plunged her into the past...

Susie had collected her at the airport. Her sister had been single then, and in a very good mood as she'd chattered about the exclusive club she was taking Ella to that evening.

'I've just finished exams and I'm really tired, Susie,' Ella had confided 'I might just go to bed and give the socialising a miss.'

'You can't do that!' Susie had gasped. 'I wangled a special guest-pass for you, so you can't let me down. Ari Xenakis and his friends will be there.'

Susie, with her determination only to mix with the most fashionable crowd, and her strenuous efforts to ensure that her name appeared regularly in the gossip

columns, was the apple of their stepfather's eye. Theo
Sardelos expected women to be ornamental and frivolous. Ella's serious nature, her championship of her
mother and dislike of pretension were all traits that
made him feel uncomfortable.

For the sake of peace that evening, Ella accompanied
Susie. The club was noisy and very crowded. Surrounded by Susie and her pals, who had nothing more
on their minds but the hottest party or man on offer, Ella
was bored. She listened dutifully to tales of how outrageous Ari Xenakis was. He had dumped his last girl-
friend by text and her parents had had to pack her off
abroad to stop her stalking him. As the stories of his
wildness, fabled riches and volatility were traded round
the table, Ella registered in amazement that there still
wasn't a girl present who wouldn't give her right arm
to date him—in spite of his evident obnoxiousness.
When he was pointed out to her across the dance floor,
she registered another reason why he was so dispropor-
tionately popular: he was breathtakingly good-looking
with black hair, brooding golden-brown eyes and the fit
body of an athlete.

If one of their party hadn't collapsed, Ella was convinced that Aristandros would never have noticed her.
Lethia, the teenaged friend of one of Susie's mates,
suffered a seizure. Ella was shocked by the way everyone
abandoned the girl as she lay twitching and jerking at
the side of the dance floor. When Ella went to her assistance, Susie was furious. 'Don't get involved!' she
hissed, trying to drag her sibling back to their table. 'We
hardly know her!'

Ignoring Susie's frantic instructions that she keep her

distance, Ella placed Lethia in the recovery position and made her as comfortable as possible while the seizure ran its course. The other girls disclaimed any knowledge of Lethia's health. Ella had to turn out the girl's handbag to learn that Lethia appeared to be an epileptic and to be taking prescribed medication.

'Do you need some help with her?' someone asked her in English. Turning her head, she found Aristandros hunkered down by her side, his lean, handsome face surprisingly serious.

'She's an epileptic, and she needs to go to hospital because she's been unconscious more than five minutes,' Ella told him.

Aristandros organised an ambulance, his cool in a crisis welcome in the overexcited atmosphere surrounding them. He also contacted Lethia's family, who confirmed that she was a recently diagnosed epileptic.

'Why wouldn't anyone else help?' Ella sighed while they waited for the ambulance.

'I suspect that most people assumed that her collapse was drug-related and they didn't want to be associated with her,' Aristandros explained.

'Nobody seemed to know that she suffers from epilepsy. I suppose she didn't want people to find out,' Ella guessed, her blue eyes compassionate. 'You spoke to me in English. How did you know I was English?'

Dark eyes glinting with amusement, Aristandros gave her a sardonic smile that made it extraordinarily hard for her to breath. 'I had already asked who you were before Lethia collapsed.'

Ella flushed, self-consciousness assailing her, because she was convinced he could only have noticed her because she didn't fit in. The other girls were like exotic birds in their skimpy designer outfits, while she was wearing a simple black skirt with a turquoise top. 'Why did you come over?'

'I couldn't take my eyes off you,' Aristandros confided. 'Lethia was just an excuse.'

'You dump women by text and then call them stalkers. I'm not interested,' Ella told him drily, switching to Greek, which she spoke fluently.

'There's nothing hotter than a challenge, *glikia mou*,' Aristandros husked, black lashes as long as fly-swats lowering on his dark, golden gaze...

CHAPTER THREE

AT NINE the following morning, Ella slid into a silver limousine and watched her cases being loaded. Her hair anchored in a knot at the nape of her neck, she was dressed with care in a narrow grey skirt and a pinstripe shirt. She was well aware that she didn't look like mistress material, but was proud of that fact. If Aristandros wanted to waste his time trying to turn a level-headed unfashionable woman into a seductive bedroom hottie who dressed to impress, then he'd one of those challenges that he so professed to love on his hands.

Ella closed restive hands round the handbag on her lap. Sex was just sex, and of course she could handle it. Technically she knew a lot about men. Most probably she wasn't the sexiest woman around—after all, she had lived for years as if sex as an activity didn't exist. Celibacy had only bothered her once, and that was while she'd been seeing Aristandros. She could feel her cheeks warming as she recalled that burning kiss on his yacht. He was so slick, so practiced, that he knew all the right moves to make. And she had always hated that sense of being out of control. Aristandros, on the other hand, would love getting her in that condition as it would crown his conviction that he was a hell of a guy both in and out of bed.

When the limo drew up by the kerb, Ella climbed out and surveyed the building before her in surprise. The sleek logo of a city lawyers' office greeted her frowning gaze. She walked into Reception, where she was immediately greeted and shown into a room. Aristandros swung round from the window to study her.

'What am I doing here?' Ella questioned before he could even part his chiselled lips. As always he looked amazing, the broodingly handsome image of bronzed good looks and highly expensive tailoring, a sophisticated business-tycoon to his fingertips. But even at first glance he was a great deal more than that, for he exuded a potent aura of power and self-assurance.

Dark-golden eyes narrowed and rested on her, roving from the full curve of her mouth to the swell of her breasts with a sensual appreciation that was as bold as it was blatantly male. Maddeningly aware of his appraisal, and conscious of the wanton awareness tingling between her thighs, Ella flushed a fierce pink.

'I have had a legal agreement drawn up by my lawyers here,' Aristandros informed her. 'I want you to sign it so that there are no misunderstandings between us in the future.'

As he gave her that explanation, Ella went very still and lost some of her colour. 'Why am I only being told about this now? For goodness' sake, I've already resigned from my job and agreed to sell my apartment!'

'Yes,' Aristandros agreed softly, not an ounce of apology in his reply.

Ella worked his agenda out for herself. 'You planned it that way? Now that I've burned my boats, I'm less likely to argue the terms?'

'What I love about you is your lack of illusion about me, *glikia mou*.' Aristandros drawled with sardonic amusement. 'You expect me to be a devious bastard and I am.'

Ella struggled to master her rocketing fury at the manner in which he had closed off any potential escape-hatches and destroyed any bargaining chips in advance. Aristandros was famed for his astute manipulative skills in business and his ability to spring a surprise on his opponents. No doubt it had been naïve of her not being better prepared for such tactics to be used against her. In fact it had not occurred to her that Aristandros might think it necessary to tie her up in some legal agreement, particularly as their arrangement was of an intimate nature.

'Did you actually discuss our future relationship with your lawyers?' Ella demanded, cringing at the idea, and incredulous that he could have gone to such insensitive lengths in his determination to bind her in legal knots.

'I always try to anticipate problems in advance. And a woman as strong-minded as you is likely to cause trouble if she can,' Aristandros forecast.

'But you discussed the fact that you want me to be your mistress!' Ella launched back at him in raw condemnation.

'It's scarcely going to be a secret when you live with me and are constantly seen by my side,' Aristandros responded in a direct challenge. 'I'm not going to pretend that you're just the nanny.'

Air scissored painfully through her dry throat as she dragged in a charged breath, for the level of his insolent indifference to her feelings infuriated her. 'You really don't give a damn about how all this makes me feel, do you?'

'*Should* I?' Aristandros raised an ebony brow. 'How much of a damn did you give when I had to tell all my friends and family that you were not, after all, about to become my wife?'

That controversial question flamed in the air between them like a physical blow. Ella paled, recalling the awful, squirming embarrassment and guilty discomfiture that she had suffered over the whole wretched mixup that night seven years ago. 'I was *very* upset about it. But it wasn't my fault that you decided to simply assume that the fact I loved you meant I would give up medicine and marry you!' she replied accusingly. 'There was no malice on my part, either. Although I didn't want to marry you, I really did care about you, and the last thing I wanted to do was hurt you in any way.'

In receipt of that spirited speech of self-defence, his dark eyes turned almost black with derision, and his strong jawline clenched hard. 'You didn't hurt me. I'm not that sensitive, *glikia mou.*'

But his anger and desire for revenge seven years on were giving Ella a very different message. Aristandros had always enjoyed a glossy air of invulnerability over a core of indomitable strength that suggested he was too tough to be easily damaged. Yet it seemed to her now that her rejection had wounded him more than she had ever dreamt possible.

'Whatever,' Ella slashed back. 'It still doesn't excuse you for calling in lawyers to talk about the possible problems of an intimate relationship! Is nothing sacred?'

'Certainly not sex,' Aristandros parried drily. 'You need

to be aware that this is not a cohabitation agreement, and you will not be my partner in that sense, so you won't be able to claim anything from me at some future date.'

'Oh, I'm getting the message now!' Ella flung at him, temper racing up through her like flame reacting uncontrollably to a draught, her pride stung to the quick by his assurances. 'You're protecting your wealth, even though you know very well that I have no designs on your wretched money! My goodness, if money had been that important to me, I'd have married you when I got the chance!'

His dark eyes blazed burning gold with anger at that blunt exclamation. 'Here.' Without further ado, Aristandros scooped a document off the table beside him and extended it to her. 'Read it and sign it.'

Her slim legs feeling a tad wobbly in the support stakes, Ella sank down into the nearest armchair. It was a long and involved contract. As her angry resentment cooled, she digested the terms of the agreement. Soon horror at the extent of his ruthlessness was assailing her as heavily as a lump of concrete settling into her stomach. He had reduced their upcoming relationship to the coldest possible set of hard-hitting demands and embargos.

In return for the privilege of looking after Callie and having all her expenses met by him, Ella was to share his bed whenever he wanted while making every possible effort to meet his expectations of her in everything that she did. She was to live, dress and travel as and where he wished. In addition, she was to accept that what was referred to as his 'private life' was none of her business and that interference in that field would be considered a breach of their agreement. Her teeth ground together and she had to snatch in a breath to restrain another angry outburst

The conditions of what could only be called her proposed 'service' were unbelievably detailed and humiliating. How could any man have dared to discuss such confidential matters with his lawyers? Where had he got the nerve to dictate such unashamedly cruel and disparaging terms?

'This....this is outrageous!' Ella told him grittily. 'Why don't you just put a collar and a lead on me and refer to me as a pet?'

'I want the job description to be accurate before you take on the role,' Aristandros traded levelly. 'I am honest about what I want and expect from you. You won't be able to say that you weren't warned.'

As Ella read on, she grew ever more tense and rattled. He was even laying down advance restrictions on her contact with Callie—she would not have the right to take Callie out without his permission and accompanying security. At all times she was to respect Aristandros's position as her niece's sole legal guardian and take note of his instructions. Any attempt to remove Callie from his custody or to claim any rights over the little girl would result in her access to Callie being denied. Ella shivered at that brutal threat and glanced up at Aristandros, evaluating the intractable expression stamped in his lean dark features. No, he wasn't joking about any of it. He didn't want a mistress, and certainly not a partner of equal status; he wanted a slave on a round-the-clock mission to please him.

'Until this moment,' she muttered shakily. 'I didn't realise how much you hated me.'

'Don't be ridiculous.' Aristandros sent her a quelling glance.

'If I couldn't even *argue* with you, I couldn't breathe!' Ella hurled back in response.

'I expect occasional disagreements,' Aristandros countered with the air of a man making a generous allowance. 'But I will not accept continual hostility which might detract from my comfort.'

Ella was mute with dismay and disbelief at the iron rule he was trying to impose on her. The written agreement was a humiliating nightmare. She felt like her wings were being clipped and she would never fly free again. Aristandros was determined to own her body and soul, and control her every waking moment.

'We have wasted enough time discussing this. *Sign*,' Aristandros ordered flatly.

'Aren't I entitled to legal advice of my own before I sign anything? I haven't even finished reading it yet!'

'Of course you're entitled to seek legal advice, but that will hold matters up for at least another couple of weeks and extend the time you will have to wait to meet Callie,' Aristandros pointed out.

'I'm beginning to understand why you're so rich,' Ellie mumbled sickly. 'You know what buttons to push, how to put on the pressure.'

'Of course…' Aristandros spread shapely brown hands in a fluid movement '…I want you and I'm programmed to fight for you.'

'You fight very dirty,' Ella whispered, bending her head to read on, still shocked by the extent of the control he was determined to exert over her. She skimmed through the financial details of the ridiculously extravagant monthly allowance he was offering her, and the even more generous 'severance package' promised as consolation at the end of their relationship. How could she fight him? All that mattered to her at that moment was the promise of seeing Callie, being able to care for her and ensure that the child received the love and security she needed to blossom. She was not prepared to risk losing that opportunity.

'Will you sign?'

'If I sign right now, when will I see Callie?' Ella pressed.

'Tomorrow.'

Ella breathed in slow and deep and got up to put the document down on the table. 'I'll sign,' she said.

He summoned two lawyers and their signatures were duly witnessed. She couldn't look either man in the eye, for Aristandros had made her feel like a whore who was selling not only her body to him but also her self-will. She found it hard to credit that the same male had once treated her with pronounced respect and courtesy. She was convinced that rejection had made him hate her.

'What now?' she breathed when they were alone again.

'This...' His hands enclosed her firmly to pull her to him. Long fingers curved to her cheekbone, tipping up her mouth, and suddenly he was kissing her and instant explosions of reaction were fizzing through her bloodstream. His masculine urgency was incredibly exciting. A savage rush of sexual hunger engulfed her. With a helpless shiver she pressed herself to the hard muscular wall of his chest, impelled by the straining sensitivity of her breasts and the liquid heat between her thighs to seek closer contact. She wanted, needed, *craved* more than that connection. He closed a hand to her hips, tilting her against him, and a low sound of response broke low in her throat as she felt the force of his erection even through their clothing, and her own body leapt with instant answering need.

Aristandros lifted his handsome dark head and dealt her a smile that was pure-bred predator. 'Frozen on the outside, meltingly hot within, *koukla mou*. How many other guys have there been?'

Ella hated him with so much passion at that instant for daring to voice that insolent question that she could barely vocalize, and her voice emerged with a husky edge. 'A few,' she lied without hesitation, determined to hide the fact that, to date, only he could extract that mad inferno of response from her. 'I'm a passionate woman.'

A tiny muscle pulled tight at the corner of his expressive mouth. His eyes were as ice-cold as a mountain stream. 'Evidently. But from here on in, all that passion is mine. Is that understood?'

Not averse to taking on the guise of a *femme fatale*, Ella looked up at him from beneath the long, silky lashes that gave her blue eyes such definition against her fair skin and pale hair. 'Of course.'

There was a moment's silence while Ella gathered her wits and her courage. 'Will you tell me what Callie's like?' she asked tautly.

Aristandros stilled in apparent surprise at the request. 'She's a baby. What can you say about a baby? She's pretty—' He hesitated, as if recognising that more than that superficial comment was required. 'She's, er, quiet, good; you would hardly know she was there.'

Ella lowered her lashes to conceal her dismay and concern at that description. A toddler of eighteen months should be lively, inquisitive and chattering, almost anything other than quiet and unobtrusive. Evidently her niece was still suffering the effects of losing her parents. 'Do you have a close relationship with her?' she queried, reluctant to say anything that he might translate as criticism of his guardianship of the little girl.

'Of course I do.' Aristandros frowned. 'Now, if that is all, the limo's waiting for you. You have appointments to keep.'

'Where?'

'I'm taking you to a gallery opening tonight. You'll need clothes.'

'I *have* clothes.'

'Not to suit my social life you don't,' he parried, drily enough to rouse colour to her cheeks. 'I'll see you later.'

Clutching her copy of the legal agreement, Ella got back into the car. She was deeply shaken by the encounter, which had imposed a challenging dose of hard reality on her. The chauffeur delivered her to a designer salon. Her arrival had clearly been pre-arranged. She was ushered from the door straight into a changing room, where detailed measurements of her figure were noted down. Within minutes a selection of garments was being brought for her to try on.

'And for the event this evening,' the senior sales-assistant murmured, fanning an elegant black cocktail-frock out in front of Ella like a bait to hook a fish, 'Mr Xenakis particularly liked this one.'

Ella breathed in deep to hold in an instant desire to state that the dress wasn't her style at all. In fact, she was stunned by the awareness that Aristandros had taken so personal an interest in what she was to wear. He had actually torn himself from the world of business to consider her appearance? Was that the true definition of a womanizer—a guy so tuned in to the female body that even choosing clothing could become a prelude to sex? She focused her anxious thoughts on Callie and achieved a state of grace equal to the task of donning the dress without comment. She was equally tolerant of every other piece of apparel presented to her, even the absurd collection of silky, frivolous lingerie. The new wardrobe was only a prop to enable her to play a part, she told herself soothingly. Unfortunately, the prospect of slipping into flimsy provocative underwear for Aristandros's benefit put Ella into a mood close to panic. Suddenly she was wishing she hadn't claimed a level of experience she didn't have.

The chauffeur took her to a beauty salon next. Ella had no objection to a little fine grooming. Indeed, it was a treat to have someone else do her hair and her nails, and the process of being made up by a professional beautician intrigued her. Colours and techniques were employed that she would never have dreamt of trying. Not for nothing had Aristandros called her '*koukla mou*'—my doll—she reasoned wryly. She was no longer required to be herself. Instead she was to be what Aristandros wanted her to be: a painted, pampered ultra-feminine remake of her former self programmed to behave like the mistress equivalent of a Stepford wife.

In an underground car-park, she got out of the limou-

sine and was ushered into a lift. Aristandros lived in a
tri-level penthouse apartment that overlooked Hyde
Park. Luxurious acres of space seemed to run off in
every direction from the imposing entrance-hall. She
and her shopping were taken straight to the master
bedroom. A swimming pool gleamed beyond the patio
doors, alongside a sun terrace and the lush greenery of
a rooftop garden. A maid, who addressed her in Greek,
proudly demonstrated the lavish appointments of the
dressing room where her clothes were to be stored,
before showing her the opulent marble bathroom.

Ella discovered that she couldn't take her attention
off the massive bed that occupied centre-stage in the
bedroom. The divan was so big Aristandros would have
to chase her round it to capture her, she thought crazily,
her heart starting to beat very, very fast. Sex with
Aristandros—something she had dreamt about seven
years earlier and now cringed at the threat of, she acknowledged ruefully. Still, if practice made perfect, he
ought to be better in bed than most.

The maid hung the black dress in readiness, while
Ella selected a turquoise voile-and-lace bra and
matching panties and then went for a shower. When she
had put on these items, she posed in front of the
bathroom mirror, noticing how the clinging fabric of the
underwear clung to the fullness of her breasts and the
swell of her hips, not to mention even more personal
parts. Just then, the door opened without warning. A
gasp was snatched from her parted lips, and she
snatched up a towel to conceal her only partially clothed
body. Her startled blue gaze was very wide.

Aristandros was in the doorway, seeming taller and

more powerfully built than ever. Having already discarded his jacket, his tie and his shoes, he was an aggressively masculine sight with his shirt hanging loose to frame a muscular brown slice of hair-roughened chest. 'You should have locked the door if you didn't want company,' he teased, eyeing the big white towel she was clutching to her chest with feverish hands. 'For a woman who has been with, and I quote *a few* men, you're very shy.'

Pride stiffened Ella's backbone and she flung her head high, blade-straight white-blonde hair feathering in a silken swathe across her flushed cheekbones. 'I don't have a shy bone in my body!'

'Drop the towel and prove it,' he advised lazily.

In a convulsive movement, her slim fingers released their grip and the towel tumbled to the marble floor. She knew it was silly, but she felt ten times more naked and self-conscious in the fancy lingerie than she would have felt in her own unadorned skin.

Aristandros looked, and made no attempt to hide the fact that he was looking and enjoying the view of her scantily clad curves. Her body tingled in all the private places as though a flame had passed too close to her skin. 'It pays to undress you, *glikia mou.*'

Ella dragged in a charged breath, the creamy swell of her breasts stirring, her swollen nipples visible below the lace. His brilliant eyes smouldered gold, and her mouth ran dry as he took a step forward and reached for her, sinking his hands below her hips to lift her up and settle her down on the marble vanity-unit as if she weighed no more than a child's toy.

'What are you doing?' she demanded.

'Appreciating you,' Aristandros husked, breathing in the soapy fresh scent of her skin as he bent over her, the hot blood pooling at his groin. *His* soap from *his* shower, *his* woman, right where she belonged. It was a moment of supreme sensual satisfaction for Ari. He pressed his warm mouth lightly to the tender skin at her collarbone, where a tiny pulse was beating out her tension. With the tip of his tongue he tasted her. His hands slid from her slim shoulders to brush the bra cups down and ease her pert breasts free of confinement. The sweetly curved mounds spilled forward, held high by the constraint of the bra, the stiff, pink crests drawing his attention.

'You're perfect.' He moulded the ripe swell of her brazenly exposed flesh and kneaded the tender tips. Taken by surprise, Ella was defenceless, mentally unprepared for a sexual challenge before nightfall. Her nipples were unbearably sensitive. Her head tipped back, and a moan broke from her throat as he stroked and pinched the distended buds. A warm, rich wave of sensational response was engulfing her even before he lowered his head to suck the rosy crests. Her control was sliding as inexorably as night followed day. Desire was sinking taloned claws of need into her treacherous body. He drove her lips apart with sudden mesmeric urgency, his tongue plundering the moist interior of her mouth while his skilled fingers traced the taut, damp stretch of material between her thighs and made her shiver violently.

At an unhurried pace, he eased below the triangle of fabric and circled the most sensitive point, teasing and toying with her delicate flesh. All lingering remnants of self-discipline were wrenched from her as he subjected her to his erotic mastery. Very soon she reached the stage where she could have wept with frustration and begged him on her knees for satisfaction. A husky sound of amusement broke from him as she dragged him closer with frantic hands, seeking the temporary consolation of physical contact that their position denied her.

'Take a deep breath, *khriso mou*,' Aristandros urged thickly. 'We have a gallery opening to attend, and I need a shower—'

'A gallery opening?' Only with the greatest difficulty did Ella extract herself from the all-encompassing sexual hunger that he had induced and return to reason again. It was like coming out of a coma to a brash new world. She was appalled to appreciate that Aristandros had virtually seduced her in his bathroom and was now trying to head for the shower while she still clung to him. She whipped her hands from him as though she had been burnt. 'Of course.'

'We have no time.' Aristandros lifted her down from the marble unit-top with strong hands. 'I don't want to treat you like a takeaway,' he murmured huskily. 'I want to enjoy you like a feast and appreciate every nuance.'

'A takeaway!' Ella repeated through gritted teeth of disdain.

Aristandros gazed down at her with shimmering golden-brown eyes fringed with spiky black lashes. 'You want me,' he countered with hard satisfaction. 'A time will come when you don't care *how* I take you…only that I do.'

That frightening forecast trickled down her taut spine like ice-water. 'Never,' she swore. 'I'd sooner die!'

A wolfish smile slashed his beautifully shaped mouth. 'I know women; I'm never wrong…'

'You were *once*,' Ella reminded him before she could think better of summoning up a recollection that could only alienate him.

His lean, dark face tensed, ruthless eyes cool on her face. 'Don't go there,' he warned her softly.

A deep chill formed inside her tummy. Regretting her incautious words, she turned her head away, shame and uncertainty clouding her blue eyes as she returned to the bedroom. For a split second she was recalling the short-lived joy of the moment when he had told her that he wanted her to marry him. Her happiness had turned to horror an instant later when he made a public announcement about their plans while spelling out the fact that she would be giving up medicine to concentrate on being a wife and a mother. Minutes later they had been engaged in a heated dispute in which it had swiftly become clear that Aristandros could be as inflexible in his expectations as a solid-granite rock and quite unapologetic about the fact too.

Rejection had swiftly followed her refusal to conform seven years back. Aristandros was very black and white. There was no going back with him, no halfway measures or compromises. The break-up had felt as swift, cruel and unjust as a sudden death. At least this time around, she reflected heavily, she knew what to expect if she crossed the line with Aristandros Xenakis. There would be no second chance to get it right…

CHAPTER FOUR

'I ALMOST forgot,' Aristandros remarked, striding into a book-lined room off the imposing hall and leaving Ella to hover in the doorway.

Ella watched him lift a small shallow case from the desk. Her smooth brow pleated.

'Come here,' he urged with his usual impatience. 'You can't go out without jewels.'

'I don't have any,' she confided with an uneasy laugh.

'I'm starting off your collection, *glikia mou*.' Aristandros detached the glittering diamond necklace from its velvet bed as she approached him on stiff legs. 'Turn round.'

'I don't want it!' Ella told him sharply for, while she had tolerated the clothing, a dazzling river of diamonds felt too much like the biblical wages of sin. Her principles had already taken enough of a hit.

'But it is my wish that you wear it,' Aristandros spelt out, purposeful fingers curving to her shoulder to flip her round. The jewels felt very cold against her skin. She shivered as his fingertips brushed her nape. He spun her back round and, with a satisfaction undiminished by her bleak expression, surveyed the glittering tracery of jewels encircling her throat

Ella was surprised by the crush at the gallery opening. She had never dreamt that she would see so many well-dressed people and famous celebrity faces grouped in the same place. Nor had she ever received quite so much personal attention for, the moment she entered the room by Aristandros's side, every female head seemed to swivel in their direction. An audible buzz of conjecture accompanied their passage through the crowds. While Ari was engaged in discussing a sculpture with its creator, Ella strayed across the room. She was studying an enchanting painting of the seashore when she was accosted by a tall, leggy redhead whose perfect body was adorned by a tiny white satin dress.

'So, *you're* my replacement!' the woman snapped, settling her furious and accusing green gaze on Ella. 'Who the hell are you? Exactly *when* did Aristandros meet you?'

Ella knew exactly who the beautiful redhead was. Her name was Milly, she was a top model and probably Aristandros's most recent ex. Ella said nothing, for she had seen the tears in the other woman's eyes and recognised her distress.

'You won't get any warning that it's over. One day you're *in*, and the world's your oyster, and the next you're *out* and there's nothing you can do about it. He doesn't take your calls any more,' Milly recited chokily. 'Every door slams in your face!'

'There has to be many safer and more rewarding options for a woman as young and beautiful as you are,' Ella told her bracingly. 'Don't give him the satisfaction of knowing that you care.'

Milly studied her in wide-eyed bewilderment. 'You're being nice to me? Aren't you jealous?'

'No,' Ella declared with innate dignity. 'I'm not the jealous sort.'

Too late, she saw that the redhead's attention had shifted from her.

'Milly.' From behind Ella, Aristandros greeted the other woman politely.

'You're *not* jealous?' Aristandros queried in near disbelief as his ex-girlfriend vanished speedily back into the crush, unnerved by his ice-cold appraisal.

'Of course not,' Ella assured him, thinking of the seven years she had spent reading about his exploits with countless other women. Familiarity, she was convinced, had brought tolerance and common sense to her outlook. Everywhere Aristandros went, he was a target for ambitious women. That was a fact of life, and as long as he remained fabulously rich and gorgeous, the situation wasn't likely to change any time soon.

Dark eyes sardonic, Aristandros guided her back to the landscape of the seashore. 'It reminds me of Lykos...the beach below the house,' he remarked, inclining his imperious head to the gallery owner hovering a few feet away. 'We'll take it.'

Aristandros had inherited the Greek island of Lykos from his mother's side of the family. Once Ella had had a picnic there with him, and suddenly the years were rolling back inside her head and she was remembering how the breeze had whipped wildly at her hair while they ate. Wrapped up warm for the winter temperatures, she had listened with interest while Aristandros had outlined his plans to revitalise the island's failing economy and prevent the population from falling any further. His sense of responsibility for the small, isolated community living on Lykos had impressed her a great deal.

'Where will you hang the seascape?' Aristandros asked as they left the gallery.

'Where will *I* hang it?' she stressed in confusion. 'Are you saying that you are buying it for *me*?'

'Why not?'

'Because I don't want you buying stuff like that for me; the way you're splashing out cash on me is indecent!' Ella hissed frantically under her breath as they headed across the pavement to the silver limousine awaiting them. Crash barriers prevented the gathered members of the press from getting too close.

Her spine rigid, Ella blinked like an owl while cameras went off all around them, and questions and comments were hurled at Aristandros. Uppermost were the demands to know the identity of his new companion. But, in every way, Aristandros remained gloriously impervious to the media presence, settling into the limo beside her, 'Of course I'm going to buy you things; get used to it!'

'I'm only here with you because of Callie. Contact with her is the *only* reward I want,' Ella proclaimed, uneasy fingers brushing the diamond necklace in meaningful emphasis of the point.

The smooth planes of his lean features took on a cold, sardonic light, his brilliant gaze narrowing. 'No man wants to be told that his only attraction is an eighteen-month-old baby, *khriso mou*.'

Ella lifted her pale head high. 'Even if it's the truth?'

'But it's not the truth, it's an outright lie for which

you should hang your head in shame,' Aristandros traded without hesitation, his beautifully shaped mouth curling with derision. 'You want me as much now as you wanted me seven years ago. Don't make the child your excuse.'

Ella had lost colour. 'It's not an excuse. I may occasionally find you…attractive, but I wouldn't have done anything about it.'

'Too spineless?' Aristandros sent her a contemptuous glance. 'I didn't meet your narrow-minded requirements, so the fact that you wanted me and I wanted you meant nothing to you.'

'Don't be ridiculous…of course it meant something!' Ella flashed back. 'But you wanted me to be something I couldn't be.'

Aristandros closed a strong hand over hers to force her to turn and look at him. 'I only wanted you to be a *woman*, not a strident feminist—'

Ella sent him a flaming look of bone-deep resentment. 'I was never strident. I was sensible. We wanted totally different things out of life. It could never have worked.'

'No doubt time will tell,' Aristandros fielded very drily, releasing his hold on her hand.

The silence that laced their return to the penthouse gnawed at Ella's nerves. She was already wishing that she didn't speak first and think later. They were about to share the same bed, and she could barely believe that, never mind accept the idea in the mood she was in. 'If the painting's to be mine, I'll be hanging it here somewhere,' she told him abruptly, surrendering to a sudden need to bridge an atmosphere filled with tense, uneasy undertones. 'Because I don't have anywhere else to live at present.'

Aristandros sent her a sudden, satisfied smile, as if that bleak assurance was a heart warming plus on his terms. 'You live where I live now.'

An involuntary shiver ran down her taut spine as the level of dependency that that statement suggested continued to chill Ella and her independent soul to the marrow.

The tall, powerful Greek closed his hands over hers to turn her back to face him. Brilliant golden-brown eyes assailed hers. 'Don't fight the inevitable, *glikia mou*. Embrace these changes in your life. You might even find that you come to enjoy them.'

'*Never*,' Ella swore in a fierce undertone.

'I hear words on your lips that no other woman has ever dared to confront me with,' Aristandros confided, his deep drawl silky with indulgence. 'You are truly unique.'

Recognising his triumph at the position he had her in, Ella shut her eyes tight. So, when his mouth came down on hers without warning, her only weapon was her rage. But even as she braced her hands to his chest to push him angrily away she thought better of that move. She had made a devil's bargain, and now payment was due. While Aristandros kissed her, she stood like a statue, unresponsive as stone. But he played with her mouth, soft one moment, teasing the next, and then hot and male and hungry, until her thoughts were no longer clear and her resistance was breaking down, sensual response beginning to quiver through her treacherous body in an ever-swelling tide.

With a masculine growl of approval, Aristandros bent down and lifted her, swinging her up into his arms with easy strength to carry her into the master bedroom.

Her heart was racing so fast she couldn't catch her

breath. When he set her down, she kicked off her shoes. A soft glide of air brushed her backbone as her dress was unzipped. His sensual mouth was like a brand on hers. The slide of his tongue between her parted lips was an indescribable aphrodisiac that sent darts of heat and tingles of excitement quivering through her entire body. For an instant she was shattered by the awareness that she wanted him as fiercely as she wanted air to breathe. Guilty unease filtered through her, cooling her head for a moment as she tasted the bitter truth that she was weaker than she had thought she would be.

'Stop it,' Aristandros growled, scorching dark-golden eyes raking her troubled face.

'Stop what?'

'Thinking whatever you're thinking which is suddenly giving you all the animation of an Egyptian mummy.'

Discomfited colour bloomed across her cheekbones.

'In fact, don't think at all,' Aristandros urged forcefully. 'This is sex. You don't need to carve it up into little intellectual nuggets to be studied below a microscope. Be spontaneous…natural.'

'*Natural*?' Ella hissed at him tempestuously. 'This is the most unnatural thing I've ever done!'

His blue-shadowed jawline clenched. 'Only because you're fighting everything I make you feel.'

That he recognised her struggle, ineffective though it was, shook Ella, for it had not occurred to her that he might understand her that well. His impatience unconcealed, he dumped her down on the bed. 'This is sex', he had said with a detachment that ran contrary to her every instinct. But if their arrangement was to work, she reasoned, she had to stop judging him and wanting and expecting more than he was ever likely to give her. She had passed the last deadline: it was crunch time.

'How many guys did you say?' Aristandros enquired silkily, watching her shimmy beneath the sheet until only her shoulders could be seen.

Ella sat up, delicate facial bones tightening defensively. 'I *didn't* say!'

The silence stretched. A sardonic edge to his expressive mouth, Aristandros undressed, taking his time, every movement fluid with a grace that caught her eye no matter how hard she tried to avoid that side of the room. From the whipcord muscles of his shoulders to his beautifully defined torso, he was a vision of sculpted masculine perfection. He was also very well endowed and fully aroused, she could not help noticing. Her mouth ran dry and her heart began to pound.

'Less than fifty?' Aristandros asked casually.

Ella shot him an aghast glance.

'Definitely less than fifty,' he decided for himself.

'It's none of your damned business!' Ella launched back at him furiously. 'Stop making a production out of it!'

'Come out from below the sheet.'

In a series of violent movements, Ella kicked off the sheet and reclined back against the pillows in the exaggerated pose of a glamour model, with her spine arched to thrust out her chest. 'Satisfied?'

Aristandros raked his appreciative gaze over the voluptuous swell of her breasts in the turquoise bra. 'Not yet. Take it all off, *glikia mou.*'

Her blue-as-sapphire eyes rounded. '*Everything*?'

Aristandros inclined his handsome head in a confirmation that was a clear challenge. For a split second, Ella was rigid with rejection, and then she scrambled off the bed. Taking up a defiant stance, she peeled off her bra and discarded her knickers.

His attention nailed to her, dark eyes flaring hungrily over her pale, slender curves, Aristandros strode forward and snatched her up into his arms. 'I already feel like I waited a lifetime for you!' he growled, claiming her soft mouth with savage possessiveness even while his hands moulded to the pert mounds of her breasts and kneaded the swollen pink tips between his fingers.

Her body came alive with almost painful immediacy. Needles of bittersweet longing arrowed from her breasts to her pelvis, and awakened a hollow feeling that was swiftly followed by a sharp stab of desire that made her tummy muscles contract. His mouth on hers suddenly became a fierce necessity. The pressure of his hard, masculine lips and the erotic exploration of his tongue went some way towards satisfying the craving taking charge of her. The stimulating passage of his hands over her sensitised body made her push against the unyielding contours of his hard muscular torso. He backed her down on to the bed. Heat and restlessness had entered her bloodstream. All of a sudden she was alight with a need that she had known only once before. Then, as now, the power of that sexual hunger scared her with its unnerving strength. Of their own volition it seemed, however, that her hips lifted and her thighs eased apart, seeking ever more intimate contact with him.

Aristandros lifted his tousled head to look down at her, his smouldering gaze scanning her flushed cheeks and the swollen contours of her mouth. 'You'll enjoy yourself much more when you let go of that rigid self-control—'

'Don't taunt me,' Ella warned him grittily.

'I wasn't.' He frowned. 'I want this to be an unforgettable night.'

Her body a playground of tingling, energised responses, all of which seemed beyond her control, Ella shivered, so wound up with tension that it was an achievement just to think. She registered that this was Ari, the ultimate alpha male at his most driven, and seemingly sex was not quite as casual an event as he had made it sound. Even between the sheets he was set on scoring the highest possible results. At the same time, he was so beautiful that just looking at him turned her heart over. He shifted, the hair-roughened skin of his chest scratching against her jutting nipples and sending a scorching dart of extreme awareness down to the swollen heat and moisture at the very heart of her. In a movement that was utterly instinctive, she sank her fingers into his luxuriant black hair to drag him down to her and urge his mouth back onto hers again. He dealt her a frank look of surprise.

'You talk too much,' Ella told him baldly.

Laughter rumbled in his chest and then he kissed her. Complaint was the last thing on her mind, for in that department he had no equal. He kissed with an unholy passion. The all-encompassing hunger surged again and she clung to him, excitement taking over and overwhelming her final defences.

'*Se thelo*…I want you,' he bit out, studying her with dark-golden eyes that smouldered with appreciation. 'When you respond like this to me, it blows my mind, *khriso mou*.'

She writhed in whimpering reaction while he explored the slick, wet flesh between her thighs. She was so tender and he was so skilled that both stillness and silence were impossible for her. Sensation engulfed her with exquisite pleasure as he teased the tiny bud below the pale curls screening her feminine mound. All restraint was gone. Her entire being was centred on the throbbing need he had awakened and the wickedly tormenting expertise of his technique. The yearning hunger got stronger and stronger until it felt as though her whole body was primed on a knife-edge of intolerable tension and longing. When he finally tipped her off that edge into climax, it was as if an explosion began low in her pelvis and slowly, wonderfully, roared in wave after glorious wave through the rest of her.

She was still awash with wondering bliss and stunned by the intensity of the experience when Aristandros slid between her thighs and sunk his hands below her hips to raise her. His iron-hard shaft probed her lush opening, and she gasped at the strangeness of a sensation magnified by the incredible sensitivity of her tender flesh. He attempted to plunge deeper, but for an instant her body seemed to resist him. With a stifled exclamation he tipped back her knees to ease his entry. Her untried feminine sheath finally stretched to accommodate him, and she cried out at the sudden shockingly sensual pleasure of his penetration. Her heart was racing as he delved deeper into her, and she arched up, on fire with excitement and renewed hunger. Nothing had ever felt so amazing. She was spellbound by the heady exhilaration of his masculine dominance and the extraordinary pleasure that was building inside her again. Just moments later she surged feverishly to another sexual peak which shattered her like glass into a hundred glittering pieces and flung her into the sun. Stunned by the explosive intensity of the pleasure, she was better prepared when it happened yet again, before he achieved his own release.

In the aftermath of that wild rollercoaster experience, Ella was in shock and as physically weak as a newborn kitten, drained by her own extravagant response.

'My every dream comes true,' Aristandros purred as he stretched like a jungle cat in the heat of the sun. Rolling back to her, he dropped a kiss on her brow and studied her with unashamed satisfaction. 'A multi-orgasmic woman who sets my bed on fire, *khriso mou*.'

Ella was hugely embarrassed at having been so wildly responsive. She could not deny that sex with him had proved to be an extremely pleasurable activity. But, whether it was fair or otherwise, she pretty much hated him for the fact that he had made her enjoy herself. Her lovely flushed face bleak as a wintry day, she evaded his keen scrutiny because she felt she had let herself down. After all, she had planned just to tolerate his love-making, not leave him with the impression that he was an amazing lover.

'And so beautiful,' Aristandros remarked, trailing caressing brown fingers lazily through the silken tangle of white-blonde hair lying across her slim shoulder. 'But remarkably inventive with the truth.'

Her hackles rose instantly. Given the excuse, she pulled away from him and snapped, 'Meaning?'

'You said you'd had a lot of lovers. But I don't think there was even one.'

'Well, you'd be wrong!' she hissed furiously.

Aristandros captured her hand to imprison her when she began scrambling out of the other side of the bed. 'I've never shared a bed with a virgin before, but you felt as tight as one,' he imparted softly.

Affronted by the intimacy of that comment, Ella wrenched her hand out of his. 'Wishful thinking, eh?' she jibed, high spots of colour burning over her cheekbones. 'You're Greek to your backbone, aren't you? You've slept with scores of women but you don't want one who's enjoyed the same freedom. In fact, your ultimate hypocritical fantasy is a virgin!'

'Don't speak to me like that,' Aristandros intoned with an icy bite to his words.

'*Se miso*; I hate you!' Ella spat at him.

Stalking across the bedroom, Ella took refuge in the bathroom. She was trembling and her eyes were scratchy with the tears she was fighting back. He had become her first lover, but she would sooner have cut out her tongue than admit that fact to him. She didn't want to give him that satisfaction—the knowledge that she hadn't got really close to any man since he had walked out of her life seven years earlier, telling her that she would regret turning him down until her dying day. She had met other men, but sadly nobody who had had the same effect on her as Aristandros Xenakis. Having loved and lost him, she had been determined not to settle for anything less. And those high standards had ensured she'd stayed single and alone.

Recognising just how far she had now fallen from her own ideals hurt. Ari made her feel vulnerable and threatened. She already felt as though he had turned her inside out. She got into the shower to freshen up, still shaken that he should have noticed that she was something less than experienced. After years of athletic activity and the egg-donation process that had resulted in her sister conceiving, Ella had been confident that he would have no reason to ever guess the truth. Her pride utterly denied him any right to that truth.

She was wrapped in a towel when a knock sounded on the door. She flung it open. 'What now?'

'What's the matter with you?' Aristandros demanded rawly. 'We're good together. Tomorrow you meet Callie. What's wrong?'

The sound of her niece's name, the tacit reminder of their agreement, steadied Ella. 'Nothing's wrong. It's been a long day, and I suppose I'm tired,' she muttered, sidestepping him to leave the bathroom.

In the dressing room she selected a strappy nightdress and got back into bed, scolding herself for her loss of temper and control. She was being stupid. Antagonising Aristandros was pure insanity. Bitten, he would bite back, and she had the most to lose. She was not necessary to him and far from irreplaceable. Any number of women would be happy to assume the role of mistress, and none of them was likely to shout at him or insult him. He wasn't accustomed to that kind of treatment and he wouldn't tolerate it.

At dawn the following morning, she listened while Aristandros showered and dressed and left the room before she drifted off to sleep again. A maid wakened her a couple of hours later and told her that Aristandros would breakfast with her when she was ready. Aware that within a few hours at most she would be meeting Callie, Ella leapt out of bed with enthusiasm and rushed to get dressed. Breathless and unbelievably tense, she entered the elegant modern dining-room.

'Good morning,' she breathed stiltedly, every skin cell in her body jumping as Aristandros cast down his copy of the *Financial Times* and rose to his full, commanding height.

Having sex with him had increased her awareness by a factor of at least a hundred. Uneasily conscious of the intimate ache between her thighs and the still-swollen contours of her mouth, she felt the hot blood of embarrassment engulf her face with uncomfortable warmth even before she met his brilliant dark-golden eyes. He gave her a steady look that betrayed nothing beyond his rock-solid assurance and cool.

For some reason she remembered their first date seven years back, when he had wakened her whole family by arriving unannounced at an early hour to take her out sailing on his yacht. Her stepfather, had fawned on him to a mortifying degree while her twin half-brothers had hovered, unsure whether to approve or disapprove of a mega-rich Xenakis with a bad reputation taking an interest in one of their sisters. Only her mother had had reservations. Ella hadn't really appreciated just how rich, powerful and well-known Aristandros was until she saw the way other people treated him.

She was surprised by how much of an appetite she had, and she ate a good breakfast before asking tautly, 'Is Callie on her way here?'

'No. She'll be waiting for us on *Hellenic Lady* with her nurse. We're sailing home to Greece,' Aristandros informed her.

Like all of his family, Aristandros was never happier

than when he was on a boat. Susie had complained bitterly about Timon's love of the water, which she had not shared.

'I hope she likes me,' Ella muttered before she could think better of revealing that admission of insecurity.

'Of course she will.' Aristandros shot her a lingering look redolent of very male appreciation.

Her cheeks warming, Ella stirred her coffee.

'She's also very lucky I let you get out of bed this morning,' he husked.

Ella dealt him a startled glance from her vivid blue eyes.

Aristandros rested a lean-fingered brown hand on her slim thigh and urged her round to face him. 'I wanted to keep you awake all night. Moderation isn't my style, *koukla mou.*'

Wildly conscious of the unashamed hunger that had flared like liquid gold in his intense gaze, Ella found herself leaning forward to speed up the meeting of her mouth with his. She could not have explained what prompted her to make that encouraging move. But that spontaneous kiss was indescribably sweet and intoxicating, and it sent every nerve-ending jumping with vibrant energy and response. A quickening sensation thrummed low in her pelvis. A moment later, his hand was meshed in her hair, holding her to him, and a moment after that he had lifted her right out of the chair into his arms. Excitement blazed through her like solar flares as he carried her back to the bedroom...

CHAPTER FIVE

ELLA was so taut with anticipation that her heart almost leapt out of her chest when she first saw Callie in the reception salon of the Xenakis yacht.

At a glance she recognised how much her biological child resembled her, with that silvery-blonde cap of hair and those almond-shaped blue eyes. She wondered with painful regret if ironically that pronounced similarity had unleashed Susie's insecurity over her role as Callie's mother. The little girl straightened up to turn away from the toy she was playing with and focused not on Ella but on Aristandros. But, instead of toddling forward to greet the tall Greek as Ella expected, Callie waved at him and smiled. Aristandros waved back.

'She always smiles when she sees me,' Aristandros commented, evidently content with the style of his greeting.

Ella went over to meet her niece and got down on her knees, her heart lurching as she studied the child, whose very blue eyes were curious. A shy little hand reached out to touch Ella's equally pale hair and then hastily withdrew again. Recognising Callie's fear of the unfamiliar, Ella began talking to introduce herself, and within minutes totally forgot the presence of Aristandros and the Greek nursemaid stationed on the other side of the vast salon. When she recalled their presence she looked back over there but Aristandros had gone.

She soon discovered that Callie lit up when she heard music and loved to dance. The little girl giggled in delight when Ella joined in, and the atmosphere became much more relaxed. When refreshments were served, Ella sat down to get acquainted with her niece's youthful nurse, Kasma, and find out about the child's routine. While the two women talked, Ella made a hat out of a napkin to amuse Callie, who was becoming fractious. Callie finally consented to sit on Ella's lap to enjoy a fruit snack. Momentarily the warm, solid baby weight of the toddler resting trustingly against her made happy tears wash the back of Ella's eyes; this was a moment that she had truly believed she would never know in reality. Just then, every sacrifice she had made seemed more than worthwhile.

Kasma had a good deal to tell her that was of interest. The young woman stood in too much awe of Aristandros even to imply criticism of her employer. Even so, what Ella learned from subtle questions soon convinced Ella that Aristandros had zero parenting skills and, quite possibly, no interest in rectifying that deficiency. By then Callie was fast asleep in her arms, and Ella followed Kasma down to the lower-deck cabin which was set up as a nursery and put her niece in her cot for a nap.

Keen to freshen up—something Ella hadn't had a chance to do earlier that day after their rushed late depar-

ture from the London penthouse—she returned to the
main cabin suite, where she took a shower in the superb
marble wet-room. She couldn't stop smiling as she relived
the afternoon that had just passed. The hours had just
melted away while she'd been with Callie. A stewardess
came to tell her that Aristandros was waiting for her in
the salon. Ella finished drying her hair, her body tingling
in outrageous tune with her thoughts, because she could
not forget the pure, erotic excitement of Aristandros's
love-making at the outset of the day, or the blissful release
she had once again experienced in his arms.

'A change of plan—we're flying to Paris in an hour,'
Aristandros announced when she joined him.

'Paris?' Her eyes homed in on him straight away and
involuntarily clung to his compellingly handsome
features. Even in the formal garb of a black pinstripe
business-suit and dark silk tie, he emanated a charge of
raw sexuality and animal energy that made her mouth
run dry as a bone. 'Why?'

'Some friends are having a party, and I'm looking
forward to showing you off.'

'But Callie's in bed and exhausted. She's just flown
in from Greece,' Ella reminded him uncomfortably.

'She can sleep during the flight.' Aristandros
shrugged, instantly dismissing her protest. 'Children
are very resilient. I must have travelled round the world
with my parents a score of times by her age. How did
you get on with her?'

'We got on great, but it'll take time for her to bond
with me.'

'You'll still be a better mother than Susie ever was,'
Aristandros forecast with a hint of derision.

Astonishment and annoyance at that criticism flared through Ella in defence of her late sister. 'What on earth makes you say that?'

Engaged in flicking through a business file, Aristandros raised a sleek ebony brow and glanced up again. 'I'm not afraid of the truth, and death doesn't purchase sainthood. You should never have agreed to your sister's request that you donate eggs to enable her to become pregnant. Susie couldn't handle it. An anonymous donor would have been a safer bet.'

'What are you talking about?' Ella demanded angrily.

Aristandros dealt her an impatient look. 'Don't tell me that you never realised that as far as Susie was concerned you were the kid sister from hell? You outshone her in looks and intelligence, and compounded your sins by attracting my interest.'

'That's complete nonsense!'

'It's not. Susie tried to lure me long before she ever looked at Timon, but I didn't bite.'

Ella was shattered by a piece of information that had never come her way before. Susie had been attracted to Aristandros? That possibility, that very private and dangerous little fact, had never once occurred to her. 'Is that honestly the truth?'

Aristandros frowned. 'Why would I lie about it? I wasn't pleased when Susie started dating Timon, but he fell hook, line and sinker for her.'

Ella had lost colour, the fine bones of her profile prominent below her creamy skin. All of a sudden things that she had not understood but which had given her an uneasy feeling were being explained—her sister's constant, tactless carping about Ari's inability to stay faithful throughout the period when Ella had been seeing him; her repeated angry accusations that Ella didn't appreciate just how lucky she was.

'No matter what your sister did, Timon forgave her because he loved her. But, when you made it possible for them to have a child together and Susie turned her back on that child, Timon couldn't accept it.'

Ella gave him a stricken appraisal. 'Susie turned her back on Callie? How?'

'She left their staff to take care of her. Having got the baby she insisted she could not live without, she rejected her. Timon was at his wit's end. He consulted doctors on her behalf. Susie refused to see them, and finally Timon began to talk about divorcing Susie and applying for sole custody of Callie. Their marriage was very much on the rocks when they died.'

Her consternation and sadness at that news palpable, Ella sank heavily down on a chair. 'I had no idea that the situation was so serious. If only I had known, if only Susie had been willing to see me and talk to me after Callie's birth, maybe *I* could have—'

'You were the last person who could have helped her. She was too jealous of you.'

'It's perfectly possible that Susie was suffering from severe post-natal depression. Didn't my family try to help her?' Ella prompted feverishly.

'I don't think they recognised the extent of the problem, or that they wanted to get involved once they realised that Susie's marriage was in grave trouble,' Aristandros said flatly.

Ella knew that in such circumstances her domineering stepfather would have urged her mother to mind her own business, and that her mother would not have had the backbone to stand up to him even if she'd disagreed. She felt unbearably sad. Had Susie been suffering from depression? Evidently, however, even Timon had been unable to persuade her sibling to seek professional help. Poor Callie had had a troubled and insecure life right from the moment of her birth. Ella thought that it was hardly surprising that the little girl was quiet and somewhat behind in her development.

'How much time have you spent with Callie?' Ella asked Aristandros.

His well-defined black brows pleated, as if he suspected a trick question. 'I see her every day that we're under the same roof.'

'But do you play with her? Talk to her? *Hold* her?'

Aristandros winced at those blunt questions. 'I'm not a touchy-feely guy. That's what you're here for.'

Ella breathed in deep and stood up. 'I don't want to offend you, but I have to be frank. At the moment, all you seem to do is wave at her from the doorway of her nursery once or twice a day.'

Aristandros frowned and threw up his hands in objection at her censorious tone. 'It's a little game we play. What harm does it do?'

Ella was hanging on to her temper only by a hair's breadth. He was not that obtuse. He could hardly believe that he was playing father of the year with a long-distance wave. 'Callie needs to be touched and talked to and played with. The reason she didn't rush to greet you today is because you've got her accustomed to only seeing you at a distance—and that's how you like it, isn't it? Hands-off parenting? But she needs real contact with you—'

'What am I supposed to do with a baby?' Lean, strong face hard with impatience and hauteur, Aristandros ground out that demand, clearly offended by her criticism. 'I'm a very busy man and I'm doing my best.'

'I know you are. You just need a little direction,' Ella murmured, suddenly wondering if the closest he had ever got to his own dysfunctional parents was a breezy, noncommittal wave from the nursery door. 'And then you'd be brilliant, because you always do well at anything you set out to do.'

His dark eyes gleamed at that assurance while a wicked slow-burning smile tilted his beautiful mouth. 'Flattery will get you nowhere, *glikia mou*.'

'Will you think again about flying to Paris—for Callie's sake?' Ella pressed softly.

'You don't do sweet and submissive well.'

Mortified by the derisive tone that let her know that he had seen straight through her attempt to talk him round to her way of thinking, Ella stood straight as a blade, colour burnishing her cheeks. 'I was trying to be tactful.'

'I don't like it. It doesn't suit you,' Aristandros spelt out without skipping a beat. 'On the very first day you meet Callie, do I need to remind you that I make all the decisions where she's concerned?'

Ella turned very pale at that blunt reminder. She met cold eyes, the warning look of a strong male who had no intention of allowing his authority to be challenged. Her tummy flipped. He made her appreciate all over again that he was the one in control, and that she was walking a dangerous path from which she could not afford to stray. It was clear that he intended to hold her to the very letter of the agreement he had made her sign. She had promised not to interfere in Callie's up-bringing. All of a sudden she was appreciating just how difficult it was likely to be to take care of Callie while following his rules.

'*We* come first in this instance, not the child. *Don't* let her come between us and cause discord,' Aristandros advised her with forbidding emphasis.

Ella wanted to tell him how selfish and unreasonable he was being, but he had just delineated her boundaries as a warning and she did not dare. Aristandros Xenakis had spent thirty-two years on the earth doing exactly what he liked at all times. She might try to guide, but he would never allow her to lead. Who was she to think she could change him? The chill in the atmosphere raised gooseflesh on her bare arms and she turned to leave.

'Where are you going?'

Her spine prickled with apprehension. 'I, er, need to work out what I'm going to wear this evening.'

'No need. As yet you don't have a proper wardrobe. My staff will organise a selection of dresses to be brought to my Paris home for you, and your maid will do your packing. There's very little that you need to do for yourself now.'

Ella flipped back round. 'Sometimes you scare me…' And the instant she voiced that admission she regretted it, but there it was: the complete unvarnished truth.

Aristandros cast aside the file and vaulted upright. His astute eyes were unreadable, his fabulous bone-structure taut. 'I don't want that.'

Ella pinned her tremulous lips closed. 'I can't help the way I feel.'

'You're one of the strongest women I've ever known,' Aristandros countered.

But he was making a coward of her because if she spoke her mind she stood to lose too much, Ella conceded bitterly. Aristandros closed a hand over hers and tugged her closer. With an imperious shift of his handsome head, he smoothed her fingers straight and linked their hands. 'If it's that important, I'll make more effort with Callie.' Unusually he hesitated, his wide, sensual mouth compressing. 'I don't know how to go about it, though. I didn't have a conventional childhood.'

Ella was well aware that even that minor admission of ignorance was a major step for him, and that any sort of change of heart on his part was to be warmly appreciated and encouraged, but she was still so tense and worked up that her hand trembled in his. 'I *know*,' she said feelingly, her heart lurching inside her, for his cruelly troubled childhood had been lived out in the full glare of the media spotlight thanks to his larger-than-life parents and was very well documented.

'My earliest memory is of my father shouting at my mother when I almost drowned in a swimming pool. They were either drunk or high…' A broad shoulder shifted, his strong face hardening. 'They were so busy fighting they left me out on the terrace and forgot about me again. I know what *not* to do if you have a child.'

'Yes, of course you do,' she agreed. 'When you're a kid it's so frightening when you see adults fighting and out of control. The first time I saw Theo hit my mother, I thought the world was going to end…' As Ella realised what she had inadvertently revealed, she was appalled by her carelessness, and she fell silent.

'Repeat that,' Aristandros urged, his narrowed gaze reflecting his stunned reaction. 'The first time you saw your stepfather *hit* your mother?'

Ella was aghast at what she had let drop. 'I don't want to talk about it. I really didn't mean to say that!'

Aristandros lifted a hand to tip up her chin so that her eyes were forced to meet his. 'But now that you have, there's no going back or denying it. Theo Sardelos is in the habit of hitting your mother?'

Ella was pale as death, and full of the shame she had never been able to shake over that sordid reality. 'I don't think the violence happens as much now as it once did…at least, I would hope not,' she confided jerkily. 'But it's been so long since I had any contact with them, I really have no idea.'

'Did he ever hit *you*?' Aristandros growled.

'No, only my mother. It's a pity he didn't have a legal agreement drawn up like you did before they got married, though I'm not sure she would have signed up if she'd known what she was in for!'

'What the hell are you saying?' Aristandros grated.

'Well, that's why he beat her up—she objected when he didn't come home at night. He was always with other women,' Ella explained grudgingly. 'I think he had affairs with every secretary he ever had, as well as with some of the friends Mum made over the years. Like you, he's very attractive to the opposite sex and an incorrigible womaniser.'

Brilliant dark eyes assailed hers with cold, hostile force. 'I've never hurt a woman in my life, nor would I.'

'I didn't insinuate that you would. That's not why you scare me,' Ella extended tightly. 'You scare me because you're so cold-blooded, so tough and determined to win every bout. It's your way or the highway, and trying not to fall foul of that is a constant challenge.'

'I don't want you to feel like that, but I can't change what I am.' Aristandros breathed, with a raw edge to his deep drawl. 'The fact you compared me to Theo Sardelos is revealing. You see us as similar personalities, a comparison which I absolutely reject. But I *am* shocked by what I have just learned. I can hardly credit that you never breathed a word to me about what was going on in your own home seven years ago.'

'It was a private matter. I grew up with a mother who swore me and my siblings to silence. We were brought up to be ashamed of it and keep it hidden. The violence was never, ever discussed. Everybody tried to pretend it didn't happen.'

'Even your brothers?' Aristandros prompted with growing incredulity. 'Susie never mentioned it to Timon either.'

'Susie just ignored it, and the twins were still quite young when I left home to go to university. I don't know how things stand now. I've always hoped it stopped, but I suspect that was rather foolish wishful thinking,' she muttered heavily. 'Look, can we please drop this subject?'

Unsympathetic to that plea, Aristandros settled his smouldering gaze on her. 'You thought I might be like your stepfather, didn't you? That's one of the reasons you wouldn't marry me.'

'I don't want to discuss this any more,' Ella told him quietly, and she turned on her heel and simply walked out of the salon. She was shaking like a leaf and cursing her unwary tongue. There was no way she could tell him the truth. Of course she had seen a similarity between him and her stepfather. But with Aristandros it had not been violence she feared, but the terrible pain, constant fear and suspicion of living with an unfaithful partner. She had loved him too much to face that prospect.

Ella was overseeing her packing when Aristandros strode into the state room. With a casual movement of one hand he dismissed the maid while wrenching off his tie with the other. 'You've kept too many secrets from me, *moli mou*,' he delivered harshly. 'I don't like that. I will tell you now—that *has* to change.'

Ella slanted a feathery brow. 'Just like that?'

Inflexible dark-golden eyes clashed with her defiant gaze. 'Just like that. Don't try to keep me out of the loop.'

'Ari…threats and warnings don't create the kind of atmosphere that encourages trust and the sharing of confidences,' Ella countered, the flush on her cheekbones accentuating the sapphire brightness of her eyes.

Aristandros shrugged off his jacket. 'Exactly when were you planning to tell me that you have had no contact with your family for years?'

Ella stiffened. 'I already told you that when I admitted that nobody contacted me to tell me that Susie and Timon had died. There was a huge row the night I said I wouldn't marry you. I haven't seen my family since then.'

Aristandros frowned. 'The rift developed that far back?'

'Yes. As far as Theo was concerned, it was my duty to marry you for the good of the family. He was livid. My brothers thought I was insane to say no, as well. They took your side, not mine, because you're filthy rich and a profitable business connection and I'm not,' she

advanced bitterly. 'If it had happened a couple of cen-
turies ago, they would have cheerfully locked me up in
a convent and left me there to rot for the rest of my life!'

'I didn't know your family had reacted that strongly.
Timon did mention that you didn't come home any
more, but I assumed that that was because you were too
busy with your training,' Aristandros admitted. 'Now
that you're with me and Callie, they can hardly continue
to behave as if you don't exist.'

'Don't you believe it. I don't get on with Theo. I
never did.'

'You don't need to get on with him or anyone else
you dislike now,' Aristandros informed her lazily. 'My
guest lists are extremely select.'

Ella tried not to think of her stepfather's rage if he
found himself suddenly excluded from the Xenakis
social circle, and stilled a shiver. She watched Ari peel
off his shirt to reveal the rugged musculature of his
powerful chest and flat, hard stomach. He really did
have the most beautiful body, she acknowledged helplessly. Her nipples tightened into taut, swollen buds
beneath her bra. A clenching tight sensation between her
thighs made her tense. She was remembering the
smooth, steely heat of his skin when she touched him,
the tormentingly sexy slide of his strong, hard body
against hers. The palms of her hands prickled. The
tender flesh at the heart of her throbbed with awareness.

Aristandros surveyed her with a sardonic amusement
that was shockingly aware. 'No,' he breathed. 'We
haven't got the time. Pleasure is all the sweeter when
deferred, *glikia mou*.'

When Ella registered that he had realised just how

she was feeling at that moment, she boiled alive with embarrassment and self-loathing. Did she really find him that irresistible? How could her body get so out of step with her pride that it betrayed her? Was she really such a sexual pushover that she could hardly wait for him to touch her again? Could the experience of physical pleasure change her so much, or make her feel so disgustingly *needy*? Ella stifled an inner shudder of distaste at that image. What was happening to her? All of a sudden she felt like a hormonal teenager suffering from an embarrassing crush that had got out of control.

Callie began crying at the airport. Over-tired and rudely awakened from her rest, the little girl was in no mood to find herself in strange places surrounded by unfamiliar faces and voices. By the time the Xenakis private jet took off, Callie was fully wound up and screaming at the top of her lusty lungs. Without a word, Ella went to assist Kasma, who was looking distinctly frazzled round the edges when Callie continued to sob in spite of all her efforts to the contrary.

'This is a nightmare. Mr Xenakis is being disturbed,' the young nursemaid said guiltily to Ella. 'That should never happen.'

Ella soon discovered that there was no magic solution capable of quickly settling an exhausted and very cross toddler who was merely expressing her distress at having her settled routine destroyed. Although Callie could be distracted for a few minutes, she would soon start grizzling again. Ella took her into the sleeping compartment, sat down on the bed and rocked and sang to the little girl. Miraculously that seemed to calm Callie down, but she then objected vociferously to Ella's every attempt to put her down again. Ella took charge of her for the flight.

'Give her back to her nurse,' Aristandros instructed when they were about to board the waiting pair of limousines in Paris.

Callie tried to cling and had to be prised off Ella, a process which caused sobs to break out again. Ella found it very hard to walk away.

'Well, I don't think we need to worry about the bonding process,' Aristandros remarked with an outstanding lack of tact and sympathy. 'You're clearly a whiz in the maternal stakes. It's only day one and Callie's already doing a great impression of a limpet.'

'She's upset,' Ella fielded tightly.

'One of life's lessons is that she can't always have you when she wants you,' Aristandros countered. 'For what is left of the afternoon you will be fully occupied.'

Indeed, Ella barely had time to catch her breath at his magnificent Paris townhouse before a parade of breathtaking evening gowns arrived for her perusal. A phalanx of beauticians followed to groom her for the party. This time Ella was less tolerant of the beauty regime imposed on her. Indeed, because she would have much preferred to spend time with Callie, she fretted through every step of having her nails, hair and make-up brought to a glossy standard of perfection that she could never have achieved for herself. A maid helped her into the rich blue dress she had picked to wear, and she surveyed her reflection. Her silvery-fair hair fell in a sleek curtain round her shoulders, the designer dress a wonderful frame for her tall, slender figure. Acknowledging that she had never looked so good in her life before, however, had no impact on her frustration at the prospect of having to go through the same prolonged beauty routine every time she went out in public.

Aristandros strode through the door. 'I want you to wear this set.'

Hugely conscious of his appraisal, Ella lifted the large jewel-case he had tossed down on the bed. As she lifted the lid on a magnificent sapphire-and-diamond necklace and earrings, she gasped. 'My goodness…I'm impressed.'

'So you should be. It's a family set.'

Ella tensed. 'Then I shouldn't be wearing it.'

'They've been mouldering in a safe for decades. Someone might as well wear them,' Aristandros decreed in a bored tone that strangled the further protest on her tongue.

Feeling more than ever like a doll being decked out in decorative trappings, Ella put on the jewels. 'I want to check on Callie before we leave,' she told him then, barely glancing in the mirror to see how the superb necklace and earrings became her.

'You have five minutes.'

Ella was dismayed to discover that her niece was still awake and crying intermittently. She had also pushed away the food that Kasma had tried to give her. Ella lifted the little girl out of her cot and examined her. She soon discovered that Callie was running a temperature and had swollen lymph-glands in her neck.

'What's wrong?' Aristandros demanded from behind her a few minutes later.

'I think Callie has tonsillitis. It's probably viral, so antibiotics won't do any good.'

Aristandros turned to the PA hovering at his elbow and instructed him to arrange for a doctor to call. Ella worried at her lower lip. Callie was miserable, and Ella didn't want to leave her. Aristandros flashed her a sardonic look, and her chin came up at what she recognised as a direct challenge. She sped over to Kasma and hastily wrote down her mobile-phone number so that the nurse could keep her in touch with developments. She squeezed Callie's hot little hand and walked away with guilty tears burning her own eyes.

'She's not seriously ill, is she?' Aristandros breathed.

'No, of course she isn't. She'll be fine.'

'So, remember that you're a doctor and stop over-reacting,' Aristandros urged. 'We're going to a party.'

'I'd rather stay here,' Ella admitted, wondering how he was contriving to make her feel guilty as well. Her desire to comfort Callie had nothing whatsoever to do with her being a doctor.

'But another doctor will be checking her out. She is in the best of hands. If there is further cause for concern, we will be informed,' Aristandros pointed out levelly.

Feeling that she was making an unnecessary fuss, Ella breathed in slow and deep, and caught her reflection in a giant mirror as they descended the sweeping staircase into the hall. She barely recognised herself with the spectacular jewels glittering at her throat and ears, and the glorious dress shimmering in the soft lights.

Aristandros closed a hand over hers. 'You look gorgeous, *moli mou*.'

CHAPTER SIX

THE PARTY WAS BEING thrown by Thierry Ferrand, an international banker and one of Aristandros's closest friends. Thierry and his wife, Gabrielle, lived on the exclusive Avenue Montaigne near the Champs-Elysées, where a huge crowd of paparazzi was waiting on the street to catch photos of the guests arriving. This time round, Ella copied Aristandros, held her head high and acted as if the members of the press were invisible.

The Ferrand apartment had been transformed with jaw-dropping extravagance into a Moroccan backdrop for the party. The colourful tented walls, hanging lanterns and the hall fountain scattered with aromatic rose petals made Ella's eyes widen. Aristandros anchored her to his side and introduced her to their hosts. She took an immediate liking to Gabrielle, a lively brunette with a contagious smile.

'I believe you're a doctor?' Thierry Ferrand remarked.

'Yes, but I'm no longer practising,' Ella replied, a touch flatly.

Gabrielle studied her in surprise. 'But why not?'

'Ella plans to devote herself to my ward and her niece, Callie,' Aristandros advanced.

'It's not easy to settle into being a lady of leisure,' Gabrielle remarked. 'I'm a corporate lawyer, Ella, and by the time my maternity leave was over I was ready to *run* back to work!'

'You have a child?' Ella asked.

Gabrielle needed no further encouragement to part Ella from Aristandros and take her upstairs to show off her adorable ten-month-old daughter who was fast asleep in her cot. The two women chatted.

'You're so normal and natural, not Ari's usual style of companion,' Gabrielle commented, her curiosity unhidden. 'Several of his exes are here tonight, and the usual squad of man-hungry singles. I shouldn't have dragged you away from him. You can't afford to leave Ari alone for a moment. Women really do go mad for him.'

Ella shrugged, still bone-deep furious with Aristandros at his stony-hearted response to Callie's illness and his determination that Ella should leave her to attend the party. As far as Ella was concerned, at that moment any woman was welcome to him. 'Ari is very well able to look after himself,' she said lightly.

Her mobile phone rang before she rejoined Aristandros, and she stayed out in the hall where it was quieter to talk to Kasma. Callie was still miserable, thirsty, but refusing to drink because of her sore throat. Furthermore, her high temperature remained a source of concern. When Ella put her phone away she registered that Aristandros was watching her. He beckoned her with in an imperious gesture that brooked no refusal. Her full lips compressed; she felt like a disobedient dog having her choke-chain yanked.

Impervious to her mood, Aristandros ran an appreciative forefinger below the pouting line of her lower lip. 'You look like a queen tonight.'

Her bright-blue eyes gleamed. 'Worthy of your investment?'

'Only time will tell,' Aristandros traded in a typically oblique response. 'But you're definitely a trophy. Every man in the room has noticed you.'

'I'm thrilled,' Ella fenced in a bored monotone.

An appreciative glint lit his shrewd dark eyes, and smouldering sensuality curved his expressive mouth. 'Not now, but you will be later. I intend to make the most of the fact that you're mine to take home, *khriso mou*.'

With his security team acting as a protective filter, a constant flow of people tried to approach Aristandros. A few were friends, most were interested in talking business opportunities, but an equal number were chancers eager to take advantage of an opportunity to meet one of the richest men in the world. Ella, engaged in watching how other women reacted to him, was constantly amazed by how much blatant encouragement and flirtation came his way, even while she stood there right beside him. He introduced her to only a handful of people.

'Let's dance,' Aristandros urged, predictably getting bored with the social chitchat, and closing his hand over hers to extract her from the crush surrounding him at speed.

It was the first time in over an hour that he had even acknowledged her existence. They had barely reached the edge of the floor when Ella's mobile phone vibrated its call signal in her clutch bag. Extracting it in spite of Aristandros's exasperated scrutiny, she left him and returned to the hall to speak to Kasma.

She learned that the doctor had visited and confirmed Ella's diagnosis of tonsillitis and the treatment she had advised. The medication was finally kicking in to reduce Callie's fever and ease the pain of her sore throat. Lighter of heart, Ella went off in search of Aristandros, wondering whether he deserved to hear the good news or not.

Gabrielle intercepted her for a chat, and it was just after parting from her that Ella's phone rang yet again. Ella was astonished when she put the phone back to her ear and heard a voice she had truly believed she might never hear again.

'Ella…is that you?' Jane Sardelos was demanding. 'That friend of yours, Lily, gave me your number.'

'*Mum*?' Ella framed, dry-mouthed with shock, wandering restlessly over to a window and staring out sightlessly at the lights of Paris.

'Where are you?'

'I'm in Paris.'

'With *him*? I understand that there was a picture of you in a British newspaper with Aristandros Xenakis. I couldn't believe it was you, until it was confirmed. What are you doing with him?' her mother pressed feverishly.

'I'm living with him and helping to look after Callie,' Ella admitted with pronounced reluctance.

'Are you out of your mind? You wouldn't marry him when he asked you, but seven years on you're happy to be his whore?'

As that horrible word struck Ella like a physical blow, perspiration dampened her upper lip. 'It's not like that, Mum—'

'Of course it is. It couldn't be any other way with a Xenakis in a leading role. We're all disgusted and embarrassed by your behaviour. What do you think this does to our standing in the eyes of family and friends? How could you be so selfish? How could you shame us like this?'

'Morals have moved on for women since the Middle Ages,' Ella protested. 'I'm in a relationship with Aristandros. It doesn't mean I've become a whore.'

'Your stepfather says that, because of you, we won't be able to visit Callie now!' Jane Sardelos complained with a sob. 'He says that if we do it will look like we're condoning the situation.'

Ella was pale. 'That's untrue and unreasonable. You're Callie's grandmother, and your right to see her should not be influenced in any way by my relationship with Ari.'

'Every picture tells a story, Ella,' her mother interrupted bitterly. 'Only last month, Ari Xenakis was with another woman, one of a *very* long line of other women. Now, all of a sudden, you're wearing a designer dress and a fortune in diamonds round your throat that you could never have afforded to buy for yourself. So, tell me—if that doesn't make you a whore, what does?'

The phone went dead with wounding emphasis, denying Ella the chance to defend herself further. A little voice asked her wryly what more she could possibly have said when it was so clear that her parent wouldn't have been prepared to listen. Numb and sick inside, and with her mother's angry accusations still ringing in her ears, Ella replaced the phone in her clutch bag. A whore: it was not a word she had ever heard on her rather prim mother's lips before. But she knew who would have voiced that abusive word in the first instance: her stepfather. Theo would have stormed and shouted until his wife was upset enough to call her daughter and pass on the official family opinion personally. It would not have been the first time that Theo had used her mother as his mouthpiece.

Gabrielle Ferrand approached and addressed Ella with a strained look on her lovely face. 'I think you'd better go and rescue Ari before a catfight breaks out over him.'

Frowning and totally distracted after her upsetting phone call, Ella followed the brunette and saw Aristandros seated in a lazy sprawl across a sofa. Three gorgeous women literally had him surrounded. They were all over him like a rash, laughing and chattering and giving him looks, little touches and signals that were blatant sexual invitations. Ella felt nauseous just watching the scene, and she waited for Aristandros to take back his own space. If ever a guy had been born to look after himself without any help from anyone else, it was Aristandros. But he made no move to rebut the advances coming his way, and when one of the women sprang up he accompanied her on to the dance floor.

'He's been on his own almost all evening,' Gabrielle muttered frantically. 'He's not used to being neglected.'

'You're saying I've neglected him?' Ella queried while she watched Aristandros and a sexy redhead salsa-dancing with considerable dexterity and enjoyment. She hadn't even known he could move like that. Seeing him smile and allow his body to connect intimately with another woman's hurt like a knife cutting through tender skin. There was an enormous amount of flirtation going on. She was glued to the spot, trapped by ghoulish curiosity and tormented by more pain than she could have believed possible.

'I didn't mean to sound critical,' her companion retorted uncomfortably.

'Don't worry about it. Ari has more than his fair share of charisma. Women always make excuses for him when he behaves badly,' Ella commented, having met with that female reaction to Aristandros on many occasions seven years earlier. 'But I'm afraid I don't.'

Unfortunately, Aristandros was simply being himself—an unapologetic womaniser set on amusement. Ella, however, could not bear to have that fact paraded right under her nose, particularly when her mother's condemnation of their affair was stuck like a giant immoveable rock in the middle of her every thought and reaction. Surely only a woman worthy of the label 'whore' would stand by and just accept Ari's behaviour?

'I can't stay, Gabrielle. Will you tell Ari I've left? But don't rush to do it,' Ella advised, turning on her heel to move towards the front door.

'Don't do it, Ella. I really like you, and he'll be furious if you walk out on him,' the other woman protested. 'I'm sure you're right. He's only flirting…it means absolutely nothing to him. Women of that sort come onto him every day. But you're different, not least because you happen to be wearing the Xenakis sapphires and possess a brain.'

Ella glanced back at Aristandros and the redhead. She felt sick with rage and hurt, and the depth of her reaction terrified her. The hand she employed to push her hair off her hot, damp brow was trembling. She travelled down in the lift to the ground floor where the concierge called a taxi for her. Cameras flared as she departed alone and in considerably less state than she had arrived. By then she was willing to acknowledge that she was running away from her own feelings as much as she was turning her back on a scene of public humiliation. But she was horrified by her over-sensitivity and the powerful emotions churning around inside her. Why should it matter to her so much what Aristandros did? Wasn't she capable of switching off her emotional responses to him? Just then she didn't care about the agreement she had signed. She refused to act like some whore he owned and to do as he expected regardless of how he himself behaved. A dignified departure from the party was truly the only option she could live with.

Back at the townhouse she headed straight for the nursery. Callie was slumbering peacefully, while Kasma was also asleep in her bed in the next-door bedroom with the door ajar. Ella gazed down at the little girl with a volcanic mixture of relief, love and pain rocketing through her. She reminded herself that Callie had managed fine before she was around, and would scarcely miss her, and that while she stayed her mother would refuse to visit her granddaughter. How could she allow that to happen?

Her maid helped her remove the dress and the sapphires and brought her a case when she asked. Ella put on jeans and a T-shirt and packed the few personal items she had brought from London. Then the heavy thud of the front door reverberated through the whole house, and she went rigid.

'Ella!'

Ella gulped at the harsh sound of her name on Aristandros's lips. 'I'm up here…'

Aristandros filled the doorway, strong features taut, eyes blazing a challenge. 'What in hell are you playing at?'

Ella settled bright-blue eyes on him, her chin at a defiant angle. 'What were *you* playing at? If you think I'm going to stand around while you carry on with other women in front of me, you have another thought coming!'

'You don't walk out on me in a public place... *ever*!' Aristandros raked back at her in a tone of fierce condemnation.

'You can tear up the agreement. I'm leaving you, so all bets are off.'

'You're all grown-up now,' Aristandros lanced back with derision. 'You're not allowed to run away when things get too hot for you.'

'I've never run away from anything in my life!' Ella yelled back at him, her temper unleashing like a dam overflowing.

'You run from anything that upsets you.'

'I'm not upset!' Ella practically screamed at him.

'This is not the calm, sensible Ella that I know.'

'But you don't *know* me!'

A sleek ebony brow listed. 'Don't I?'

'No, you don't!' she repeated squarely.

Aristandros settled scornful dark eyes on her. 'I have to confess that I didn't expect quite such a hysterical reaction.'

'Who are you calling hysterical?' Ella threw the demand at him furiously. 'And why the use of that word, "expect"? Are you suggesting that you deliberately chose to flirt with other women to get a reaction out of me?'

His brooding gaze locked to her hectically flushed and lovely face, Aristandros spread brown hands in a graceful gesture that neither confirmed nor denied. 'Would I do something that calculating?'

'Yes!' Ella's seething gaze was glued to him, her accusing stance unabated. 'Yes, you would if it amused you, because you are the most naturally devious and manipulative man I have ever met.'

'I could simply have told you that you were behaving badly,' Aristandros sliced back. 'It's ill-mannered to keep on taking phone calls in company.'

Outraged by that censure of her own behaviour, Ella looked at him in raw disbelief. 'How *dare* you tell me that I was behaving badly?'

His sculpted jawline squared even more, and he settled his steady gaze on her with considerable cool. 'It's the truth. Your behaviour was atrocious this evening. You went out in a sulk and you never came out of it.'

'That's a ridiculous thing to say!'

'Is it? You didn't want to leave Callie.'

'So, I'm human and caring, which is more than anyone could say of your attitude tonight. You didn't give a damn that she was ill!' Ella condemned him hotly.

'Then why did I ensure that I spoke to the doctor who attended her? And why did I check back with Kasma after that?'

Ella ground her teeth together, while giving him a look that would have withered a lesser man. 'I didn't know you'd talked to the doctor...you didn't mention it.'

'In short, I was as informed as you were, with regard to your many phone conversations,' Aristandros skimmed back, smooth as glass.

An almost overwhelming desire to slap him threatened Ella's cracking composure. 'Maybe you did speak to the doctor.'

Aristandros dealt her a tough look. 'I'm not lying. I

may not get all emotional and dramatic like you do, but that doesn't mean that I wasn't also concerned about Callie tonight.'

In receipt of that cutting, hard-hitting reproof, Ella snatched in a deep, steadying breath. 'I apologise if I misjudged you on that score.'

'You did,' Aristandros drawled, rubbing salt in an already open wound.

'But I do not sulk…and I certainly wasn't sulking earlier!' Ella slung back at him angrily.

'Maybe you have another word for it, but you were definitely in a strop.'

'I was annoyed with you,' she admitted grudgingly.

'I'm not so thick-skinned that I didn't get the message, but it was juvenile to parade your mood in public.' Aristandros sent her a grim look. 'I'm a very private man and I value discretion, but tonight you made a scene for the gossip columns. Do it one more time and I'm sending you back to London.'

Ella sent him a fiery look of sheer loathing. 'You don't need to send me any place. I'm leaving. But, my word, you are good at turning the tables, You haven't said one word about your own inappropriate behaviour, except to imply that you were giving other women encouraging signals purely to rile me.'

Aristandros laughed out loud, the unexpected sound of his amusement shattering the tense atmosphere in the room. 'Not to rile you.'

'I don't give a damn what you do,' Ella hissed, slamming the case shut and closing it.

'Liar,' Aristandros framed silkily. 'For a woman who doesn't do jealousy, you were red-hot with it tonight.'

Ella went rigid, shot him a fuming appraisal and swung the case down. She was so mad she wanted to throw things at him. How dared he accuse her of being jealous? How dared he have the power to divine feelings she had not even admitted to herself? As she stalked across the room in a rage, he cut across her path and snatched the case off her. 'What the heck do you think you're doing?' she shouted at him.

'I'm preventing you from doing something very stupid, *moli mou*,' Aristandros growled, throwing open the door of the dressing room and slinging the case in there with a resounding crash.

'I'm not some whore who's going to take whatever you throw at her!' Ella flung at him wrathfully, adrenalin pumping like crazy through her veins and making it impossible for her to stay still or even think with any rationality. 'I'm not interested in your money or what you can buy me. I'm not impressed. Nothing you could give me would persuade me to tolerate the kind of treatment you gave me tonight!'

'Even if I admit that the only woman I want is you?' Aristandros chided, leaning elegantly back against the door to close it. 'Yes, I conducted an experiment tonight, I wanted a reaction.'

'An experiment?' Ella parrotted with raw incredulity.

'A harmless one. Only a very possessive woman would get so worked up at the sight of me dancing with another woman.'

Her slim hands clenched into fists. So much emotion was hurtling round inside her that she felt frighteningly violent, and yet terrifyingly vulnerable at the same time.

'But that's all that I did,' Aristandros continued steadily. 'Nothing else.'

The hard truth of that statement struck Ella like an avalanche powerful enough to knock her off her feet. So he had danced with another woman and smiled and laughed...big deal! Social interactions of that ilk were normal at parties. What had made her overreact to such an extent? Why did she feel like rage was ready to explode out of her because she couldn't contain it? He had wanted a reaction and she had given it to him. *Only a very possessive woman...* And in spite of all her denials she *was* possessive, wasn't she? Violently possessive, with feelings and responses born from years of sitting by on the sidelines looking at photos of Ari with other women and reading about his affairs. Lily had suggested it was an unhealthy obsession, and so it was, for it had fostered a bone-deep streak of jealousy that she had not even recognised for what it was.

'Maybe I overreacted.' Ella voiced those words as though they were composed in a foreign language she found hard to pronounce. It was an acknowledgement of folly which cost her pride dear. For a moment she was standing outside herself and wondering in horror at the raging mindless jealousy that had consumed her and almost persuaded her to burn every one of her boats. Had she truly been willing to sacrifice Callie in that conflagration as well? She was genuinely appalled.

The silence stretched, drawn tight by her strain.

Ella focused on Ari's lean, classic profile, her nervous tension at an incredible high. He had set her up to see how she would react to his flirtation, and he would have had to torture her to get an apology out of her. She hated him, not only for doing that to her, but also for appreciating that what he had made her feel scared her. Suddenly she did not want to probe the precise nature and cause of the madness that had overpowered her common sense. 'The last couple of days—all the changes in my life—have been an incredible strain,' she said instead, her low voice tight and stilted, because her pride was cringing at the excuse she was using.

'Of course,' Aristandros breathed with an almost instantaneous agreement of that explanation that took her aback.

She was standing beside a mirror, and she looked at herself. The illusion of perfection was gone now, replaced by tousled hair, smudged mascara, lipstick and a T-shirt bought at a rock concert.

'Sometimes I push too hard.' Aristandros murmured that concession without any expression at all. 'But don't ever walk out on me like that again.'

Ella jerked her head in agreement, her throat taut with self-restraint. He had pushed her so hard that he had almost broken her. She was scared that she was going to cry as her jangling emotions continued to surge without any hope of being vented. She was fighting to reinstate intelligence and control. He reached for her before she could seal shut the dangerous gaps in her mental armour. The intoxicating sensuality of his mouth met hers in a hot, melting collision.

She fell into that kiss like a drowning swimmer in search of air. Hunger exploded through her every nerve ending in a chain reaction. Her hands delved deep into his thick, black hair. She could feel the raw passion pent up in his powerful body, and even the clothing between them couldn't douse her awareness of the bold ridge of his erection. The sure knowledge of his desire made resisting her own need impossible. The taste of him went to her head, and she felt dizzy and breathless. He curved his hands to her hips and settled her on the side of the bed where he proceeded to dispense with the barrier of her jeans.

'I can't salsa dance like that,' Ella heard herself say abruptly. 'Like that redhead—'

'I can take care of that,' Aristandros declared, pushing up the T-shirt and burying his face in the scented valley between her high breasts, impatiently while he peeled her free of the expensive scraps of satin and lace that still separated him from her slender curves.

Her chest rose and fell rapidly with the short, straining breaths she drew. She was hyper-aware of his every move. The abrasive brush of his stubble against the smooth slope of her breasts sent a violent shiver through her. The scent of him that close left her liquid with longing. 'I want you,' she admitted in a driven undertone.

Lush black lashes lifted from scorching golden eyes. 'I have died and gone to heaven,' Aristandros breathed softly. 'I thought I was never going to hear those words from your lips.'

'We've only been together two days!' Ella protested.

'Since when have I had patience?' Aristandros traded, long fingers skating over the tormentingly tender flesh between her thighs with a provocative skill that caused a startled gasp to part the swollen contours of her lips.

Her head tipped back against the pillows and her spine incurved. A glorious, heavy lassitude was spreading through her limbs, closely followed by energising darts of erotic sensation. She strained up to him, moaning out loud when he used his sensual mouth to tease and taste her urgently sensitive nipples. There was a sweet, painful tightness gathering in her pelvis as her inner muscles tensed and her hips squirmed in a rhythmic pattern against the sheet. She wanted, *needed* him. He turned her over on to her stomach and raised her on to her knees.

For a split second Ella didn't know what he intended but, an instant later he plunged his fully engorged manhood into her yearning flesh. Shock and wild excitement gripped her in an overpowering wave. His every deep thrust sent a hot, primitive charge to electrify her. The erotic pleasure of his virile dominance ravished her sense, and she whimpered her delight, encouraging him with every yielding flex of her hips. The seething tension and disturbed emotions she had stored up were blown away by a spellbinding orgasm that flooded her body with ecstasy and drained her of energy.

'Better?' Aristandros muttered thickly, curving her into his arms in the dizzy, dreamy aftermath when she honestly felt that she would never move again.

'Still floating,' she whispered before she could think better of it.

He leant over her, keen dark eyes lustrous as polished jet beneath the fringe of his black lashes. 'So why do you fight me?'

Ella rested her head against a brown muscular shoulder, revelling in the intimate connection of their bodies and the gloriously familiar scent of his skin. 'I like a challenge?'

His incredibly handsome features taut, Aristandros closed his arms round her and studied her with sardonic force. 'Stop it now, *hara mou*. Making me angry is a bad idea.'

Ella let her fingers trail along the line of his ruthless but aesthetically beautiful mouth. 'It makes you more human, and no matter how hard I tried I couldn't ever be all giggly and flattering and submissive.'

'That's not what I want, either. Be natural, be yourself…the way you used to be without even trying,' Aristandros urged.

Ella lost colour and turned her head away, knowing there was no going back to the young woman he was remembering. Was that what he wanted from her—the impossible? The turning back of time? How could she be twenty-one years old again and in love for the first time in her life? Even thinking about being that vulnerable again turned her stone-cold with fear inside. Loving Ari again would be a one-way ticket to hell.

'If you stop looking for problems, you'll soon find that you can enjoy what we have,' Aristandros intoned with blistering conviction. 'We're sailing back to Greece tomorrow.'

But Ella was already recalling the crazy weeks when she had been twenty-one and madly in love with him. Everybody who was anybody had spent those weeks warning her that Ari Xenakis would quickly lose interest in her. That was his track record, and his appetite for beautiful women ensured that he had an intimidating reputation as a heartbreaker. Ella, however, remembered feeling ridiculously happy during that period. Cool reflection hadn't got a look-in. She had not continually rehashed their dates in her mind looking for hints that he might be considering a future with her, either, for that possibility had not even occurred to her. She had simply adored being with him and had lived for the moment.

He had taken her out sailing a lot, for long drives and lengthy meals, rarely inviting others to join them. They hadn't gone to many parties or clubs, and when they had they hadn't stayed long. They had talked constantly and she had been herself, for she had not known how to be anything else in those days. Hard as it was to credit now, she had believed she had met her soulmate in Ari. The second time she'd called a halt to their love-making he had just laughed and made no further attempt to persuade her into bed. When he'd invited her to his grandfather's seventy-fifth birthday celebrations, she'd been overjoyed, because she had known how close Drakon was to his grandson and had felt honoured to be invited to meet him.

Now, a good deal older and wiser, she lay in the darkness, dully, painfully, reliving that final evening.

'I love you,' Aristandros had told her squarely, and she had responded with the same words. And, although he had afterwards accused her of insincerity, she had really meant what she said.

'I want to be with you. Will you marry me?' he had asked.

And her heart had bounced as high as a rubber ball, since it had not occurred to her then that he might have made the offer with sacrificial restrictions attached, a sort of trick question which was likely to come back and haunt her and leave her heartbroken. She had dimly assumed that they would get engaged and that Ari would visit her in London and marry her once she had completed her training. When he had got up to make a speech in honour of his grandfather's birthday, he had announced their engagement—along with the news that she would be giving up medicine.

Reality had swiftly burst her bubble of happiness. After a ferocious argument he had dumped her, and minutes later retracted the announcement he had made. Her family had taken her home in disgrace, unable to believe or come to terms with the startling idea that she could possibly have refused to marry a Xenakis.

Aristandros catapulted her back into the present by hauling her up against his lithe, muscular frame. Blue eyes very wide, she clashed with his heavily lidded, smouldering, dark-golden gaze. This man, she acknowledged with a fast-beating heart, already had the power to make her feel bitterly jealous and act in an irrational way. He was dangerous, was a very dangerous threat in every way to her peace of mind.

'Once is not enough,' he growled sexily, half under his breath. 'I still want you, *moli mou*.'

And some very basic element in Ella exulted in her sexual hold over him. In that instant, her heart racing, her pulses quickening and her treacherous body quivering with anticipation, she was a slave to the promise of the pleasure he would give her and she had no time to spare for agonising over the label that other people might affix to her position in his life.

CHAPTER SEVEN

TEN days later, Hellenic Lady arrived in Athens.

Ella was still in bed in the yacht's magnificent main state-room and she was devouring the British newspapers, several of which contained items about her. It was an extraordinary experience to suddenly see herself appear for the first time in print in the guise of a celebrity. In her case, however, her fame was purely borrowed from association with Aristandros. She was variously described as his 'new companion, Dr Dazzler', 'Calliope's sexy aunt' and 'the family black-sheep'. Her fascination only died when she came on a disturbing couple of paragraphs that suggested that her family had shut the door on her because she was a promiscuous wild-child.

Aristandros strode in, clad today in a dark pinstripe suit of faultless tailoring that made the most of his tall, well-built body. He was said to electrify a room when he walked into it, and Ella was certainly not immune to that effect. She tensed against the heaped-up pillows, sapphire-blue eyes very wide in the heart-shaped delicacy of her face.

'I've been working for four hours. One glimpse of you,' Aristandros husked, strolling over to the side of the bed, neatly sidestepping the sprinkle of discarded toys that betrayed Callie's visit earlier that morning, 'And I want to get straight back into bed.'

Her body tingled, nerve-endings uncurling in anticipation, heart rate speeding up. It was just sex, and she regularly told herself that fact. But she still had to acclimatise to the magnetic draw of wanting to rip his clothes off every time she saw him.

With an impatient sound he scooped up the heap of newspapers on her lap. 'Haven't you learned yet? You don't *ever* read your own publicity. I pay my lawyers to read it for me,' he confided, discarding the tumbled, crackling newspaper sheets in an untidy heap on the carpet. 'I did appreciate the Dr Dazzler line, but not the wild-child tag. Someone's confused you with your sister Susie, and an official apology will be appearing this week.'

Her full lower lip had parted from the upper. 'Are you saying you've complained?'

Aristandros shrugged and removed his jacket, pitching it on to the ottoman by the wall and removing his shoes. Smouldering dark-golden eyes assailed her as he straightened to his full six-foot-three-inches of height. 'I'm still convinced that you've only ever been a wild-child with me.'

'Well, you'd be wrong.'

'You're all talk and no action,' Aristandros quipped with a razor-edged challenge in his gaze. 'In bed you don't know how to do anything until I do it first!'

Cheeks as red as ripe strawberries, Ella slung him a

furious look. 'I suppose you think that that kind of crack is funny?'

'No, I find it highly entertaining that, while most women prefer to minimise the number of their past lovers, you want to claim more,' he drawled, smooth as silk.

'Why on earth are you getting undressed?' Ella demanded abruptly, finally taking notice of that fact.

'And, in spite of that scarlet past, she still has a mind as pure as driven snow. Haven't I corrupted you in any way?' Aristandros mocked, skimming off his boxers in a manoeuvre that soon made it blatantly obvious why he had stripped off.

'Oh...' A darting little frisson of sexual heat travelling through her slender length, Ella sank back into the pillows in a manner that might almost have been labelled inviting as he joined her in the bed.

'Oh...' Aristandros teased, reclining back and drawing her to him with clear intent. As her slim fingers found the bold, jutting length of his arousal, he emitted a roughened groan of appreciation. 'Oh *yes*,' he growled hungrily. 'You beat the hell out of a coffee break, *khriso mou*.'

For a split second, that quip made Ella hesitate, but in truth she found his sexual spontaneity and raw potency as irresistible as she found him. His sensual mouth on hers was like a brand that burned to create a flame that was never quite doused. No matter how much he kissed her, enough was never enough. His tongue thrust between her lips and released a flood of excitement that lit a feverish trail of response through her entire body. He wrenched her nightdress out of his path and closed his lips on a swollen pink nipple.

Sweet sensation gripped her while his knowing mouth

travelled between one taut peak and the other, laving and teasing her sensitised flesh until she moaned. With the impatient stroke of his forefinger, he probed the slick, wet welcome at the heart of her before pulling her under him with an unashamed urgency that thrilled her. He plunged into her hard and fast, and her eager body rose to meet his. Excitement was as intense and searing as a fire inside her. He pleasured her with long, forceful strokes, pushing back her knees to gain even deeper penetration. She felt like she had hitched a ride to the stars, and the spellbinding pleasure devoured her. She heard herself cry out and buck under him as breathtaking heat and the waves of ecstasy roared through her. In the sheer power of that sensual conflagration, she was helpless and mindless in her response. He slammed into her one last time with an uninhibited shout of satisfaction.

For a timeless moment she lay under him, rejoicing in his weight, the pound of his heart and the rasp of his breath. At that instant she felt as she often did, overwhelmed by the level of mind-blowing pleasure. But not so overwhelmed by physical sensation that she didn't enjoy the brush of his mouth against her brow in a salutation, and the tightening of his powerful arms around her in what might almost have been a hug. He didn't do hugs, but she lived in hope. She loved what he did to her in bed, but she loved the closeness in the aftermath even more, and never, ever stirred a muscle to break their connection before he did.

It was a shock when Aristandros tensed, voiced an unmistakeable Greek curse and pulled back from her in a violent movement that spoke more of rejection than of anything else.

Hard eyes struck her questioning gaze in a near-physical blow. He struck the wooden headboard with a powerful fist, and made her flinch back from him in consternation.

'What?' she gasped in bewilderment.

'I forgot to use a condom,' Aristandros bit out rawly.

'Oh…dear,' was all Ella could think to comment in that unbearably tense moment. The date when she was to start taking the contraceptive pill had not yet arrived, and she had warned him that other precautions would be necessary for the first couple of weeks they were together. Until now he had followed that rule with scrupulous care and had left no margin for error.

Aristandros sprang out of bed like a hungry tiger leaping on prey and swung round to glare at her. 'Is that all you've got to say?' he demanded icily. 'I don't want a child.'

A chill ran through Ella, and she wondered why that statement should feel like a slap in the face when she was equally as keen to avoid the trauma of an unplanned conception. She was frantically working out dates inside her head, which was difficult, as recent changes in her routine appeared to have unsettled her once-regular menstrual cycle. 'I'm afraid it probably wasn't the best time to overlook the precautions,' she admitted ruefully. 'I could be at my most fertile right now.'

'I can't believe I forgot!' Aristandros grated as if she hadn't spoken. 'I'm never careless.'

'Either of us could be infertile,' Ella remarked. 'You'd be surprised how common it is.'

Aristandros gave her a look of outrage and compressed his handsome mouth, as though the suggestion that he might not be able to father a child was a gross insult to his masculinity.

Ella stayed where she was until he had showered and departed. She was in shock, but she also felt that she had just received a much-needed wake-up call. For the past ten days she had been with Aristandros almost round the clock. He got up before six every morning to work with his personal staff. At eight, he joined Ella and Callie for breakfast. If he hadn't yet reached the stage of being able to totally relax and play with the little girl, he was at least unbending from his rigidity around her, and developing the ability to talk to her and get to know her.

Life on the vast luxury yacht was excessively comfortable and easy. The crew attended to their every need, and very often even before Ella realised that something was required or even available. She was waited on hand and foot and encouraged to be a lady of leisure, with nothing more important to consider than her next visit to the well-equipped beauty salon and its staff on the deck below. It was a lifestyle that could never have come naturally to her, but it gave her the opportunity to spend a great deal of time with Callie. The bond between Ella and her biological child already ran deep and strong. While she would never have chosen to frolic in a swimming pool for her own benefit, she was happy to do so when the purpose was to teach Callie to swim, and the occasions when Aristandros had joined them had proved by far the most entertaining.

'Sailing home to Greece' as Ari had termed it, had been more of a leisurely cruise than a straightforward trip between A and B. *Hellenic Lady* had called in at several islands. Aristandros had taken her out clubbing on Crete, and out to dinner on Corfu. Afterwards they had walked through the narrow streets of the old town hand-in-hand. And who had reached for his hand? Ella clamped cool palms to her agonised face. Hand holding? She felt ill. Just then her mortification was so intense that she honestly wanted to slap herself hard. How could she have been so stupid as to initiate such a foolish gesture? Romance had nothing to do with their relationship.

She was his mistress—the woman currently meeting the demands of his high-voltage sex drive—not his girl-friend, his fiancée or his wife. And, just as he had wanted, she was always sexually available, and not because she was afraid to be in breach of that outrageous contract that she had signed! No, indeed; the nagging hunger of desire that tormented her had nothing to do with contractual obligations or pride. She couldn't keep her hands off him, in or out of bed. The need to touch, to connect, was like a fever, a terrible temptation she fought day and night. She was appalled by how attached she had already become to being with Aristandros.

Yet nothing could have more clearly delineated the gulf between them than his reaction to the possibility of her falling pregnant. Somehow he had made her feel like a one-night stand he had picked up, a stranger he barely knew, a female body in which he had no interest once he had sated his most pressing sexual need. If she con-ceived, he would view it as a disastrous development, and she could only hope that the situation didn't arise.

Fresh from the shower and with a towel wrapped round her, she was walking back into the state room when Aristandros entered. 'Did I mention that I'm staging a social gathering at my Athens home this afternoon? No?' he queried lazily, when she gave him a look of frank dismay. 'I have some business to tie up with fellow investors and you'll be acting as my hostess.'

'Thanks for the last-minute warning!' Ella gasped.

'At least you don't need to worry about booking time in the beauty salon,' Aristandros quipped.

They flew from the yacht direct to the property. His villa on the Greek mainland was set in an unspoilt area of countryside. Surrounded by olive groves and vineyards, it enjoyed superb views of the mountains. Ella was surprised by the rural setting, for when she had last known Aristandros he and his grandfather had been very firmly rooted in the vast Xenakis townhouse in Athens.

'Drakon still prefers life in the city, but I like to escape the skyscrapers and the traffic at the end of the day, and here I'm still less than half an hour from the airport,' Aristandros advanced. 'I spend a lot of time on the island now. I can work from home, and it's very private.'

'It's beautiful here as well,' Ella commented, wondering just how many different properties he owned round the world, and even if he knew himself without having to think about it.

'The pearls look good on you.'

In receipt of that remark, Ella brushed the magnificent necklace at her throat with uneasy fingertips. It was matched by the pearl-drop earrings she wore, and most probably worth a fortune. A slender diamond-studded designer watch also encircled her wrist. She had no idea how much her growing collection of jewellery was worth, since nothing as vulgar as price was ever men-

tioned when Aristandros insisted on buying her a gift.
The previous week an imposingly correct jeweller had
flown out to the yacht with a magnificent selection of
world-class gems for Ari's private examination. He had
decided on the pearls, which were reputed once to have
belonged to an Indian maharajah. Ella had already
decided that when she and Aristandros parted she would
leave all such unsolicited presents behind her.

Presumably Aristandros was accustomed to rewarding the women in his bed with gifts of extraordinary
generosity. But the glorious jewels made her feel more
like a trophy piece of arm-candy than ever, and frighteningly deserving of the offensive label her mother had
fired at her: *Whore.* Was that how other people saw her
as well—a costly parasite earning a rich reward for
pleasing her tycoon lover in bed? She cringed inwardly
at the suspicion that she had sunk so low. Ironically, at
a moment when she was dressed from head to toe in
designer clothing, and sporting fabulous gems, her
once-healthy self-esteem was at a very low ebb. She was
very much afraid that on Ari's terms she was just an expensive accoutrement, like a flash car—and, just as he
only drove the world's most expensive cars, he wouldn't
dream of showing off a woman without the spectacular
looks, clothing and jewellery that paraded his wealth.

Catering staff already had the food and drinks for the
reception organised. The house was immaculate, very
contemporary in design, and perfect for large-scale en-
tertainment. A svelte figure in a knee-length plum silk
cocktail dress and stiletto heels, Ella joined Aristandros
on the outside terrace where drinks were being served
just as the first guests arrived. It was not very long

before her cheeks were hot with self-consciousness. While everyone was scrupulously polite, it was brutally obvious that she was the focus of a great deal of curiosity. She tormented herself with worries of what stories might already have appeared in the local press about her. Ironically, it was the arrival of Ari's courteous grandfather, Drakon, which caused her the greatest embarrassment.

'Ella,' the dignified older man murmured, stooping to kiss her cheeks in a kindly salute of polished Xenakis charm. 'Is it rude to admit that, while I am delighted to renew our acquaintance, I very much regret meeting you in these circumstances?'

Lean, strong face broodingly dark and taut, Aristandros answered for her. 'Yes, it is rude, and quite unnecessary, Drakon. What circumstances?'

The elderly Greek's shrewd eyes withstood the challenge of his grandson's grim appraisal. 'Don't pretend to be obtuse, Ari,' he advised drily.

Rigid with mortification, and keen to escape the fallout and any further discussion, Ella was quick to move away to intercept Callie, who was toddling across the room to greet her. Helplessly smiling as the little girl came full tilt into her arms, Ella hugged her. Callie, adorable in a little blue-cotton dress, was as pretty as a picture, and already noticeably more confident and talkative than she had been when Ella had first met her. Callie expressed a desire for the toy rabbit that she took almost everywhere with her, and Ella was taking her back to Kasma to ask where it was when she heard the raised voices sounding from a room off the hall.

Behaving as if there was nothing untoward occurring,

the young nurse lifted Callie and took her back upstairs to look for the rabbit.

'If Callie is Ella's as you say,' Drakon Xenakis was thundering in Greek, 'Give her to Ella and let them both go!'

'I'm not prepared to let either of them go,' Aristandros drawled as quietly as if he was in church, his audible calm a striking contrast to his grandfather's anger. 'I had a very comprehensive agreement drawn up that suits Ella and I very well—'

'A *legal* agreement? Is this what I raised you to do— to corrupt a young woman who only wants access to her own child? Is this what it takes to appeal to your jaded appetites now, Ari? If you had a single streak of decency left, you would marry her, for you've destroyed her reputation!'

'The days when women needed to be whiter than white are long gone, Drakon. Thankfully I live in a world with far more enlightened sexual mores,' Aristandros retorted bitingly. 'Whether you believe it or otherwise, Ella is happy with me—'

'She's worth more than any of the gold-digging sluts you specialise in, and you're treating her worse than all of them! The only thing I see in this scenario is revenge, Ari…and it's ugly and unworthy of you.'

Nausea stirring in her stomach, and her blood running cold in her veins, Ella stumbled away from the partly open door before she could be caught in the act of eavesdropping. Drakon's opinion hit her as hard as a physical blow, because Ari's grandfather knew him well, indeed far better than she did. She had been quick to discard the idea of Aristandros acting in revenge—too quick? Certainly she had much preferred to believe that the secret of her ongoing attraction was more her being a *femme fatale* whom he had never forgotten. But how likely was that interpretation? Was it not more likely that Aristandros was taking revenge for her rejection all those years ago? He had made her walk away from her career, her home and even her principles. He had made her enjoy her captivity in the gilded cage of his life. No; he hadn't *made* her do anything, she acknowledged, trying to be honest with herself—she had made the choices she'd had to make to be with Callie, the daughter of her heart, and to be fair he had kept his promises.

Even so, revenge struck her as the more apt explanation for Ari's continuing interest in her. Why else would a man who could have the most beautiful women in the world settle for an inexperienced and unsophisticated doctor who was ill at ease with a party lifestyle? He would not have sacrificed his own desires and preferences for Callie's benefit. In fact, most probably Callie had merely been used as a weapon to put pressure on her biological mother. Having acquired the child, he had also acquired the perfect means to make Ella dance to his chosen tune, and that was exactly what he had done.

In the shaken-up state she was now in, it was the wrong moment for Ella to set eyes on her family for the first time in seven years. Her stepfather, a heavily built man with thick, grey hair, was standing on the terrace with a drink in his hand. Her mother, a slight, fair-haired woman in a pink dress, was by his side. Behind them stood two tall, dark young men—her half-brothers, grown to adulthood without her knowledge. Ella paled when Theo Sardelos looked right through her, and her mother, her face full of painful discomfiture, turned her head quite deliberately to avoid seeing her only surviving daughter. Her twin half-siblings, disdaining such pretences, stared stonily back at her, their scowling attitude one of pure belligerence.

Ella was very angry that Aristandros had put her family on the guest list without telling her. Conscious that she was not the only person present capable of noting that her family was giving her the cold shoulder, she forced herself to address her stepfather with a perfunctory greeting before turning to her mother to say, 'Would you like to come and see Callie?'

'No, she would not,' Theo Sardelos growled, slinging his stepdaughter a look of profound distaste as he answered for his wife, a controlling habit of his that Ella remembered with repulsion. 'Your presence here makes that impossible.'

Her olive branch broken and discarded unceremoniously at her feet, Ella did not respond. She knew the older man well enough to appreciate that he would relish any opportunity to embarrass her in front of an audience. Although it took considerable courage, she kept on smiling and moved on, beckoning a waiter to ensure a clutch of late arrivals were served at the buffet. Kasma brought Callie back down, and the little girl, her stuffed rabbit now tucked securely under her arm, sped back to Ella's side to clutch at her skirt in a possessive hold.

It took real effort for Ella to continue to play hostess and chat and smile as though nothing was wrong. Every so often she bent down to touch her hand gently on Callie's head and remind herself of what she had gained, and why she had forged her devil's bargain. Her thoughts were tumultuous. Aristandros had only told the truth to his grandfather: she *was* happy with him. Did that mean that at heart she was a slut? Sharing Ari's bed and being with him was more of a pleasure than a punishment. It shook her to admit that to herself. He had held her to ransom over an innocent child's head, and yet whenever he wanted her she was still his for the asking. What did that say about her? Shame and confusion engulfed her in a hot, creeping tide of remorse.

Lily had texted her only that day: *are you his Dr Dazzler by accident or design?*

Ella still didn't know how to answer that question. While the original design had been Ari's, it now sometimes seemed to her as though she had simply surrendered, and had used Callie as her excuse for doing so. When Aristandros touched her, she went up in flames. What had started out purporting to be a sacrifice had become a delight. If she was a victim, of revenge she was a willing victim and that reality made her cringe.

Lean, breathtakingly handsome face cool as icewater, his carriage as always superb, Aristandros strode towards her. Nothing in his expression revealed any sign of annoyance over his recent dispute with his grandfather. Her heart lurched behind her breastbone, her mouth running dry as he rested a hand at the base of her spine and whispered, 'Why aren't you with your family?'

CHAPTER EIGHT

ELLA shot him a darkling glance of disbelief. 'Why on earth did you invite my family when you knew there was a rift between us all?' she flung at him, half under her breath, furious that he had set her up for such a confrontation even after she had told him that her family was at odds with her and had been for years.

'I thought the invitation would help...I even thought you might be pleased to see them!' Aristandros responded, his strong face taut

'It was a serious mistake. You shouldn't have interfered. My family don't want to be around me when I'm with you,' Ella revealed in a bitter surge of confidence. 'In fact, Theo says they can't have anything to do with Callie while I'm here.'

Aristandros rested his stunned gaze on her, and swore below his breath. 'That's outrageous, *khriso mou*. He cannot insult you below my roof. Anyone who does so is an unwelcome guest.'

'There's not much you can do about it. He's a very stubborn man. Just ignore it, as I am, and hopefully in time he'll get over his pique. You shouldn't have asked them here.' Ella's teeth worried anxiously at her full lower lip as she absorbed the stormy flare of gold immediately lightening Ari's spectacular eyes. Assurances that he should *not have* done something went down like a brick with a guy who had based his entire life on doing what he wanted to do on every occasion. Callie vented a cross little sob and tugged at Ella's dress, while resting heavily up against her legs as tiredness took her over.

'Sardelos has upset you,' Aristandros growled. 'I will not tolerate that.'

'Stay out of this, it's not your business,' Ella hissed in a frantic undertone as she bent to comfort Callie, and lifted the child up into her arms. 'If you interfere any more it'll just cause endless trouble and resentment. I'm going to put Callie down for a nap. Promise me that you'll mind your own business.'

Aristandros dealt her a sardonic look of disbelief. 'You *are* my business. If they insult you, they insult me, for it is my wish that you be here and I will not tolerate any show of disrespect.'

Anchoring the little girl on her hip, and keeping her there with one straining arm—for Callie was no lightweight—Ella rested what she hoped was a soothing hand on his chest. 'Nobody is being disrespectful of you,' she hastened to assert in an effort to pour oil on troubled waters. 'Please don't get involved...*please*. Don't play with fire.'

With that final, urgent plea for forebearance, Ella headed off with Callie. Kasma offered to carry the little girl upstairs, but Ella demurred; in the mood she was in, the feel of Callie's clinging arms was comforting. The very last thing she needed was for Aristandros to wade in to an already delicate situation. She was all too painfully aware that her mother invariably suffered when Theo lost his temper

When she glanced down from the landing, she saw the male guests were gathering in the hall, and then moving on into Ari's office-suite, where a conference room would house the investors' meeting he had mentioned. The sight of what had to be an excellent diversion for unreliable masculine tempers and egos filled her with a giant sense of relief. When business was at stake, Aristandros would surely not waste his energy thinking about anything else.

'Shoos,' Callie sounded importantly as Ella removed her sandals. 'Socks.'

'Very good,' Ella applauded, turning up Callie's earnest little face to drop a kiss on it.

'My goodness, she's talking now…'

Ella almost jumped out of her skin, and twisted her head round to focus on the older woman in the doorway. 'Mum?'

'Theo's gone into the meeting, and I asked a maid to bring me up,' Jane Sardelos explained in a harried undertone. 'He would be furious if he knew I was here with you.'

'He gets furious far too easily. Why won't you leave him?' Ella asked in a pained, heartfelt undertone that betrayed her incomprehension on that score.

'He's my husband and he loves me. He's been a good father and provider. You don't understand,' the older woman proclaimed, just as she had throughout Ella's teenaged years. 'Let me see my grandchild… She's the very image of you, Ella.'

Ella noticed that the little girl showed no sign of recognising her grandmother. 'You haven't seen much of her, have you?'

'Susie was very difficult after the birth,' Jane murmured sadly as she stared down with softening eyes at the sleepy little girl and sat down beside the cot. 'She didn't want my advice, or anyone else's, and it was obvious that her marriage was breaking down and she didn't care. I saw Calliope a few times when she was very young, but Susie really didn't want to be bothered with visitors, and she was quite unpleasant on several occasions.'

'I think that Susie very probably had post-natal depression,' Ella contended gently.

'She wouldn't see a doctor, though.' Jane Sardelos shook her head heavily. 'I did what I could, but your sister was always very wilful and I'm afraid she paid the price for it. But I don't want you to pay a price as well.'

'Let's not talk about me,' Ella cut in hurriedly.

'Half the world is talking about you since you moved in with Ari Xenakis. He might want you today, Ella, but there are no guarantees for the next day, or the one after that. I shouldn't have called you what I did, but I was very upset when I found out that you were living with him.'

'I can't discuss Aristandros with you. I'm an adult and I've made my choice. I don't expect you to agree with it, but there's no point arguing about it, because it won't change anything. Mum, it's seven years since I even saw you,' Ella reminded the older woman painfully. 'Let's not waste this moment.'

'A moment is really all we have,' the older woman acknowledged tautly, scrambling up to wrap her arms round her taller daughter in a sudden jerky movement that betrayed the precarious state of her nerves. 'I've missed you so much, particularly after Susie passed away. But Theo is outraged by this situation. He says that because of your very public affair he's lost face.'

Ella hugged her mother back with warm affection. 'For goodness' sake, he always exaggerates—he is only my stepfather.'

'You've embarrassed the whole family,' another voice delivered in condemnation from the doorway.

Ella focused on her half-brother, Dmitri, as her mother backed away from her. 'Stop making excuses for your father,' Ella urged. 'He found fault with everything I ever did because I stood up to him. He doesn't like me and he never will.'

'Mum…in a few minutes Dad will be looking for you. You need to come back downstairs.' Having issued that warning, Dmitri turned away from Ella, who was livid with him for behaving like a pompous prat.

'Do you still live at home?' she asked her brother. Watching her mother turn pale with fear as she'd registered the risk of her husband discovering that she had defied his dictates took Ella back to all the years that she did not want to recall. Years blighted by sudden violence and discord, and Jane's increasingly pathetic attempts to make their warped family life seem normal.

'Not for years. Stavros and I have an apartment.'

'So, I can't ask you to look after Mum tonight,' Ella remarked stiffly.

Immediately grasping her meaning, Dmitri reddened, said nothing and concentrated on hurrying the older woman out of the room. He was as desperate to avoid conflict with his father as Ella had once been. She would

never forget the tension of living in the Sardelos household, where everyone had worked hard in speech and
action to avoid doing anything that might annoy Theo.
While the initial conflict in the marriage had arisen over
her stepfather's infidelity, he had soon found plenty of
other issues to set his temper off.

'I'll try to phone you.' Jane flung the promise over a
thin shoulder.

'Any time, and for any reason. I'll always be here for
you.' Ella returned that assurance with a slight wobble in
her strained voice. Until she had seen her mother again,
she had not allowed herself to acknowledge how much
she had missed the older woman's presence in her life.

Ella settled Callie for her nap, and left the nursery to
return to the female guests milling round the terrace and
the spacious drawing-room. She discovered that she
was very much the centre of attention, and was reminded of how curious people always were about
Aristandros—his lifestyle, his possessions, his women,
his family and background, all of which had supplied
years of gossip fodder for newspaper and magazine
articles. Tactfully sidestepping the more intrusive questions, she moved from one knot of women to the next.

The men filtered back in little groups to their
partners, and the guests began to go home. Drakon
Xenakis made a point of bidding Ella goodbye before
his departure. She was filled with consternation, however, when she saw her stepfather halt on the threshold
of the room and simply jerk his head in her mother's
direction in a peremptory signal that he wanted to leave.
Even at a glance she could tell that the older man was
incensed with anger, the colour high on his fleshy face,

his mouth compressed into an aggressive whitened line. As she watched her stepfather, her brothers and her mother trooped out without a further word to anyone.

Ella tracked Aristandros down to the office that connected with the conference room.

'What the heck did you say to my stepfather?' she demanded curtly.

His personal assistants froze in incredulity, and she flushed, wishing she had exercised greater self-control, and waited until she could speak to him alone.

Face impassive, Aristandros lounged back against the edge of the desk behind him and viewed her with hard, dark eyes. 'Don't address me in that tone,' he told her with a chilling bite.

Ella was mortified when only then did he dismiss his staff with a meaningful shift of one authoritative hand. 'I'm sorry,' she muttered. 'I should have waited a moment.'

'All that I ask is that you remember your manners,' Aristandros responded grimly.

'I was concerned—I saw Theo stomping out in a complete rage. What happened?' she pressed, anxiously pacing the carpet in front of him.

'I informed Sardelos and your brothers that they are not welcome here if they cannot treat you with respect.'

Ella shot him an appalled look. 'I don't need you to fight my battles for me!'

'I invited them, and this is my house. Their behaviour was unacceptable. What I say goes, *khriso mou*.' Aristandros spelt out that reminder without a second of hesitation

'I've never seen my stepfather so angry, and no wonder! You humiliated him in front of his sons, and he'll blame me for that as well!' Ella lamented. 'I could kill you for interfering in something that has nothing to do with you.'

'I defended you and you're behaving as if *I* did something wrong?' Aristandros growled, his eyes smouldering dark gold with angry disbelief. 'You've let your stepfather bully you for so long that you can't see the wood for the trees. He needs to be shown his boundaries by someone he can't influence or control.'

Ella spun away from Aristandros, her thoughts heavily preoccupied with the likely fallout from the comeuppance which Theo had been given. Her stepfather set great store on his association with the Xenakis family; the sudden loss of that favourable social standing would not only humble him but also harm his business prospects. She wanted to yell and shout at Aristandros for acting with a heavy hand, but knew he had no comprehension of the likelihood that her mother would ultimately pay for her husband's sins.

'You interfered by inviting them here when you knew there was a serious rift between us,' she accused tautly. 'For goodness' sake, my mother phoned me in Paris to tell me that they thought I was acting like a whore with you!'

Aristandros went rigid. 'A *whore*?'

'Nobody suffers from the illusion that *I'm* the one paying for the designer dresses and the jewellery!' Ella slashed back bitterly. 'How do you expect people to view me?'

His brilliant gaze semi-screened by his lush, black lashes, Aristandros stared broodingly back at her, his eloquent mouth clenching hard. 'It's not a question I paused to consider—'

Ella raised a dubious brow. 'You didn't? Well, my goodness, you considered everything else that related to image. Why else was I repackaged as a dress-up doll?'

But Aristandros wasn't listening. He was frowning darkly. 'So that's why you walked out on me in Paris…'

Ella tossed her head, her pale hair fanning back across a flushed cheekbone and brushed away by an impatient hand. 'That phone call may have made me a little touchier than I should have been.'

He treated her to an austere appraisal. 'But once again it underlines how little you listen to what I tell you, *khriso mou.*'

The intimidating tension in the atmosphere was ringing alarm-bells in Ella's head. Aware of his renewed anger, but at a loss as to its cause, she blinked in bemusement. 'I'm not sure I know what you're getting at.'

'That you should have told me about that phone call that distressed you,' Aristandros grated impatiently. 'And don't you *dare* tell me that it was none of my business, because your behaviour that night spoke for you! I don't like the way you keep secrets from me. It's dishonest.'

Ella sucked in a startled breath at that hard-hitting denunciation. She could not credit what he was saying to her. 'You have some nerve to say that to me!' she slung back. 'Maybe there's a lot about you I don't like: a guy who uses lawyers to blackmail me into an indefensible agreement to let him do whatever he likes, while I do *only* as he likes. Is that what you call having a relationship? No wonder none of them last longer than five minutes! On what basis do you think I would give you my trust?'

'Stop there before this gets blown out of all proportion,' Aristandros advised harshly.

But Ella was trembling with pent-up emotion, and she could no more have held back what she was feeling inside than she could have contained a tornado. Her blue eyes were as bright a blue as the heart of a flame. 'Do you think I could trust a man who once told me he loved me and wanted to marry me, but who dumped me less than an hour later? And why—because I couldn't match the perfect blueprint of a wife that you had in your head? Because I had the audacity to want something more than love and your money to focus on? Would you have given up business and the art of making money to marry me?'

Aristandros had lost colour below his bronzed skin, and it lent a curious ashen quality to his usual healthy glow. He stared steadily back at her, however, predictably not yielding an inch of ground. 'We're not having this conversation,' he told her.

'I'm not asking for permission, and I'm not having a conversation. You may not have noticed yet but I'm *shouting* at you!' Ella yelled at him at full tilt, inflamed by his stony resistance to her verbal attack and his refusal to respond.

'*Stamates*…that is enough,' Aristandros bit out icily.

'I hate you…even your grandfather thinks you're treating me badly… Yes—not content with having lousy manners, I listen outside doors as well!' Ella threw wildly at him, tears burning her eyes, and rage swelling like a giant balloon inside her to restrict her breathing. 'I'm definitely not the perfect woman you think is your due. You'd better pray that I'm not fertile!'

And with that final parting shot, which was as low as she could think to sink, Ella fled out past the clutch of his staff in the hall who were trying to act like everything was normal and avoid looking at her. She took the stairs two at a time, with a huge sob locked halfway up her throat, and raced into the master bedroom—her fourth since she had moved in with him.

Ella very rarely cried. A sad film or a book could make the moisture well up, but it took a great deal to make her cry. Now she flung herself across the bed and sobbed her heart out. She was worried about her mother having to go home alone with an enraged and violent man who liked to use her as a punch bag. But, most of all, she was distraught over the row she had just had with Aristandros. It had started out a small argument and just grown and grown until it had torn apart the fragile fabric of the peace they had established, and destroyed the bonds they had somehow contrived to build. Now there could be no hiding from ugly but revealing truths, such as his fear that she might conceive a child he didn't want.

Why was she getting upset over being at odds with him? At least she had spoken her mind on the trust issue. She had trusted him once seven years back and look where that had got her—dumped, heartbroken and rejected by her family. Aristandros, however, had picked himself up in time-honoured Xenakis style from the debacle of the engagement that had only lasted five minutes with a widely reported cruise round the Mediterranean, where he had stopped off at various ports to booze and carouse non-stop with promiscuous women. Ella struck the mattress with a clenched fist. She was still so angry she wanted to scream. She hated him; she truly *hated* him!

But it was almost time for Callie to have her evening

meal, and Ella cherished her bedtime routine with the toddler. She hauled herself off the bed and groaned out loud when she saw her swollen eyes and ruined make-up. No longer having access to the beautician's tools, and in possession of very few cosmetics of her own, Ella did her best to conceal the ravages of her uncontrolled crying-jag.

Callie was a delight and a consolation that evening. Ella played with her in her bath, dried her little wriggling body and cuddled the little girl while she read her a story.

Callie was happily making quacking sounds when Aristandros appeared on the nursery threshold. 'I fancy eating out tonight,' he announced.

'I don't care if I never eat again,' Ella lied, for in truth she was starving, but could not have borne letting him get away with pretending that nothing had happened—even if she did suspect that that might be a wiser approach than running the risk of a post mortem about the row.

Callie slid off her knee and padded barefoot over to him, holding her arms up and demanding to be lifted. Possibly relieved that someone appeared to appreciate his presence, Aristandros crouched down and swept her up into his arms as if he'd been doing it for years. But in fact he had never done it before, and Ella watched slyly from beneath her lashes as Callie explored his hair, smothered him in wet kisses and yanked at his tie before settling down happily, trying to steal one of his shiny gold cuff-links.

'Quack,' Callie told him importantly, and then she stuck out a foot. 'Socks,' she added.

'You're not wearing any,' Aristandros pointed out.

Callie pouted. 'Shoos.'

'You're not wearing shoes either.'

'She's trying to dazzle you with her new words, not have a conversation,' Ella explained.

'It's more appealing than conversation,' Aristandros remarked, shrewd dark eyes skimming from Callie's smiling little face to Ella's frozen expression. 'You're sulking again.'

'I'm not sulking,' Ella pronounced through gritted teeth. 'I'm just can't think of anything to say to you.'

'Is there a difference?' Aristandros strolled across the room to lower Callie gently back down on to Ella's lap. As their eyes connected in an unexpected encounter, she was shockingly aware of the raw charge of his masculinity, and her mouth ran dry.

'I'm going out,' he said casually.

Ella almost called him back to say that she would go out after all. Watching him go out alone had no appeal whatsoever. Her contentment at her relaxing session with Callie ebbed fast. No woman in their right mind would encourage Aristandros to go out by himself—but no woman with any pride would accompany him after the day that had just passed and the words that had been exchanged, Ella reasoned with spirit. When Callie was safely asleep she went downstairs and ate a light meal without appetite, while she watched the clock and wondered how long he would stay out and who he was with. Athens was a lively, cosmopolitan city with many clubs.

Having decided on an early night, she went for a bath, then phoned Lily and finally told her friend everything she had previously withheld.

'He's a total bastard!' Lily hissed in disgust.

Ella winced, finding that opinion not as much to her taste as she might have hoped. 'Occasionally he's…very challenging.'

'I don't believe what I'm hearing. You're making excuses for him?'

'That wasn't an excuse,' Ella protested uncomfortably.

'Ella…in all the years of our friendship I have never understood your essential indifference to men. Now, finally, I do. You're insanely in love with Ari Xenakis— and I do mean *insane*, because by the sound of it he's already running rings round you!'

'Of course I'm not in love with him,' Ella retorted crisply. 'We have absolutely nothing in common. He's cold, selfish and arrogant, and I could never care about a man like that!'

'On the other hand,' Aristandros added lazily, striding into the bedroom without warning and startling her into dropping the phone, 'I'm very rich, very clever and very good in bed—a combination of traits which seems to keep you very well entertained, *khriso mou.*'

Ella fumbled clumsily for the phone again.

'It's okay…I heard,' Lily admitted. 'I think you've just met your match, Ella.'

Ella replaced the phone and stared at Aristandros. Her nipples stirred and peaked below her nightdress, becoming uncomfortably sensitive. His scrutiny burned like molten gold over her upturned face, and pink colour warmed her cheeks while her tummy performed a wicked little somersault of response. The atmosphere sizzled. She closed her eyes tight and snuggled down beneath the sheet, awesomely conscious of his presence, and tensing to the rigidity of an iron bar when the mattress gave under his weight

'*Se thelo*…I want you,' Aristandros breathed thickly as he eased her back into his arms.

'I thought you'd be out half the night,' she framed flatly, staying stiff and unresponsive against the hard, muscular heat of him.

'Not when you're in my bed waiting for me, *moli mou*.'

'I wasn't waiting for you!' she yelped.

Brushing back her tumbled silvery-blonde hair, he pressed his sensual mouth to the slender column of her neck, and she quivered beneath the erotic brush of his lips across her skin. 'Of course you were. Do you think I don't know when a woman wants me?'

'Quack,' Ella pronounced flatly.

Aristandros vented a husky laugh above her head. 'Meaning?'

'That normal dialogue is a waste of breath with a guy as vain and arrogant as you are.'

Aristandros extracted her from her nightdress without receiving or even appearing to need the smallest assistance from her. He proved that he was more than capable of rolling with the punches of that negative character-assessment. He nibbled at the tender skin below her ear, while his hands roved from the urgent jut of her swollen nipples to the slick, wet flesh between her thighs. She clenched her teeth and gasped, striving to resist temptation until he teased the tiny nub of arousal below her feminine mound, and suddenly resistance was more than she could bear. She twisted round in a violent movement and found his tormenting mouth for herself, burning for him and burning with shame simultaneously. He held her to him with strong hands and plundered her parted lips until she was breathless with desire. Then he lifted her over him and pushed up into her slick, tight depths with a long, guttural groan of pleasure.

'As long as you know that I still hate you,' Ella mumbled shakily, struggling not to lose herself entirely in the pleasure he had unleashed.

'I love the way you hate me,' Aristandros husked, long, brown fingers on her hips controlling her rhythm, and then rising to cup her swaying breasts and roll the sensitive crests.

She was dizzy with excitement and beyond thought. The waves of pulsating pleasure began low in her pelvis and slowly spread out in ever-increasing circles in a white-hot surge of shattering pleasure. She cried out, and her head fell back on her shoulders as the wild convulsions of ecstasy engulfed her.

Aristandros cradled her limp body and rolled over to a cooler spot in the big bed. 'Tomorrow we'll be on Lykos, and I don't think I'll let you out of bed for a week. You make me insatiable, *khriso mou.*'

Her brain kicked back into gear and she flinched, loathing herself for surrendering to the passion. 'I meant everything I said,' she told him doggedly.

'What a temper you have,' Aristandros mused lazily, his unconcern on that score palpable.

Her body still throbbing from the primal urgency of his possession, Ella pulled free of him and shifted over to the far side of the bed.

'No,' Aristandros said succinctly, and he reached for her with hands that brooked no argument and hauled her bodily back into contact with his long, powerful body. 'What you sow, you must reap, and I'm not finished yet.'

'I am!' But, as she spoke, the familiar signature tune she used on her mobile phone broke out in the tense silence.

'Ignore it,' Aristandros instructed. 'It's after midnight.'

Ella, by comparison, was accustomed to reacting with urgency to calls during the night, and she broke from his loosened hold and snatched up the flashing mobile-phone on the bedside table to answer it. An instant later, she threw her legs off the side of the bed and stood up to switch on the lamp. Although she couldn't yet understand what her mother was saying, she realised that the older woman was crying and that something was badly wrong.

'Calm down; I can't follow what you're saying. What happened? Did he hit you?'

Ella felt Aristandros pull himself up behind her. 'Are you still in the house?' she prompted her parent. 'Where is Theo? Look, whatever you do, don't go back in there,' Ella warned the weeping older woman. 'Stay where you are and I'll come and get you. No, of course it isn't a problem. Don't be silly, Mum. All I care about is you.' Putting her phone down, she turned to Aristandros. 'I need a car.'

Aristandros was already talking into the house phone and getting out of bed. He broke off to demand, 'Did Sardelos attack your mother? What happened?'

'What always happens,' Ella responded wearily. 'He has a few drinks, blames her for everything wrong in his life and hits her. He's in bed. She's in the park across the street. Why are you getting dressed?'

'I'm coming with you.'

Ella was already pulling on a pair of trousers. 'That's not a good idea.'

His handsome features were grim. 'I'm not leaving you to handle this alone. Your stepfather left my house in a rage this evening, and I was to blame for that.'

'You're not to blame for anything. Theo is the baddie here. I warn you: Mum won't report him to the police. I've tried a dozen times to persuade her to have him charged, but she won't, so he gets away with it every time. She's like an addict,' Ella muttered heavily. 'She won't give him up.'

'Are you planning to call your brothers?'

'I'll do what Mum wants me to do. I notice she phoned me rather than either of her sons.'

Twenty minutes later, Ella was approaching the park bench where her mother was huddled like an old discarded rug, her shoulders hunched, her head bent, so that even in the street light her face couldn't be seen. When Ella got her first proper look at her, she had to bite back an exclamation. Her face swollen and puffy with one eye almost sealed shut, Jane Sardelos was almost unrecognisable. Her lip was cut and distended, and she was cradling one arm as though it was hurting her.

'What's up with your arm?' Ella asked.

'Let's get her into the car first,' Aristandros urged.

'You brought him with you?' the older woman gasped in horror.

'I couldn't shake him off.' Ella helped her mother stand up and guided her towards the waiting limo. Once they were safe in the passenger seat, she bent to examine the arm and realised that the older woman's wrist was badly broken. 'We'll have to go to the hospital.'

'No hospital…I'll go to a hotel or something.'

'You don't have a choice,' Ella broke in. 'I think your wrist needs surgery, and the sooner it's done the better. Do you want me to call the boys?'

Jane shook her head in an urgent negative. 'No point in upsetting them as well.'

Aristandros raised a brow but made no comment. During the drive to the hospital and then their subsequent arrival, after he had called in advance, she was surprised by how gentle he was with her battered mother, who had never been one of his biggest fans. She was wryly amused when his natural charm began to draw the older woman out of her shell.

It was a very long night. After the x-rays had been carried out, Jane was given a thorough examination, and Ella was appalled by the bruising she saw on her parent's thin body. It was obvious to her that, if anything, her stepfather's attacks had become even more violent over the years. Surgery was immediately scheduled for her wrist. The police arrived beforehand, and Ella braced herself for her mother's usual evasive efforts to shield her husband from arrest and prosecution. Aristandros asked if he could speak to Jane privately for a moment and Ella stepped outside the room, curious as to his motive, but so sleepy that she was grateful for the chance to move around and wake up a bit.

She was shocked when she realised on her return that her mother was finally willing to give a true statement of events and press charges against Theo. She also seemed stronger, steadier and less afraid than she had been. While she was in the operating theatre, Aristandros made a series of phone calls.

'What did you talk about with Mum?' Ella asked.

'She wants a fresh start, and I pointed out that she can't have it without having Sardelos charged with assault, because only that will make him leave her alone. I also pointed out that she could well die during one of his assaults. I asked her to accompany us to Lykos to recuperate, but she wants to stay with your brothers until she's feeling better. I called them. They should be here soon.'

Ella was disappointed that Jane wouldn't be coming to the island, but she knew that her mother would very much enjoy fussing over her adult sons for a few weeks. She was amazed that Aristandros had triumphed where she had so often tried and failed. Her stepfather was finally going to be taken to court, and that was a source of tremendous relief to Ella. But perhaps it wasn't so strange, she conceded. Jane was always more easily impressed by a strong man than she was by a strong woman, and Ari's intervention and advice had been warmly appreciated and respected.

They remained at the hospital until Jane emerged from the operating theatre and had regained consciousness in the recovery room. The surgery had been long and complicated but successful. Ella fell asleep in the limousine, and wakened only when Aristandros settled her down on the bed.

'You were really great tonight with Mum,' she mumbled drowsily. 'I wasn't expecting that.'

'I'm not always the bastard you like to think I am,' Aristandros retorted with level cool.

Her heavy limbs sinking into the comfortable mattress,

Ella focused wryly on his lean, compellingly handsome face. 'I'm not stupid,' she told him. 'Leopards don't change their spots.'

CHAPTER NINE

THE island of Lykos had undergone some changes since Ella's last visit seven years earlier. Aristandros had made the harbour much bigger and deeper to accommodate his yachts. The fishing boats looked like colourful children's toys beside *Hellenic Lady*. The island's little town, composed of lime-washed white houses adorned with traditional blue paintwork, stretched up the hill in neat tiers behind the harbour. The wedding-cake church with its ornamental bell tower sat in the shade of the plane trees edging the main square, and a windmill, long defunct but nonetheless charming, punctuated the winding road that led down to the far end of the island and the Xenakis house. Beyond the town stretched lush green hills studded with cypresses and olive groves and rather more buildings than she recalled.

'The last time we were here you told me that you wanted to get married in a church exactly like that,' Aristandros murmured.

'Did I...really?' Standing by the rail as the yacht docked, Ella was still suffering from the loss of the previous night's sleep. That reminder almost made her choke on the coffee she was drinking to wake herself up, and she secretly cringed over the knowledge that she could ever have been that gauche. 'I don't remember that.'

'I liked the fact that you didn't watch your every word around me. My parents got married here in the church of Ayia Sophia. My mother thought it was cute as well.'

'Lykos originally belonged to her family, didn't it?'

'Yes. She was an only child and a great disappointment to a shipping family, who longed for a son.'

'I just remember the portrait of her in the house. She was absolutely gorgeous.'

'She still holds the trophy for being the vainest woman I ever knew,' Aristandros remarked with a cynical shake of his proud dark head. 'In many ways she was lucky to die young. She could never have handled growing old.'

Ella thought it was sad that he could be so detached from the memory of his mother, a habit he had probably acquired for self-protection when he was a boy, cursed by not one but two wildly irresponsible parents who had refused to grow up and behave like adults. Too alike to stand each other for long, the warring pair had divorced by the time he was five years old.

Although Doria Xenakis had grown up with great beauty and wealth, both attributes had only been a means to an end for a young woman obsessed by her dream of becoming a famous actress. While his mother had chased endless drama-classes and roles, and thrown constant parties to entertain influential celebrities, Aristandros had been seriously neglected. He had twice been removed from her home by social workers for his own safety. Doria had finally died of a drug overdose at the age of thirty, and was only remembered in the film world for having starred in some of the worst movies ever made. Ari's father, Achilles Xenakis, an inveterate gambler, womaniser and drunk, had worked his way through multiple partners and repeated visits to rehabilitation centres after an unending succession of financial and sexual scandals. Achilles had died when he crashed his speedboat. Orphaned, Aristandros had moved in with Drakon at the age of fourteen.

Ella, Callie and Aristandros climbed into one of the cars waiting by the harbour while their luggage was stowed in another. Ella gazed out at the turquoise-blue sea washing the inviting white strand that circled more than half the island and, appreciating its emptiness, said, 'Are you still trying to keep the tourists out?'

'Why would I want to share paradise?'

'It would be the easiest way of revitalising the economy and persuading the younger people to stay on. A small, exclusive development near the town wouldn't interfere with your privacy.'

'Remind me to keep you well away from the town council. They'd elect you immediately,' Aristandros asserted. 'In recent years, I've brought in several businesses to provide employment, and the population is currently thriving—without the tourist trade and its attendant problems.'

Ella gave him a sunny smile. 'I'm sure you know what works best in your own personal little kingdom.'

'I do not regard the island as my kingdom,' Aristandros growled.

'I didn't mean to be controversial,' Ella declared unconvincingly.

Aristandros skated a long, reproving forefinger along one slender thigh clad in coffee-coloured linen trousers. 'Liar. You always liked getting under my skin, *moli mou.*'

'Constant agreement and admiration is bad for you. Too many people behave as if your every decision is an act of sheer brilliance.'

'It usually is,' Aristandros fielded. 'That's how I make so much money.'

Involuntarily, Ella grinned, for his self-assurance was immense and always bold as brass. She studied the big house perched like a land-locked ship on the cypress-studded hillside. The villa, designed by his late mother, overlooked a secluded cove where the clear waters reflected the sky.

'I have a project for you while you're here,' he said, greeting the staff assembled in the hall while Ella retrieved Callie from surging towards the stairs as fast as her little feet could carry her. 'Revamp the house and drag it out of the eighties. It always reminds me of a film set.'

The big screen was undoubtedly what had inspired his mother's opulent choice of décor, and the vast sunken living-area, marble floors and theatrical Greek columns. Ella was amazed that he had still not had the house renovated, and it made her wonder if he was more sentimental than he would ever be willing to admit. Doria's portrait still adorned one wall, along with many photographs of her taken with famous people.

Aristandros bore not the slightest resemblance to his blonde, brown-eyed mother. He did, however, look very like his handsome father. In terms of attractiveness, though, he easily outshone both his parents, Ella decided, shooting him a keen appraisal. While he had Achilles' looks, he had inherited his grandfather's sharp intelligence and business acumen. Daily exposure to Aristandros had simply made her more aware than ever that he was an extravagantly beautiful, intriguingly clever and challenging man. On paper he ticked all her boxes.

Turning pink as he intercepted her lingering scrutiny, Ella walked out hurriedly on to the sweeping terrace and wondered if Lily was right: was it possible that she had never got over loving Aristandros? Had she never moved on properly after that first disillusionment? The suspicion appalled her, for she liked to see herself as being sensible. The sort of woman who could continue to harbour a strong, secret preference for a notorious womaniser struck Ella as being silly, weak in resolution and certifiably insane.

'In three weeks' time we'll be attending a major charity performance at the opera in aid of the Xenakis Foundation. Dress formal,' Aristandros announced.

Ella suppressed a sigh. 'Where's it being held?'

'Athens.'

Ella saw Callie installed in the nursery, which the little girl clearly saw as home. Callie toddled over to a basket of toys and smiled as she dug out familiar favourites, her satisfaction at rediscovering them unhidden. Later, when Callie was in bed and Ella was dining out on the terrace with Aristandros, she breathed in deep. 'You know, I've barely been with you two weeks and this will be the sixth different bed I've slept in.'

Aristandros shifted a broad shoulder with nonchalant cool. 'Change is stimulating.'

'I know you don't want to hear this…'

Aristandros shifted a fluid brown hand in a silencing gesture. 'Then don't say it,' he advised drily.

'It's not fair to Callie. She needs a more settled home.'

'I don't normally trail her round the world with me as I have done recently,' Aristandros finally admitted. 'She's usually based here on the island.'

Guilt assailed Ella as she grasped the heart of the dilemma. 'She's travelling because I'm in the picture now and you know I want to be with her,' she guessed ruefully.

'While I want you to be with me. We're the perfect threesome,' he quipped. 'Be practical.'

Ella toyed with her delicious, light seafood starter, her appetite ebbing. *Be practical—remember the agreement you signed, remember who calls the shots around here, remember who says what goes as far as Callie's concerned.* But his lifestyle was unsustainable for a toddler, Ella reflected. More than anything Callie needed stability and routine to thrive, not to mention the same people around her.

Dark eyes reflective, Aristandros sipped his wine. 'I have a business trip next week. I'll leave you here.'

'Great.' Ella knew she was being thrown a consolation prize, but ironically she just as quickly found herself wondering whether his sudden willingness to leave her behind could relate to the fact that he was getting a little bored with her. Why not? she asked herself. Two weeks was a sizeable length of time for Aristandros to stay committed to one woman. And, if he was losing interest, how would she handle it?

Extinguishing that incendiary thought from her mind, for she saw no advantage in borrowing trouble in advance, she phoned her mother, who was still in hospital, after dinner. Jane was in reasonable spirits. Stavros and Dmitri were visiting her and had passed on the news that their father had been arrested and charged. Freed from the fear of her husband's violence, Jane had decided to go for counselling.

'Mum's dealing with this better than I thought she would,' Ella commented to Aristandros when he wandered out of the bathroom, only a towel linked round his lean hips and drops of water still sparkling on his hair-roughened chest. She would never have dreamt of adding that her mother thought she had misjudged him seven years earlier and had underestimated his potential for reliability. In her mother's eyes, Aristandros had suddenly become a knight in shining armour worthy of the highest praise.

'Hopefully it will give her a new lease of life. Sardelos had sucked all the energy out of her,' he pronounced grimly.

A slender figure in a shimmering emerald-green nightdress edged with lace, Ella shivered. 'I was only a child when they married, but I still remember how different she was before she met him—lively and outgoing. He turned her into a doormat.'

'Not something anyone could accuse you of.'

Her blood sang in her veins as she studied him. He made her feel like a teenager—a hopelessly infatuated teenager, who got a thrill every time he looked at her. 'Sometimes you make me very angry.'

A wicked grin slashed his handsome mouth, and her heart hammered as if he had pressed a switch. 'You make me hot in a very different way, *khriso mou*.'

For the first time Ella took the initiative, crossing the room to slide up against his hard, masculine body, revelling in every point of physical connection with an earthy streak she hadn't known she possessed until he'd brought it out in her. The very boldness of his arousal thrilled her. He parted her lips and let his tongue delve hungrily, deeply, and her bones seemed to melt beneath her skin while languorous heat and heaviness slowly uncoiled between her thighs. She detached the towel and looked up at him while she traced the impressive length of his erection.

'There's no hope for you in the wanton stakes,' Aristandros husked. 'You're still blushing.'

'Of course I'm going to blush if you're planning to offer a running commentary!'

'So, take my breath away, *moli mou.*'

And she did, kneeling down gracefully at his feet to deploy her slim hands and her full, sensual mouth to the task she had set herself. She used her knowledge of the male physique and her infinitely more intimate aware-ness of what he liked to pleasure him. Ella was always a high achiever at anything she set out to do. Ripples of helpless response began shuddering through his power-ful frame. He withstood her provocative attention for a very short time. His breathing audibly fractured, and then suddenly he was pulling her up and backing her down on the bed with scant ceremony.

'You excite the hell out of me!' he groaned, coming down on top of her and ravaging her luscious pink mouth until her senses swam.

He made love to her with mind-blowing power. Afterwards she lay shell-shocked with the intensity of the pleasure in his arms, her willowy body magically indolent and peaceful after her explosive release. He smoothed her hair gently back off her warm face. She kissed a smooth, muscular shoulder, catching the faint scent of cologne mingled with his own male scent, and drank in the smell of him like an addict. Right and wrong, she registered, no longer seemed so well-defined.

On some level she couldn't hold back what she was feeling any longer, and wasn't even sure that there was a point in such restraint while she lived with him and Callie. Sexually she found him irresistible, but his hold on her went much deeper than that. She was possessive of him and she cared about him as she had never yet cared for any other man. Yet he wasn't the young man she had fallen in love with any more. Those seven years apart had altered him. He was harder, more cynical and self-contained, and willing to go to any lengths to get what he wanted. Was it terribly wrong of her to feel special because he had gone to such extremes to get her back into his life again? And what was he doing to her once-firm moral compass?

In the early hours of the following morning she wakened and frowned at the familiar little cramping pains low in her stomach. A moment later she got out of bed and went into the bathroom to check out her suspicions. No, as she had thought, she wasn't pregnant, and it was time to start her contraceptive pill. The necessities taken care of, she returned to bed.

Aristandros was still fast asleep in a careless sprawl which took up more than his fair share of the bed, outsized though it was. With his jet-dark lashes almost long enough to hit his hard cheekbones, blue-black stubble outlining his angular jaw and sculpted mouth, and with his classic, aquiline profile relaxed, he looked gorgeous. Her insides chilled at the thought of how he might have reacted to an inconvenient pregnancy. He liked to control everything, and she couldn't have allowed him to exert control or influence in that field. She was grateful that the situation hadn't arisen.

'Hmm…' He shifted position and found her, a hand splaying across her stomach and then rising to cup a small, firm breast with a drowsy sound of masculine contentment. '*Ella…*'

'I'm not pregnant!' Ella just blurted it out, keen to get the news out, mortified by the idea that he was secretly dreading the possibility that she might have conceived.

Spiky black lashes lifted on startled dark-golden eyes. He was as instantly awake as if she had doused him with a bucket of cold water. 'Are you sure?'

'One hundred percent,' she declared.

His lean, strong face clenched. 'I would have taken care of you. You needn't have worried on that score.'

'We have enough problems without that particular one.'

'You still don't want children?'

'I didn't say that.'

'Just not children with me?' His expression sardonic, Aristandros released her and vaulted out of bed. 'I need a shower.'

Ella was bewildered by his behaviour. 'I assumed you would regard a pregnancy as a disaster and that you'd ask me to have a termination. You did tell me you didn't want a child.'

A bronzed vision of pagan masculinity, he surveyed her with brooding force from the bathroom doorway, and shrugged a broad shoulder. 'Then I thought about it and I reckoned I could live with it. Callie would probably enjoy having a playmate,' he murmured lazily.

'I wouldn't have suggested a termination. The main reason my father divorced my mother was that she tried to have me aborted—he stopped her on the way to the clinic. That kind of knowledge gives you a different take on an accidental pregnancy.'

Shocked by the content of that entire speech, Ella nodded slowly. 'I suppose it would.'

She tried to get her thoughts in order. Every time she thought she had Ari pigeon-holed, he confounded her expectations again. Think of him casually commenting that Callie would enjoy a playmate, admitting that, at the very least, he was uncomfortable with the idea of terminating a pregnancy that was merely inconvenient! *I reckoned I could live with it*—he could live with her having his baby. Well, she was still relieved that she wasn't about to face that challenge. He would have needed to be a good deal more enthusiastic and they would have had to have discussed the idea in advance before she could have allowed herself to regret the fact that she hadn't conceived.

Swallowing hard, she got back into bed. She had on several occasions in recent years gone through the experience of feeling broody, when the very sight of a baby or tiny clothes brought a lump to her throat and a powerful craving, but she would never have admitted anything so personal to him. Indeed her longing to see and hold her biological daughter had almost broken her heart for eighteen months. But, now fully aware of how incredibly lucky she was to have a loving healthy child like Callie in her life, she expected nothing more from Mother Nature.

Ella prowled round the modern building housing the doctor's surgery and emergency facilities which

Aristandros had funded on the outskirts of town. It was a rural doctor's dream, but apparently two doctors had already come and gone, bored with the lack of a social life on a small island and the inconvenience of having to step on a ferry to visit friends and family. Currently the position was vacant. Having checked out the patient numbers, Ella reckoned there was really only enough work for a part-time doctor, and she very much would have liked to put her name forward.

'We would be honoured to have you here,' the town mayor, Yannis Mitropoulos, assured her, having intercepted her and offered her a tour after she had been seen peering wistfully through a window.

'Unfortunately, I'm not looking for a job at present,' Ella advanced uncomfortably.

Had she been, she was convinced she would have been in harness within five minutes of accepting the job. Aristandros had devoted two days to showing her round the island, and had introduced her to many of the locals. But he had *not*, offered her an inspection of the unoccupied state-of-the-art medical building he had built, or admitted that Lykos lacked a doctor's services. Ella had only found out those facts for herself when she'd taken Callie into town. Whilst enjoying cold drinks at the taverna overlooking the picturesque harbour, she had found herself slowly and steadily being surrounded by hopeful people in search of off-the-cuff medical advice. Aristandros, however, appeared to have no conscience about keeping the only doctor on the island confined to home, hearth and bedroom.

In spite of that truth, over the past three weeks Ella had settled happily into life on Lykos. Aristandros had twice flown off on business trips without her, and she had been dismayed by the discovery that she missed him when he was out of reach. He was, however, surprisingly sexy and amazingly addictive during late-night phone conversations, she conceded with a covert smile.

She had come to terms with the fact that she loved him, and that she probably loved him a great deal more than she had seven years ago, which struck her as especially ironic when he had behaved so badly this time round. Back then she had expected perfection, a soulmate who shared her every thought and conviction and made no awkward demands of her. Now her expectations were rather more human-sized and, in any case, she knew that she and Aristandros were diametrically opposed by the simple fact that she was a modern female and he was very old-style macho male. Although she felt that Aristandros was being totally selfish and unreasonable in refusing to allow her to pursue her medical vocation, she was beginning to suspect that his being the centre of her world, the only other person she really had to think about besides Callie, was something he prized above everything else in their relationship. He was as possessive as she was, and seemingly unwilling to share her.

Ella had managed to adopt two homeless dogs since her arrival on Lykos. One, Whistler, a fluffy mongrel of indeterminate breed, had been injured by a fish hook and brought to her for attention for there was no vet on the island either. Ella had dealt with the little animal's lacerations and had offered to keep her while she healed. The second dog had arrived on the slender strength of the assurance that 'everybody knows the English are mad about dogs'. Bunny, inappropriately named by

Callie, was a boisterous Great Dane pup with paws the size of dinner plates, and he was accused of having sneaked off the ferry unattended. Both dogs were brilliant with Callie.

Aristandros had been taken aback by the sudden addition of two animals to the household, but had adapted wonderfully well after a lot of cool brow-raising over their antics, and had admitted that his mother had hated dogs and that he had never been allowed a pet. Ella thought his heart had been touched by Callie's enthusiasm for the dogs: the sight of the trio gambolling on the beach was quite something.

Of course Aristandros was learning to love Callie which was very entertaining to watch. For instance, he tried to teach Callie to say 'toes' and she continually came up with 'socks' or 'shoes'. She saw his pleasure when her daughter rushed to greet him and hug his knees. The child's innocent affection and playfulness drew him out of his cynical shell and made him patient and much less driven. When his mobile phone had been found in a vase of flowers, he'd insisted he had somehow dropped it in there, when everyone in the house knew that Callie was always trying to get her hands on his phone because the colours it flashed attracted her like a magnet.

It no longer mattered to Ella that Aristandros had fenced her in with an outrageous legal agreement. She had signed up for the long haul and was beginning to dare to hope that he might have as well. She was happier with him than she had ever dreamt she could be. The gift of a grand piano had been his most well-received present to date, and she was able to play her music every day on a superb instrument with wonderful tone, and she was already looking forward to teaching Callie. But the piano was only one of a number of fabulous presents with which he had surprised her. She had acquired designer handbags, perfume, sundry outfits and a fantastic sculpture of a sylph-like dancer that he had said reminded him of her. As she did not have endless legs and a large bosom quite out of proportion to the rest of her body, she had decided to be flattered by the unlikely comparison.

Aristandros was now accustomed to seeing her without make-up or a fancy hair-do, but dressed instead in casual beach-wear or jeans, and none of it had put a single dent in her apparent desirability. Her mother and her twin siblings had visited, and he had taken her brothers—who were not the world's most entertaining guys, out fishing and sailing without even being asked. She had been grateful, for her family now accepted their relationship, which made life a great deal smoother.

He had proved surprisingly understanding when she had been overjoyed after receiving a letter forwarded by Lily from Alister Marlow. As asked, Alister had notified the cleaner about the photo Ella had mislaid, and the small, faded snapshot of her late father had been found behind a piece of furniture. Ari had been sympathetic when he'd grasped that Ella had no memory of her father, who had died when she was only a baby. He, too, had been a doctor.

'Is that why you went in for medicine?' Aristandros had asked.

'No, I wanted to be a doctor from quite a young age, and as I got older it appealed more and more. I loved the idea of being able to fix people's bodies and solve their problems, but of course it's only occasionally that straightforward.'

But, when it came to the lack of commitment in relationships that Ella saw as Ari's most pressing problem, she convinced herself that she had the solution. If their sex life was good, Ari would surely have no reason to stray—but she despised herself for thinking that way and for being willing to accept those boundaries. Her pride told her she deserved more, but her brain told her that she already had as much as she could reasonably expect from Aristandros Xenakis in terms of attraction, attention and time. Even the newspapers were talking about what a quiet life he was leading of late.

In honour of the charity opera performance she was to attend that very evening, she had shopped for hours in Athens for a gorgeous dress and had promised to wear the sapphires with it. Aristandros had flown out the night before on a helicopter, and she was being picked up early evening. The beautician who worked on *Hellenic Lady* came to the house to do the honours, and Ella was admiring how well her hair looked when Ianthe, the housekeeper, came to her bedroom to tell her that Yannis Mitropoulos had phoned to ask if she would come and see his daughter who was pregnant and unwell.

Ella wasted no time in driving into the town to the surgery, with Ianthe in tow. Grigoria was a young first-time mother-to-be who was almost eight months' pregnant with twins. Her husband was in the army and away from home. Grigoria was very nearly hysterical, and clung so tightly to Ella that she had to prise herself free to examine her patient. What she learned was not good. Grigoria's blood pressure was sky high, and her hands and feet were swollen. Her condition was made more complex by the fact that she was a diabetic. Ella told Yannis that they needed the air ambulance, for she was convinced that his daughter was suffering from pre-eclampsia and needed urgent hospital treatment. It was a dangerous condition which would most likely only be cured by the delivery of the babies. She checked the records and rang the relevant hospital to forewarn them and get the advice of the gynaecologist on duty.

'You'll come with me?' Grigoria pleaded, clutching at Ella's arm frantically.

'I would be very grateful if you would,' Yannis added jerkily, tears in his eyes as he took her to one side and began to tell the very sad story of how his late wife had once gone on the same journey and, for possibly the same reason, and had died shortly after Grigoria's birth.

His daughter's state of mind was not helped by that inopportune recollection of her mother's demise. Ianthe ventured to remind Ella of the opera engagement, and the reminder cleared Ella's frown away; she was quick to work out how she could be in virtually two places at once, for both destinations were in the city. Determined to stay with Grigoria, Ella instructed the housekeeper to have her evening dress and jewellery delivered to Ari's house in Athens where she would be able to change for the evening, having left the hospital.

The flight in the air ambulance to Athens was fraught and tense; Grigoria was suffering increasing pain, and was seriously ill. It was a great relief to reach the hospital. Ella, preoccupied with her patient's condition, spared not a thought for her disrupted social arrangements until Grigoria's twins, two little girls, were safely delivered by Caesarean section. Her anxiety about Grigoria soothed by the knowledge that the young woman was receiving the best possible treatment, Ella only then registered that she had not even tried to contact Aristandros to tell him where she was. In a passion of dismay that she had been so thoughtless in relation to an engagement which he had made clear was an important event, she texted fervent humble apologies to him. She wasted no time trying to explain what had happened, but instead promised to join him by the time of the intermission.

More precious time was wasted while she found a taxi willing to take her out of the city. She contacted Ianthe to check that the dress had been delivered. Reassured on that score, Ella began worrying about how Aristandros would react to her appearance just before the end of the evening. Her heart sank. He hadn't responded to her text, which suggested to her that he was furious. Furthermore, she didn't feel she could blame him, since he had always been meticulous about contacting her well in advance in similar situations. Also, telling him that she had simply forgotten about him and the opera date because of a medical emergency was scarcely likely to prove a comfort to a male accustomed to the very best treatment when it came to the female sex.

By the time the taxi trundled up the long driveway to the imposing villa, Ella was very tense, because she was running against the clock and not doing very well. She rang the bell and, after a few moments, the housekeeper appeared, and her look of consternation was suf-

ficient to warn Ella that her arrival was unexpected.
Ella hastened past the older woman with a muttered explanation and apology. She sped upstairs, where she
assumed her evening gown awaited her. There was no
sign of it in the master bedroom, but she stilled in
surprise on the threshold when she saw the scattered
pieces of female clothing littering the floor. She frowned
at the sight of the frilly black-and-turquoise bra and
matching knickers, and wondered who on earth they
could belong to. Unfortunately, she did not have to
wonder for long.

The mystery was immediately solved when the
bathroom door opened and a breathtakingly lovely
blonde appeared, wearing only a towel. It was difficult
to say which of them was the most discomposed by the
unexpected meeting.

'Who are you? What are you doing in here?' Ella
heard herself demand.

Aqua-green eyes challenged her. 'As I was here first,
I could ask you the same thing.'

And, even as Ella parted her lips to speak again, a
sick sensation took up residence in her tummy and perspiration beaded her brow. She wondered if she was the
only woman in the world stupid enough to ask a beautiful half-naked woman what she was doing in her
lover's bedroom. After all, the answer was so obvious
the question didn't need asking. Striving to save a little
dignity in a confrontation that had burst upon her with
the abruptness of an earthquake, Ella retreated back to
the doorway. She discovered that it was horrendously
difficult for her to peel her stunned eyes from the blonde
in the towel. A revolting, terrifying curiosity had her

staring, and striving not to make bland comparisons. Her mind marched on regardless: she herself was older, less exciting in the curves department and, although her skin was good, she knew it wasn't quite as flawless. Rejecting those crazy, unsavoury evaluations, she spun on her heel and headed down the sweeping stairs at such a speed that she almost tripped over her own feet.

'Dr Smithson.' The housekeeper began speaking anxiously to Ella as she threw open the front door for herself, simply eager to be gone and leave the scene of her humiliation behind her. 'I'm sorry, but I didn't know you were coming.'

'It's okay. I'm fine,' Ella burbled, not wishing to deal with the woman's visible embarrassment. It was obvious that the housekeeper had a very good idea of what Ella had found upstairs. She just fled, hurrying down the drive as though a gale-force wind was powering her from behind. Her mind was a total blank. She didn't know what she was doing. She didn't know where she was going either. Shock had wiped her thoughts out, and fear of the pain of those thoughts was protecting her from them.

Aristandros had another woman. *Well, whoopee, Ella—what were you expecting? Did you think he had signed a one-woman-only pledge just because he had taken up with you?* It was not as if Aristandros had promised to be faithful. Indeed, he had gone to some trouble to declare that he was promising her no such thing in that wretched agreement. For all she knew he had a stable of other women stashed around the globe at his various properties or, indeed available to come at a call whenever he felt like a little variety.

Aristandros had gone into his Athens headquarters today, finished his day's work during the afternoon and had then come home with or to the very beautiful blonde and gone to bed with her. The bed had been made again. So the very beautiful blonde was tidy as well as clean! She pictured Ari's housekeeper telling him what had happened and flinched. Seeing a bus trundling along the road in the distance, she speeded up to reach the stop and flagged it down. It didn't matter where it was going, just as long as it got her safely away from the vicinity of the villa where she might be seen. Her phone vibrated in her bag and she dug it out and, refusing to even look at the message, she switched it off. She wasn't in any fit state to deal with Aristandros.

It was a warm, humid evening. Ella felt hot and her skin felt clammy, though her teeth kept on threatening to chatter in shock. She got on the bus and sat down at the back, her body lurching and swaying as the vehicle swung round corners. Why was she so shocked when Aristandros had only done what had always come naturally to him? Such a very beautiful girl, as well. If a man had always wanted the diversity and excitement of other sexual partners, he was unlikely to change. And no doubt, if she asked him, he would be honest with her about it.

Her mind went into free fall at the thought of him being *that* honest with her. Any admission of infidelity would cut like a knife and leave scars, haunting her for ever. But the images already tormenting her were no more comforting, she acknowledged wretchedly, for the idea of Ari in another woman's arms was her worst nightmare and always had been. Now it had finally happened, she was reeling from the pain she was experiencing.

But wasn't the extent of that pain her own fault, a self-induced punishment? What woman in her right mind would have fallen in love with Aristandros Xenakis and hoped for a happy ending? Countless women had tried and failed with him. Yet she was still crazy about him. She had held nothing back. In fact, a week ago, when she had watched Ari building a sand-castle with Callie—a real boy-toy skyscraper version of a sandcastle—she had wondered if she had made an ap-palling mistake when she'd turned his marriage proposal down seven years back. She had wondered if, against the odds, they might have found happiness together. She had known that although she loved her career and lived for its challenges it had never brought her the sheer, soaring happiness, excitement and con-tentment that he could just with his presence.

Her cheeks were wet with tears when she climbed off the bus at the terminal. What was she planning to do—run away and leave Callie behind? That option was ab-solutely out of the question. Hadn't Ari already accused her of running away when anything upset her? Ella bristled at that recollection. But exactly what was she doing now? She couldn't give up on Callie; she just *couldn't*! Whatever happened, whatever else she had to bear, there was no way she could give up on the little girl she loved. At the same time, however, she needed a few hours' grace to pull herself back together before she had to face Aristandros again. She decided that the wisest option was to find a hotel for the night.

She walked for ages before she came on a small es-tablishment sited in a quiet street. Checking in, she was conscious of the receptionist's swiftly veiled curiosity, and when she saw her reflection in the mirror in the *en suite* bathroom of her hotel room she grimaced in horrified embarrassment at the state of her face. Her mascara had run, and her eye shadow had smudged where she'd wiped her eyes, and her hair was all messy. She freshened up and then made herself switch her phone back on. She couldn't stage a vanishing act for very long. She had also left Aristandros standing at the opera. Although that was the very least of what he deserved, it would have gone down like a lead balloon.

Her phone rang within seconds of being switched on.

'Where the hell are you?' Aristandros growled.

'I'm sorry I didn't make it, but I need some space tonight.'

'No!' It was thunderous. 'No space allowed. Where are you?'

'In a hotel, a little place, not one you'd know. I really do need to be alone for a while,' Ella breathed flatly, wondering how she could possibly stand to be with him ever again, how she could ever contrive to live with him and the knowledge of his infidelity.

'You're not allowed to walk out on me under any circumstances,' Aristandros intoned in a fierce undertone. 'I will not tolerate it.'

'I'm not walking out on you.' Ella framed those words with a sob trapped in her throat.

'Ella…' he breathed huskily.

Ella cut the call before she could let her turbulent emotional mood betray her into revealing more than she should. But he would soon find out through his staff that she had met his trollop. No; where did she get off calling another woman a trollop just because she had slept with Ari? After all, she wasn't married to him. He was still a free agent in the eyes of the world.

Tears choking her, Ella, her slender body trembling, sank down on the end of the bed. As she always feared, her love for Aristandros was tearing her apart at the seams, destroying her strength and self-esteem, when really the only person she ought to be thinking about was Callie, who was safely asleep in her cot and blissfully ignorant of the messes adults could make of their relationships. But Ella recognised at that moment that she had to find a way to sort this mess out, because it was unlikely that she could trust Aristandros to make that effort.

More than an hour later, she jumped in surprise when a knock sounded at her door. Glancing out through the peephole, she could see nothing but a large probably male shape and she opened the door on the chain.

CHAPTER TEN

'Open the door, Ella,' Aristandros instructed harshly.

Ella was shattered that he had found her so quickly. She shut the door, undid the chain and opened the door again. 'How on earth did you know where I was?'

His tension palpable, Aristandros was staring at her, his brilliant dark gaze roving from the crown of her head down to her feet and swiftly back up again. 'I have tracking devices in your mobile phone and your watch, so it was just a matter of switching on the surveillance equipment to locate you—'

Ella gaped at him aghast. '*Tracking devices*?' she parrotted.

'A precaution in case you were kidnapped, a standard security procedure,' Aristandros proclaimed matter-of-factly. 'I'm a very wealthy man, and it's possible that someone could try to target you because of your connection to me.'

'You fixed tracking devices on me?' Ella condemned him in angry disbelief, still back at that first admission. 'And you never said a word about it either.'

'I didn't want to make you nervous or scared. But

I'm not going to apologise for it, either,' Aristandros added in an aggressive undertone. 'I needed to be sure you were as safe as I could make you. It's my job to protect you.'

'A tracking device,' Ella muttered shakily. 'Like I'm a possession…a stolen car or something.'

'You are a hell of a sight more important to me. It was no big deal until you went missing tonight and, let me tell you, you've put me through complete hell in the space of a few hours!'

Pale and drawn, Ella slowly breathed in. 'Have I really?'

'Why didn't you phone me from the hospital? You could have let me know what had happened, not cleared off in an air ambulance as if I didn't exist!' Aristandros launched at her, his strong bone-structure rigid beneath his bronzed skin. 'Ianthe was out and I couldn't get hold of her, so I had no idea an emergency had come up. All the domestic staff knew was that you had gone off somewhere with her. I was worried about you—'

'Why? What could possibly have happened to me on the island?' Ella couldn't believe she was managing to stay so calm.

Aristandros glowered at her as if that was a very stupid question. 'You could have had an accident. I knew something must have gone badly wrong when you didn't show up at the opera house, because you're usually very reliable.'

'Oh…'

'And then Yannis phoned after you had left the hospital to rave about how wonderful you had been with his daughter, and I began to understand what had happened. But you never arrived at Drakon's house because he checked.'

'Drakon's house? Why would I have arrived there?' Ella questioned uncertainly.

'That's where you sent your dress.'

'Ianthe organised that.' Ella hesitated. 'I assumed it had been sent to the villa outside Athens.'

'Ianthe knew I had a bunch of guests staying there this week, so she wouldn't have sent it there.'

'Guests?' Ella echoed weakly.

'I understand that you may have met *one* of them,' Aristandros pointed out with laden emphasis.

Suddenly the atmosphere was so thick it could have been cut with a knife.

Ella was very still and she stood very straight. 'Is that what you call the young woman I met—a guest?'

'So you did rise—or should I say *sink*—to the worst possible conclusion,' Aristandros gathered, his sensual mouth compressed into a grim line of disapproval. 'Eda is my niece, the daughter of my father's youngest sister.'

Her stress level rising as his explanation gathered pace, Ella's brow had indented. 'Are you saying Eda was the girl I ran into? And that she's a relative of yours? If that's true, why was she in the master-bedroom *en suite*?'

'I have no idea. Her parents left her at the villa while they attended the opera because she refused to go. She's something of a handful, and fairly spoilt. Maybe she was trying out the facilities or just exploring while she had the house to herself. How should I know?'

Ella was mentally running through the explanation to see if it could fit what she had seen.

'You can ask her when you meet her tomorrow.'

'I'm going to meet her?' Ella framed uncertainly.

'I'm throwing a party on the island for my relatives tomorrow.'

As Ella began to hope that she had totally misinterpreted the girl's presence at the villa, her legs seemed to go hollow, and her head swam. That physical weakness was her body's response to the powerful rush of relief assailing her. 'Oh, my goodness,' she framed. 'I thought…'

Aristandros reached for her hands and pulled her closer. His dark-golden eyes were raw with reproach. 'Yes, you immediately assumed that I was *shagging* a sixteen-year-old behind your back!'

'She's only sixteen?' Ella mumbled, clinging to his hands to stay upright while she acknowledged that the girl had indeed looked very young.

'I prefer rather more mature specimens of womanhood, *khriso mou*,' Aristandros spelt out levelly. 'Although that does make me wonder why I'm with you, because sometimes you seem to react more like an impulsive airhead of a teenager than the intelligent adult I know you to be.'

A flood of hot moisture engulfed her eyes in a tide, and she blinked repeatedly while staring down at their still-linked hands. 'Her underwear was lying on the bedroom floor. She was only wearing a towel. I did think you must have been with her…'

'No.' His handsome jaw clenched. 'For that matter, I haven't been with anyone else since you came back into my life.'

Ella was so relieved by that admission that a sob escaped her. 'But that agreement said—'

'That was just me acting like a gorilla and beating my chest to ensure you had some healthy respect for me,' Aristandros admitted, gripping her hands so tightly in his that she was convinced they would go entirely numb. 'I'd like to go home now. I appreciate that it's late, but the helicopter is standing by at the airport, and I very much want to get back to the island tonight.'

'Okay.' Ella's voice was small and breathless, and she nodded in confirmation; the terrible, frightening tension and the fear of an unknown impossible future was leaving her piece by piece. There *was* no other woman in his life. He hadn't been with anyone but her since they'd got back together again. She had misunderstood, deemed him guilty when he was innocent. Her world had horizons and possibilities again, but she was almost afraid of accepting that fact.

'You're really shaken up,' Aristandros remarked, draping her bag over her shoulder and guiding her out of the room. 'I should be shouting at you for thinking the worst of me and putting me through a hellish evening of frustration and worry. I don't even like opera at the best of times, but tonight I felt trapped.'

'I'm sorry,' she muttered in the lift, and she wanted to lean up against him and cling but wouldn't let herself act that weak and feminine.

'You're never going to trust me, are you? Why do I get the feeling that I'm paying for your stepfather's sins?'

Ella ducked her head as he tucked her into the limo waiting outside. She had made a hash of things again. A sniff escaped her and then another. Aristandros wrapped both arms round her and almost squeezed the life's breath out of her. 'Don't be silly. You have nothing to cry about.'

'Maybe it was stupid, and I know I misunderstood, but I honestly thought you must have slept with her I was devastated!' Ella gasped out strickenly. 'And I didn't know what I was going to do because I couldn't give up Callie to walk away from you—I *couldn't*!'

Aristandros held her back from him. 'That's one worry you don't have to have ever again.'

'What do you mean?'

'I care too much about Callie to use her to control you. You were right. I shouldn't have involved her in our arrangement. That was inexcusable.' His darkly handsome features were taut and grim as he made that statement. 'Whatever happens between us, I will share custody of Callie with you. You love her and she loves you, and I have watched her blossom in your care. I will never try to separate you from her and you will both always enjoy my financial support.'

Ella was astonished by that far-reaching promise and the conviction with which he spoke. 'Why are you saying this now? Why have you changed your mind after forcing that iniquitous agreement on me?'

'I recognise that what I did was wrong from start to finish: using Callie as bait to trap you, forcing such an unscrupulous contract on you. Drakon was right in what he said, and he didn't know the half of what I imposed on you. Worst of all, I knew that what I was doing to you was wrong even as I did it. Yet I *still* went ahead with it,' Aristandros recounted heavily, his handsome head turned in profile to her, his mouth harshly compressed.

'Why, though? Was it all about revenge?' she pressed, desperate to understand what had motivated him

The silence lay like a blanket and the tension in his

big, powerful frame was so fierce she could feel it even though they were no longer touching. The limousine was already pulling in at the airport.

'Ari…?' she prompted. 'I need to know.'

'I told myself it was purely an act of revenge, but it wasn't. The truth is usually the most simple answer—and the simple answer is that I just wanted you, and that agreement bound you hand and foot to ensure you couldn't walk away again. I needed that protection before I could let myself get involved with you again,' he breathed in a driven undertone. 'But now I realise that I don't want to keep you only because I've got legal custody of your daughter.'

'So, if I want to leave and return to my life in London,' Ella whispered unevenly, 'You'll let me go and allow me to take Callie with me?'

'Letting you both go would kill me, but I won't go back on my word to you,' Aristandros declared with raw emphasis as the door beside her was whipped open by his driver.

Surrounded by his security team, they walked through the airport in silence. *I just wanted you.* Four little words that made a heck of a difference to Ella, and that kept on rhyming back and forth through her head, providing a much-needed mantra of hope. In spite of all the other options he must have had, he had returned to his past and blackmailed her back into a relationship with him. For the first time she registered that she had been and still evidently was much more important to Aristandros Xenakis than he had ever been willing to admit. He didn't want to lose either her or Callie, but he was willing to let them go free if that was what she decided she wanted.

As they waited in a VIP lounge, Ella was conscious of his scrutiny. She knew he was desperate to know what she intended to do next. He had removed the one threat that could have forced her to take whatever he threw at her. No longer did she need to stay with him purely for Callie's sake. His ferocious pride couldn't live with that concept. Blackmail, he had finally discovered, did have its drawbacks.

They were walking towards the helicopter with a neat, respectful space between them when Ella reached abruptly for a lean, brown hand across that divide. 'I want to stay with you,' she told him tautly.

Right there and then, Aristandros turned round and swept her straight into his arms, plunging his mouth down urgently on hers with a passion that blew her away. He had to practically carry her on board the helicopter after that. She was stunned by the level of his relief at her announcement, and could not have doubted his level of ongoing satisfaction over that news when he gave her a heart-stopping smile and retained a hold on her hand throughout the flight. The engine was so noisy that there was no chance of any further conversation until they arrived back on Lykos.

Ella kicked off her shoes just inside the front door when they arrived and padded off straight to the nursery to satisfy her desperate need to see Callie. When she looked up from the cot and the peacefully sleeping child, Aristandros was on the other side of it.

'I really screwed up tonight—the opera thing,' Ella said ruefully. 'I know it was important. I'm sorry I didn't make it.'

Aristandros gave her a wryly amused appraisal. 'You

left me standing. But then I'm used to you embarrassing me in front of my family.'

Ella blinked. 'Your...er...*family*?'

'Yes. Pretty much the whole tribe attended that benefit, and I was planning to show you off to them all.'

'My word; truthfully?' Ella prompted as she followed him out of the nursery. 'Why did you want to show me off?'

'Because I very much hope you're going to marry me, but I wasn't so stupid that I was going to make an announcement without thoroughly discussing terms with you in advance,' he explained smoothly.

Her bright-blue eyes grew very wide. 'You're proposing *again*?'

'A tactful woman would have left out that last word,' Aristandros told her, walking her out on to the terrace where a champagne bottle and glasses sat on the table. 'Are we celebrating or not?'

Ella winced. 'I'm totally, madly in love with you and just like the last time I really, really want to marry you and be with you for ever. But I also spent a large chunk of my life training to become a doctor.'

'And you can *still* be a doctor.' Aristandros frowned as she looked at him in shock. 'I was being very selfish, which I hate to admit comes naturally to me around you. My mother was so obsessed with the film world that she had no time or energy to spare even for me, never mind my father. I don't want a marriage like that. I once resented your medical career because you chose it over me.'

Her lovely face was pensive in the moonlight. 'No, I think I used it as my get-out clause because I'd suffered

Theo as a horrid example of a womaniser and I was so afraid of getting hurt. I should have had more faith in you.'

'We didn't have enough time together.' Aristandros lifted her hand and slid a ring on to her engagement finger. 'It's the same diamond I planned to give you seven years ago, but I've had it reset.'

'It's glorious.' Ella watched the glittering stone sparkle like starlight on her hand and a warm, deep sense of happiness began to fill her.

'We were too young then,' he admitted ruefully. 'If we'd been more mature we would have tried to find a compromise and a way of being together that we could both live with. Instead I lost my temper with you because you made me feel foolish, which was very superficial.'

'You really broke my heart,' Ella confided, ready to be totally frank now that she had his ring on her finger and a proper secure future to look forward to. 'I couldn't believe you'd ever loved me.'

'I loved you so much that I never found anyone else to replace you. With you I thought I could break the Xenakis tradition of bad marriages. I believed that settling down while I was still quite young into marriage would give me a much better prospect of happiness than, for instance, the life I've been leading since then.' His rich, golden eyes were full of regret. 'But I fell at the first challenge.'

Ella wrapped her arms round his neck, her fingers gently feathering through the silky, black hair at his nape. She wished she had understood him better seven years earlier and recognised that his troubled background had made him crave a much more stable life with one woman rather than a succession. 'You were so all-or-nothing about everything, and then you just walked away from me and I never heard from you again.'

'You just walked away too,' he reminded her. 'I was too proud to chase after you, although I thought of looking you up when I was over in London at least fifty times.'

'There's never been anyone else for me. I never stopped loving you although I didn't realise that until recently.'

'I fell in love with you on our first date. You got drenched with sea spray and you laughed. Every other girl I knew would have thrown a fit.'

'I'm not vain, but I'm a jealous cat,' she warned him, cherishing the ease with which he could look back through those years and recall one tiny incident, in much the same way he had remembered her admiring comment about the church on Lykos. The idea that he loved her was becoming more and more real and credible with every passing second. She smiled, and soon discovered that she couldn't stop smiling.

'I've sown my wild oats, but I didn't enjoy myself so much that I want to do it again, *agapi mou*,' Aristandros confided with blunt sincerity. 'I wanted a second chance with you. I wanted to hear you say you'd misjudged me. But when I found out about your wife-beating stepfather I got a step closer to understanding why you were so unwilling to trust me. When you threw that jealous scene after the Ferrand party, I was overjoyed, because that proved that you still had feelings for me just as I did for you.'

'So, what do you want now?' Ella enquired tightly.

'All I really want now is more of what we already have. I'm very happy with you. To be frank, I was disappointed that you weren't pregnant. I want to have a baby with you.'

Ella released a happy sigh at the prospect and beamed at him. 'How soon can we start trying?'

Aristandros laughed with rich appreciation. 'Would tonight be too soon?'

Ella regarded him with eyes as starry as the night sky above. 'No; I'm available without appointment whenever you want.'

'I should warn you that I want you pretty much all the time, *latria mou*,' Aristandros admitted, bending down to press his mouth to hers and kissing her slowly and skilfully until the blood drummed through her veins in a passionate response. 'It's an effort to go away on business when I've got you in my bed.'

'I don't want you going anywhere right now,' Ella confessed, her hands curling into the lapels of his suit jacket at the mere mention of him needing to go away from her. 'I want you all to myself. Will we get married on the island?'

'Yes. And soon,' he urged. 'Speaking as a guy who was once engaged for about five minutes, I don't believe in long engagements.'

'Neither do I,' Ella agreed fervently, while she busily thought about wedding dresses and Callie as a little flower girl, not to mention the provision of a baby to keep Callie company. She was so happy at the prospect of those delights that her heart felt as though it was overflowing.

Fourteen months later, Ella watched Kasma tuck Ari's son and heir, Nikolos, into his cot.

At three months old, Nikolos was already revealing Xenakis traits of character. He was very impatient, and screamed the place down if he wasn't fed immediately if he felt hungry. He truly adored an audience of female admirers and basked in their attention. He was advanced for his age in size and development. He already looked as though he was likely to be as tall as his father, and he had definitely inherited his father's heartbreakingly charismatic smile.

These days Drakon Xenakis spent more time on Lykos than in Athens. He was enchanted by his grandson's perfectly ordinary family life with Ella, Callie and the new baby. It was what he himself had never managed to achieve with his own late wife and children, and he appreciated the commitment it took for such a busy couple to make it work.

The house had been virtually rebuilt during the extensive renovations Ella had organised and was now a much more comfortable family-orientated home. It had not been easy to live in the house while all the work had still been going on, particularly while Ella was pregnant, but with her mother's help, and that of the staff, Ella had managed.

Jane had got divorced. Theo was still in prison serving time for that final assault on his ex-wife, while Jane lived in a city apartment and enjoyed a healthy circle of friends with whom she shared interests. At least once a month the older woman visited her daughter and, if both Ella and Aristandros were abroad together, she came to stay and took charge of the household.

But actually Aristandros was travelling a great deal less than he once had and worked more from home, while Ella was putting in part-time hours as the island doctor and taking an interest in the charitable endeavours of the Xenakis Foundation. Just as Aristandros had gone to a good deal of trouble to ensure that business rarely parted them, Ella had been equally careful to ensure that her job didn't steal too big a slice of her time and energy, and after a year she reckoned that she had got the balance exactly right. Plentiful help on the home front had been invaluable, and Callie currently attended a play group in town several mornings a week. That winter the whole family would be moving to the Athens villa to enable Ella to undertake a paediatrics course at the hospital.

Ella was blissfully happy. She and Aristandros had enjoyed a huge engagement party, and her wedding a couple of months afterwards had been the fairy-tale event that she had always secretly dreamt of having. Although Ella had been just a little pregnant at the time, she hadn't been showing. Lily had been her chief bridesmaid, and was currently applying for a surgical job at a Greek hospital after meeting up with a Greek businessman of her own at the wedding.

Ella had been surprised when she'd fallen pregnant so quickly, while Ari had merely had his unshakeable faith in his own virility proven to his full satisfaction. Callie was just at the age when a baby brother was a source of fascination to her, and had had to be dissuaded from treating Nikolos like a living, breathing doll. Ella and Aristandros had formally adopted Callie, and although they were careful to tell the child only as much as she could currently understand about her true beginnings and Timon, the little girl regarded them as her mother and father.

When Ella heard the buzz of the helicopter passing overhead, she grinned and headed out to the terrace to watch it land. Lean, dark and stunningly handsome in his business suit, Aristandros strode towards her.

'How was New York?' she asked.

'I had a frantic schedule. I'm just glad to be home with my beautiful wife and children.' As Callie raced towards him chattering in excitement, Aristandros swung the little girl up and hugged her with an ease that would have been foreign to him a year earlier. He paused beside Ella and lowered his dark head to kiss her.

Tingles of sensual awareness ran up and down her spine and into more private places. 'I like the dress,' he growled.

'Daddy's talking like a bear,' Callie giggled, sliding down to the ground to run off again.

Ella twirled so that Aristandros got the full effect of the short, red strappy dress swirling round her slim legs. 'Happy anniversary,' she told him.

'What's on the agenda for tonight?'

'Dinner on the yacht, and we're spending the night on board so that we can have lots and lots of private time without being interrupted,' Ella told him cheerfully.

Her candour brought a deeply amused smile to his striking features. 'You know how to keep me happy.'

'I certainly hope so. I love you loads,' she confided, wrapping her arms round him.

'And I love the way you love me as much as I love you.' Aristandros gazed down at her with brilliant dark eyes. 'I want you to know that this has been the happiest year of my entire life, *agapi mou*.'

Ella knew that that was an admission to be truly treasured, and felt almost overwhelmed by emotion.

Over dinner on *Hellenic Lady*, they caught up after his three-day absence and he gave her a sapphire eternity-ring engraved with their son's name. Hand-in-hand they walked to their state room, which was adorned with fresh flowers, to share a wonderful night together, and an early morning disturbed neither by a baby's cries for attention nor a toddler's wistful demands for company.

But that rare silence felt a touch weird to both of them and, after a quick breakfast, they got in the speedboat to sail back to shore and they spent the rest of the day on the beach as a family…

HIS VIRGIN
ACQUISITION

MAISEY YATES

Maisey Yates was an avid Mills & Boon® Modern™ romance reader before she began to write them. She still can't quite believe she's lucky enough to get to create her very own sexy alpha heroes and feisty heroines. Seeing her name on one of those lovely covers is a dream come true.

Maisey lives with her handsome, wonderful, nappy-changing husband and three small children across the street from her extremely supportive parents and the home she grew up in, in the wilds of Southern Oregon, USA. She enjoys the contrast of living in a place where you might wake up to find a bear on your back porch and then heading into the home office to write stories that take place in exotic urban locales.

To the MH mavens, my dear sisters.
Thanks for your insight, your support,
and most of all your friendship.
And to my husband, Haven.
Without you I wouldn't know what romance is.

CHAPTER ONE

"I THINK the numbers speak for themselves. Marriage is definitely the most profitable course of action."

It seemed Elaine Chapman had finally come to the end of her lengthy presentation.

Marco De Luca scanned the expanse of his office, looking for hidden cameras or some other sign that she was here on assignment from a reality show. There was no way she could be serious.

He didn't spot a blinking camera light anywhere, nor did he detect an ounce of insincerity in her tone. He stopped his search and locked his eyes onto her determined face. She *was* serious. Although why that should come as a shock he wasn't sure. Ms. Chapman was known for using whatever means necessary to get ahead. Including her body.

Marco's gaze swept her up and down. "Marriage? To you?"

Elaine's face heated at the incredulous note in his voice. She knew she wasn't exactly Miss New York. Clearly Marco did too, as she seemed to recall reading somewhere that he'd once *dated* Miss New York, but she wasn't *that* bad.

"Of what benefit could that possibly be to me?"

He leaned back in his chair and put his hands behind his head, delineating muscles that weren't at all concealed by his tame button-up dress shirt. She forced her eyes back to his face. Who cared about his muscles? So he had them? Men did, after all. She did not need this distraction right now, or ever.

"Didn't you pay attention to the chart?" She held up the colored graph for his further inspection.

"I heard what you said. But none of it was worth hearing. I've allowed you to waste twenty minutes of my valuable time, time that you couldn't begin to afford to re-imburse me for, and the business proposal you were sup-posed to come here and offer me turns out to be a marriage proposal? You're lucky I haven't called Security."

He studied the tired, bleak-looking woman standing in front of him. He had only seen her on a few occasions, and even then it had been from a distance, but every time, even at formal charity balls, she had been in some variation of a black or navy blue pantsuit, her blond hair scraped back into a tight, unforgiving bun.

She was one of those women. The kind who seemed to think that they had to look like a man in order to compete in the business world. The sort of woman who took great care to disguise every trace of femininity she possessed. And this one did a particularly excellent job. He also knew that if she *could* use her femininity to her advantage she would do so without shame or scruples. Though he hadn't experienced that personally.

"I've already explained how it benefits you." She straightened her shapeless suit jacket and continued. "You're a smart man, Mr. De Luca. You want the bottom line, so here it is: married men make more money than single men. That's a fact. And you can't pretend the statistic doesn't interest you. Your reputation for expanding your company at almost any cost is legendary. A marriage between the two of us is a business strategy. A valid one."

James Preston. The name swam through his mind. James was holding out on a multi-million-dollar deal because he couldn't imagine handing over his beloved resort to a man who had no concept of the joys of a loving family. So instead he was out to find some family man to take it over. A family man who would have neither the time nor the drive that Marco had to offer the resort. Marco wanted the deal, no denying that, and as it stood he wasn't going to get it. It had been gnawing at him for weeks. He didn't do failure. Not anymore. He'd had enough of it.

But marriage seemed like an extreme solution; he'd spent thirty-three years avoiding the institution, and he had no desire to enter into it now.

"And you honestly think I'm going to stoop to marrying you to increase my profit margins?"

She pursed her lips, clearly unhappy with his choice of words. "Yes. I do. You're a legend in the industry. Not just for all that you've achieved, although that's impressive enough, but also for your ruthlessness, and that is something we share. Although my aim is considerably lower."

"And how does this benefit you, Ms. Chapman?" He stood up from his position behind the desk and walked around to the other side of it, so he was standing directly in front of her, his arms crossed. "Because, businesswoman that you are, there has to be an angle."

Elaine took a deep breath to steady herself. She had answers to all of his objections carefully prepared, but being on the receiving end of his intense dark gaze caused her well-rehearsed argument to get jumbled in her head.

She had never seen a man as gorgeous as he was on

this side of the silver screen. He was the epitome of tall, dark and handsome, and he made her want to ditch her normally feminist persona in favor of that of a swooning Southern belle.

Swooning? Where had that come from? She'd never swooned in her life! She wasn't even sure what swooning was.

She tried to collect her thoughts and continue on as rehearsed, but it was hard to concentrate when he was standing so close being all tall and handsome and intimidating and *handsome*. His masculinity was so potent it nearly reached out and grabbed her, or made her want to reach out and grab him. She had never had a fantasy before that she could recall, and here she was in the middle of a business presentation, entertaining predatory thoughts about the man to whom she was making her pitch. He was throwing her completely off balance.

She was starting to think she'd made a serious miscalculation. A very serious, very tall, very sexy miscalculation.

Taking a deep breath to banish her rogue thoughts, she pressed on, "My father, like most men his age, thinks a woman's place is in the kitchen. And while I have no problem with a woman being in the kitchen, if that's what she wants, it's not what I want. *I* want the company, and he doesn't seem to think I'm capable of running it."

"*Are* you capable of running a company?" He leaned back against the desk and her eyes were drawn to his big hands, which were clutching the edge of the desk, supporting his weight. They were nice hands, masculine and callused. She hated smooth hands on a man. Well, theoretically she hated smooth hands on a man. Actually, she hadn't given it much thought before.

She was letting herself get distracted again. This was not the time for latent hormones to be popping up and making themselves known. She wanted this. She needed this. Attractive or not, she was not letting this man stand in her way.

She drew up to her full height, which in her chunky heels put her at the bottom of his chin. "I am more than capable, and more than qualified. I have a business degree, I interned at a Fortune 500 company, and I'm currently working as the head accountant for a small marketing firm. You can rest assured that, with or without those qualifications, if I were my father's son he would hand over the reins of the company to me with pride."

"If you're so incredibly competent why haven't you simply branched out on your own?"

Her lips, lush when they weren't pinned together in an uncompromising line, tightened, and she narrowed her eyes. "I would have. But my father had me sign a non-compete clause when I worked for him back when I was in college. I'm banned from starting a new business that might compete in any way with Chapman Electronics."

"And you were foolish enough to sign it?"

He enjoyed watching the pink flush creep into her ivory cheeks. It made him wonder if she flushed the same color when she was aroused, which made him wonder just what it would take to arouse passion in a woman like Elaine. Spreadsheets, most likely.

"At the time I assumed the business would pass to me when he retired, so it seemed like a non-issue," she said curtly.

"And you think that a marriage of convenience is going to help you out of this little situation you've landed yourself in?"

"I told you, I've done my research." She took a step

closer to him and put her hands on her hips, pulling that awful jacket tight, revealing a small waist and the gentle rounding of her breasts. "You're set to acquire my father's company upon his retirement."

"And how exactly does marriage work to your advantage?"

"The contracts have already been signed, haven't they?" He nodded in confirmation. "So he can't back out now."

"Well, he could try, but it would be unpleasant for him." His voice held a hard edge that left her in little doubt that he was telling the truth. He seemed completely ruthless. She liked that.

"So I marry you, and as your wife I'll own half of your assets, which makes me half-owner of my father's business. I would have come to simply negotiate a sale, but there's a clause in your contract that says if you sell to me you'll forfeit the company."

"Yes, I am aware of the clause you're talking about. I got a little bit of a chuckle out of it, actually. But I had to wonder if it was added because of your gender or your competence." His deep, mildly accented voice held a hint of mockery that made her bristle.

"My father is the consummate male chauvinist. Ideally I'd send him to a therapist to explore his issues, and maybe we could reach some sort of agreement that way," she said dryly. "But that isn't likely. So here I am. My father's a good businessman, a worthy adversary. But I'm better. I found a loophole, a rather gaping one. The contract says I can't *buy* the business, however, there isn't anything in there about me inheriting the company—say, through a divorce." She couldn't disguise the self-satisfied note that had crept into her voice.

She studied his face, searching for a hint as to what he

might be thinking, but there was nothing. The man was solid granite.

Marco laconically flipped through her stack of data. "It seems to me, Ms. Chapman, that you've presented a one-sided deal. You get your family company and I get what? An increase in profits based on hypothetical statistics? I don't think so. That's not how business is done."

He took great satisfaction in seeing her unflappable cool slip for a moment. "I know how business is done," she snapped. "I'm fully qualified. I went to Harvard."

"Time in a classroom does not teach you the reality of the business world. You know numbers. You know text-book scenarios. You don't know how things really work. As proved by your willingness to sign whatever piece of paper your father put in front of you."

She thrust her chin up in a gesture of defiance. "I know how things work. Money makes the world turn. And this will mean money for you. You'll make more in gross profit from this than you ever could have made with my father's small potatoes business. Chapman Electronics barely makes fifteen percent of what *one* of the De Luca Corporation's subsidiaries pulls in annually. Marrying me has the poten-tial to boost profits by ten percent in each of the companies owned and operated by the De Luca empire."

The tip of her tongue darted out and slicked over her bottom lip. Her lips were actually very full and tempting when they weren't pinched together. He could easily imagine them parting beneath his own as she granted him entry into her mouth. Imagine her shedding some of her hardened shell and melting beneath him.

She did a wonderful job of downplaying her natural femininity. Such a good job that most people would miss it entirely. But natural beauty like hers was impossible to bury completely. She had large, generously lashed china-blue eyes, finely arched eyebrows, and clear pale skin. She wasn't made-up and finished to a highly glossed sheen like the women he typically went out with, but there was a freshness to her look that intrigued him.

It had been a long time since a woman had intrigued him at all. In his experience women were all very much the same in the presence of a rich man. Flirtatious, transparent and, once the sparkle wore off, boring.

"And how long do you see such a marriage lasting?" It was the sheer mercenary quality of the proposition that had him asking questions. It was interesting to meet someone as committed, as driven as he was, to the pursuit of success.

"Certainly not 'till death do us part'. I figure twelve months should be enough to make it look as though we gave it a legitimate try. Sadly…" she gave a little shrug of one of her padded shoulders "…as happens with more than fifty percent of marriages, ours just didn't stand the test of time."

This was where the real bottom line was revealed. He still didn't believe she would want only Chapman Electronics. She was right in her assessment of it as small potatoes. And a woman who was willing to sell her body for a contract would not be interested in small potatoes.

"And after that twelve months is when you think you'll get your hefty settlement? Are you going to cry abuse? Say that I was unfaithful?"

"Hardly! I told you I want the company. Nothing more or less than that."

"But what will become of my newly increased profits when we divorce?"

"That's the beauty of it," she said, her smile had become a smirk. "When your wife leaves you and breaks your poor heart, your profits will increase even more. I've done my research."

"So you've said."

She gave him a pained look and continued. "Empathy is a very powerful emotion. Most of the men you'll be doing business with have been divorced, generally because commitment to their business outweighed commitment to their wife. When your wife leaves you, you'll have the whole lot of them standing around ready to dole out cigars and sympathy."

Everything in him was on high alert. His blood was pumping faster, just as it did when he knew he was on to a profitable deal. He lived for this. Lived for the challenge—the danger, even. And it wasn't in him to shy away from either.

He didn't need more money. No question. But he wanted it. The boy who had slept in grimy alleyways and crowded homeless shelters craved the security. Needed to push farther and farther away from those low points, keep pushing past all that he had been. Needed constant success, where before there had only been failure and struggle.

"There would have to be a prenup. And don't think for one moment I'll be content to let you or your lawyer draw it up and start making demands. The way I see it, I could send you out the door and I will have lost nothing. You, on the other hand, will have lost everything. Where I only stand to gain, you could lose."

She was slightly shocked that he seemed to be on the verge of accepting her offer. Obviously she had hoped that he would, but a very large part of her hadn't believed she had a prayer. "I have no issue with you having a prenup drafted. I don't want anything from you but what's rightfully mine."

He looked her up and down in a way that made her feel as if she was on the auction block.

"Would we be consummating this marriage?" It seemed important to know. Surprisingly, he found his body responding to the idea. The faint hint of a figure he'd caught lurking under her masculine attire was more than a little enticing. And there was something about her high-necked don't-touch-me blouse that just begged to have the buttons released one by one...

He was amused when a tide of color crept up her neck and rushed into her cheeks. He hadn't seen a woman blush since... Well, maybe never. The women he associated with were not the blushing kind. They were like him—jaded when it came to life and relationships. He liked a woman who knew how to please a man. A woman who understood that sex was not love. A woman who knew the score.

Normally he didn't go for the whole bashful innocent façade, and he knew it *was* a façade, but somehow she was even more beautiful when she blushed. The layers of composed, hard-edged businesswoman seemed to fall away and reveal a woman who was capable of being soft and sexy.

"No!" She hadn't meant to sound so flustered by his question, but she wasn't a good enough actress to pretend she was unaffected by his blatant mention of sex. The topic wasn't exactly something she was used to discussing in the broad light of day with a man. Or with anyone, at any time. "I mean you're free to do whatever you want, with *whoever* you want. With discretion, of course. I sincerely doubt that any of those conservative old businessmen would have any sympathy for you if they knew you had been running around...philandering behind your wife's back!"

He let his eyes wander over her body, and he suddenly

saw the appeal of women concealing more than they revealed. It was making him unbearably curious.

He wondered what it would take to get her to loosen up a little, to get her to let her hair down. He could picture her with her blond hair loose around her face; her cheeks flushed pink with passion, her gorgeous mouth swollen from kisses. His kisses. She would be an aggressive lover, he decided. A woman so bound and determined to give as good as she got in the boardroom would very likely behave the same in the bedroom.

He felt himself getting hard thinking about it. He let his eyes wander over her figure, catching hints of the lushness that lay beneath her loose cut clothing. Oh, yes, beneath that armor she was all woman. Slender, yet soft and curvy.

"Whoever I want?" He lowered his voice and brushed his knuckles gently across her cheek.

Elaine had never had a man look at her like this. As if he was seeing straight through her, with all of his desire reflected in his eyes. Desire for her. She was momentarily immobilized by the flash of attraction that raced through her. She'd never felt anything like the fluttering, twisting sensation that was curling low in her belly.

"What if I told you that I wanted you?"

She realized that she was starting to lean towards him, her lips parting slightly, as if in invitation, her eyes drifting closed…

She backed away from his touch as if she'd been burned, mortified heat flooding her face again.

"No! No. No. I mean, this is a business deal, and I've no desire to…muddy the waters by introducing anything physical, and anyway it's…it would be inappropriate." Her face was burning, and she knew she was glowing like a beacon. She was starting to wish she hadn't come. She was totally and completely out of her depth with him.

He laughed. She was absolutely priceless, clinging to her prim and proper persona. "Point taken."

It would be better that way. Much better to keep business and pleasure firmly separated. Especially when there was a marriage license involved. He didn't want to be tied to one woman for a year, and he had a feeling that if he did sleep with her, the "anyone at any time" offer would be revoked.

And anyway, if he changed his mind he could have her if he wanted her. He had seen it in her eyes, in the rapid beat of her pulse at the base of her elegant neck. She wasn't immune to him. But in his experience very few women were. They loved his status, his wealth, and his skill in the bedroom. Sometimes they even loved him. But *he* didn't love *them*. Ever.

"You would have to move into my penthouse," he said.

"Absolutely not!" And there it was again, that flustered look that made her seem soft, maybe even feminine. That made her seem so desirable.

He took a step toward her. "I can't exactly have my new wife living across town. I do have a reputation, after all. Any woman of mine is always kept as close as possible."

The low, seductive timbre of his voice caused a shiver to race up her spine. When she'd imagined this little arrangement she hadn't pictured them living together, somehow. The thought of being in such close quarters with a man as…disturbing as Marco made her feel…hot.

But she could do it. To get the business she would do anything. She wasn't about to let her life's ambition go. She would find the whole thing much more tenable if she brought him to her turf. Really, she'd find the whole thing much more tenable if he was living on another continent, but as that wasn't an option… "If we have to live together, *you* can move in with *me*."

"No," he countered, "*you* will move in with *me*." Poor Elaine. She really was so painfully naive. The first rule in a business dealing was to know your adversary. And she clearly didn't know him. Marco De Luca did not negotiate. "And you'll take my name."

"What?" Her face was red again, but this time he was fairly certain it wasn't from embarrassment. "I wouldn't do that if I was entering into a *real* marriage with you! It's anti-feminist! Making a woman lose her identity just because she's getting married! It's an archaic form of control!"

He shrugged. "So call me a caveman, then. I'm not exactly a modern, sensitive male. And the closest I get to 'enlightened' is ordering a latte. When it comes to relationships, just like in business, I'm in charge. No one would believe it if *I* moved in with *you* and you kept your maiden name. My distinguished conservative clients would lose a lot of respect for me if I let my little wife run rough-shod over me in her ugly clogs."

She curled her toes inside her sensible footwear, hating him for making her feel self-conscious about her appearance. She had made the decision a long time ago, and with good reason, not to put emphasis on her looks—in fact, she did the opposite. And she refused to be made to feel silly for wanting to be taken seriously based on her qualifications instead of how sexy her legs looked in heels and a mini-skirt!

"Fine," she said through clenched teeth.

"And—" his lip curled into sneer "—I expect you to understand that as my wife my satisfaction is your priority. I am expecting to take full advantage of all of the perks this arrangement can afford me."

Her mouth dropped open. "I told you I'm not sleeping with you. Don't you dare make me sound like a…a…*prostitute*!" She clamped her mouth shut again, her pulse pounding in her ears. The absolute rank arrogance of the man!

He barked out a laugh. "That isn't what I said. I won't have any trouble finding a woman to share my bed. What I need is a woman to hold on to my arm and gaze at me adoringly during business functions. When I have an engagement that requires your presence, it takes priority. Not your work. Not your social life."

He could see the internal argument she was having with herself play out in her blue eyes. "Fine. I agree to your terms."

He gave her a hard look. "There is no chance that I might be tempted to make this arrangement permanent. That isn't how I operate. Even if you do wind up in my bed, it will only be until I'm finished with you. Don't fall in love with me, because I certainly won't be falling in love with you." It was a slightly more blunt version of the standard disclaimer he presented at the beginning of every relationship. If there was one thing he hated it was a woman getting overemotional and acting shocked when it was obviously time to end the relationship. And relationships always had to end.

"I'll try," Elaine said dryly. She was grateful for that little slap back to reality. He was a domineering womanizer, the sort of man she despised. And she'd do well to remember that.

Don't fall in love with him? She nearly laughed out loud. She wasn't even sure she liked him. And anyway, how could you fall in love if you'd written off the entire emotion?

"Plenty of women before you have fallen for me. Or my wallet, whichever the case may be."

"Trust me when I tell you I'm not interested in your heart or your wallet. I'm fully capable of supporting myself financially, and as for my taste in men…well, it doesn't run toward relics from bygone eras."

A slow smile spread across his face. "We have a deal," he said.

She stuck out her hand and he shook it in mild amusement. The woman was all business. Except when she blushed.

"Well, Mr. De Luca, it will be a pleasure working with you." The professional smile she had entered with was pasted firmly back into place. "I'll have my lawyer contact yours, and they can begin drafting the prenuptial agreement. Send me a copy of your calendar so that we can make a decision on the wedding date."

"Of course," he said. She turned to go, her pants tightening against her pert, rounded backside as she strode to the door. "Ms. Chapman?" She stopped and turned to face him again. "I'll pick you up tomorrow at eight. We're going to go shopping for an engagement ring in the morning."

She looked as if she wanted to say something. Her lips quivered, then hardened, but she remained silent.

"Oh, and be sure to wear something…feminine."

CHAPTER TWO

ELAINE glared at her bedside clock as the shrill alarm reminded her that it was time to get out of bed. She hadn't slept at all. She'd just twisted around in a tangle of sheets, second-guessing everything that had taken place the previous day.

She was no romantic—far from it. She was a pragmatist right down to her ugly shoes. Marriage, at its heart, was only a business arrangement anyway. The signing of a contract to legally bind two people together, with certain penalties applying should the agreement be broken.

But suddenly it seemed so much bigger than just signing a contract. She was actually *marrying* the man.

She swung her legs over the side of her bed and padded over to her closet. Wear something feminine, he'd said. If only she didn't need his help so badly she would have told him exactly where he could stick his opinions on her style of dress. But she wasn't about to blow this deal by being stubborn over every small demand. She would save up for the big things. This, although a blow to her pride, she could do.

She rifled through the tightly packed closet. Nothing but severe-looking suits in dark colors. Practical, but not exactly pretty. Certainly not *feminine*.

Although his idea of feminine was probably a corset and fishnet stockings!

There was a pale yellow dress wadded up into a ball and stuffed in the far reaches of the closet. She picked it up and shook out the wrinkles. It had flowers. And it was a dress. That, she supposed, would qualify it as *feminine*.

She took a quick shower and shaved her legs hurriedly. She got out and propped her leg up on the vanity, dabbed at the razor cut on her knee, then made the fatal error of looking in the mirror. She grimaced at the face staring back at her. There were deep purple shadows under her eyes from lack of sleep. She looked like a raccoon.

It had been a long time since she'd tried to play up her looks. These days she took care to tone down her beauty by wearing suits that camouflaged her hourglass figure and by pulling her long golden hair into the tightest bun she could manage. She didn't like the way she looked, but at least it had made the guys at work stop patting her on the behind and sending her off to make coffee.

She looked at her make-up bag, shoved against the back of the vanity. It was actually dusty. She did a mental calculation on when she'd gone to her last charity ball. Six months ago. That was how long it had been since she'd touched make-up. But it was desperately needed now.

Even without the raccoon eyes she would feel inadequate enough on the arm of a man who looked like Marco De Luca.

He was the perfect example of how it was different for men and women in the workplace. Where his looks were an asset to him, hers made men treat her like their own personal Barbie doll and made women treat her as if she was the enemy.

In the beginning she hadn't disguised her body. She hadn't felt she was at a disadvantage being female. But she had learned very quickly. It had only taken one incident to have her blacklisted from every decent real estate firm in the city; one tiny rumor that everyone had believed without so much as a photo to confirm it.

Even the man involved in the incident had denied it, but that hadn't made a difference to any of the city's gossipmongers. In the end the man had been allowed to keep his job, and at the age of twenty she had learned exactly where she stood in the male-dominated corporate world.

She applied the bare minimum of make-up needed to cover up the dark circles, and put on a little blush, mascara and lipgloss to play up her features as subtly as possible. She was reasonably satisfied with the results. She wouldn't be winning any beauty pageants, but the make-up highlighted her features nicely, made them look softer.

She checked her bedside clock. She had five minutes. She raced to her dresser and sifted through her massive collection of underwear, pulling out a pale yellow lace bra and thong. Her affinity for girlie bras and panties was her one concession to femininity. And it was safe, because no one knew about it.

The doorbell rang, and the sound put an uncomfortable jittery sensation low in her belly. She clamped a hand to her stomach in an attempt the squelch the feeling. The last thing she needed was to start acting like a silly teenage girl with a crush. She hadn't acted like a silly teenage girl when she'd *been* a teenager. No reason to start now that she was nearly at the halfway mark of her twenties.

"Coming!" she shouted, still trying to clasp her bra.

She gave herself one last glance as she raced by the bedroom mirror, and grimaced. Her hair was starting to curl, and in no time it would turn into frizz. Normally she didn't dare let her hair dry naturally, but at the moment she didn't have time to worry about it.

She slipped the dress over her head as she hurried out of her bedroom. It was shorter than she remembered, ending above her knees, and the scoop neck showed a lot more cleavage than she remembered too. The last time she'd worn it had probably been her sophomore year of high school. But it was too late to change now.

She swung open the door and her heart slammed against her ribcage. If he'd been handsome yesterday in his suit, he was devastating today in dark blue jeans and white button-up shirt. The color of the shirt enhanced his golden-brown skin, and he had the sleeves scrunched up to his elbows revealing his muscled forearms.

That tightening sensation was back, winding through her midsection and sending electric pulses through her bloodstream. Muscled forearms were something else she liked, apparently.

She was staring. *Oh, no.* She was staring and she couldn't stop. Thankfully, he didn't notice. Or maybe he pretended not to. Or he was just so used to women gawping at him that he took it as his due.

"You're ready," he said, in a tone she wasn't certain was complimentary. He assessed her slowly, his brown eyes taking a leisurely tour of her body. She had to fight the urge to try and cover up. "Typical female behavior demands that you keep me waiting for at least half an hour."

"I haven't picked up my copy of *The Rules* lately, so I must be out of the loop," she said waspishly.

He chose to ignore her biting retort and let his eyes roam over her body again. "Don't you think it's a little chilly out for a dress that skimpy?" The dress ended well above her knees, showing off killer legs she'd done a great job of camouflaging with her baggy pants.

"Skimpy?" She tugged at the hem, as if trying to add length to it. "It's perfectly decent. Besides, it's all I had that was appropriately *feminine* for you." She said it sweetly, but he could feel her barely contained annoyance radiating off her in waves.

Fine. That made two of them. The last thing he wanted to do was take a woman shopping. Much less take a woman shopping for a ring. Commitment, and anything resembling it, had been something he'd always endeavored to avoid. He'd spent too much of his life looking out for the needs of others, being the stable influence. As soon as his younger brother had turned eighteen Marco had taken his life back, and he wasn't about to forfeit it again by thrusting into the claws of some greedy female.

Usually if he was going to buy a woman jewelry, or some other gift, he had his PA sort it out. Anything else was much too personal and might convey intent that was most definitely not there.

But this was a necessary evil. It would call attention to them. Give the press a bone to gnaw on. Which was exactly what he wanted.

"It's fine," he said, trying not to give away just how fine he thought the dress was. "Just get a jacket."

"Well, as long as it meets with your approval, Mr. De Luca." She grabbed a light jacket and swept out the door.

Marco walked behind her, trying not to pay too close attention to the sway of her hips and the flare of that dangerously short dress. He felt his body tighten and he nearly groaned out loud. Who knew that Elaine Chapman had been hiding legs that could bring a man to his knees? And that image brought to mind a host of interesting possibilities.

He pulled his keys out of his pocket and pressed a remote unlock button, making the headlights of a low-slung black Ferrari flash.

"I expected it to be red," she mused.

He chuckled. "I hate to be too obvious."

She had to bite back a laugh. Marco was completely obvious in every way. His clothing screamed wealth, from his custom-made suit jackets to his handcrafted Italian leather shoes. And his body screamed sex, from his broad shoulders to his bold swagger.

He wore his confidence with the ease of a second skin, and it made her envious. She doubted he did anything based on the approval or disapproval of others. He simply succeeded. He lived to please himself. She wanted that.

He opened the passenger door and gestured for her to get in. She stopped in her tracks and gave him a look that could have melted ice.

He quirked a dark eyebrow at her. "You don't allow men to open doors for you?"

"I can open my own doors." She was being pigheaded, and she knew it. She let men open doors for her all the time if they offered.

She saw a glint of something dangerous in his eyes. Something exciting. "Yes, I'm sure that you can. But as of today you are my woman. And that means that I will treat you as I would treat a lover, *bella mia*." He purred the endearment, and she felt it vibrate all the way down to her toes.

Her knees wobbled slightly and she gave in and sank into the car's plush leather seats to avoid giving herself away.

An arrogant grin lit his handsome features. "Now, let's go find you a ring. Something to show the world that you are mine."

* * *

When they entered Tiffany & Co. a thousand childhood dreams that she'd never actually had converged on her, and a wave of emotion swamped her. The sophisticated surroundings and the man standing next to her made for an intoxicating romantic fantasy.

"We have an appointment," he whispered, and placed his hand on the small of her back, guiding her past tall, elegant glass display cases filled with rows of sparkling, exquisitely designed jewels.

She could barely concentrate on the jewelry. All her concentration had gone to the spot where Marco's hand rested, low on her back. Other than the handshake, and when he'd tortured her with that soft, sensual brush against her cheek, this was the first physical contact she'd had with him. Actually, other than handshakes and the hand on her cheek, this was the first physical contact she'd had in a long time. She hadn't realized how starving she was for it.

A tall, spindly saleswoman moved from behind one of the counters and greeted Marco with a double kiss on the cheek. "Ah, Mr. De Luca. We have the private viewing room open for you. If there's anything particular you have in mind, you need only to ask," she said, in a French accent that Elaine assumed was fake.

Private room? "I don't need anything extravagant," Elaine protested.

"Nothing is too extravagant for you, *cara mia.*" Marco's voice was so sticky sweet she was surprised it didn't rot his teeth.

The woman reached out and lifted up Elaine's hand. "Very nice fingers. Very slender," she remarked. "She should fit the sample size perfectly."

She was starting to feel as if both Marco and the twiggy saleslady saw her as nothing more than a living mannequin.

"This way." The woman gestured to a curved flight of stairs and led them into a chic, simply adorned room with sleek, modern furniture and a rich color palette.

A platter with fresh fruit and champagne had been laid out for them, and soft, soothing music was being piped in. Life was certainly different when you had billions of dollars at your disposal.

The woman went over to the streamlined desk and unlocked a drawer. She pulled out a cream-colored velvet tray filled with sparkling gems. "These are from our Signature collection. For the woman who wants to stand out."

The rings were all so large, so ornate. They were beautiful, but the idea of choosing one of these special rings for this…this fraud seemed wrong somehow.

"I don't know…"

"This one." Marco picked up an antique-style ring with a startlingly blue square-cut diamond in the center. "It would be perfect."

She pasted a smile on her face. So the offer of *carte blanche* really meant she got whatever he wanted. A ring that size was the equivalent of an animal marking its territory. Really, he might as well just skip the ring and tattoo the word "mine" on her forehead.

"Yes, but you know me," she said through gritted teeth. "I really do hate to be too obvious." She repeated his earlier words back to him.

She scanned the tray, looking for something that wouldn't make such a bold statement. Her breath literally caught when she saw the delicate emerald and platinum ring nestled in the bottom corner. Diamonds wove around the larger emeralds, giving it an old-fashioned, romantic feel.

The image that appeared in her mind of Marco slipping that ring onto her finger, his eyes full of some tender emotion she didn't recognize, caught her completely off guard.

Of all the times to romanticize!

He moved closer to her—so close that she could feel the heat radiating off his body. "That's the one you like?" His warm breath touched the back of her neck and made her stomach drop to her feet.

"I don't know." The thought of that perfect ring being a part of this sham almost made her feel sick.

"It seems very you. It's unique," he said, keeping his voice down to a husky whisper.

No wonder women fell at his feet. Everything about him was so dangerously seductive. She wanted so badly to buy into the fantasy. Just for a moment.

She closed her eyes. If she was honest with herself she knew she was never going to have a real wedding. Never going to experience this moment for real. Why not enjoy it?

"She would like this one, and a band to go with it," he told the saleswoman, not waiting for Elaine's response.

He was still standing too close, darn him! Her brain cells had gone on strike.

The woman went off to find a selection of wedding bands, leaving her alone with Marco. Her breath caught in her throat.

"Calm down," he whispered in her ear. "You're going to have to look like you enjoy my touch. Like it reminds you of pleasures we've recently shared." He ran his hand up from her waist to the underside of her breast. A tremor shot through her body and it made her shiver. She hadn't had this kind of contact *ever*.

He laughed low, his breath hot on her neck. "I don't think you'll have to *pretend* to like it."

His arrogant statement was enough to pull her out of her

sensual haze. She moved away from him, fighting hard to regain her sanity. She pretended to study one of the paintings on the wall, her body still tingling where his hand had made contact—and, more disturbingly, tingling in places he had *not* made contact.

The woman came back into the room with a simple platinum band, contoured to fit the asymmetrical design of the ring, in her hand. "This will be perfect."

"We'll have them wrapped, if you don't mind," Marco said, keeping his eyes trained on her. "I'm going to wait and present them to her later." The smile he gave her was so warm and intimate. And so not meant for her. It was for show. She didn't want to know what the cold, pressing sensation in her chest meant.

An hour later their purchases were wrapped up and they were back out in the morning sun, the warm rays banishing some of the chill that had been lingering in the air.

Marco's cellphone rang. "De Luca." He paused for a moment. "Yes. Go ahead and put me down for one hundred thousand." He paused again, and Elaine could hear a man's excited chatter on the other end. "Not at all. It's a worthy cause. Thank you. You too." He ended the call and put his phone back in his suit pocket.

"Was that for a charity?" she asked, feeling something soften inside her.

He nodded briskly. "A charity that provides financial support for the families of children with special needs. I make frequent donations to them."

"That's nice of you."

He stopped walking. "I'm not a nice man, *cara*. The sooner you realize that, the easier your life will be for the next twelve months."

"But you donated all that money…" She trailed off.

"And it benefits me. It will be a very high-profile donation. Philanthropy can be good for business." He turned away from her and started walking again, his strides so long she had to take two to his every one.

All of the soft feelings vanished. She knew he was ruthless when it came to business. His reputation was legendary. The man who, ten years ago, had become the youngest billionaire in the world. The man who crushed competition without a hint of conscience. He was well known for destroying any obstacles in his way, regardless of the fallout to anyone else. The bottom line was king. Wasn't the fact that he'd agreed to a marriage with her to boost his profits ample proof of that? Of course she supposed, as the marriage was her idea, she fell into the same category.

His reputation with the opposite sex was just as legendary as his business acumen. A couple of years ago he'd broken up with an Italian supermodel and she'd sold her story to one of the gossip rags. She'd spilled a lot of shocking details, and ever since then he'd become serious tabloid fodder. Elaine doubted that even half of what the woman said about him was true, but what she knew for sure was that he managed to be photographed with a different beautiful woman on his arm every weekend.

She had come in prepared for that. Prepared for the fact that he was sexy and that his charm was lethal enough to affect most any woman. But she had underestimated him. She had assumed that, with her practiced indifference to the masculine gender, she would be immune. The stark reality was that she was not.

It was the only downside to their little arrangement. She'd known he was handsome, she'd seen him at charity balls, around her father's office and in grainy magazine pictures, but she hadn't been prepared for how amazingly attractive he was up close. His face was square and undeniably masculine, yet his eyes, for lack of a better word, were beautiful. They were rich chocolate-brown with golden green flecks, framed by a fringe of long dark lashes. It was enough to make her mouth water. His body was another problem altogether.

She slowed her pace a little and allowed herself to take in the view. A frisson of something new and scary shivered through her. He had a broad, well-muscled chest that tapered down to a lean waist and narrow hips that led to— heaven help her, but she *had* noticed—the most heart-stoppingly sexy backside she'd ever seen. And she'd made those observations when he was fully dressed. If she lived with him, the odds of catching him without a shirt or— the image made her knees quake—in a towel were overwhelming.

He turned and quirked a black eyebrow at her, the glint in his eye letting her know that he was well aware that she'd been taking advantage of her position by checking out his assets.

She quickened her pace so that she was beside him again, the distracting view, as well as her erotic thoughts, placed out of sight. "Well, aren't you the master of the public image? A fiancée and a large charitable donation all in one day!" she returned tartly, banishing the images that were parading through her mind's eye.

"That's half of doing business, Elaine. You should know all about that."

Angry color rose in her cheeks. Leave it to this arrogant, infuriating man to remind her of her own personal black moment. "I do. I'm just not accustomed to seeing a public image that's so well crafted and so far removed from the true individual."

"Image is half, but business acumen and unflinching ruthlessness make up the rest."

She felt as if his dark eyes were looking into her, as though he could see through her polished, smooth façade, to the insecure girl inside her. She didn't like it.

"You have the ruthlessness, and a mercenary streak a mile wide. Selling yourself to me proves that."

Heat spiked through her. "I did not sell myself to you. Don't make me sound like a harem girl. I made a business deal with you. Yes, I used unconventional means, but there was no other way. Believe me, if there had been I would not be standing here with you."

"You misunderstand, *cara mia*. I admire your ability to shut off all of your finer feminine emotions in favor of marrying for mutual gain." He jerked open the passenger door of his car, which was parked closely to the curb. "So long as you remember that all you'll be getting out of this is your father's company."

He dipped his head close to her, his dark eyes blazing. She smelled the clean, musky scent of his aftershave and it made her stomach feel as if it had inverted.

She swallowed. "As I've already assured you, I have no interest in a husband. Nor do I have any interest in your vast fortune. I want what belongs to me. As my father's only child, I don't think it's outrageous for me to expect to inherit the company. I know I can do it, and if he would give me a chance he would know it too."

"Is that what all this is about? Proving yourself to your father?"

She ground her teeth together. "No. I want to take

control of my life and make something of myself. Surely you can understand that."

She sank into the car and he slammed the door behind her. He got in and turned the key aggressively, the engine of the car purring like a big exotic cat. "I'm a self-made man. Whatever I have I've worked for." He shifted into second gear as he eased into traffic and the engine growled as if emphasizing his point. "Including my reputation. A solid reputation is difficult to build, and one indiscretion can undo decades of work. That's why image is so important. I'm sorry if you find it duplicitous." His tone made it perfectly clear that he wasn't sorry in the least.

"It's why you need a wife," she said, trying not to sound smug.

He laughed—a low, dark sound. "I don't *need* you, *cara*, but I will certainly find use for you." He flicked an unconcerned glance at his wristwatch—a watch that undoubtedly cost more than her annual salary. "I have an appointment this evening that I cannot break." He turned to look at her, his dark eyes heating her, filling her with a longing that was nearly unbearable. "But you and I have a date tomorrow night."

CHAPTER THREE

THE phone had been ringing all day. How reporters had gotten hold of the extension to access his office line, he didn't know. Once the phone stopped ringing he would have to interrogate his staff.

Granted, he wanted press. That was the point of the arrangement. But he certainly didn't want the paps to have *personal* access to him. It was his PA's job to field phone calls, and he paid her handsomely for it.

The trip to Tiffany's had done its job, just as he'd planned. The picture of Elaine and himself entering Tiffany's together, and exiting holding the telltale robin's-egg-blue bags, had spawned a host of articles in every news source from the *New York Times* to *TMZ*—the latter speculating that it was a Mafia arrangement. His Italian heritage was all he could credit for the creation of that rumor. But then, when did a tabloid need anything silly like facts to come up with a story?

That, combined with strategically leaked information about his reservations at La Paz, a trendy restaurant in Manhattan, had the press engaged in a feeding frenzy to extract more information about Marco De Luca and his mystery woman.

He answered the phone midway through the first ring. "I'll tell you the same thing I've told everyone else. Ms. Chapman and I will comment when there is something to comment about." Denial, in his experience, was the best way to fuel a rumor. The more he downplayed it, the more interest would be piqued.

"That's a shame. I thought you'd be a little more straightforward with your own brother."

"Rafael." He was pleasantly surprised to hear his younger brother's voice. Despite living less than half an hour from each other, with Marco being a workaholic and Rafael being a family man, it was hard for their schedules to coincide. "I take it you picked up the paper this morning?"

"Actually, Sarah showed me. She loves all forms of gossip media. Though I doubt you're getting married to this woman to save her father from a mob hit."

Marco laughed. "Not even close. The Mafia has recently quit asking my opinion on whose knees they should break."

"Why *are* you getting married, then?"

Marco picked up a pen and started doodling on his day planner. "Oh, the usual reasons."

"Love?" Rafael asked, in what Marco thought was a hopeful tone. His brother had drunk the love Kool-aid a couple of years ago, and seemed to think that he should want to do the same.

"No. Financial gain." He explained how the arrangement had come about.

"Well, that sounds typically you," Rafael grumbled.

"That's because it *is* typically me, little brother. We can't all be happy running a dinky little real estate office. Some of us have ambition."

"My 'dinky little office' is a multi-million-dollar operation. And anyway, I have a wife I like to go home to every night."

Marco cut him off. "Well, that's fine for you. But I've raised one kid already, and I'm not planning on willingly doing anything like it again. Commitment of any kind is not on the agenda. This is for business."

Rafael cleared his throat. "I know that taking care of me wasn't easy. But I'm grateful for it."

"I don't need your gratitude, Rafael. You're my brother and I did it gladly. But this marriage, if you want to call it that, is strictly a business arrangement. The length of the marriage isn't indefinite. The longest it will last is a year. If neither of us has achieved our goal by then, we'll go our separate ways—no harm, no foul."

"And the woman? She knows that you're not madly in love with her?"

Marco huffed out a laugh. "I'm a ruthless bastard, Rafael, but not even I'm that bad."

Rafael sighed. "You're going to go ahead with this no matter what I say, aren't you?"

"Always. But you will agree to be my best man? It's the only chance you'll have."

"Of course I will. No one else would do it."

Marco barked out a laugh. "That's probably true. Now, let me get back to work, little brother. Some of us work for a living."

Marco turned back to his computer and tried to get on with his work day. The phone rang again.

The phone in Elaine's workspace rang for what seemed like the twentieth time since she'd come back from lunch.

She looked at it dubiously. It was either a reporter or,

worse, her father again. He'd called her at work early this morning, beside himself with glee that Elaine had managed to snare herself such a rich husband, and even happier that Elaine was finally settling down. Probably because her marriage, especially such a suitable one, would go a long way in blotting out that "unfortunate incident" from a few years back.

Thankfully he didn't seem suspicious about her marrying the man who'd just bought his company. He was too busy congratulating himself for raising a daughter who had finally wised up to the fact that a woman's place was in the home, not behind an executive's desk. And probably too confident in his skills as a businessman to even begin to think that his *daughter* could have seen a loophole that he hadn't.

She had ended the conversation with her father feeling renewed determination. That was exactly the reminder she'd needed for why this was necessary.

She picked up the phone. "Hello?" she said curtly.

It was another reporter, rattling off questions at light-ning speed that were both personal and degrading. She hung up on the man mid-sentence, and rested her forehead on the cool veneer surface of her desk.

Her head popped up when she heard a knock on her office door—or, to be more accurate, her cubicle wall.

Marco's handsome face appeared around the corner, followed by the rest of him. Her mouth went dry at the sight of him. Her memories of how gorgeous he was didn't do him justice. And it had barely been twenty-four hours since she'd last seen him.

"Have the press been hounding you?"

She blew out a breath. "Yes. My phone has been ringing all day."

"The cost of doing business."

"So it seems." She sighed. "You know, I'm not putting myself through this just because I feel some sort of sense of entitlement—like I deserve it because I'm my father's daughter." It seemed important somehow that she tell him the details to make sure he understood what she'd accomplished and why she felt the way she did. She shouldn't care what he thought, but even as she reminded herself of that, she did care. "Four years ago Chapman's nearly declared bankruptcy. I identified a flaw in the system and helped my father rework the way products were shipped. It shaved four points off the cost and brought the company back into the black. I proved myself. I saved the company. My *family's* company. And still he'd rather let your corporation absorb what he built up from nothing than give it to me. All because I'm a woman. Do you see why I feel the way I do?"

"If everything goes according to plan, you should be getting exactly what you're entitled to." Truth be told, Marco wasn't the most modern guy. He was of the opinion that in general women should stay home and take care of their kids. But he could understand why she wanted to claim what was rightfully hers. It was a feeling he understood very well.

"Well, Miss Chapman." He took her hand and pulled her from her sitting position. "I believe you and I have a date."

"I'll just pop in and change. You can wait in the living room." Almost as soon as Elaine closed the front door to her apartment someone knocked on it. She opened it to a woman with spiky pink hair and a man whose eyebrows were more immaculately groomed than her own. "Can I help you?"

"I'm not sure how to say this tactfully, so I won't bother.

You need some help if you're going to look believable as my fiancée," Marco said from behind her.

Elaine stared blankly at him, the realization of what his statement meant slowly dawning. "You're giving me a makeover?"

"I'm not; they are." He gestured to the two people still standing at the threshold.

Her ears were burning. *A makeover!* "I'm not your dress-up doll, De Luca. You can't just mandate things like this!"

He sighed in exasperation. Why was *he* exasperated? She was pretty sure she ought to have the market on exasperation cornered at that moment.

"Why bother to fight me on this? You need it—trust me—and I'm going to get my way, so you might as well sit your cute little butt down."

She gave an indignant squeak and stood facing him with her mouth open.

"What? No snappy comeback?" he mocked. "I think I should notify the press."

She could not remember ever being so angry before. He was taking control from her bit by bit, and there was nothing that threw her off more than losing control.

She gave him a look that would have cowed most men. Leave it to her to get engaged to the one man who didn't seem to find her the least bit intimidating. "The measure of a woman is not her looks."

"Very nice sentiment. It's also patently untrue."

"It is not!" Great. Now he had reduced her to petty playground tactics.

"It most certainly is. And the same is true for a man. If you dress the part you'll be more likely to get the part. If I showed up at a board meeting in swimming trunks I wouldn't be taken seriously, and your feeble, stereotyped sense of style is hardly going to earn you any respect."

Neither had dressing feminine, but she certainly wasn't going to get into *that* with him. "Be that as it may," she said crisply, "I'm not here to play trophy wife."

He continued to smile for the benefit of the stylists, who were busy pretending to ignore the fight. She wasn't fooled by the grin frozen on his face. It had hardened, and his jaw shifted, the muscles in his shoulders bunched tight. "You're here to be whatever I ask you to be. And if I ask you to be my trophy then that's what you'll be. We *do* both want this marriage, don't we…*cara mia*?" The threat was implicit.

Icy fingers wrapped around her heart. She couldn't lose this deal. She had worked too hard. And she certainly wasn't going to lose it over something as trivial as a hair-trim and a little lipgloss.

She sat in the chair that was moved for her, keeping her face carefully neutral.

The petite hairdresser talked animatedly while she worked, waving her scissors every now and then to empha-size her point. She put a row of foils on the top of Elaine's hair, turning it a lighter, less brassy shade, and cut six inches off the length, bringing it up so that it just skimmed her col-larbone, and added long layers to give it body and movement.

The man, Giorgio, was there for make-up and, Elaine wasn't terribly surprised to hear, eyebrow waxing. Her face was scrubbed and peeled and waxed and finally painted.

Giorgio stepped back and examined her like an artist looking at his masterpiece.

"I'm brilliant," he said as he handed her a mirror.

She barely recognized the woman looking back at her. She had fun, modern hair that looked full and healthy. Her face glowed, probably from the gold powder that Giorgio had brushed all over it, and her eyes looked larger and brighter with the expertly applied eyeshadow and her newly shaped brows. She hated so much to admit that it was an improvement. But it was.

Marco took her by the hand and pulled her up out of the chair, and dropped a light kiss on the tips of her fingers. Her legs wobbled.

"You look beautiful."

A new knock on her door broke the moment, and Elaine wrenched her hand from his. "I assume you know who that is too?"

He nodded, and walked to the door and opened it, taking a garment bag and tipping whoever it was that had made the delivery. "Your dress for dinner."

He placed the hanger in her hand, and she stared at it. He was changing everything about her, from her hair to her wardrobe, in order to make her look like his type. Either that or he was just trying to drive her insane.

She opened her mouth to offer up a sour comment, but the frosty look in his deep chocolate eyes stopped her cold. This was her end of the bargain—the part she had to keep in order to get what she wanted. She swallowed the comeback and went to her room, making her footsteps heavier than necessary, and unzipped the garment bag, revealing a filmy golden-brown dress with beaded spaghetti straps.

It fit her perfectly. *Too* perfectly. The gown clung to her curves like a second skin, showcasing her small waist and full bust, and revealing a little too much cleavage for her comfort.

Marco hadn't even asked her size. He'd guessed. If there was a more potent reminder of just how much of a womanizer he was, she couldn't think of it. And what was even worse was that she had a sneaking suspicion that the boiling feeling she got in her tummy when she thought about him with other women just might be jealousy. Which was a completely futile road to walk down. Men like Marco De Luca could have, and *did* have, any woman they wanted. And women like her were not exactly the women that men like him wanted.

She exited her bedroom, fighting the desperate urge to cover up her exposed figure. There had been a time when she might have liked the dress, might have felt beautiful. Not anymore. Now she just felt exposed. And the heated look Marco was giving her did not help. He evaluated her slowly, his chocolate eyes slowly caressing her curves. Heat flared in the depths of his eyes and it made her insides tighten. It felt as though someone had reached inside her and stolen the air from her lungs.

"Almost perfect," he said, reaching into his jacket pocket and pulling out a slender velvet case. "I went back to Tiffany's today." He opened the case and revealed the most beautiful necklace she'd ever seen.

The chain was made up of gossamer strands of white gold gathered together by delicate round-cut diamonds. The center pendant was a showcase of delicate craftsmanship, with intricate winding vines of platinum, and a large, perfectly cut emerald at the center.

He moved behind her and swept her hair to the side, his warm fingertips brushing her nape, sending a shimmer of sparks through her. "You're a beautiful woman, Elaine. Truly beautiful." She sucked in a breath when the cold jewelry touched her skin, the pendant settling between her breasts. "Your power is in your beauty. You should use it. Not hide it."

Heat curled through her. Pleasure, she realized. She liked having him say she was beautiful. She liked feeling beautiful. And she wasn't sure how she felt about discovering that weakness.

He put his hands on her bare shoulders and turned her to face him. "Now you look like my fiancée."

It was one of Manhattan's trendiest nightspots. A Latin-fusion restaurant decorated with old-world South American art, mingled with the clean, sleek lines of modern design. The hostess led them to his personal table, which was situated by the wall of slanted windows, overlooking the brightly lit city streets. But tonight he didn't fully appreciate his surroundings.

His thoughts were completely occupied with the woman walking next to him. He had thought the makeover would be helpful, but he'd had no idea that she would be transformed into a supermodel. No, not a supermodel. There was nothing angular or androgynous about her. She was all soft, curvy woman. Her looks weren't cookie cutter, or trendy. She was classic. Her perfect bone structure gave her the kind of beauty that not even age would diminish.

He'd thought she had a beautiful face when it wasn't enhanced with make-up, but with the subtle colors playing up her eyes and making them sparkle, making her lips look fuller and more inviting, she was stunning. One of the most beautiful women he'd ever seen.

Her hair, which he'd only ever seen in that schoolmarm bun or hanging wet down her back, was styled into soft blond waves that fell down past her shoulders and ended right above the swell of her lush breasts. And that necklace fitted right in the dip of her cleavage, touching her where he wanted to touch her.

This was the woman he had heard about. The one who could drive a man to do something stupid and reckless and condemn the consequences to hell.

And she didn't want to consummate their marriage.

He ran his hand down the length of her arm and moved it to the small of her back; he saw her pulse jump at the base of her neck. He fought the smug smile that tugged at the corners of his mouth. So she wasn't as unaffected by him as she wanted him to believe.

He pulled her chair out for her, and for once she simply accepted his offer.

She sat ramrod-straight, a strained look written across her delicate features. He reached across the table and took her hand, rubbing his thumb across the pulse of her wrist. "Do you ever relax?"

"No. Do you?" Her heart fluttered rapidly in her chest and a knot of excitement coiled in her stomach.

He leaned his head in so that his nose was nearly touching hers, and her fluttering heart stopped for a moment. "Only when I'm with a beautiful woman."

The intimacy of the moment was shattered by a flash-bulb that momentarily blinded her. She looked and saw a photographer sitting at the bar, trying to look nonchalant as he sat and drank his beer. "Is it always like this for you?"

He gave the photographer a sideways glance. "Not always, but being spotted together two days in a row is bound to have the paparazzi descending in droves. The prospect of me settling down has them chomping at the bit to get the scoop."

"I guess it's a good thing." Another flashbulb went off. Elaine's head whipped in the direction of the light. "We do want the word to get out."

She tried to feign indifference at the constant flashes punctuating their conversation, but it was almost impossible when she felt as if she was an actor in a play. Being on show was getting tedious, and it had only just begun.

By the time dessert arrived they had engaged only in small talk, and made no mention at all about the impending nuptials. It was starting to make her nervous. She knew he hadn't brought her here to discuss how well the Knicks were playing this season. Marco De Luca didn't do anything without a purpose. She didn't like feeling like this: unprepared, out of the loop. She had intended on retaining control of the deal, but he was wresting it away from her inch by inch.

Before she could take a bite of her tamarind white chocolate mousse, Marco stood and grasped her hand, then pulled her up so she was standing beside him. She had been afraid he was going to do something like this.

"Can I have everyone's attention?"

Elaine's heart rate kicked into overdrive. Oh, he was *not* doing what she thought he was doing.

"I have something I would like to ask this beautiful lady."

Yes, he was.

The press started snapping pictures like mad. It was the reminder she needed to try and look happy. She didn't need to try and look surprised.

"Elaine Chapman." He turned and looked her in the eyes, covering both of her hands with his. "Would you do me the honor of becoming my wife?"

He pulled out a small velvet box, and even though she knew exactly what was in it everything in her tightened up. She couldn't breathe properly. He opened the box and held the ring out to her. She stood frozen, unable to get a word out around the lump of emotion that was blocking her throat. She could only nod. He gave her a smile that stopped her heart; he looked like a man who had just proposed to the love of his life.

He slipped the brilliant ring onto her finger, and in that moment she could almost believe that he wanted her—almost believe that all of this was real. She felt tears sting the backs of her eyes, because she knew this moment would never be real. Not for her.

The people in the restaurant started to clap. Her knees started to buckle. Marco put his arms around her and pulled her up against him, bringing her flush against his hard body, and then he lowered his head and covered her mouth with his.

She stood completely still for a moment, so shocked she couldn't respond. Then he changed the angle of his head and teased her lips open with his tongue. She whimpered and wrapped her arms around his neck. His lips were soft and firm and she didn't care that the moment was being caught on film by a hundred cameras. She didn't care that they were in the middle of the restaurant. The only thing that mattered was this.

It had been so long since she'd been kissed. Years. But she couldn't think clearly enough to figure out how many. And she'd never been kissed like this.

He ran his fingertips down the length of her spine and she tangled her fingers in his thick black hair. She felt as if she was going to melt into a puddle at his feet. His tongue swept across her bottom lip and she abandoned all her reason to revel in the moment.

She thrust her tongue into his mouth and felt his body jolt. He anchored his hands on her hips. Her breasts felt heavy and an unfamiliar ache started to throb between her thighs.

Then he released her, and she wanted to grab his head

and pull him back to her regardless of the fact that they had an audience.

He smiled at her and leaned in to whisper in her ear, "I think that looked pretty convincing, don't you?"

The high she'd felt when his lips had touched hers crashed. It was all for show.

And as the flashes continued to go off, and people continued to clap, she stood with a smile fixed on her face and all she wanted to do was go home, crawl into her bed, and cry.

CHAPTER FOUR

"I CAME over so we could discuss the terms and conditions." Marco swept past Elaine and entered her tiny apartment without waiting for an invite.

"I told you I would have my lawyer contact you." She didn't want Marco and his disturbing presence in her apartment. It was her sanctuary, her refuge from the frenetic pace of her life. Bringing him into it seemed wrong somehow. She hadn't seen him since their faux engagement had gone into effect. Hadn't seen him since that kiss.

"I assume you've had contracts drawn up?" he asked.

She glanced at her briefcase. "Yes." She'd had them drafted as soon as she'd found the loophole in her father's contracts.

He smiled sardonically. "It's necessary that we discuss precisely what each of us expects from this union before anyone signs anything."

"All right," she said slowly. She studied the layout of her shoebox apartment. Papers covered most surfaces. It was a very orderly mess; everything was stacked neatly and organized. The kitchen and living area served as her office, and since visitors were rare she usually left everything out rather than sticking it back into neat little folders.

"We can work at the coffee table." She gestured to the low table in the middle of the living room.

She bent and picked up a stack of documents and moved them to the large metal filing cabinet in the corner. When she turned, Marco was leafing through one of the binders she'd left on the table.

He looked up at her, his dark eyes keen. "Your business plan?" She nodded and watched, feeling tense for some reason, as he skimmed the pages. "You have some very good ideas," he said finally, setting the black book back in its spot.

A flush of pleasure crept through her traitorous body. "Yes. I think I can double the profits inside of two years just by implementing basic technologies. There haven't been a lot of advances at Chapman's in the past few years. My father isn't the most modern of men."

Marco gave her a wry smile. "So I gathered."

She rushed on as if he hadn't said anything, the fire and excitement burning in her now. "I want to set up a website with online ordering. I also think the way the warehouses and call centers are run could be streamlined for greater efficiency and lower operating costs."

Her heart was beating a little faster, as it always did when she talked about the company. The man sitting on her couch had nothing to do with it.

"Very good." To his credit he didn't sound surprised, but still it made her feel defensive.

"Thank you. I'm actually pretty smart, you know." She couldn't resist adding, "I graduated from high school two years early, and I was at the top of my class at Harvard."

"And look at all you have to show for it."

She narrowed her eyes. "Is that an insult?"

"Only if you're unhappy with what you have to show

for it." And, judging by his critical expression, he thought she should be.

"Hey! He tells jokes," she said balefully.

"I'd do a song and dance but…I know where my talents are best served."

"And, as you know, sticking to what you're good at is the key to success."

He nodded, his hard features serious. "That and perseverance."

She would be shocked if Marco De Luca had ever had to practice much perseverance. He seemed like the kind of man who'd had everything handed to him in life—mostly because she couldn't imagine that very many people were brave enough to deny him anything. And even if they were brave enough, he was a very charismatic man. He drew people to him. She was sure he was very good at getting what he wanted, using honey *or* vinegar.

"So, what is it that you hope to get from our arrangement?" Marco asked.

"I want exactly what I said upfront. I want my father's company. Nothing more or less."

"You're an ambitious woman, Elaine. I find it hard to believe that you would be content with just your father's company when you could try and obtain so much more."

"Why? You think because I'm a woman that my highest end goal is to just marry some rich guy and spend my days lunching and shopping? I respect myself far too much to have my happiness be determined by a husband or anyone else."

Her own mother had been pathetic that way. Chasing after men in an attempt to gain the attention of an indifferent husband, searching for some sort of acceptance and validation at the hands of others. Elaine was making her own way, her own success. She certainly wasn't going to become the kind of simpering female her mother had been.

She'd worked so hard to distance herself from that sort of behavior. Ironic that one small rumor about her and her direct supervisor at Stanley Winthrop had undone every ounce of her work. Marco had been right about reputations: they were difficult to build up but so very easy to tear down.

A snide comment made from a co-worker she'd dated briefly, who'd taken offense at the fact that she hadn't jumped at the chance to sleep with him, had spread amongst other jealous interns until it had somehow blossomed into its own entity. She'd been sick when it had finally reached her. The story was that she'd been having illicit sex with her very nice, very married boss. And the man who had relayed it to her had gleefully given her all the graphic details that he'd heard.

It had been indescribably painful, knowing that someone she'd cared about, someone she'd kissed, had said such awful things about her, had set out to ruin her because she wouldn't hop into bed with him. She'd avoided men since then. No dates. And she honestly hadn't had many before that. Which was why, at the ripe old age of twenty-four, she was still a virgin. Which was fine with her. Hormonal awakenings had kind of passed her over. Until recently.

Marco settled on the couch, his dark eyes trained on her. "Just as well that you feel that way, as I have no intention of being tied down by a wife. Not permanently, at least."

"At least we agree on that point." She had a feeling it might be their last agreement of the evening.

"And we need to agree on another one. You cannot get pregnant. If you do, you forfeit the company, and you can forget any sort of financial allowance from me. I don't want a wife, and I definitely don't want diaper duty."

She blinked, shocked by the words that had just come out of his mouth. "I thought we'd already established that I wasn't going anywhere near your bedroom during the course of this…this marriage. And, seeing as you and I both know it isn't the stork that brings babies, I think fatherhood is the last thing you have to worry about." She wrinkled her nose. "Well, the last thing you have to worry about with me. I can't comment on behalf of your other lady-friends."

"I always practice safe sex."

It was the absolute truth. Marco had no intention of becoming some woman's meal ticket for eighteen years, and he was totally scrupulous in his sexual practices for both the sake of his health and his checkbook. But that didn't mean that some of his mistresses hadn't tried to find a way around the precautions. He'd caught one woman with an open box of condoms and a needle, and he'd watched as she'd put a tiny puncture in each plastic packet before putting them neatly back into the box.

Then there had been the woman who'd tried to pass another man's baby off as his. Never mind that she'd been eight weeks along and he'd only known her for two.

He was well familiar with the female mind and how it worked. Financial security and wealth was the highest goal for the vast majority of the fairer sex. His own mother had prized it above everything, even her two children.

"Well, you won't be practicing any sort of sex with me," she said, twin spots of color high on her cheekbones.

Her prim exterior amused him—especially knowing what he did about her. She made for a very intriguing challenge.

"What exactly are your other *terms and conditions*?" she said tartly, as if reading the tenor of his thoughts.

"Simple. I'm only agreeing to this for the benefit of my company. I need to be sure that I'll be gaining much more than I would lose by forfeiting Chapman Electronics. That means I need you on call twenty-four hours a day, seven days a week."

Elaine didn't like the sound of that, although the odd fluttering in her stomach seemed to indicate otherwise. "What am I on call for?"

"Business functions, personal dinners. Whatever I might need my *wife* for."

"What about my job…my *life*?"

"I thought the company was the most important thing in your life."

Desire burned in her chest. Desire to prove herself to her father, to everyone. "It is."

"Then that means for the next twelve months I'm your number one priority. I'm in negotiations right now with James Preston. He's selling one of his resort properties in Hawaii, but he doesn't want to turn it over to someone who might turn his nice family vacation spot into some debauched spring break hangout."

"Which is why you *need* a wife," she said, feeling triumphant.

The corners of his sexy mouth twitched with humor. "It's why a wife will be useful to me, yes."

"So I'm supposed to be evidence of your transformation from playboy to doting husband?"

"Something like that."

Oddly, she felt a little indignant for Marco. His personal life had nothing to do with what a good businessman he was. Apparently not even men were exempt from the archaic viewpoints of others. Not that she condoned the way Marco treated women, but it was still separate from how he ran his business.

"So it seems like we need each other," she said.

"It isn't a necessity for me. I want the resort just as I want to experience a profit increase, but you're the only one who really *needs* this arrangement. Don't forget that."

"You mean I should remember that when you pull me out of work in the middle of the day and drag me off to some art gala at which you expect me to play trophy wife?"

A slow grin spread across his face. Her heart beat a little bit faster. "Something like that."

"What is *this*?" Elaine slapped the thick stack of documents onto Marco's pristine walnut desk.

He didn't look up from his computer screen. "The prenuptial agreement that my lawyer drafted. Or was that not made clear by the heading?"

"Oh, that was made perfectly clear. It's *this*." She picked the papers back up and rifled through them before setting them down again. "*This* is what I'm talking about!"

He flicked the offending lines a glance. "The infidelity clause?"

"Is that its official title?" She'd never been so angry in her entire life—and that included the day she'd confronted Daniel the Rat about the salacious rumors he'd spread about her. "If I have an affair I lose the company, yet there are absolutely no limitations imposed on *you*! It's a blatant, unrepentant double standard!"

His dark eyes collided with hers; the heat of his gaze warmed her whole body. Rage was coursing through her veins, nearly blinding her with a red mist, and still he was making her body tingle with anticipation for something she didn't even have a name for.

"If that's how you see it." He shrugged in a classically

Latin manner. "I see it as protecting my…" he looked her over her in a way that made her squirm "…assets."

She crossed her arms over her chest, trying to disguise her stinging nipples. "I'm not your asset! We are supposed to be a team!"

He stood and rounded the desk, the sheer height and breadth of him as awe inspiring as it was intimidating. "No, Ms. Chapman, we are not a team. Do I need to remind you, yet again, that I'm the dominant party here? That means that you will do as I say." He picked the prenuptial agreement up from his desk. "You will remain out of other men's beds for the duration of our marriage. If you need sex, you get it from me. If there's even a hint or rumor of impropriety on your part the company stays with the De Luca Corporation."

She tried to fight the hot tide of embarrassment that washed through her. What was it about this man that rattled her so? "And what about you? You're still free to do whatever you want?"

He nodded, his jaw fixed. "With whoever I want, as I recall."

"That is the most disgusting double standard I have ever heard! You didn't mention *this* a few days ago when we were discussing 'terms and conditions'."

"I'm simply covering every possible eventuality. I can't afford to have my wife seen with other men. In a real marriage it would never happen. No woman runs around on me. And I don't share."

"Then neither do I. Enjoy the next twelve months of celibacy."

"And you think you can resist me?"

She laughed. "No question."

He hauled her to him, pressing her breasts against the

muscled wall of his chest. "I don't believe that." His lips crashed down on hers, his tongue pushing past her lips and tangling with hers.

She couldn't resist. She didn't want to. She just wanted this moment, this heady, sensual moment, so far removed from her normal life.

He lowered his hands to her bottom and pulled her tightly against his body, pressing his erection against her belly. She gasped and moved against him, enjoying the electrifying sensations pulsing through her, exulting in the fact that he was as turned on as she was. That she had been the one to turn him on.

Her breasts ached for his touch, their shameless peaks announcing to him just how aroused she was. A pulse throbbed hard between her thighs. She wanted him. She wanted him to show her everything she'd never even cared to learn about. Everything she'd always steadfastly ignored about herself and about men.

She moved her hands over the muscles on his back, then around to his chest. He was so firm. So hot. So perfect. Just what a man should feel like. She wanted to feel his body without layers of clothing between them. She wanted….

She pulled away from him and jumped back as if she'd been burned. "I'm sorry," she said.

Her lips felt tight and swollen, her breathing was ragged, and she knew some of her hair had escaped the confines of her bun.

"There isn't anything to be sorry about. We're going to be married in two weeks' time. We might as well sleep together. It would add to the *convenience*."

It was the last part that kept her from saying yes. Without that scathing reminder that it would mean nothing to him she might have agreed. But there was no way she could view sex as casually as he did. She didn't have the experience or the sophistication to treat it as a recreational activity. Combined with the fact that she simply didn't have the time to devote to discovering her sexuality.

"I can't do that. I don't…I don't see sex as a *convenience*." She took a breath, trying to conjure up that steely businesswoman she knew lived inside her somewhere. "What I mean is, I don't sleep around."

Marco stared at her flushed face, her red lips, her eyes still dark from passion. She wanted him, even if she couldn't admit it yet. Or perhaps she was holding out until she felt it was most advantageous for her to give in. "That's fine. But the clause stays in. If you want sex, you get it from your husband."

She swallowed hard, trying to keep her face neutral. "I don't think I'll be wanting any in the near future."

He shrugged. "It's up to you. I don't have to coerce women into my bed."

That was the absolute truth. He couldn't remember the last time a woman had turned him down—if there had ever been a time. He didn't like it now. He liked it even less that his body seemed to have some sort of fixation on a woman who wasn't fixated on him. It must be the novelty of it. It was unusual for him to have to pursue a woman. They came to him—frequently and easily. If he didn't end up in bed with Elaine it would be easy enough to find someone else, seeing as there was nothing forbidding *him* from doing exactly that.

But the idea of Elaine being with another man while she was wearing his ring had made him see red. He had told the truth when he'd said he didn't share. And in his mind marriage, even one of convenience, made her his. Old-fashioned and unenlightened, yes, but there wasn't anything he could do about it.

"You have an appointment with a bridal gown designer tomorrow at nine."

"I have work," she said sharply.

"I don't care. The wedding takes priority right now."

She put her hands on her hips. "Is this how it's going to be, then? For the next twelve months you're going to treat me like your personal doll?"

Marco shrugged. He seemed entirely unaffected by the kiss, and with her heartbeat still going erratically it irritated her.

"If that's the way you want to look at it. Or you could simply view this as your newest job opportunity."

"You know, you have a real talent for making me sound like a call girl."

"And you have a real talent for wasting my time. If you want to see me, next time make an appointment."

She drew up to her full height, but was careful not to get too close to him again. Desire and anger were still struggling for pride of place inside her. "I am your fiancée."

"No. This is a business deal, as you're so fond of pointing out, which makes you one of my business partners. Which means you make an appointment like they all do."

She leaned all her weight onto one leg, pushed out her hip and settled her hand on it, in her best indignant pose. "And do you kiss all of your business partners the same way you did me?"

"If any of them looked like you, I might. As it is, I've never been tempted to try."

It was difficult to decide whether to embrace anger at

his sheer male arrogance, or enjoy the sneaky glow of feminine pleasure she got from his underhanded compliment. In the end, it was the anger that won out. "I see. So you decided that because I'm a woman you can just kiss me whenever you like?"

He moved toward her, his dark eyes blazing with fury and something more compelling. "No. I kissed you because I wanted to. And *you* wanted me to."

"Your ego is impressive." She took a step back. "I didn't want you to kiss me. As you mentioned, this is a business deal, and I never mix business with my personal life." At least she was certain she wouldn't if she *had* a personal life.

The mockery in his smile told her he didn't believe her for a moment. "I know that this is all an affront to your feminist sensibilities, but for the purposes of this deal I'm your boss. You will do as I say. You will sign the prenup, and you will meet with the wedding coordinator tomorrow morning to choose your wedding dress."

Everything in her raged out of control. Her hormones were still on red alert from the kiss, and her temper had just about reached its breaking point. She sucked in a calming breath. This was where years of training kicked in. Where she played the game. This was business. You fought the battles you could win, not the ones you were destined to lose.

"And will *you* be attending this bridal gown extravaganza?"

"Absolutely not. It's bad luck for the groom to see the gown before the wedding."

"I would imagine that it's bad luck for the marriage to have a predetermined end date," she returned crisply.

He acknowledged her comment with a slight smile, then turned, walked back to his desk and settled behind it. Apparently she was dismissed.

She turned to go.

"Elaine?"

She stopped at the sound of that sweet, honey-coated voice saying her name, sending waves of sensation through her body. Well, wasn't *she* one to dramatize?

"I hope you don't have plans tonight."

She turned and arched her eyebrow. "Would it matter if I did?"

"Certainly. I would feel bad for asking you to break them."

"You most *certainly* would not."

The left corner of his mouth lifted into a half-smile. "You're right. I wouldn't at all. I have a dinner party that I'm expected to attend tonight and I need a date."

"Did you misplace your little black book?"

He gave her a pained look. "I don't have a black book." He picked up his gleaming cellphone and waved it. "That would be old-fashioned."

She felt her lips thinning into an unattractive line. "You're straight out of the Dark Ages. A BlackBerry isn't going to fix that."

"Nice to know you hold me in such high regard, *cara*. Did you drive here?"

She eyed him warily. "No. I took a cab."

"Perfect. You can ride with me."

"And if I have plans?"

"Cancel them. As per our agreement," he said.

"As per your *demands*."

"If you like." He seemed completely unconcerned by her anger, which only fanned the flame. "But I can hardly show up at this dinner without my new, highly publicized fiancée."

"Just tell them your fiancée has a life, and doesn't just hang on your arm professionally twenty-four hours a day."

"Oh, they know you don't do that. I'm sure they think you spend at least twelve hours wrapped around me in bed."

She flushed, her vocal cords failing her. The images that were pinging through her brain were graphic, and much more intriguing than she'd like to admit.

She had done so well, burying any interest in the opposite sex beneath piles of ambition. Then she'd walked into Marco De Luca's office and her long-ignored hormones had sprung to life and hadn't left her alone since.

"In any case, I need you to play your part. This is business, remember?" He said the last part with a mocking edge to his voice.

"I won't forget."

The dinner party was hardly the intimate affair she'd imagined. There were at least two hundred of Manhattan's most elite social movers in attendance, and it made it hard for her not to be grateful for the dress Marco's efficient PA had provided for her at the last minute.

It was too short and too tight for her taste, but judging by the similarly bedecked Barbie dolls that were hanging on their date's arms the look was par for the course.

Marco gave the stunning, reed-slim hostess a kiss on both cheeks before putting his hand on Elaine's back and introducing her. "This is my fiancée, Elaine Chapman. Elaine, this is Caroline Vance. She's the chairperson of the De Luca House charity."

"Nice to meet you." She shook the other woman's perfectly manicured hand, and held back the questions that were forming in her mind. Marco had never mentioned that he had a charity, but his fiancée would certainly know all about it. Well, a real fiancée would at any rate. She was clueless.

"Nice to meet you too." Caroline smiled warmly. "I didn't think I'd live to see the day when Marco would settle down. He's always preferred life in the fast lane." She shot Marco a teasing look. "I guess you're merging into the carpool lane, huh?"

The smile on Marco's face looked forced to Elaine, but Caroline didn't seem to notice. "Yes. It was time. When I met Elaine I knew I couldn't let her get away."

"Welcome to the club. You'll enjoy it." She gave Marco's arm a squeeze.

Marco paused and pulled his checkbook from his pocket, and filled in an amount that made Elaine's eyes widen.

Caroline took the check from Marco's hand, a broad smile on her pretty face. "He's generous to a fault," she said, her comment directed at Elaine.

Elaine smiled back, hoping she didn't look as confused as she felt. "Yes, he is."

Marco chuckled darkly as Caroline fluttered off to greet the next couple that was entering the ballroom. He took her arm and led her to a cluster of tables that were designed with intimacy in mind. They were small—so small that when she took her seat and Marco took his their knees brushed beneath the table. Her heart sputtered.

"All of the food, and all the prep work that went into the food was donated," he explained. "The guests paid two hundred dollars for each plate. All of the proceeds will go to the De Luca House."

She smiled. "That's great. What is the charity for?"

A shadow passed over his face for a brief moment. "Homeless children. It's an issue that's close to my heart."

She realized at that moment just how little she knew about the man sitting across from her. His background wasn't exactly a mystery, but there hadn't been a lot of information on his childhood either. She'd found out through her careful research that his father had been a wealthy Sicilian businessman who had moved his family to New York when Marco had been a young teenager. But between that event and his meteoric rise to success in the real estate industry and beyond she hadn't been able to find any details about his life. She'd just assumed he'd been growing up. Now she wondered. Marco claimed he was a self-made man, which meant that he'd built his empire up without the aid of his father's riches.

She looked at him. He was engaged in a conversation with the couple next to them, his speech pattern eloquent, his manner perfect. His profile was aristocratic, and he wore tuxedos as though the whole concept of formalwear had been built around his physique. He didn't look like a man who had ever struggled for anything.

At that moment, though, no amount of research into his background could have prepared her for the very disturbing effect Marco was having on her. She could hardly taste the gourmet dinner that had been prepared for the evening. Every few minutes her knees would brush Marco's beneath the table, or someone would come to speak to Marco and congratulate them on their engagement, and Marco would take her hand and look lovingly into her eyes. Or, worse still, he would draw her hand to his lips and press a tender kiss to her knuckles and send the butterflies that had taken up residence in her stomach into tailspins.

When the plates were cleared, after-dinner drinks were served—which Elaine declined. Her defenses were weakened already. No sense at all throwing alcohol on the burning fire of her attraction to Marco. So instead she sat still in her chair, ramrod-straight, trying her best to smile at everyone who cast a glance in her direction, and trying not to jump a foot in the air every time Marco's leg made contact with hers.

Tinkling crystal distracted her, and Elaine looked across the room at Caroline, who was standing on a riser at the far end of the room.

Caroline cleared her throat and the hum of conversation diminished. "I'd like to thank everyone for coming this evening. Your support means a tremendous amount. And I'd like to introduce the founder of De Luca House—Mr. Marco De Luca."

Marco gave her a wry smile, stood from his seat and bent down to drop a lingering kiss on her cheek before he crossed the long expanse of the room. She couldn't help but notice the sheer masculine grace his movements possessed. He stepped on the stage, his magnetic presence drawing the attention of everyone in the room and holding them, spellbound, in the palm of his hand. Her included.

"Thank you all for being here." His rich velvet voice rolled over the room. Her stomach tightened. "In these economic times I know making large contributions might seem like a lot to ask. But I ask you to remember that these children have likely never had the most basic necessities, even in the best of times. They don't have food, or clothing, or even shelter. They give no thought to four-star restaurants when they would give anything for a loaf of bread. What does fashion mean to them when they don't have a coat to protect them from the elements?"

Elaine felt her throat constricting as she looked into his earnest dark eyes. Something near her heart shifted, and she wished more than anything that she could make it shift back. Because lust was bad enough, new enough, scary enough, without there being emotion involved.

Marco continued, his slight accent making his speech

all the more compelling. "And how can we be concerned about keeping our summer homes when they do not even have the bare minimum of shelter?"

His speech went on, his words impassioned. He cited heart-wrenching statistics about how many of New York's homeless were children who had fallen through the cracks in the system. The charity worked to provide those children with homes that would give them a sense of family, an education, and even occupational training. The vision was to provide them with a base they could always come back to, even after they reached legal age.

When Marco had finished, many of the guests were blinking back tears, and she had a feeling the emotions Marco had brought out in them would be reflected in their donations.

Marco made his way back to where she was standing, pausing at intervals to shake hands and direct people to the donation area.

When he came back to her side he wound his arm around her waist and her heart did a freefall into her stomach.

"That was…" she struggled to sound unaffected "…a very nice speech. I had no idea there was so much need."

His dark eyes were clouded. "Many people assume that the government is taking care of all of the displaced children, but that is not the case."

It hadn't been the case for him. He and Rafael had been abandoned—first by their father, then by their mother. And no one had stepped in. No one had known about the two young teenagers who had been left to fend for themselves.

"Many people are unaware of what goes on in their own backyard. I consider it my duty to educate them and to do what I can."

She chewed her lush bottom lip, and he had the strongest urge to use his tongue to soothe away the marks her teeth had left in the tender pink flesh. "So not all of the nice things you do are for public image?"

He chuckled darkly. "Not all. But most."

A pianist began to play a slow, jazzy song, and couples started to migrate to the dance floor. Her body language was screaming that she didn't want him to ask her to dance.

"Elaine, I think I should have this dance with my fiancée."

He was amused when she pressed her lips into a thin line, her tension palpable. What would it take to kiss those lips into soft, willing supplication?

She was the epitome of hot, sexy woman in the skin-tight black dress that showcased curves so tempting they would make a priest sin, and still she maintained that untouchable aura of hers that she always threw up like a shield unless he kissed her.

She looked at the people around them, as if evaluating the situation to see if she could get away with a refusal. "All right." She said it as though he'd offered her a jail sentence.

It was a source of fascination to him that this woman, who was so obviously attracted to him, so responsive to his touch, his kiss, acted as though physical contact between them was anathema to her.

Elaine tried to quiet the pounding of her pulse. She looked at the couples on the dance floor, their bodies entwined as they moved in a rhythm that seemed far too…sexual to simply call it dancing.

Marco trained his bright white smile on her, but this smile was different than any other he'd given her before. It was almost predatory. He extended his hand. "Dance with me."

Not a question, a command. And for some reason a thrill ran through her rather than the anger that she'd expected, *needed*. Something about him was breaching her defenses, softening her. He was surprising her. He wasn't just a shallow playboy, and she had been much more comfortable with him when she'd been able to just write him off as such.

She accepted his offered hand, hoping he didn't notice that her own was damp with perspiration, and allowed him to lead her onto the dance floor. *Not smart*. Her practical inner voice was all but screaming at her.

Necessary, she countered, ignoring the churning pleasure in her stomach when he took her in his arms and brought her close to the heat of his body. Dancing with her fiancé was necessary. It wasn't about anything but keeping her end of the bargain.

The music was sultry, captivating, and she found herself swaying in time to the rhythm. One of his hands held onto hers, the other was low on her back, holding her to him, bringing her breasts into contact with his hard muscled chest. Her nipples tightened, ached. It was so unfamiliar, unexpected, and no matter how much she wanted to she couldn't hate it. She couldn't even muster up a faint dislike for it.

Her heart was pounding and she was certain he must be able to feel it. Certain he would be able to see the fluttering pulse that she could feel moving at the base of her throat.

Marrying a stranger didn't frighten her. Standing up in front of family and friends making vows she wasn't going to keep didn't bother her in the least. The thought of running a company wasn't scary at all. Not next to this— this attraction that she didn't want or understand. She always had control, and this sudden absence of it was terrifying. And oddly exhilarating.

She gripped his broad shoulders more fiercely in an instinctive effort to keep her knees from buckling beneath her. She regretted that instinct almost immediately.

He chuckled low, his hot breath fanning across her cheek, his grasp becoming stronger. Everything in her suddenly wanted to lean into him, kiss him again, to feel his mouth, hot, hard and insistent on hers.

She pulled away from him, her breathing labored, her body sluggish from unfamiliar desire. He looked amused. It was infuriating. Even worse that he knew exactly how he had affected her.

"Why do you pull away from it, Elaine?" he asked, his dark eyes compelling. Tempting.

"From what?" Playing ignorant was pointless, and she knew it, but pride and a desperate need to gain some sort of control pushed her to try anyway.

"From this." He hooked his arm around her waist and drew her to him, tilting his hips so that she could feel the length of his hardened arousal.

She drew in a shaky breath. "Because I don't feel the same way."

He chuckled. "This isn't about feelings. This is about lust. Want. Need. And you *do* feel it." He stroked a thumb across her hot cheek. "It's written all over your pretty face."

And just like that he was back in the slot she'd placed him in at their first meeting. It was a relief. But it didn't cause her own arousal to lessen. Her breasts felt heavy, sensitive, and she felt an embarrassing slickness well up between her thighs. She didn't have to be an expert on sex to know that her body was getting ready to experience it.

Too bad.

"I'm not interested in getting played, Marco. When I proposed to you it was so I could have the company, not a fling." It took every ounce of willpower she possessed to make her voice even and steady.

"Elaine Chapman?" Elaine turned to face the source of the voice, and her stomach sank to her toes when she recognized the man who had spoken her name.

"Yes?" She tried to appear poised, blank. She had perfected the act over the past few years. Better to be seen as an ice queen than to be seen as a slut.

A sick sensation weighted down her stomach. Daniel Parker. The man who had ruined her reputation because she hadn't slept with him. She knew he wasn't going to pass up the opportunity to fling a few insults at her now.

She straightened her posture and mentally braced herself. It simply wasn't in her to shy away from a challenge. She would not allow this man to intimidate and demean her. He'd gotten away with it once; she wasn't letting it happen again.

Marco cupped her elbow and stuck his hand out toward the other man. "Marco De Luca. I'm Elaine's fiancée."

"Really?" Daniel drew the word out, extending it several syllables. He shifted his focus to Elaine. "Your taste in men hasn't changed, then."

She bit her tongue. She didn't want to have this conversation, now or ever. Living through the humiliation and condemnation, and her subsequent barring from every decent firm in the city, had been bad enough. Rehashing it now just seemed stupid—especially when the man in front of her seemed to be out for blood. In a very sophisticated way, of course. There was no other way amongst the Manhattan elite.

To Marco's credit, he didn't comment. To Daniel's discredit, he pressed. "You always did prefer a more powerful man."

"I just prefer a man with as much ambition as I have," she answered waspishly, tightening her hold on Marco's arm. The fresh scent of his aftershave tickled her nose and, along with the surge of anger, quickened her pulse. "And they're difficult to find."

Daniel's smile turned cruel. "I would have thought it would be difficult to climb the corporate ladder lying flat on your back."

Her face heated unbearably, and she felt a surge of adrenaline infuse her veins with trembling energy. From the curious and condescending glares the other guests were giving her she knew no one in the immediate vicinity had missed Daniel's sleazy allegations.

"At least I don't feel as though I have to step on others on my way to the top," she said coldly.

"Of course not, Elaine," Daniel said, his eyes glinting. "You've just had to straddle others on your way to the top."

Adrenaline surged through her, and she clenched her fists to try and still her shaking hands. Daniel didn't wait for a response from her; he simply took the arm of his graceful, cold-looking date and walked away from them.

Marco put a hand on her elbow. "Do you want to leave?"

She looked around the room. People were still staring. She set her jaw. "No."

He regarded her closely. "You look like you might break at any moment. I think for the sake of your pride it would be best if we left."

She swallowed the lump that was rising in her throat and nodded her consent. She wasn't going to cry, she wasn't a crier by nature, but there was a very real danger that she might end up dumping a drink on Daniel's head.

Marco thanked Caroline for hosting the event and

slipped his arm around Elaine's waist, leading her down to the limousine that was idling at the curb. He opened the door for her and she slid inside. He got in and sat beside her, sitting closer to her than was strictly necessary.

"Are you all right?" Marco asked, studying her drawn face. The encounter with that man had disturbed her. She had kept her wits in place, not letting him cow her, but it had affected her.

She angled her face away from him, keeping her eyes trained on the brightly lit streets. "Of course. People like that are a part of life, aren't they? People who resent the success of others."

"Perhaps just their methods," he said coolly.

"Perhaps. But if I really was climbing the corporate ladder I doubt I would be stuck in a cubicle."

"I doubt you would be stuck in a cubicle if you hadn't been caught messing around with your married supervisor. Word spreads."

Her head whipped around. "And sometimes word is wrong. I can't beat the rumors, Marco. Believe me, I've tried. No one believes the truth, and the lie makes me a liability that nobody wants around the office. So I've found my way around it. Hard work isn't going to be enough—not with all of that—" she gestured toward the direction of the hotel "—hanging over my head. But I'm not the woman Daniel says I am, and I refuse to be punished for sins I didn't commit."

Marco shrugged. "Frankly, I don't care what happened. Whether or not you slept with your boss is wholly irrelevant to me. But I must warn you that while some men might be easily blinded by generous curves, I'm not. You can't use your body to get to my heart or my bank account."

She clenched her teeth. "My body isn't on offer."

"Really?"

She was angry, he could see that, and it was genuine. At being called out or at being falsely accused, he wasn't certain. He knew she was calculating—he had known it before she'd walked into his office. But it was no matter to him. He was hardly going to become a victim of her machinations like her foolish supervisor had supposedly been. He wasn't going to be swayed by her tempting mouth and her lush curves. He was far too jaded for that.

Of course she was welcome to try. It would make the next twelve months interesting.

"Really," she stated emphatically. "For what it's worth, I have too much pride to seduce my boss into promoting me."

He studied the haughty tilt of her chin. It was very possible that she did have too much pride to do anything like that—now. She had been very young after all.

"It's no matter to me one way or the other."

She scoffed. "Not worried that I'll take advantage of you?"

"Not in the least." He had infinite experience with conniving women. "Although you're welcome to try."

Angry color suffused her milk-pale skin. "I don't think that will happen. We have a deal. I already have what I want," she said stiffly.

He moved his hand to her soft cheek, letting his finger drift along her silken skin. He felt a sharp tug in his midsection and his shaft hardened. What was it about this woman that made her such a temptation? "But what if you could get more? Doesn't that appeal to you?"

She blew out a breath, its heat fanning across his hand. "No. I only want what I earn."

A slow smile spread across his face. "That could be taken many different ways, *cara mia*."

"You know what I mean," she said tightly.

The limo pulled up at the curb in front of her small, shabby apartment building. Neither of them moved.

She parted her lips and slicked her tongue across their surface. She was pure temptation. And he wasn't used to resisting.

He leaned in, half expecting her to draw back. But she met him in the middle, her soft lips clinging, her mouth molding to his, her tongue testing him almost shyly. He cupped the back of her head and crushed her to him, delving deep inside her mouth, tasting her.

She pulled back abruptly, shoving hard at his chest, her blue eyes rounded, her lips pinched. "That shouldn't have happened."

"It was only a kiss," he growled, knowing he sounded as frustrated as he felt. But he had been ready to take her in the back seat of his car, with only the privacy shield and tinted glass between them and the world.

"And it shouldn't have happened," she insisted.

She ran her hands over her tightly knotted hair. Even after their passionate interlude there wasn't a lock out of place, he noticed with wry humor.

She drew in a sharp breath and thrust her chin high, her prim façade firmly back in its place. "I would invite you in," she said tartly, "but I don't want to."

"You want me to come in. You're just afraid of what might happen if I do."

She looked thoughtful. "You're right. This might be the perfect opportunity to seduce you out of your millions. But, darn it all, I have a headache."

He laughed. At least she was amusing. "I guess even temptresses need a night off now and then."

She gave him a humorless smile and stepped out of the car.

"Elaine?"

She paused, her expression cautious.

"Next time I see you you'll be wearing a white dress."

CHAPTER FIVE

THE wedding had become sort of much-anticipated society event, despite how little time had passed between the announcement and the actual ceremony—or maybe *because* of that reason. Elaine couldn't help but think that the haste of the marriage was part of what made it interesting.

She felt half the eyes in the historic church examining her flat stomach speculatively as she walked down the long aisle.

The air was heavy with the perfume of flowers, compliments of her overzealous wedding planner, and the late-afternoon sun streamed through a round stained glass window, throwing squares of blue light onto the stone floor. It was a beautiful wedding. But it was someone else's wedding. None of it was to her taste except for her simple dress. But none of that mattered. All that mattered was what would happen twelve months from this moment. When the company she had worked so hard for would be hers.

She raised her eyes and looked at her groom, waiting for her at the head of the aisle. She had never seen him look so handsome. His tuxedo was black and well fitted, showing off broad shoulders and a tapered waist. He was in fantastic shape, but hours in the gym weren't the biggest contributing factor to his immense appeal. He was handsome, criminally so, his chiseled features the perfect blend of masculinity and beauty. But it was his charisma, his raw confidence, his power that made people gravitate to him. He wasn't like any man, any person, she'd ever met. And she was about to marry him.

She swallowed. Her throat felt like the inside of a pin-cushion.

This is nothing but a business deal. Nothing but another contract.

She shifted her bouquet and took her groom's hand.

Elaine had no idea how she'd managed to make it through the ceremony, the receiving line, and four hours of the reception. Her feet hurt from wearing her extremely imprac-tical shoes, and her face hurt from all the overly cheerful smiling. And dancing with Marco, clinging to his arm, trying to pretend that she wasn't melting from the heat he was making her feel, had been as taxing as it had been torturous.

She sank into the limo with a sigh, and rested her head on the back of the seat. "That was exhausting."

"New brides usually say that *after* the honeymoon."

Heat flooded her face. Her treacherous mind was all too willing to offer up possible ways Marco could tire her out. She did *not* need this. Not now, and not with this relic from the Dark Ages.

The limo, which had been decorated with over-the-top script writing that said "Mr. and Mrs. Marco De Luca", pulled up to the curb in front of Marco's penthouse. She didn't wait for him to open the door for her. She got out and waited for him by the entrance of the building.

He caught up to her and passed her by, his long legs

taking strides much faster than her own legs could carry her. She'd changed after the reception into a white silk pencil skirt and a green sweater, but she was still wearing the ridiculous stilettos, which made walking fast a little tricky.

She trailed after him down the long marble corridor. This was the sort of love den she'd expected a man like him to own. His women probably fawned over it. Then over him.

Her stomach lurched at the thought of him bringing other women back here. How many had there been? More importantly, how many would she have to see during their marriage? Would she be able to *hear* them as she lay in her own bedroom trying to sleep?

"This is my elevator."

"You have your own personal elevator?" All those little tarts he paraded though here probably *loved* that.

"Yes, it acts as the main door to my house. It would be a security risk if everyone could use it." He spoke to her as if she might be a small child.

"Does everyone have their own elevator?"

"No, just me." He offered a smug grin at that.

He entered a key code into the number pad that was on the lift and the doors opened. The ride up was a long one; he was on the top floor, naturally—what penthouse wasn't? When the ping signaled that they had reached their destination, the doors opened and revealed a bright, airy living room. It didn't match with the rest of the building at all. Nothing tacky or overdone about it. No gold filigree on the windows. No champagne glass hot tub dominating the room.

Far from any of the glittering garishness she'd imagined, it was a contemporary design with clean, sleek lines that didn't suffer from the impersonal, cold feeling of some modern décor.

White walls and vaulted ceilings added to the feeling of openness, along with floor-to-ceiling windows that afforded a fantastic view of the sparkling Manhattan skyline.

The kitchen and living room flowed into one another seamlessly. The countertops in the kitchen were granite, and the appliances were top-of-the-line stainless steel. It was a modern luxury Mecca. The kind of home she'd always imagined setting up for herself. Of course her overcrowded one-bedroom apartment with its mismatched secondhand furniture could hardly compete with Marco's spacious, state-of-the-art penthouse. She just didn't have the cash to own such high-end things. Loath as she was to admit it, living here wasn't going to be a trial.

"You like it?" Marco asked. His husky, sexy voice sent a tremor through her body, and she had to tamp down the wave of longing that threatened to rise up and swamp her. No, it was going to be a trial, all right. Just a luxurious one.

"I do. It's very tastefully decorated, and the view is amazing. Although the windows don't offer much privacy, do they?"

"Will we be needing privacy?" He raised his eyebrows, his expression one of keen interest.

Her face went hot. "No! I just meant…I mean because people could see in."

"They can't. It's one way glass. But I'll make a mental note that you intend to do things in my living room that require privacy." He gave her a look that was so hot it nearly melted the soles of her ridiculous shoes. "I'll make it a point to work from my home office more often."

It was at times like this that she really wished she could come up with some witty, off-the-cuff remark, but his casual innuendos always left her a mess.

She cleared her throat and tried to salvage some dignity. "Where is my room?" Anything to escape.

"Down the hall, last door. You have your very own *en suite* bathroom, so you'll have all the *privacy* you need. I'll be in my office; I have some work to do." She didn't watch to see which direction he went—didn't even try to. She just headed down the hall, the promise of a hot bath keeping her going.

Her bedroom was white, like the rest of the house, and she was pleased to see that she had a view of the city skyline out of her window as well. It certainly beat the view from her own apartment, which consisted of a brick wall and her neighbor's bedroom window.

All of her worldly possessions, except for her furniture, had been brought over by movers earlier today, and most everything was still packed away in boxes and stacked neatly in the corner. She wrinkled her nose. She wasn't going to be unpacking tonight. All she wanted tonight was her bath and then bed. An image of Marco, his chest bare, his skin tan against her white sheets, flashed in her mind.

Alone. She would be going to bed *alone*.

She padded into the bathroom and her heart nearly stopped. There was a separate shower and jet tub, all tiled with caramel-colored Italian marble. The tub was so deep it looked as if she could sink in up to her neck and lose herself completely.

She went back into her bedroom and rummaged around until she found her iPod, then gave a casual scan for the bag she'd packed her clothes in. She didn't see it, and decided to forego searching for pajamas until after she'd had a chance to let the warm water work the knots out of her muscles.

It took a while to fill up the massive tub, but it was worth the wait. Elaine submerged herself in the warm water and felt the tension slowly recede from her tightened muscles. She laid her head back and closed her eyes, letting the events of the day slip from her cluttered mind.

Her quiet moment was shattered by a rush of cold air. She jerked her head up and scrambled to cover anything that might be showing when she saw Marco standing in the doorway.

"Good—glad to see you're making yourself at home."

"Get out!" She had never been naked in front of a man before. She very likely hadn't been naked in front of anyone since she'd been in diapers. She was the type to avoid public locker rooms and showers.

"Spare me your maidenly modesty."

He had no idea how apt a description *that* was.

"It's nothing I haven't seen before, and often."

Her ears burned at his casual reference to his love-life.

"I had hoped that we could put this off for a day or two, but I'm needed in Hawaii to close a very important deal," he went on.

"Can we have this conversation when I'm not naked and dripping wet, please?"

Marco clenched his teeth. The images that statement evoked were so erotic he nearly hauled her slippery body out of the tub so he could show her just what he could accomplish while she was naked and dripping wet.

He had thought that by walking in on her bath he could remove the mystery, and in so doing remove some of her allure. But far from it. The hints of peachy skin he could see beneath the water had him hard and wanting her with a ferocity that shocked him.

Her attempts to cover herself had pushed her cleavage higher above the surface of the water, and he was having trouble tearing his eyes away so that he could look at her face when she talked. He'd seen plenty of naked women—plenty of beautiful, naked women. Why should this one be special? She shouldn't be. But she was.

"Fine, I'll wait for you in the living room."

As soon as he left the room, Elaine scrabbled out of the tub. She wrapped a towel around herself and cautiously peeked into her room. After she'd verified that a certain arrogant, pain-in-the-butt hunk wasn't in there she set about looking for something more substantial than the towel that was currently the only thing separating her from total exposure.

Privacy? Ha! They were apparently using different dictionaries.

She opened the closet for the first time, and almost choked on her tongue. There wasn't a black or navy blue suit in sight. The closet was filled with clothes that she was certain bore designer labels, and every last one of them was as far removed from her general uniform as possible. This whole arrangement just got better and better. He was still playing dress-up with her.

She rifled through the clothes. Cashmeres, silks and cottons. Reds, golds and blues. The small girlish part of her that generally lay dormant was delighted by the selection. It was like shopping in her own home.

It's like being bought.

And she wasn't going to accept that. But she wasn't going out to talk to him in a towel either.

She heard Marco pacing the hardwood floor in the living room. She fingered a beautiful silk dress that hung on one of the hangers. It bothered her immensely that she was thinking about wearing it, thinking about what Marco's reaction might be to it.

She shoved the dress and the clothes next to it aside

fiercely, banishing the thought of Marco's touch burning her through thin silk.

Everything in the closet was extremely feminine, and extremely flimsy. She selected a dress made of a stretch cotton, by far the sturdiest piece of clothing available, and folded it over her arm as she went to look in the dresser for underwear. It wasn't a big surprise that the same man who'd most likely hidden her sensible wardrobe approved of her lingerie.

Her face heated at the thought of his hands on her lacy bras and panties. It seemed so intimate, so unbearably sensual. She picked a pair of red underwear and a matching lace bra. She let her fingers glide over the material. Had Marco touched them like this? Imagined her wearing them? She clenched her thighs together to try and quell the rapid pulse that was beating at their apex. Her nipples beaded shamelessly against the rough terrycloth of the towel that was still wrapped tightly around her.

Elaine put a fierce stop to her runaway imagination. She put the offending underwear on hurriedly, before slipping the wrap dress on and tying the sash around her waist as tightly as possible. The neckline dipped low, and she was tempted to look for a safety pin to bring the edges of the v-neck together.

"Elaine?" Marco's rich voice floated down the hall and she hurriedly left the room. The prospect of him coming into her bedroom was a bit more than her abnormally alert hormones could bear.

Marco turned when he heard Elaine enter the room. He'd hoped that he would have managed to get his rampaging lust under control by the time his new wife had dressed and come out to meet him. And he might have, had she not appeared in the living room looking like every man's fantasy.

The red wrap dress was held onto her luscious body with a bow, making her look like a present that had been wrapped up just for him. A present he wanted very much to unwrap.

His fingers itched to pull the end of the bow and reveal the pearly skin that lay beneath the dress. He ached to see each gorgeous inch of her delectable body laid bare before his eyes, to touch her silken skin, to taste the hollow beneath her throat.

The seam on his pants bit into his growing erection and he shifted, trying to disguise his reaction to her.

"So, now that I'm decent, you were saying…?" She sat on the couch. Her breasts moved with her, their gentle bounce drawing his attention. If she was wearing a bra it was a flimsy lingerie piece, meant to showcase a woman's breasts rather than conceal anything. He could see the perky outline of her nipples through the thin cotton. Would they be pale and pink like the rest of her? He gritted his teeth. She had to be doing this on purpose. No one could look that provocative by accident.

She was even better than he'd given her credit for. The guise of straitlaced businesswoman had put him at ease, but she was slowly dropping the charade and showing glimpses of the real Elaine. She had acted embarrassed when he'd walked in on her during her bath, but he sincerely doubted that a woman so seductive would be put off by something like that.

She'd done a wonderful job concealing the provocative, sexual part of her nature. Despite her reputation she'd nearly managed to convince him that she was an uptight prude. He could see now what a good little actress she was.

The woman sitting in front of him was a woman who *knew* the effect she had on men. Her cheeks were flushed and her eyes were bright, giving her the look of a woman who had recently indulged in hedonistic passions. There was simply no way she could be unaware of the sheer sex appeal that she exuded.

It might be fun to play her game, to take what she was offering for a while, as long as they were both sharing the same home. It was definitely tempting. He knew she had an agenda, but it was of little concern to him. He would be more than able to enjoy her physically and not get snared in her trap.

Later, when the deal with James Preston was ironed out, he would consider taking her up on the offer to use her delectable body.

He cleared his throat and sat in the chair opposite her. He looked to Elaine as if he was readying for a board meeting. Still, looking as formidable as he did, he was the sexiest man she had ever seen.

"What did you do with my clothes?" she asked, one eyebrow quirked.

"They're still in a box somewhere," he said, waving his hand dismissively.

"You didn't think you should consult me before giving my wardrobe a complete overhaul?"

"It needed one. You can trust me on that."

"I don't relish feeling like you're buying me."

He chuckled. "But that's basically what I've done. I'm paying you with Chapman Electronics to be my wife. And if you're going to be playing the part of Mrs. De Luca you need to look the part. Actors are provided with costumes. If it makes you feel better, then look at it that way."

She opened her mouth as if she was going to offer up one of her tart one-liners, then closed it again as if she'd thought better of it.

"You already know that I've been eyeing one of James

Preston's resort properties in Hawaii, and that he's reluctant to sell to me because of my reputation?"

"Yes, I remember. The Hanalei Bay Resort."

James Preston was a legendary hotelier. His resort property on the island of Kauai was the "it" spot for corporate retreats, celebrity weddings, and romantic getaways for the über-wealthy.

He gave her a wry smile. "That's the one."

"Is he still unsure about you?"

"He's getting there, but he wants to meet with me personally before he agrees to anything."

"Naturally."

He nodded. "And of course I'll need to do a thorough sweep of the property before I make a final decision."

"How long will you be gone?"

"*We* shouldn't be gone for more than a couple weeks."

"We?"

"Yes. We."

"What about my job? You just expect me to pick up and go gallivanting off to paradise and leave them in the lurch?"

"Yes, Elaine, I do. Think of this as an extended job interview. If you do things to my satisfaction, in the end you'll get the company. However, if my goals are compromised so are yours. Remember that."

Marco could see the war that was being waged behind her eyes. The fierce light that had glinted in their blue depths when she'd thought about arguing, the anger when she'd realized she had no choice but to accompany him, to hold to her end of the contract. Then, finally, he'd seen acceptance.

"When do we leave?"

CHAPTER SIX

THE vibrant colour of the island rushed up into Elaine's vision as the plane began to move closer to the viridian land. The trees were so dense she could hardly see the runway, and it felt as though the plane was going to crash into the thick palms and kukuis that lined the coast.

"It's so beautiful," she said.

Marco barely looked up from his laptop. He was sitting across from her in a captain's chair that was adjacent to the small loveseat she was perched on.

His private plane was the size of her apartment, and was lavishly furnished. She'd probably looked completely gauche when she'd boarded the plane back in New York, her mouth hanging open as she took in the absolute indulgence and luxury of her surroundings.

"Yes. It is. Which is why it's such valuable real estate."

Even the matter-of-fact statement sent a shiver of wanting through her. He could recite baseball statistics and still sound unbearably sexy. She'd had her own bedroom and *en suite* bathroom for the duration of the thirteen-hour flight, but not even that little bit of privacy had been enough to keep her from feeling horribly, embarrassingly aware of the man.

It bordered on being infuriating. Where was her focus? She was so close—twelve months away—to reaching the ultimate prize, and half of her mind, and all of her body, were homed in on Marco.

Maybe it was the natural order. Maybe hormones and normal adult desires could only be ignored and suppressed for so long. Maybe they'd spent the last ten years building up in her system, only to be unleashed on the first desirable male to come within five feet of her.

It wasn't as though she'd never had the opportunity. There had been plenty of men who'd showed interest in her, especially in college. And she'd even liked some of them, dated some of them. But in the end their lack of ambition had made her crazy, while her driving need for success had driven them away. There had been kisses— none of them overly passionate, all of them ending at the front door. There had never seemed to be the time or the adequate desire for a physical relationship.

And then there had been Daniel. Whom she'd liked a lot. Whom she'd been attracted to—whom she'd very nearly said yes to when he'd asked that all-important question at the door. But in the end she'd turned down his request to come in, nerves or maybe even morals stopping her from accepting.

That moment of refusal had changed everything. The next day Daniel had started spreading the rumors, and by the end of the day everyone *knew* why she'd been getting promoted. At least they'd thought they did. Nobody would believe that she'd gotten the promotions on her own merit, and her co-workers had been more than willing to believe that she'd slept with the boss rather than believing she might actually be good—better than they were—at what she did. And just like that her career had been killed before it had started.

Which brought her full circle to where she was now. On a private plane that had just landed in Hawaii, with her mercenary husband, whom she was appallingly attracted to, and twelve months of marriage to a man who threw her thoroughly off kilter looming ahead of her.

Marco stood when the plane came to a halt, his laptop secured in its travel case. "We will go straight to the Hanalei Bay Resort and get settled into our accommodations. Later we will be having dinner with James and his wife."

"Our accommodations? As in, we're sharing?"

Marco watched as hectic color flooded Elaine's face. It was a source of amazement to him that a woman of her age could blush so easily. He preferred a more sophisticated type of woman, the kind of woman who didn't expect anything from a man but a few nights of mutual satisfaction. The only sort of pink any of those women got in their cheeks came from their make-up bag. He found it an interesting sort of challenge, making her blush.

"No, actually I was planning to have you installed down the hall, so that I could use your services by day and entertain my mistress by night."

Color reddened her neck and slowly climbed into her face, staining her cheeks a deep crimson. "Well, the stipulations of the prenup would certainly allow it," she said stiffly.

He chuckled. "You're not getting rid of me so easily, *cara mia.*" He strode across the cabin of the plane and leaned down, cupping her chin and tilting her face up so that she was forced to meet his eyes. "I'm here to play devoted husband." He smoothed his thumb along her lush bottom lip. Lust attacked him, hot and hard. "And we're on our honeymoon. That means you will be staying very, very close to me."

Her tongue darted out to moisten her lips and the pink tip slicked across his thumb. Electricity shot from his hand to his groin. Her eyes widened, her pupils dilated. She wanted him. She probably wanted his money even more, but there was no denying that she wanted him physically.

And he ached to take her. To pull her to the floor and have his way with her, pound into her while those gorgeous, endless legs were wrapped high around his waist, as she whispered soft, feminine sounds of pleasure in his ear.

He was so hard it hurt.

But he didn't have any protection with him—and not by accident. He wasn't taking any chances with this mercenary woman he'd married. His own parents had given him an early crash course in the essence of human nature. Greed and self-satisfaction were at the core of every human being. Even the most honest and good could be corrupted for the right amount. With enough incentive a father could throw his family out onto the streets to fend for themselves. A mother could leave her children when she got a better offer than sleeping in alleyways. Yes, the right incentive could entice people to commit all kinds of sins.

He didn't trust the woman. Her motives were anything but pure. He was certain of that. She had lied to her own father and married a stranger, all for her personal gain. He had no intention of falling prey to her. She was a fabulous manipulator. She was a calculating businesswoman, the embodiment of sex appeal, a ruthless competitor…and a blushing innocent?

Until he was able to ascertain exactly what her true motives were, exactly which of the characters she portrayed reflected the real woman, he would have to keep his distance.

His erection pulsed in protest.

She turned her face away and picked up her purse. When she faced him again her composure was intact. The face of the flustered girl covered by the mask of a perfectly collected, icy businesswoman.

She was either a very good actress or a very naïve young woman who was in way over her pretty blond head. It bothered him immensely that he wasn't able to figure it out for certain.

She pushed past him, and the tips of her breasts brushed lightly against his chest. Her eyes widened fractionally and she hurried to break the contact. It seemed natural, like an honest mistake. But if there was one thing he knew about women it was that they practiced looking natural until they had it honed to a fine art.

"Well, there had better be two beds." She craned her long, elegant neck and lowered her eyelids, the light lashes fanning across her cheekbones.

He studied her beautiful, haughty profile. Everything about her was designed to entice men. Even, he was discovering, her ice queen routine. She was a challenge—a challenge that roused something in the most primitive, unenlightened, masculine part of him.

A man who really understood female beauty would be able to see hers—be able to appreciate the rarity of it, the quality, even buried beneath the layers of boardroom armor. And any man who recognized her beauty would want a taste of it. Would want to draw from her a response. Would want to make her shed her inhibitions, to take the tight knot of her hair down and sift it through his fingers. Kiss her, make her cry out in pleasure. Make her lose every bit of that hardened exterior until she was soft, pliant, and all out of that control she seemed to prize so much.

He was beginning to think she'd been cleverer in crafting her persona than he could have imagined.

He chuckled at her uptight expression. "I don't think honeymoon suites are typically outfitted with two beds. Unless the newly married couple wants to experience a change of scenery now and then, I don't really see the point."

"If this is some sort of childish trick to get me into bed…"

He reached out and hooked an arm around her slender waist and drew her close to his body. "I don't have to stoop to subterfuge to get a woman to sleep with me." He trailed his finger along the line of her collarbone, and he didn't miss the shiver of awareness that racked her slight frame.

She wiggled, extricating herself from his hold. "Well, I'm not going to become another of the legions of notches on your bedpost. Besides, if you add any more notches the whole bedframe is going to collapse—and where would that leave you and your lovers?"

"The floor."

Elaine's heart stuttered. Images of twined tanned and lily-white limbs flashed through her mind's eye. Marco kissing her passionately, desire overwhelming them to the point that they couldn't make it to the bed, Marco taking her gently to the floor, settling between her thighs…

She blinked, trying to stop the erotic slideshow.

The look in Marco's dark eyes told her that they were experiencing a moment of identical thought, and that was enough to bring common sense and sanity back.

"Classy." She sounded prissy even to her own ears.

"Class is sometimes overrated. Particularly in the bedroom."

The fact that he was always ready with some casual, off-the-cuff response was infuriating. She couldn't hope to compete with him there. She lacked both the sophistication and the experience to fake nonchalance when he said things like that. Before this moment sex on the floor had never even crossed her mind, and she was way too busy grappling with the new, unsettling notion to try and be witty.

"Where is my luggage?" she asked, hoping he wouldn't comment on the abrupt subject change.

His wicked half-smile told her he knew exactly what had prompted her to shift the gears of the conversation. "One of my flight staff will see that it gets put in the rental car."

She held back a comment about the excesses of having staff on a private plane. They were going to be meeting James Preston soon and they were supposed to look like blissed-out newlyweds, not tense strangers.

She followed Marco out of the plane and into the balmy outdoors. A warm salt breeze was blowing in off the sea. The tang from the salt mingled with the smell of moisture and tropical flowers to create a heady perfume. It smelled like sensuality, and it made her acutely conscious of her body. And Marco's.

"Aloha oe."

They stepped onto the tarmac and a woman with glossy black hair and burnished copper skin slipped a fresh flower *lei* over Elaine's head, then Marco's. Elaine didn't think it was her imagination that the double-cheek-kiss the woman planted on Marco lingered longer than was strictly necessary.

"Aloha," Marco said, his husky voice making the word sound exotic and sexy—like an invitation. An invitation to engage in bedpost-demolishing activity. It wasn't as

though she could blame the woman. Marco was a walking advertisement for the pleasures of the flesh.

Elaine saw the woman slip a card into the pocket of Marco's pants and a strange, heated emotion rolled through her stomach, causing it to cramp and twist. Jealousy? She'd never actually experienced the emotion before, and it wasn't the time or the place to start feeling it now. Or the *man* to feel it for.

A glossy silver Mercedes McLaren was parked near the edge of the tarmac, the convertible top down, the keys in the ignition. She ought to have figured that Marco didn't go to the rental counter like mere mortals.

Marco opened the passenger door, his smile aimed only at her. He looked every inch the devoted husband. He wouldn't have any trouble convincing James Preston he'd reformed.

As long as he doesn't convince you.

She brushed the thought aside as soon as it popped into her mind. She didn't care if he did truly reform and decide he wanted love, commitment, and two point four kids. He could find them with some other woman who actually *wanted* those things. She wanted to realize her full potential, not become a casualty of marriage—a mere accessory to a husband who valued her about as much as he did his brand-new Rolex.

She'd seen it happen to her mother. Seen the decline of her self-esteem. Seen her make an absolute fool of herself over male attention, craving validation from her husband and, when that failed, from her many young lovers, unable to find value in herself. Elaine had vowed she would never be that woman. She would never pin her hopes, dreams and sense of self-worth on someone else.

Marco put his hand on the small of her back, and she

all but leapt into the car to escape the burn of his touch through her thin button-up blouse. The cool, butter-soft leather of the seat helped to douse some of the flames that his touch had ignited, but the embers still burned in her veins. She hoped he didn't notice how much he affected her physically. One look at his dazzling grin as he sank into the car told her he was acutely, absolutely aware of what he did to her.

The virgin and the playboy. It was an unfair pairing. She had never felt this level of desire for a man in her life, and she certainly didn't have any practice suppressing it.

The high-performance engine roared to life and Marco tapped the gas pedal, taking the sleek sports car from zero to sixty in a fraction of a second.

Elaine's eyes widened when she looked at the speedometer. "Slow down!"

Marco took a sharp corner on the narrow two-lane road with ease. "A car like this isn't meant for slow."

After a few moments she relaxed. The car handled with total precision, and Marco was in complete control of the roaring beast. He tamed it, harnessed its power, drawing from it the response he wanted—a response only he could command…and just like that her mind was back on sex.

He had that effect on women, *all* women, she thought sourly, as she remembered the forward actions of the gorgeous native woman.

"Did that…did that woman at the airport give you her phone number?"

He reached into his pocket and pulled out the card, setting it in Elaine's lap. "I hadn't checked."

The digits on the card confirmed what Elaine had suspected. "That's nice. We're here on our honeymoon and she's trying to pick you up."

He chuckled, low and throaty. "It makes a case for there being two beds in our honeymoon suite."

Her face heated, but not from embarrassment this time. "That's disgusting."

"You're the one who made the rules of the arrangement, Elaine."

"I hardly imagined you bringing another woman back to our *shared* hotel room."

"Give me a bit more credit than that," he said, sounding darkly amused. "It isn't as though I've slept with every woman I've been photographed with. My bedpost actually remains pretty sturdy."

She didn't know why, but the knot of tension that had settled in her chest loosened a fraction. "I guess we're both victims of false press."

He shrugged. "It's all part of having ambition. There are a lot of people who want to get to the top. They want fame and fortune, and if they have to take others down in the process they're more than willing. Your downfall opened doors for more than one person at your firm, didn't it?" She nodded in the affirmative. "It's probably why your colleagues latched onto it with so much glee. Your descent from grace was the secret to their success."

"I guess I lack the killer instinct. Maybe I should have spread some gossip of my own."

"I sincerely doubt you lack the killer instinct." He reached over and took her left hand, lifting it so that her engagement ring and newly acquired wedding band caught the sunlight. "This is proof."

"What does it say about you, then?" she huffed.

He laughed. "No one has ever accused me of being a soft touch."

Not outside the bedroom. He didn't have to add that last

part, her imagination did it all by itself. She imagined that in bed he could be a soft touch, or a demanding touch— whatever his lover desired.

She slammed the brakes on her runaway imagination and concentrated instead on the lush scenery that surrounded them. The water was clear and brilliant. Spinner dolphins swam alongside the coastline, seeming to follow them as they drove down a road that was slowly winding up the heavily forested green mountainside.

The road dead-ended at the top of the mountain, ending at a heavy wrought iron gate with a number pad and intercom mounted on it. Marco leaned in and entered a series of numbers with his long tanned fingers. She couldn't stop herself from enjoying his hands again.

The gates opened and they continued up the steep drive.

The hotel was built into the side of the mountain, the balconies for each room segmented and private, overlooking an impossibly gorgeous bay with surreally bright water and a luxuriant natural landscape, with an abundance of vibrant tropical blooms.

Everything on the island seemed like a sensory overload to her. The air was thick with salt from the ocean; mist was rising from the fresh rainfall and the perfume of flowers. The colors were overly saturated. The blanket of green that covered the mountain was thick and dense, a shocking contrast to the ever-brownish haze of smog that blanketed the city of New York. It was like having a veil ripped from her eyes and having her five senses fully realized for the first time.

Not necessarily a good thing, since her awareness of the man who was her temporary husband had also gone up several notches.

Marco slipped his arm around her waist and led her to

the front entrance of the hotel. Pink and orange sunset vines clung to the stone exterior. Far from giving it a rustic appearance, the invasion of nature upon the man-made structure made it look all the more exclusive.

A small crew of sharply dressed men exited the hotel and greeted them with broad smiles. A young man with blond hair shook Marco's hand firmly. "*Aloha*, Mr. De Luca. Mr. Preston is in a meeting, and is regretful he is not able to greet you and your new bride. My name is Jonathan, and I would love to take care of any needs you might have. The Ano Lani villa has been reserved for you. It's nearly half a mile up the coastline. If you like, myself or one of the other men can drive you and assist in the unloading of your luggage."

"Thank you, but it won't be necessary. Perhaps just a map of the resort?"

Jonathan reached into his suit jacket and pulled out a sleek brochure. "If there is anything else in particular you need, the concierge will be pleased to see to it."

"I don't think the charger for my BlackBerry made it into my luggage," Marco said. "I would like to have one delivered to the villa as soon as possible."

After receiving the make and model information Jonathan and crew went back into the hotel to complete their mission.

It was amazing the kind of service money could buy. Her family were well off by most standards, but they would hardly have been able to aspire to be guests at a place like this. Marco only had to sign a check and he would *own* it. The intensity of that amount of wealth, that amount of power, was staggering. She understood why he was concerned with guarding his assets. Even the most scrupulous of people would be tempted to try a taste of what Marco enjoyed so freely.

She wondered if he even realized just how incredible it was that he was in such a position. He probably didn't. He had been born into wealth, and from it had fashioned almost immeasurable riches. No wonder he was so arrogant. Asking him to understand her position was like asking Zeus to step down from Mount Olympus to play cards.

"You didn't forget your charger," she said accusingly as she got back into the small sleek car. As if he would forget any detail—no matter how small.

He shrugged. "No. But I will be keeping Jonathan on as an employee if he manages to show up with one in the villa in the next couple of hours."

"Testing the staff?"

"Why not? I'm not an easy boss to please, Elaine. I don't coddle employees. At a resort of this level I will expect nothing less than impeccable service from those who work here. I would like to keep the passing of the hotel's ownership as smooth as possible. Keeping the same staff would help immensely. However, I'm not running a charity here, which means I expect perfection or they don't have jobs."

Marco glanced over at her. Her expression was disapproving. A little line creased her alabaster forehead, and her mouth was pursed into an ungenerous pucker.

"You have a problem with this?" he asked, entertained by her show of humanity.

"It doesn't really seem fair to just fire someone if they don't get a BlackBerry charger to you in time."

"If you're going to run a company you're going to have to adopt the same mindset I have. Time is money—clichéd, but very true. When people on your staff waste time, they waste your money. When they leave a client dissatisfied, they cost you money. You have good ideas, but if you can't execute them, if you can't hire a team to *help* you execute them, you won't get anywhere."

The crease between her brows deepened. "I guess I'm a walking example of the lows one has to stoop to in order to make it in the business world."

He laughed darkly. "Just treat everyone the way you treat me and you'll have no trouble being ruthless."

"There's a thought."

Marco watched as Elaine's expression changed from one of recalcitrance to one of wonder.

The car eased around the last curve and the villa came into view.

The Ano Lani villa was made secluded by dense native foliage, and a pond had been built to encircle the house, with a small wooden bridge granting the only access into the grand structure. Floor-to-ceiling windows exposed the villa to billion-dollar views of the crystalline water and the surrounding mountains. It was obvious that the villa itself, no matter how stunningly luxurious, was only a part of what the guests were paying for. The real star was the serene natural beauty of the bay.

"This is… I suppose people pay a lot of money to stay in a place like this?"

He nodded. "Thousands of dollars a night. And with the proper marketing they would pay more than that."

"I can see why you want it."

"It will be a nice addition. Normally I build my resorts from the ground up, but the Hanalei Bay area is essentially full, and new construction wouldn't be practical."

They got out of the car, and Marco pulled their luggage out of the trunk of the small vehicle.

Elaine followed, the sight of her temptingly long legs

stretching from the McLaren almost more temptation than his starved libido could handle.

"Did you always know you wanted to get into real estate? Your father did manufacturing, didn't he?" she asked.

Coldness invaded his chest—that chill that always pervaded his being when he thought of his bastard of a father. "My father had no bearing whatsoever on my chosen field." His voice was hard, clipped, and he could tell by the wounded doe look in her eyes that it had shocked her. He didn't really care at that moment. "I've built my business from nothing. It was pure accident that I got work at a real estate office, but not accidental at all that I chose to excel at it—and everything else my corporation has ventured into over the past thirteen years."

He'd figured she would pry further. It was inevitable. Women always wanted to know what a man was thinking. Instead she averted her eyes and began a closer inspection of the villa.

She hurried across the little wooden bridge, running a slender, elegant hand over the rail in a movement so unconsciously seductive that all thoughts of his father were driven straight from his mind. The way her delicate fingers caressed the wood was symbolic in ways he did not need to dwell on.

She walked up the stairs and onto the wraparound deck. He didn't even try to keep his eyes from lingering on her curvaceous figure, on her pert little bottom and her narrow waist.

He noticed that her shoulders visibly sagged with relief when she walked into the expansive living room. "Plenty of places to sleep," she said softly.

He should have had them remove everything but the bed, so that she was forced to choose between the bamboo floor or a night in his arms. Although he'd told her the honest truth when he'd said he'd never had to coerce a woman into his bed. Women usually went all too willingly. But something about her resistance was enticing in a way he hadn't imagined it could be. Of course, something different and new when it came to sex was a rarity for a man of his experience. It was no wonder he found her so intriguing.

He was used to blatant women. Women who stared openly with hungry eyes and practically begged him to take them before they even made it to dinner on the first date. He was a man who enjoyed sex, and had a healthy appetite for it, but lately the game had started to turn him off. It had all started to seem vaguely distasteful. Which was why he'd put off finding an available woman to take the edge off his desire. And probably why Elaine looked as tempting as original sin.

"We'd better get ready for dinner."

Elaine jumped when Marco's husky voice penetrated her thoughts. She turned to look at him and her heart did that weird flipping thing it did whenever she was caught off-guard by his sheer masculine beauty. Which was every time she looked at him.

She might need to get ready for dinner, but he looked as perfect as ever. Not a dark, gleaming hair out of place, his white shirt unbuttoned at the collar, the sleeves pushed up, revealing those delicious forearms again. His black trousers didn't have a wrinkle. With her blond hair frizzing from the humidity, and her blouse and pants showing every hour of the long journey, she felt like one big crease standing next to his perfectly pressed beauty.

She gratefully escaped to the luxurious bathroom. Standing there with him, in a space that was made for lovers, had probably housed hundreds of them, had seemed much too intimate. And, if she was honest, too tempting. She suddenly knew why it had been so hard for all the girls in high school and college—why so many of them had made fools of themselves over boys. It had been easy for her to act above it all, but the simple fact was that she'd never desired a man in a sexual way before—not truly. Now that she did, she understood the struggle.

There was something about attraction that she'd missed before. She'd liked men, had felt little bouts of butterflies in her belly when the object of her affection had walked by. But this…this was different. There was something primitive about it. A physical response that was unrelated to any of the finer feelings she possessed. She might not have any experience with sex, but her body knew what it wanted. And its demands were getting louder with each passing minute spent in her *husband's* company.

She pulled her make-up case out of her luggage and set it on the marble countertop. She turned the handle on the basin sink and splashed cold water on her face and her pulse points in an effort to cool her heated hormones down to a low simmer.

There was no curtain for the shower, only a thick, clear panel of glass. So no privacy—although she had a feeling that she'd have to shower in a sweater and pants to feel comfortable with Marco so near. Especially given what had happened the last time she'd gotten naked with him nearby. The memory of him walking in on her in the tub made her feel hot with embarrassment. At least that was what she was pretending the heat was from.

She stripped quickly and stepped into the shower, not minding that the water was cool. She rinsed as quickly as possible and ran a razor over all the necessary places before hopping out and dressing in the simple, figure-hugging coral cocktail dress that had been pre-selected by Marco for the all-important dinner.

In a rare moment of honesty she admitted to herself that it wasn't the prospect of being walked in on by Marco that had made her cut her shower short. The pulsing spray of the water on her sensitized skin had been too much for her already fired-up hormones to handle. It had made her think of his hands, his fingertips, gliding over her body, and the heavy ache of her breasts and the dull pulsing between her thighs had reached a nearly unbearable level.

She finished getting ready as quickly as possible, tying her frizzing hair into a loose bun and applying a thin layer of make-up before putting on the ridiculous high heels that Marco had chosen for her to pair with the dress. She hurried back into the living room, still fastening the clasp on her delicate silver necklace.

"Ready?" Marco looked as though he'd also just stepped out of the shower, his dark hair damp and curling at the nape of his neck.

She closed her hands into fists, letting the bite of her nails on the tender skin of her palms ground her in reality as she fought the urge to cross the room and sift her fingers through his damp curls. Her heartbeat quickened its pace and a surge of longing washed over her.

She licked her suddenly dry lips. "Yes." Her shaking fingers slipped and she missed the clasp on the necklace.

"Need any help?"

Her heart pounded harder. She was sure, absolutely sure, that he could hear it. "Yes… No…"

He chuckled. "You aren't sure if you need help?"

I'm certain I do need help.

But not the kind he meant. If she were even the tiniest

bit sane she would have refused his offer. But it had been one temptation too many.

He moved behind her, his warm, moist breath fanning across her neck. She felt an answering wetness building between her thighs. He put his hand on her nape, his fingers lightly massaging her in small circles, and pleasure radiated from his touch and spread through her body. Her knees started to feel unsteady.

"You'll have to let go, Elaine."

Oh, she was. She was letting go of everything. Of everything she'd ever believed to be true about herself—of every conviction, every tightly held belief. There was no room for anything but this moment, and everything else—all the fear and the doubt—had to go unheeded.

"Elaine, let go of the necklace."

Her fingers released their hold on the dainty silver chain and a hot flush stole across her cheeks.

His skillful fingers moved against the sensitive skin, and far too soon he'd finished fastening the clasp for her. He pulled his hands away, and the loss of his touch left her feeling bereft somehow.

Slowly the fog of her arousal, the fog that had descended the moment they'd entered this tropical paradise, began to lift. She couldn't let this happen. He was the kind of man who used and discarded women with all the ease that most people had changing socks—definitely not the kind of man to get involved with. Even if he hadn't been the absolute wrong man, it was absolutely the wrong time for her to get involved with someone. But that didn't stop the restless ache of desire that left her feeling hollow and unsatisfied.

"Thank you," she murmured, hoping he didn't notice the throaty tone her voice had suddenly adopted. She stepped away from him, hoping that distance would bring some sort of relief from the intense, unconscionable attraction that she felt for him.

He reached out and took her hand, drawing her back into the warmth of his body. "Ready for dinner, *amore mia*?"

CHAPTER SEVEN

MARCO couldn't help but be impressed with Elaine's performance over dinner. She came across as bright, confident and witty. James Preston was eating from the palm of her hand in a matter of minutes. The older man was completely taken in by her charm and intelligence. Which Marco knew should please him. Instead, primal possessiveness surged through him.

He moved closer to Elaine, wrapping his arm around her delicate waist and drawing her to him, smoothing his fingers along her silk-covered flesh. He felt a slight tremor race through her body at the light contact.

"So, Marco," James said, sliding nearer to his own wife, "I understand you find it old-fashioned of me to have a vested interest in what will become of the resort when I retire and sell out. But I built it up from the ground. This was my first great success and it has sentimental meaning to me. I want to be sure that I'm passing it on to someone who will preserve the integrity of the property."

"And I intend to. I will be keeping it privately owned, so that I retain total control of what goes on. My vision is to keep it exclusive—perhaps even make it more so." Marco began to outline his plan for creating an even more exclusive clientele base for the hotel, while increasing profits and improving the local economy.

"And your lovely wife will be involved in the process?" James gave Elaine a glowing look, and Marco tightened his hold on her.

"*My* wife will be as involved as she wishes." He couldn't keep the biting edge from his voice.

James raised his gray eyebrows. "Well, he's quite possessive, isn't he?" He directed his question to Elaine.

A mischievous glint shone in her eyes. "Marco's such a charming antique." She ran a slender hand down his arm and gave him a look that was so falsely adoring he could have laughed had he not been so concerned about the words that were coming out of her mouth. "He has quite a reputation with women, as I'm sure you know, but I've tamed him pretty successfully. Of course there are moments when his inner caveman appears."

James's redheaded wife Kim quirked a smile, and spoke for the first time since they'd sat down at the dinner table. "Isn't that the way it is with all men?"

"You behave," James said playfully.

And just like that the tone of the conversation swayed from business and onto personal topics.

Marco had to admit that Elaine had a way with people. She could be engaging when she wanted to be, and none of her usual frosty reserve was on display for the Prestons.

Marco made an appointment to meet with James in the morning, and cut the dinner short before more drinks. As a rule he didn't drink much. He didn't like to dull his senses. And around Elaine Chapman he was going to need his mind functioning at its best. The last thing he needed was to have his decisions made through the soft, smoky haze of alcohol.

She walked ahead of him out of the restaurant, her hips swaying, encased lovingly in that form-fitting little dress. She was like a bright tropical flower, or a piece of luscious fruit. Forbidden fruit. He had made her off-limits. A notion that was completely foreign to him. A notion that made her appear all the more succulent.

She moved to the passenger side of the car, her body hidden from him by the dark shadows of the azalea bushes that lined the asphalt. He caught up to her and pulled her against him. The little hitch in her breath was the only sound she made to express her surprise. "So I'm a caveman, am I?" He placed his hands on her waist and drew her nearer, allowing her to feel the steel of his erection pressed against the curve of her bottom.

"It's not the first time I've said it," she said, her voice breathless.

"You were supposed to behave yourself," he growled low, bringing his lips so close to her ear that he brushed the tender skin.

"You mean I was supposed to play silent accessory, like James's wife?"

"Men like women who do as they're told." He skimmed his fingers from the indent in her waist to the underside of her breasts.

"Well, that's too bad. I don't suppose I'll be having much luck with men."

He chuckled. "*Cara mia*, I don't believe that for a moment. You are walking temptation."

She drew in a breath. "Even when I'm being mouthy?"

"Especially then."

She leaned her head back for a moment, her body relaxing, her curves molding to fit against him. He pressed a kiss to her neck and she stiffened. "Stop."

He released her. "Why?" Somewhere between the restaurant and the car he'd decided he didn't need to fight his attraction for her anymore. As long as he stayed in control of the situation, and there was no doubt that he would, there could be no harm in indulging in an affair with her. He found it easy to indulge in the pleasures of the flesh without engaging his emotions, and in his experience a modern woman viewed sex much the same way.

Elaine lowered her eyes. "It will make things…complicated."

He cupped her cheek and tilted her face up, forcing her to meet his gaze. "There's nothing complicated about sex."

"Maybe not for you."

But Elaine knew that for her it would be. Dinner had been akin to torture. Watching him talk business, seeing him in his element, a ruthless light in his eyes as he spoke about his plans for the resort, the confidence he exuded, the arrogance… It had been the most spectacularly sexy thing she'd ever seen in her life. More than that, he'd made her *feel* far too much. Not just desire, but other things. She'd been proud of him, had felt possessive. She hadn't liked the way Kim Preston had eyed Marco's spectacular physique—not that she could blame the other woman—but then Elaine's gaze had locked on the platinum wedding band on Marco's left hand and one word had run through her mind: *mine*.

And that was wrong. He wasn't hers. And he never could be. Neither should she want him to be!

She felt as if she was dangling from the last thin shred of her resistance. If she let go, if she lost her grip, she was going to go tumbling down into the abyss beneath her, and climbing back out would be nearly impossible.

"There's nothing complex about this," he said, his voice

a low, sexy whisper that vibrated through her, sending shockwaves of longing through her being. "This is the most basic thing in the world. Man and woman. Desire and satisfaction."

The promise in his voice almost stole her resolve then and there. "Marco, I'm tired and jet lagged. Let's go back to the villa."

She knew the absence of a firm no coming from her lips did not escape his notice. She honestly hadn't been able to muster up the will to give him one. She knew it was dangerous, going back to the Ano Lani without a definitive decision in place, but maybe that was what she wanted. She was honest enough to admit, at least in that moment, that she wanted to leave the door open a little bit. She didn't want to lose all possibility of making love with him—not when so much of her desired it so intensely.

They took the ride back to the hotel in silence. Elaine tried to steady her breathing, to get a handle on the riot of sensations and emotions that were tumbling through her usually predictable body. Where was her cool head now? When she most needed that level, analytical part of her personality it had deserted her like a rat off a sinking ship. Almost as if it wanted no part in the impending disaster.

No. There would be no disaster. She could control herself. The problem was that she wasn't entirely certain she *wanted* to control herself.

She leapt from the car the moment it came to a stop in front of the villa, needing desperately to put some distance between Marco and herself so that she could clear her head.

She felt rather than heard him enter the room behind her. "I'll sleep on the couch," she offered quickly. "You're a lot…bigger than I am."

He shrugged. "Suit yourself. I have some work to finish up before I head to bed. I'll be in the office."

"Did the BlackBerry charger show up?"

He chuckled, the sound spreading through her like melting butter. "As a matter of fact it did."

"So the staff shall live to see another day?" She didn't know why she was instigating conversation, why she was so reluctant to let him go, to let him end the evening. She hadn't completely closed the door on them making love tonight, but he obviously had. She should be relieved.

"So long as their performance remains up to par."

He turned away from her, and she couldn't keep herself from admiring the view. The broad set of his shoulders, his lean waist and his muscular butt were far too tempting a treat to pass up. She had to get her thrills somewhere. And before Marco it had been a long time since she'd gotten any. And those had been innocent thrills, mild in comparison to the kind of sensations that were pinging through her body now, electrifying the blood that was charging through her veins.

"I'll probably just go to bed," she said.

Marco turned and watched her look forlornly at the long couch. She was probably weighing her need to keep up her hard-to-get act versus her need for a good night's sleep—although she wouldn't find a good night's sleep on the couch *or* in his bed.

He went into the office without bothering to watch her make her final decision. His body ached with need and it unsettled him. Yes, it had been a long time since he'd been with a woman, much longer than he was accustomed to, but that did not excuse the intensity of the desire that had him hard, throbbing, and unable to concentrate.

Ironic that he had never come close to proposing

marriage to a woman in his life, and the one he *had* married seemed to avoid physical contact with him at all costs. But she desired it as he did. She wanted him too. But something was stopping her from making the final step. It could all be part of her act—playing at reluctance in order to build his level of sexual frustration to a fever pitch. Or she could be genuinely opposed to conducting a physical relationship. He couldn't discount that possibility.

But, whatever her reasoning, he was still left with a raging hard-on and no satisfaction in sight.

He clenched his fists and turned his attention to his laptop, trying to turn his normally high-performing mind to the task at hand. It was a futile attempt. His body was talking much louder than his brain tonight.

And he wasn't the type of man to practice self-denial.

Despite the fact that as far as her body was concerned it was the early hours of the morning, she knew she was far too keyed-up to get any sleep. She wandered through the villa, pausing to enjoy the native Hawaiian-style artwork before wandering into the bathroom.

She needed a bath to settle her mind and her body. But the bathroom that was at the "safe" end of the villa—the end that didn't take her anywhere near Marco's office or bedroom—only had a shower, and she was desperate for her nightly ritual.

She opened the glass door that led to the outdoor courtyard. Low stone walls and a vine covered lattice roof offered privacy, but also allowed her to see the jade-green bay, turned gray by the silver moonlight.

A massive jet tub sat in the corner of the courtyard. A freestanding wooden rack with towels and a white silk bathrobe was situated by the tub. She sighed. Stress relief was at hand. It wouldn't relieve any of her other physical issues, but it would help loosen her knotted shoulders.

She turned the gilded taps and experimented with the assorted essential oils that had been placed on the towel rack. Candles were placed on the four corners of the tub, and a lighter had been left nearby. She bent over and lit each candle. It was the perfect setting. Relaxing. Sensual. Romantic. It was a bath designed for two. But only one would be taking it. And it was better that way.

She slipped out of her clothes quickly, her eyes darting to the door, praying that Marco didn't pick that moment to explore this portion of the villa, and stepped into the tub. Or maybe, a treacherous voice spoke up, it would be more interesting if he did. She banished the unapproved thought and sank beneath the water, letting the scent of mint and vanilla wash over her, relaxing her body and her mind.

It was so easy to imagine Marco sitting behind her, her head pillowed on his muscular chest, her body wedged between his masculine thighs, the rough hair abrading her soft skin… Her heart began to pound heavily, and her body began to feel a whole different kind of languor.

She stood from the tub abruptly and reached for one of the jade-green towels, drying her over-sensitive skin quickly before wrapping herself in a robe. She stepped out of the water and welcomed the slight bite of the night air. She needed something to cool her down.

She padded over to the far end of the courtyard and out the gate that led to the large wooden deck that was attached to the villa. She leaned against the railing and gazed down into the koi pond, watching the fat orange fish swim lazily through the water. Her heart was still pounding and her breath was coming out in short, uneven bursts.

She drew a shaky hand over her face. She had a

feeling she was fighting a losing battle. Maybe the key was to stop fighting. She wanted Marco. She didn't want to get married for real, and fall in love—at least not in the foreseeable future—but she honestly didn't want to die a virgin either. Not that she'd ever worried about it much before.

If she slept with Marco she ran the risk of getting in too deep. She knew that women sometimes underestimated the effect sex had on them. But if she went into it with her eyes open and viewed it as a learning experience, was able to be detached…maybe then it would work.

"I was looking for you." Marco's husky whisper drew her from her reverie. She turned to face him and her throat dried. He was so impossibly handsome, so amazingly, sensationally masculine. He made everything feminine inside of her quiver with expectant longing.

"I took a bath," she said, hoping the silver moonlight disguised the blush she knew was staining her cheekbones. "It helps me relax."

He moved closer to her, his eyes black in the dim light, the planes of his face thrown into sharp relief. He reached a hand out and cupped her cheek, stroking it lightly with his thumb. She shivered, and she felt her nipples tighten and press against the thin, insubstantial fabric of the robe, her aching flesh calling for his attention, his touch.

He tipped her chin up and she met his eyes, shocked by the stark hunger she saw in them—a hunger that reflected her own. "If I kiss you I won't stop," he said, his voice a rough whisper. "Not until you're naked beneath me, crying out my name."

She licked her lips. He remained still, his uncompromising gaze locked on hers. He was putting her in control, making her take the final step. She couldn't refuse him.

Not again. She didn't have the willpower or the desire to walk away from him.

"Marco." She hoped he didn't notice the tremor in her voice. "Kiss me. Now."

And then his mouth was on hers, hot, hungry and consuming. He pulled her into his body, pressing his insistent arousal against her center. She moved her hips reflexively, and gasped at the sensations that radiated through her.

He parted her lips and thrust his tongue deep into the recesses of her mouth. She let her tongue glide against his, the friction nearly buckling her knees. She had never been kissed like this, so deeply and passionately. The ember that had been smoldering low in her belly caught fire and burned through her, white heat streaking through her veins. Every nerve ending, every cell, was on high alert. Every feeling was magnified. Desire had become something wild and uncontrollable. Want had become need, desperate and as necessary as her next breath.

Marco moved his hand to her waist and the flimsy robe slipped from her body, leaving her totally exposed to the cool night air and to him. He drew back for a moment, taking in the sight of her body. She wanted to cover herself, but fought the urge. She'd never been naked in front of a man before, and she was overwhelmed by a surge of self-consciousness, but she didn't want to look like the gauche virgin that she was. She wasn't about to confess to that. Not now. Not with him. He would probably laugh at her, if he believed her at all. She closed her hands into fists and managed to keep them at her sides.

"You are such a beautiful woman." He stroked her aching nipple with one callus-roughened thumb and she gasped at the exquisite sensation that arrowed from her breast to her core.

A broken cry escaped her lips, and any thoughts of modesty flew from her mind. She moved to embrace him again, pressing her naked body against him, not caring that he was still fully clothed. He gripped her rear end and drew her tightly into him. The buttons of his shirt teased her breasts, his belt buckle, and beneath that his cloth-covered erection, pressed into her belly. This time her knees did give way. Only his firm grasp kept her from melting into a puddle at his feet.

He locked his lips over hers again and smoothed his hands up her body, skimming them lightly over her curves. She was beginning to feel lightheaded. Tension was coiling in her pelvis, so tight it was nearly unbearable. He cupped her breasts with his hands, rolling his thumbs over their taut peaks. The muscles at her feminine core pulsed and she gasped into his mouth.

He removed one of his hands and cursed. He drew away from her and she saw that he'd been reaching for his wallet.

"What?" she asked. Her body was so tense, so needy. She needed his hands again, his mouth.

"I don't have a condom," he said simply.

She laughed weakly, not quite able to believe she was having this conversation with him. "The hotel has an excellent concierge."

He groaned. "It will take far too long. I need you now, *cara mia*."

A thrill of feminine power shot through her. His need was the same as hers. He felt just as desperate and aching and close to the edge.

"I'm on the pill," she blurted, silently thanking the doctor who had suggested she start taking birth control to regulate her cycle.

He looked at her for a moment, his expression implacable. "I'm healthy. I always use condoms. Even when the woman is on some other form of birth control."

"I'm healthy," she promised. On that point she was certain.

And then she was back in his arms, his kisses fierce and possessive. She began to undo the buttons on his crisp white dress shirt with shaking fingers, her heart thundering in her ears. When the shirt fluttered to the floor all she could do was stare dumbly in admiration at the perfection that she had uncovered.

"I want to touch you," she said.

He chuckled. "Be my guest."

His breath came out in a hiss when her cool hands came into contact with his hot, sweat-slicked skin. She could feel his heart pounding heavily beneath her palm, the erratic rhythm mirroring her own. She let her hands roam over his lightly hair-roughened pectoral muscles and down his washboard flat abs, reveling in the hardness and heat that radiated from his gorgeous body. She trailed a finger down the line of hair that disappeared beneath the waistband of his pants.

He sucked in a breath and gripped her wrist, halting her exploration. "I think it's time to find a bed," he ground out.

"I thought you were accustomed to making do with the floor." She didn't recognize the husky, sultry voice that came out of her mouth.

"Minx." He lifted her off her feet and into his arms, taking long strides into the house.

"Caveman," she said, breathless.

He crossed the large villa quickly, his heavy footfalls echoing the pounding of her heart.

"You bring that out in me," he said, setting her on her feet in front of the canopied bed.

"I do?" she asked, her voice breaking as he pressed a kiss to the hollow of her throat.

"Yes. You make me feel dangerously uncivilized."

He kissed the valley between her breasts, and she couldn't have responded to his comment if she'd wanted to. Then he moved his head and took one straining peak into his mouth. She closed her eyes, stars dancing across her vision. Molten desire pooled hot in her belly and dampened her core.

Marco took her hands and placed them on his belt. With shaking fingers she undid the buckle and let it hang loosely. She looked at the outline of his bulging erection, pushing aggressively against his black pants and quickly undid the closure before nerves could overtake her arousal. She lowered the zipper and the back of her hand made contact with his hardened shaft. His body jerked, and he groaned in obvious pleasure.

Emboldened by his response, she encircled his heavy length through the thin fabric and squeezed gently. He closed his eyes and tilted his head back. "You're a dangerous woman."

She laughed shakily and started to work his pants down over his lean hips, taking his underwear with them. It suddenly seemed very important to see him, to get her first glimpse of a naked man, so she could assess exactly what she was dealing with.

The sight of his nude body took her breath away. He was beautiful. He was also very big—much bigger than she'd anticipated a man could be—and she had to wage a small battle with her nerves. She inhaled and wrapped her fingers around him. His skin was even hotter there, like a flame. She moved her hand over his velvety skin, exploring him, learning what he liked and what made him moan with pleasure.

"Enough teasing." He picked her up again and she

found herself lying flat on her back on the cool white comforter.

He drew a nipple into his mouth, sucking it, laving it with the flat of his tongue, before moving his attention to the other breast and repeating the act. Heat flared in her pelvis and all nervousness fled, pushed out by the intense longing that was pouring through her body in waves.

Marco pulled back and looked at her, his eyes glittering with passion. He let a finger drift up her inner thigh, coming close to her pulsing wet center. She shivered, anticipation of the unknown coupled with her intense arousal making the muscles in her legs quiver.

Testing her readiness, he slid the tip of one finger inside of her tight channel. She gasped, her hips bowing up off the bed. "Beautiful," he murmured.

He leaned down, spreading her thighs wide with his broad shoulders. Then he touched the sensitive bundle of nerves with his soft lips.

"Marco!" she pushed against him.

He chuckled and pulled her hands down, pinning them to the bed. He lowered his mouth again, sliding his tongue gently through her damp folds, sucking her moist clitoris. The tension in her pelvis tightened until she thought she would shatter into a million pieces if something didn't give.

He repeated the motion, penetrating her with his tongue, and the tension snapped. Pleasure rolled over her like a tidal wave, and for a moment there was nothing. Nothing but feelings so acute, so all consuming, that they overtook her completely, leaving her spent and breathless in the aftermath.

When she came back to herself Marco was above her, positioning himself at her slick entrance. Her orgasm had taken the edge off her need, but she was still unsatisfied.

She ached for him, for his possession. She cupped his tight buttocks with her hands and urged him forward.

He surged into her—and the pain blinded her for a moment, the tearing sting bringing tears to her eyes. She bit her lip to keep the scream that was building in her throat from escaping and lay rigid beneath him, trying to catch her breath.

"What the—?" He began to move away from her, but she gripped his hips, pulling him back to her.

"No. It's getting better. Just be still for a moment." She wrapped her feet around his calves, anchoring him to her.

Gradually the stinging subsided and gave way to a feeling of fullness that was exquisite beyond words. Arousal flared to life inside her again, all discomfort forgotten.

Marco remained still, the cords of his neck standing out, showing the effort it took for him to maintain self-control.

"Now," she begged.

Then he began to move. The sensation was so shattering, so amazing. She was lost in the steady rhythm of his thrusting. The fractured sounds of their breathing. She felt the muscles in her pelvis spasming. The feeling tightened more still, radiating down to her internal muscles. She was reaching for something—something that seemed much too high for her to grasp.

Then she found it. It was so deep, so all-consuming that she couldn't keep it all inside of her. She let out a hoarse cry as the pleasure rushed up and crashed over her like a wave. She gripped his shoulders, using him as an anchor, as her release went on and on, until finally she was left spent and breathless, floating in the swirling surf.

Marco stiffened above her and pushed himself firmly against her, freezing for a moment while he gave himself up to his own orgasm. He collapsed on top of her and held her close, his accelerated heartbeat reverberating through her, matching the beat of her own.

She brushed a lock of hair out of his eye and traced the features of his face lightly with her fingers. He had shown her a side of herself she hadn't believed existed; he had made her more than she had been.

It was impossible in that moment to shut off the emotion that washed through her. Her heart was full and she felt tears begin to slide down her cheeks. She didn't want to guess at why she felt whole with Marco joined to her... why she felt she might break when he withdrew.

In that moment she was very much afraid that she *was* the naïve fool she'd promised herself she would never become.

CHAPTER EIGHT

MARCO rolled onto his back, his breathing labored, his blood roaring in his ears. His whole body was still on fire from what had been simply the most amazing sexual experience of his life. And the most reckless, stupid act he'd ever committed.

He'd had sex with her without a condom, taking her word for it that she was on birth control. She'd been a virgin. A *virgin*.

He'd never so much as kissed an innocent, and now he'd taken one to bed and initiated her none too gently. He was torn between immense guilt at the realization that he'd taken her virginity, and a building rage at the thought that she might have contrived to trap him.

He turned and looked at the woman lying in bed with him. Tears were rolling down her pink cheeks, her bottom lip, swollen and red from his violent kisses, was trembling. His gut twisted, and guilt overrode the anger.

"Did I hurt you?" he asked, catching a tear with his thumb.

She shook her head and then grimaced. "Well, it didn't hurt for too long."

"Why didn't you tell me that you were a virgin?"

She grimaced at the word. "I didn't think it would matter. I kind of hoped you wouldn't notice, actually. And anyway, you wouldn't have believed me."

"You don't know that." He knew she was right. He would never have believed her. He would have thought it a ploy of some kind—just another tactic to get him to drop his guard and do something stupid and irresponsible. Of course even without her admission he'd managed to be stupid and irresponsible.

A few more tears slid down her cheeks.

"I *did* hurt you," he said.

"No." She swiped at the moisture on her face. "I don't know why I'm crying. I really don't. I'm not normally a crier."

"A woman's first time is very emotional."

Her face pinked. "Are you very experienced in the matter?"

"I can only claim this single experience."

Something that looked like relief flashed in her tearful blue eyes. He'd meant to ask her about her birth control pills, about whether or not they really existed, but he couldn't bring himself to interrogate this new incarnation of Elaine, this vulnerable innocent with the wide, unguarded eyes.

She flushed scarlet and began to search the room visually, carefully avoiding his gaze.

He cupped her chin and turned her face to him gently. "Something you need?"

She blushed to the roots of her blond hair. "I don't have any clothes in here."

He chuckled. "I've seen and tasted every inch of you, *cara mia.* Your modesty is too little, too late."

"Well, that was different. We were…and now we're…"

She pulled hard on the sheets and coiled them around her curvy body, before sliding out from beneath the white duvet and standing up.

"Where are you going?"

Her flush intensified. The spot on her chest where his beard had abraded her delicate fair skin turned a deep mottled rose. "I was going to go get my birth control pills, and then I was going to go to sleep on the couch."

That answered his question about the pills. "You're not sleeping in another room."

"I didn't think that men liked to talk…you know… after…"

"Come back to bed, Elaine. After you get your pills, of course."

She scurried off, her steps restricted by the tightly wrapped sheet.

The woman made absolutely no sense to him. She didn't come across as being naïve or sheltered in any way, and she was extraordinarily beautiful. That she had come to his bed without experience just added another piece to her personal puzzle. He prided himself on being able to read people. Business was about more than numbers: it was about gut feeling, it was about intuition. With Elaine his intuition seemed to be on vacation. He was no closer to figuring her out, or her motives, than when she'd first walked into his office with her outrageous proposal.

She came back into the room, her face pink and fresh-scrubbed, her luscious body wrapped in the silk robe they'd discarded on the porch, the sheet draped over her arm.

"See—I wasn't lying." She waved a small pill packet. "I wouldn't risk the company like that." She placed the pills on the nightstand and stood with her arms wrapped around herself. She looked so young and innocent. Some long-ignored protective instinct had him rising from his position and reaching out to her, drawing her down onto the bed.

"So why did you suddenly decide to go to bed with me? Obviously you've made it a point to save yourself."

She shrugged. "Not really. It's like you said—desire and satisfaction. It's not very complicated." A shuddering breath shook her small shoulders. "I've never really wanted to be with anyone like that, and I didn't see the point of taking the step if it wasn't something I really wanted to do." She hesitated for a moment, and then turned onto her side so that she was facing him. "There was one guy that I thought I might… Well, anyway, when I told him I wasn't ready he seemed okay with it. Then the next day at work I found out he was telling everyone I was off-limits to all the guys in the office because I was the boss's plaything." She gave him a pointed look. "I know you've heard the story. Anyway, I haven't been that inspired to try my hand at relationships again."

Her words held a ring of truth to them, and they sent a sharp pain through his chest. The image of a young, naïve Elaine being dragged through the mud by world-weary cynics, her heart broken, her reputation left in tatters, affected him far more than he was prepared for. He didn't want to be a part of that—part of the ugly world that had stolen her innocence in so many ways. But he *was* a part of it. They had stolen her idealism, her emotional innocence, and he had taken that last piece—her physical innocence—for himself. He wouldn't use it against her, but he had nothing to offer her either.

"This isn't going to be a relationship in any sort of permanent sense. That's not how I do things." He despised the bluntness of his words, but he would not give her time to entertain fantasies of a future for the two of them. That was one reason he'd so carefully avoided women with no experience. They thought of love and sex as two things inextricably linked, and he honestly didn't have any of that kind of love available.

She straightened her spine, her blue eyes emotionless. "I know that. And I don't really want a relationship either."

Once again the woman managed to surprise him. She never said or did what he expected her to do. He'd expected her to be clinging to him and asking him about his feelings, but instead she'd been cool, almost aloof, since returning to the bedroom.

"Then what is it you want?"

Her face turned a deep crimson. Now he knew that the blushing wasn't an act. She'd blushed like a virgin because that was exactly what she had been.

"The company," she said, her chin set stubbornly.

"I meant what is it you want from me?" A slow smile curved his lips. "What are your terms and conditions?"

Elaine didn't know how to have a conversation with a naked man. It was difficult to concentrate on words when they were so close, with him naked and her clad only in the thin, barely there robe. All she wanted to do was lean in and kiss his lips, run her hands over his bare skin, feel him filling her again, bringing her the ultimate release. Harder still to tell him what she wanted when she had no idea *what* it was that she wanted or expected.

Could she honestly have a no-strings physical relationship with him?

Yes! her body screamed enthusiastically.

Yes. Her mind confirmed it. When things went back to normal, when Marco was out of her life and she had assumed her position as owner and CEO of Chapman Electronics, her life would be even more consumed by work than it already was. She would never find the time for a relationship. She had to take this, now, while she had the chance.

And when it was over she would always have the sweetest memories of what it was to be held in Marco's arms. She honestly couldn't imagine ever being with another man, sharing the intimacies that she had shared with Marco. Perhaps it was her inexperience, but she really felt repulsed by the idea of another man touching her. That was why she had to seize the moment. Men did it all the time—satisfied physical needs with no feelings involved. Why shouldn't she do it for herself?

"Twelve months. The physical relationship lasts for the duration of the marriage. Neither of us will be unfaithful, and at the end both parties go away with what we agreed upon," she said, shocked by the steadiness of her voice.

He gave her a wicked grin that made her breasts heavy and caused a pulse to start pounding at the apex of her thighs. "A business deal, Ms. Chapman?"

"Is there any other kind, Mr. De Luca?" Far from being steady, her voice was now quivering again, this time at the lascivious intent that was written all over Marco's face.

He wrapped an arm around her waist and pulled the sheet away, revealing her body to him. "I think it's safe to say we're officially mixing business with pleasure." He rubbed the pad of his thumb over one aching nipple and she felt herself melting into him, ready and willing for whatever he wanted to do to her.

His lips closed over hers and conscious thought became difficult. Her heart was thudding heavily, and new, strange emotions were swelling in her chest. She felt her eyes growing wet with tears again. If she could keep this purely physical, if she could stop herself from feeling, then everything would be all right. She could indulge in her craving for Marco and come away unchanged.

The thought of leaving him sent a ripple of pain through her body that matched the pleasure being delivered by his skilled hands. And then all thought became impossible as she was pulled down into the swirling undertow of sensation.

"Good morning." The sound of a husky male voice pulled Elaine from her comatose sleep. Gradually her senses returned to her. There was a large masculine hand splayed across her belly, and she could feel…oh…she could feel Marco's erection pressed against her backside.

The events from the night before came flooding back to her with brutal clarity. She'd slept with Marco. He knew she'd been a twenty-four-year-old virgin. She had agreed to a twelve-month sex only relationship.

She had officially lost her mind.

His hand drifted up and began toying gently with her nipples. She moaned. Yes. She'd lost her mind. And if he kept touching her like that it was going to be lost to her forever.

"Good morning." She tried to squirm out of his hold, away from him and back into a realm where critical thinking was possible, but that only brought her into more forceful contact with his burgeoning hardness. The twitch of his member and the accompanying moan of pleasure sent a shockwave of longing all the way down to her core. She wasn't going to find her sanity anytime soon.

"No need for you to get up. Breakfast will be delivered in a few minutes."

She increased her struggle to get free. "I'm not getting caught naked in your bed!"

"We're newlyweds," he said innocently. "Where else would they expect to find you?"

He rolled over and pinned her on her back, his smile playful. He raised her hands above her head and held them, effectively trapping her. It should have made her angry. It really shouldn't have turned her on. He brought his mouth down and kissed her deeply, passionately. He pushed one hair-roughened thigh between hers and she voluntarily let her legs fall open.

The intercom buzzed and Marco moved away from her. "I don't mind getting caught in bed with you, but I don't relish being found in the middle of lovemaking." His smile turned rueful. "I lose my control with you, *cara*." He looked utterly mystified by the thought.

She couldn't stop herself from openly admiring his naked body as he strode across the room and picked a pair of well-worn denim jeans from the closet. She watched him slide them up his legs and over his tight rear end. Knowing he wasn't wearing underwear was going to kill her at some point today.

She'd assumed that making love with Marco might take the edge off her desire. She'd been very wrong. Now that she knew what he could make her feel, now that she knew that every promise his sensual lips made, all the dark sexuality his lithe body proclaimed, was understated when compared to the fulfilled promise, she could think of nothing else but tasting him again.

Now that she'd discovered sex, she wondered how in the world people got anything done. That was why, she reasoned, people were so obnoxiously cheerful and scatterbrained at the beginning of an affair. Because good sex scrambled your thoughts and plastered a goofy grin on your face you couldn't erase.

She looked at her reflection in the vanity mirror that was positioned across the room. She definitely had the goofy grin. Her skin was red from the scrape of his whiskers against her delicate face and throat. She knew that if she examined her inner thighs she'd find the same sort of burns. *That* made her blush to the roots of her hair.

She slipped out of the bed and contemplated taking a chance on going to the bathroom to find her suitcase. She hadn't unpacked yesterday. She'd been resigned to sleeping on the couch, and the idea of hanging her clothing in the same closet as Marco's had seemed like an intimacy too far. Which was just about laughable at this point, since there weren't any physical intimacies left—not any that *she* knew about—that she hadn't shared with Marco the night before.

Marco walked back into the room at that moment, shirtless and carrying a tray laden with pastries, fruit and meat. He was every woman's fantasy.

She leaned over and snatched up the sheet in a belated attempt to cover herself.

He laughed and shook his head before setting the tray down on the foot of the bed. He gripped the edge of the sheet and unwound it, leaving her exposed again. He pressed a soft kiss to her lips that left her knees weak.

"No need for you to cover up. I much prefer you naked." He brushed a swath of blond hair out of her face. "You look so much softer."

She looked pointedly at the hard cut of the muscles on his torso. "I can't say the same."

"Yes, but that's one of the many wonderful things that are different about men and women. Our differences complement each other."

A small smile tugged at her lips. "I hadn't thought of it that way before."

"Hungry?" he asked, sitting on the bed and gesturing to the tray.

"Starving." She joined him on the bed, still undressed, wondering where the fleeting moment of sanity she'd had when she'd woken up had gone off to. She felt that silly grin spread across her face again as she looked at the handsome face of her lover. *Her lover.* The grin widened and she knew she looked like the cat that had gotten into the cream and licked the bowl clean. "What's on the menu?"

"Guava, French toast and fresh fruit. And I think that's Spam." He gestured to the pink square slices of meat that were fanned out on the silver tray.

"You're kidding?"

"It's a local favorite."

"I'll pass." She reached over and picked up a slice of mango.

It felt ridiculously decadent, sitting on the bed with him and sharing a tray, eating with their fingers. When he slipped a bite of guava between her lips and lapped up the juices that dribbled down her chin, the entire breakfast, and any resolve she might have hoped to claim, disintegrated.

After they'd made love they went to separate showers to prepare for the day. Marco had tried to cajole her into his, but she knew that she would give in to the temptation of his naked body and they would end up cloistered in the villa all day. Her body was more than willing to take that option, but she felt she needed to get a grip on the situation, and she wouldn't be doing that if she kept allowing Marco to turn her brain to mush with his expert hands and mouth.

She rummaged through her suitcase and found a pair of white linen shorts and a spring green halter-top made of a slithery, silky material that felt decadent against her bare skin. She had never been so aware of her body before last night, before Marco had shown her what it meant to be a woman. She found she didn't want to blend in with the boys anymore. She wanted to celebrate her femininity, embrace the power of it.

Giddiness fizzed in her veins as she quickly tied back her wavy hair and walked out into the main living area of the villa. "So, what's on the agenda?" she asked.

Marco looked up, and was momentarily frozen by the pang of lust that hit him square in the gut and the swelling of emotion that tightened his chest. She looked so young, so vibrantly beautiful. All of her haughty, don't-touch-me demeanor had faded, giving way to a soft, well-loved expression. She looked like a thoroughly satisfied woman, and he couldn't help but glory like a caveman over the fact that he'd been the man, the *only* man, to make her feel that way. He had brought her to the pinnacle of pleasure and caught her as she fell. He had been the only man to kiss her lush breasts, to join his body to hers. The novelty of it was extraordinary. No, he wouldn't even call it a novelty; it was much more than that.

He still had no idea what her game was—if there *was* a game. For the first time he considered that she might be everything she claimed to be. That she wanted her father's company out of a sense of pride and fairness—that she'd entered into their marriage with all her cards laid out on the table. That she had slept with him because she desired him. It hardly made sense, but then it had never mattered one way or the other to him if he understood the inner workings of his mistress's minds. He enjoyed their bodies, but as for their shallow dreams and desires he couldn't have cared less.

Elaine should be no different. She was his wife—*that* was different—but the marriage was nothing more than a business contract. Their proposed affair was an entirely different matter. It was strictly physical, and if Elaine had designs on making the arrangement permanent, or on scamming him out of his vast fortune, she was sadly out of luck. He wasn't the type of man to be bewitched by sex, even if it was fantastic sex. His emotions and his mind always stayed separate. There was absolutely no way Elaine could ensnare him.

"Business." He flashed her a grin and was gratified to see her cheeks turn rosy pink. She still blushed like an innocent, and in spite of himself he found he enjoyed it fully. "I have a meeting with James to discuss my business plan for the resort."

The look of undisguised longing in her eyes—not when she looked at him, but when he mentioned a business meeting—nearly made him laugh. "Would you like to join us, Elaine?"

A sparkle caught in her blue eyes, and he tried to ignore the surge of satisfaction her happiness gave him. "Well, if you wouldn't mind…"

"It's in the bag," Elaine said confidently as they left James's office later that afternoon.

Marco took in her confident smirk with great amusement. "You think so?"

She nodded vigorously, freeing tendrils of hair from her ponytail and bringing them down to frame her face. "Your figures were astounding, not to mention accurate. From what you said in the meeting I can see that your plans will up the revenue by thirteen percent in just two years."

"That's a more generous figure than I had calculated."

"Oh, good—then you hadn't thought of this," she said, almost gleefully. "The very new upscale nightclub you're planning to build on the property can bring in profit from patrons of other hotels and resorts. You don't have to open it to everyone, but making it more inclusive will certainly help it pay for the expense of building it and then some."

"It's definitely a thought."

"It's a good one."

She leaned into him, and the intoxicating scent of her assaulted his senses. He'd had her this morning but his body still felt deprived of her softness, of the fulfillment he'd experienced with her.

"You're very certain of yourself." He leaned in too, and pressed a kiss to her neck, enjoying the little shiver that racked her body.

"You should know that confidence is the key to success," she said breathlessly.

"I thought it was image."

A tortured groan escaped her lips. "I can't remember with you touching me like that!"

"Like this?" He kissed the curve of her neck again.

"Yes. Like that."

"I think it's time to go back to the villa."

"I agree."

The next few days passed in a kind of sensual haze. The sale of the resort was nearly finalized, and James had commanded that Marco take the weekend to romance his wife. In Elaine's opinion, he'd done a pretty good job of it. Breakfast in bed, intimate candlelit dinners, and of course amazing sex. She wouldn't let herself think of it as making love. It was too dangerous. Almost as dangerous as when Marco held her hand during a walk on the beach, or when he held her tenderly against his chest while they were in bed, his arms cradling her close to his body.

Monday morning she expected Marco would be back to business as usual, so it was a surprise when he exited the bathroom wearing a pair of shorts and a threadbare T-shirt. "I thought we would spend the day together," he said. "Did my PA happen to buy you a pair of hiking boots?"

She tried, and failed, to quash the giddy sensations that were fluttering through her. For all she knew his taking time out of his busy schedule to spend with his mistresses was perfectly normal.

The term brought her up short. Was she his mistress? No. She most certainly wasn't. They were equals in their relationship. She wasn't dependent on him, and she certainly wasn't expecting to be a kept woman. She had a job, and her ambitions extended far beyond that.

"I don't think I have hiking boots. I have a pair of tennis shoes, though."

"That should be good enough. You don't get seasick, do you?"

"I have no idea."

His teeth flashed bright white against his tan skin and she felt her limbs go slack. "You're going to find out today."

A slim stream of white sand backed by thick foliage came into view. Elaine leaned over the railing of the small yacht to try and get a better view of their destination.

She inhaled the salt air and was thankful, again, that she apparently didn't suffer from seasickness. The yacht cut through the water like a hot knife through butter, the waves parting and giving deference to the bulk of the sleek ship, which virtually eliminated the feeling of being on water.

Marco walked up behind her and cocooned her in his

firm embrace. "This is the island of Kapu. It means forbidden, or taboo." The wicked words sent a shiver down her spine. "It's for sale, and I'm considering purchasing it and building a luxury villa on the grounds. It's the ultimate vacation rental. A private island."

"You're going to buy an island?" There was simply no pretending to be nonchalant over this extravagant show of wealth.

"It's a lovers' paradise. The fantasy of being the only two people on earth realized, with all of the modern luxuries you could ever want."

She could imagine it all too easily. She and Marco marooned on an island, with nothing more pressing to do than give each other pleasure. She bit back a moan. "So you're thinking of it as an extension of the resort?"

"In a sense. But it will be kept separate, in that only staff and invited guests will be allowed on it when it's in use."

"That sounds…decadent."

He chuckled—his hot breath warming her down to her toes, the sound of his laugh rumbling through her body.

"That's the idea."

It didn't take long for Marco and the small crew to bring the ship into the floating marina. He moved like a man who had been born at sea, his movements sure and swift, his deft fingers tying knots with ease.

"Did your family sail often?" she asked, keeping her eyes trained on the shifting muscles in his forearms as he worked.

He stopped and straightened, a shadow passing over his handsome face. "No." He crossed the deck and climbed up onto the ship's railing before dropping down onto the dock.

She moved to follow him and he stretched his arms up, preventing her from hitting the wooden planks with the force that he had done. "You just seem like a seasoned pro."

Marco never talked about his family, and up until that point she'd thought it might have been an oversight. She should have realized that Marco didn't commit oversights. His avoidance of the subject was very purposeful, and if he didn't want to share the reasons there would be no persuading him. She had been right when she'd guessed that he wasn't a pillow-talker. He wasn't that much of a talker full-stop—not about anything personal—which had suited her fine since she didn't exactly want to rehash *her* disaster of a childhood either. But now it didn't seem enough to limit conversation to the weather and the stock market. She wanted more. And that was very, very dangerous.

"I bought my first boat when I was nineteen. Sailed it from Puerto Vallarta to San Diego and then had it transported across the country. Money was no object," he said ruefully. "I enjoyed it very much."

She could just imagine him on board a sleek white yacht, with women in scanty bikinis draped across the deck…and across Marco. Unbidden, a flame lit in the pit of her stomach. She knew Marco had an unfathomable amount of experience compared to her, and generally she could let it go, but she would be a liar if she claimed it didn't bother her. The thought of other women touching him made her stomach churn.

"I sold it a few years ago," he continued, "because I no longer had the time to take extended boating excursions."

"Cut into your social life?" she snapped, the image of beach beauties pawing at him still at the forefront of her mind.

He gave her a withering glare. "I don't sleep with every woman I'm photographed with."

She tried to look casual at his admission. "Oh?"

"I think you are jealous, *cara mia*." He looked very entertained by the notion. And, worse still, he was right.

"And my being with other men wouldn't bother *you*?"

He stepped nearer to her and claimed her mouth in a fiery kiss. When they parted their breathing was labored, their heartbeats erratic and audible in the near silence that surrounded them. "They would not live to taste your sweet lips. I would not allow it."

She tried to think of a tart comeback, something pertaining to his origins in the Neolithic era, but every fiber of her being was too busy basking in the pure pleasure of knowing that Marco wanted her and wanted no one else to have her, that he felt possessive of her in the same way she felt possessive of him.

Forsaking all others.

She quickly shook off the remembered snippet of her wedding vows and followed Marco from the dock to the pristine white sand beach. There were no footprints to mar its natural beauty, only gentle, sloping waves caused by the coastal winds.

"I'm told that back in the jungle there's a natural waterfall, if you're up for a walk."

"Most definitely," she said, keeping pace with him as he walked into the thick trees.

To think that only a week ago she'd been sitting in her gray cubicle, crunching numbers. It seemed another lifetime away. She could hardly reconcile the two points of her existence, and yet they were both real.

They moved through the sun-dappled undergrowth, vines reaching out and grabbing them around the ankles every so often. "We need a machete," she grumbled as she tripped over a wayward root.

He turned and quirked a grin at her. "Just a little bit farther. I can hear the water running."

They followed the sound until the treeline ended and

they were standing in a grassy clearing. A waterfall was spilling down a lava rock formation and into a clear pool of deep water.

Marco came to stand beside her, his arm wrapped around her waist, the heat of his body seeping through her clothes, warming her from the inside out.

"This almost doesn't seem real," she breathed. "It's like a fantasy." And she didn't only mean the scene; the man was included as well.

"Do you think it will appeal to those seeking a romantic hideaway?"

"I'd say it's absolutely perfect."

"Want to test the water out?"

She eyed him skeptically. "I thought we were here for business."

Marco felt himself grow hard as he thought about getting her in the water, her body slick, her nipples beaded tight from the coolness of the natural pool.

"We're here to test out the facilities," he said sagely. "I never buy a car without test driving it first. I'm not going to buy an island without sampling some of its attractions."

An impish grin lit her face and she untied the flimsy strings of her halter-top. The close-fitting top had been tormenting him all morning. She pulled the silky shirt over her head and revealed a skimpy electric-blue bikini that barely concealed the fullness of her curves. Her nipples were hard and pressing tightly against the Lycra. He ached to touch her, taste her, to lave his tongue over the small raspberry buds until she cried out for fulfillment.

"See something you like?" she asked.

"I don't know. Keep going."

She rolled her eyes at him and pushed the khaki shorts she was wearing down her long, shapely legs. The bottom to the bikini was just as tiny and insubstantial as the top, the tight blue fabric hugging the round curve of her bottom and revealing hints of peachy flesh.

Her irises expanded, obscuring the color in her eyes, as her body responded to his blatant appraisal of her. "Your turn," she said, her voice taking on the husky quality that he knew signaled her arousal.

She watched as he stripped down to his swim-trunks, her eyes roaming over him with unconcealed desire. She was an anomaly when compared to any of the other women he'd known. She didn't lower her lashes coyly, but neither was her look one of bold invitation. There was nothing contrived in her response. She had such total honesty in her desire. She wanted him, and she did nothing to hide that fact from him, but neither did she strut around like a cat in heat to try and gain his attention.

The pure need in her soft blue eyes was his undoing every time. He hooked his arm around her waist and drew her into his body. Shy excitement lit her face. It amazed him every time she blushed. A surge of emotion caught him off guard, and despite being on solid ground he had the strangest sensation of being unsteady.

He gripped her tightly and took two big steps to the edge of the water before jumping in and submerging them both in the aquamarine depths.

She came up sputtering, her blond hair plastered to her face. She moved the curtain of hair aside and gave him her best evil eye. His charming grin undid her, and all her pique was forgotten. She registered the heat of his skin, warming her in the cool water, the strength of his body as he held her locked against his hard, muscular chest. If she'd been standing her knees would have buckled.

She slithered out of his grasp, submerging herself again,

and swam to the waterfall, aware that he was following behind her, feeling a primitive feminine thrill over being pursued. She climbed up onto a rock that rose out of the pool at the base of the waterfall and sat down on the moss-carpeted surface, curling her legs beneath her.

Marco hoisted himself from the water and onto the rock with ease, his muscles bunching and shifting beneath his tan skin. Slick moisture pooled at the apex of her thighs, but it had nothing to do with the waterfall and everything to do with the supremely gorgeous man who was moving toward her, his dark eyes blazing with intent.

"Pouting?" he asked, trailing his finger along the line of her collarbone.

The contact was almost innocent, yet it made her thoughts turn wanton and wicked.

"Yes, well, you got me wet."

His eyes flickered. "Careful, a man could let that go to his head."

He moved his finger, dipping in the valley between her breasts. She gasped. "Is it always about sex with you?"

"Not always. But when I'm with you that seems to be the subject more often than not." He cupped her breasts, teasing the straining peaks with the pads of his fingers. She shuddered.

She flicked a glance at the dense jungle, looking for any signs of movement in the thick growth of plants. "Marco, we're right out in the open." She couldn't summon enough conviction to give her scolding any weight.

"It's a private island. And the crew is still aboard the yacht."

He leaned in and pressed a kiss to the curve of her neck. Her body went slack, leaning into his, surrendering to the feelings he aroused in her so effortlessly.

He untied the strings on her daring bikini, the one that she'd vowed never to wear on her first inspection of her new wardrobe, and left her bare to his hungry gaze.

He groaned. "You're so gorgeous." He moved his thumb over her tight nipple and she squirmed. She wondered if anyone had ever died from longing, from wanting a man so much it took the breath right from her body.

He moved his hand beneath the falls and let water pool in his palm. Then he brought his hand to her and tilted it slightly over her, let the water trickle slowly over her flesh, so it trailed down the dips and swells of her body, over her already aching breasts. The contrast of concentrated drops of cool water on her overheated skin made her gasp. It also wrenched her arousal up another untenable notch.

She reached behind her head, feeling for something to grip, something to keep her rooted to the earth. She found a fern frond and grasped it in her hands, holding it so tightly that the leaves bit into her palms.

He gathered more water in his hand, tormenting her again with the sharp chill as he let it fall in beads over her bare breasts, this time lapping up the drops with his tongue. She arched into him, begging him silently to possess her, to fill her and take them both to the heights they so desperately craved.

He leaned in and drew her nipple into his hot, moist mouth, and she let out a shocked cry that was swallowed up by the roaring of the water. She released her hold on the plant and gripped the back of Marco's head, holding him to her, needing him to stop for fear that she would shatter, needing him to go on forever, needing to keep experiencing the wicked sensations that were coursing through her body.

He escaped her hold and untied the flimsy bikini

bottoms, his dark eyes turning black with the force of his desire as he looked at her naked body.

"I'm at a disadvantage," she said. She was almost shocked by her growing boldness as she gripped his aroused length through the thin fabric of his swim-shorts. She squeezed him, loving the look of surrender that passed over his handsome face.

She put a hand in the center of his chest and gently shoved him back, moving his shoulders beneath the cascading water. She moved her hands over his bare chest, sliding her fingertips over his slick bare skin.

She hooked her fingers into his shorts and pulled them down his legs, smoothing her hands up his muscled thighs, skimming the area around his erection. His shaft jerked at the near contact and she thrilled at his response. She would never, ever get enough of his body. She would never tire of looking at him. He was the perfect example of what a man should be. Hard, hot, rough and smooth.

She leaned over and took the tip of him into her mouth. He gripped her hair, weaving his fingers into the wet strands. She didn't know if he meant to pull her away or keep her there, but when she slid her lips down over his full length his hand froze, his grip tightening, whatever his original intention had been lost.

She pleasured him that way until his thighs began to quiver beneath her hands, and then he pulled her away, bringing her up the length of his body and taking her mouth in a fierce, deep kiss. When he broke the kiss his breathing was labored, his eyes dark with intensity.

"Was that okay?" she asked.

"Okay?" A strained chuckle escaped his lips. "Any more and this would have been over before it started."

He settled her onto his lap, so that she was straddling

them. The water was showering them both, but doing nothing to cool their mutual desire. He lifted her and settled her onto his erection, gently sliding into her damp core, stretching her, filling her.

He cursed, and she cut him off by pressing her lips to his, absorbing his masculine groan of ecstasy as she began to move.

She rode him, their eyes locked, their breathing fractured. She felt the onset of her climax, but it felt like too much too soon, as though her body couldn't possibly contain it. He moved his hand between them and rubbed her clitoris. She shattered. She screamed, not caring if anyone heard, not mindful of anything but the intense, pulsing sensation that was centered at her apex of her thighs and radiating out through her whole body, filling her so completely that she thought she might burst with it.

Marco thrust hard into her one last time and followed her over the edge, his harsh groan of completion shifting something inside her chest.

He rested his head against her breasts, his arms holding her tightly to him. She cradled his head, holding him to her, craving his closeness to a degree that frightened her.

She had been foolish to believe that she could conduct this affair as if it was business. She would never be free of him after this. He was part of her, in her. He'd changed her.

She had done exactly what she'd been so determined not to do—what she'd thought she would be incapable of doing. She'd committed the unpardonable sin. She had fallen in love with her husband.

CHAPTER NINE

"YOU'RE in the mood for Spam this morning?" Marco asked incredulously.

Elaine swallowed the bite she'd been working on and shrugged. "It looked good. Very salty," she said, taking another bite and relishing the flavor. She'd declined the local favorite every other morning during their breakfast in bed sessions, but this morning it had looked mouth wateringly amazing.

They'd been in Hawaii for nearly a month. The sale of the resort had been finalized, and Marco had been working on negotiating a deal for the island of Kapu. Her face, and other parts of her, heated as she thought of the afternoon they'd shared on the forbidden island, making love beneath the waterfall.

The days since then, since the realization that she loved him, had been a sweet kind of torture. On the one hand she felt more alive, more inspired than ever before. She felt things more deeply; her mind was more attuned to the things around her. On the other hand it nearly broke her heart every time she looked at his impossibly gorgeous face and realized that their relationship had a timer ticking on it.

She looked at the plate in front of her and was shocked

to see that she'd polished off more than her share of their breakfast. She gave him a sheepish grin. "I guess I was hungry."

Marco dropped a kiss on her nose and a strange, hot, melting sensation flowed through her body, weakening her limbs. "Sex burns a lot of calories. At least if you do it right. Which we most definitely do."

In spite of the fact that she'd shared every intimacy with him, she blushed. "I can't argue with you." She reached for the remaining piece of meat on their shared plate.

"Plans for the day?" he asked.

Because their "honeymoon" had gone on for so long, she'd been working remotely, doing the accounting for her firm, and she'd continued to actively work on her own business plan.

"No. I finished approving payroll last night while you were at your meeting."

"Excellent. I have to meet with Mr. Naruto briefly this morning, to discuss a final price for Kapu, but after that we can spend the day together."

A sweet feeling of absolute contentment stole over her, leaving her fuzzy. If she could pause everything right then, and just live in this stolen piece of time, she thought at that moment that she would. And that desire frightened her a lot less than it should.

"I might head into town for some supplies," she said.

"You could have the concierge send over whatever you need."

"I know, but then what else am I going to do? I'm not comfortable lying back and being served—especially not when I'm more than capable of going to a grocery store."

Marco could only stare at her determined face. Not a

single one of his ex-mistresses would have opted to run menial errands when they could have been sunbathing or shopping for a designer wardrobe.

His chest tightened. He didn't want to admit that Elaine was in any way different from his other mistresses. He didn't want to admit that she was touching him, thawing some of the hardened, ice-encrusted edges of his heart.

He clenched his fist and turned away from the woman on the bed. She was a hundred times more deadly than the air-headed gold-diggers he'd dated in the past. Because Elaine Chapman's beauty was mixed with a keen mind and a driving ambition that nearly matched his own. The connections their marriage could afford her were limitless. A merger with his corporation once she was at the helm of Chapman Electronics would be priceless. She had to know those things, and while it was easy for him to drop his guard when they were together, when she was offering to do down-to-earth things like grocery shopping it was of the utmost importance for him to remember that her highest goal was power.

Her brand of potent, innocent sexuality made it easy to forget to remain on his guard. But he had to wonder if she was using her innocence to her advantage as well. She was a smart woman, and she certainly wasn't ignorant of the way men viewed a woman's virginity. Perhaps it had seemed advantageous for her to give it to him, for her to use it to make him feel bonded to her? And he'd been allowing her to do that—allowing her to meld herself into his life.

Callous as it sounded, he didn't typically share a room with his women if a trip were going to last so long. He valued his space, his privacy, far too much, and he certainly didn't want to give a woman the wrong idea. But he had dropped his guard with Elaine, and it was a mistake he couldn't continue making.

Marco strode across the room and began to dress. Elaine had seen the shutters come down over his dark eyes, but she couldn't for the life of her figure out what had caused it.

Shrugging off the chill, she rose from the bed and chose her clothing before going into the bathroom to shower. When she surfaced, Marco was gone. His not saying goodbye hurt far worse than she should allow it to.

PMS. That was her excuse for being such an emotional wreck. She'd taken her first blank pill last night, and she was due to start her period any moment. Her body ran like clockwork, thanks to the miracle of her birth control pills, and she no longer had to deal with debilitating cramps and a cycle that ran on a timetable all its own.

She went to the bathroom to prepare for the impending event and was brought up short by the fact that she hadn't started yet. Not even spotting. She placed a hand on her abdomen, expecting at least a slight ache—something to signal the arrival of her period. There was nothing.

With shaking hands she put the necessary items in her purse and made her way out of the villa. She would start soon. Any moment. She had to. Because if she didn't that meant she'd broken a binding part of their agreement.

She slid behind the wheel of the car and tried to ignore the pounding of her pulse. She wasn't pregnant. There was no way. She was on the pill.

The refrain repeated in her mind as she drove the car down the winding road and into town, stopping at the nearest department store.

No way. Not pregnant.

She made a pitstop in the restroom, hoping that nature would grant her a definitive sign that she had not conceived Marco's baby. Still nothing. But it was too early to panic.

Yes, her body had run like clockwork, nearly to the hour, for the last five years, but that didn't mean that there was a baby.

Not pregnant.

Numbly, she moved through the store and into the family planning aisle, pausing at a box of condoms that seemed to mock her with their promise of a ninety-nine percent success rate, and stopped finally in front of a wall of products she'd never looked at in her life. Pregnancy tests.

She placed her hand on her stomach, almost expecting it to be rounded. She began to shake as she examined the boxes. Digital readouts. Early results. Traditional lines. In the end she grabbed three different brands and hurried to checkout, trying to look as nonchalant as possible about buying potentially life-altering items.

With her bag gripped tightly to her chest, she raced out to the parking lot and into the car. She gripped the steering wheel, trying to still the tremors that were racking her body. She couldn't be pregnant. It was a coincidence that she happened to be late for the first time in her memory. After becoming sexually active. A coincidence.

That was what she told herself during the drive back to the hotel. That was what she told herself when she took all three tests and set them gingerly on the vanity top, too afraid to check the results.

Not pregnant, she begged silently.

Finally she stood and stared down at the tests. Two lines on the first test; the digital test proclaimed "pregnant" in stark black and white; two more bright pink lines stared up at her from the final test. There was no questioning the evidence.

Her knees buckled and she sat down on the toilet, gripping the edge of the countertop to keep herself up and conscious.

For one selfish moment all she could think was that her life was over. She'd lost the company—her driving force, the thing that she'd worked so tirelessly for. She'd signed the prenup, mentally shaking her head as she'd done so over the lunacy of even having to make such a deal when she knew there was no chance Marco would be getting close enough to her to make her pregnant.

A baby. She didn't know anything about babies. She didn't want one. She never had. Yet morally she felt she had no option other than to carry the child. Adoption was a possible solution…

Blinding pain, as real and severe as the shock and fear she'd felt upon reading the positive tests, assailed her as she imagined lying in a hospital bed, sweaty and exhausted from labor, handing a tiny squalling baby over to someone else. Never seeing the baby again.

She couldn't hold back the anguished cry that escaped her lips. She couldn't do that either.

She stumbled into the bedroom and sat on the edge of the bed, her eyes so dry they stung, the tears that would give her relief nowhere to be found.

That was how Marco found her an hour later.

"Did your shopping go well?" he asked.

She didn't respond. She only sat on the edge of bed, her knees folded up to her chest, looking smaller, more fragile than he'd ever seen her. She looked as if she was in shock, her lips chalky white, her eyes glassy.

"Are you all right?" He knelt down in front of the bed and gripped her hands. They were freezing. "Has someone hurt you?" Primitive male anger rushed up inside of him, and he felt capable of destroying whoever had dared lay a hand on her, capable of taking them apart piece by piece.

Her eyes snapped up to meet his. "No. I'm okay." She sounded as though she were trying to convince herself.

"Well, you don't look okay. You look like death warmed over."

A broken laugh escaped her lips. "Just what every woman loves to hear."

"You're avoiding the question," he said tersely, the gnawing fear in his gut making his voice harsher than he'd intended.

"I'm pregnant." Her bald statement fell flat in the heavy tropical air, leaving a thick silence in the room.

"You said you were on the pill." His voice held an air of deadly calm—much more terrifying than if he'd started shouting.

"I am. I haven't missed one. I don't know…I don't know how it happened." She looked up into his eyes. They were cold, flat. Somehow that was worse than the force of all of his rage. Yelling she could fight, but this dead silence, this calm, cold wave of anger, she didn't know what to do with.

"You don't know how it happened?"

"Marco, I swear I didn't plan it. Why would I? Legally I've lost the company now. I'm as shocked as you are. This isn't what I wanted!" she exploded.

His dark brows snapped together. "You don't want the baby?"

"No! I mean, I don't know. I haven't had any time to process this. It changes absolutely everything."

"You put on a very good show, *cara*. But you and I both know this only *benefits* you. Access to my power, my money, for far longer than the twelve months agreed. Child support. The prospect of our union becoming permanent. All things that would be very beneficial to you. Although legally, as you said, that means you forfeit the company. I can't imagine you being a very effective CEO with a baby on your hip."

"You honestly think I planned this? That I planned to conceive your baby?"

"You would hardly be the first woman to try and snare me by using pregnancy. You're simply the first one to succeed."

"How could I have possibly planned for this to happen? I was on the pill."

He waved a hand to silence her. "Perhaps. At the very least I think you planned to find a way to make our arrangement more beneficial to you. Whether you planned on using a baby to accomplish your goal, I don't know. But I've suspected that you had ulterior motives since the moment you stepped into my office proposing marriage."

His words cut through her like a knife. He had suspected her from the beginning? Had there ever been a moment when he'd trusted her? When he'd felt something for her? Anger rushed through her, rescuing her from the flood of tears that were threatening.

"If you suspected that I was nothing but a gold-digger, then what does that make you for conducting a relationship with me?"

"It was not a relationship. It was an arrangement," he spat. He turned away from her, shutting her out, his shoulders rigid, his back straight. "Out of curiosity, what was the going rate for your virginity? A price none of the other men were able to pay but one you thought you would be able to extract from me?" He walked out of the villa, his parting shot hanging in the air.

Violent nausea overwhelmed her and she leaped up from the bed and raced across the room, barely making it to the toilet before being sick. She leaned her head against the cool wood of the vanity and let the first of today's tears roll down her cheeks.

Marco breathed in the heavily perfumed air and nearly gagged on the floral scent. That woman, that *puttana*, had made a fool of him. She had made him feel something for her. And all the time, every single moment, she had plotting against him.

And now she was carrying his child. His *child*.

He had thought he could safeguard himself against anything she was planning, but this… In this she had won, because he would not abandon his child. He would not be an absentee parent. His child would be his focus. He would love him and care for him in a way his own parents had failed to do for him and his younger brother. In that he was absolutely determined.

And he would not let his child's mother leave him. His child would want for nothing, and that included both parents in the same household. And he knew how to ensure that that happened.

He strode back into the villa, his mind absolutely made up.

"Elaine."

She appeared in the doorway of the bathroom a moment later, her face white, a sheen of sweat on her brow. His heart clenched and he hardened it, shunning the tender feelings she still managed to rouse in him.

"There is only one way to solve this."

She put a hand over her stomach. "I'm not giving up the baby."

"I am not asking that of you. We will remain married. It is the only option."

Elation and horror vied for top position inside of Elaine. "What?"

"It is not what I would have chosen, but the simple fact is that I will not be a part-time father. Neither will I deprive a child of his mother. That leaves us with one option."

"Millions of people share custody of their children—"

He cut her off. "I will not be one of them. It is never in a child's best interest to be treated as though they are an incidental. My own parents could not be bothered. My father threw us out onto the street—my mother, my brother and myself—when I was just twelve. After a couple of years of scraping by and living in homeless shelters my mother met a wealthy man who did not want children, so she left us to fend for ourselves while she pursued a life of luxury. I will never let a child of mine go through life feeling so insignificant. I will never subject my own flesh and blood to that kind of indifference."

The charity for homeless children and Marco's passion for the cause, his reluctance to mention his family, suddenly made horrifying sense. He had been homeless. Not orphaned. Far worse than that. His parents had been alive and too absorbed in their own vacuous existence to worry about the survival of their children.

Her heart ached for the boy he'd been and the man he had become—a man who could not trust and did not believe in love. Yet how could she blame him? How could she even hold his reaction to her pregnancy against him when she knew what he'd had to endure at the hands of those who should have loved him more than they loved anyone or anything else? She felt his pain as though it were her own, and it destroyed the anger that had been growing inside her.

"If you agree to stay in the marriage I will have a new

contract drafted, guaranteeing you the ownership of Chapman Electronics plus a generous allowance."

She hadn't forgotten about the company, nor had her desire for it dissipated in any way, but she wouldn't stay in the marriage for that reason alone—not when the nature of their relationship had changed irrevocably; not when she knew what he thought of her. But knowing what she did now, about his childhood, about the way he had been forced to survive on his own, caring for his younger brother, she knew she could not deny him this chance to have a family, this chance to repair the things that had been broken in his life.

"I accept," she said, the ridiculously formal words sounding wrong for the situation.

He laughed cynically. "I had a feeling you would see it my way."

Her defense caught in her throat, stuck behind a lump of grief. Her heart felt broken—for him, for herself, for everything they'd shared together. Everything they'd lost.

They flew back to New York the next day. Marco was silent and avoiding her while burying his head in his work, and she was trying to do the same. She spent a good portion of the flight in the bathroom being sick. Her morning sickness, which did not see fit to limit its active hours to the morning, had hit with a vengeance once they'd hit the sky, and it hadn't let up.

When the plane touched down in the city she walked on wooden legs to the car that was waiting for them and slid inside. The drive back to the penthouse was as quiet as the miserable plane ride. Marco hated her. He had already tried her and found her guilty based on the past actions of those in his life.

Not that she could blame him. She knew what it was like

to be so shaped by past experience; to carry deeply etched scars inside yourself that were not visible to the naked eye.

Her own life had been one desperate attempt at separating herself from her father's perception of her, from the influence of her mother. She had wanted so much to achieve what her father thought her incapable of, using that drive to steer clear of the self-destructive nature she feared she might have inherited from her mother.

Her mother, who had been so weak, so needy for someone to fill the gap in her life, so desperate for the attention of a husband who did not love her that she had sought solace in the arms of countless lovers in addition to drugs and alcohol. Her mother had self-destructed: a combination of narcotics, a Ferrari and a tree ending her life when she was much too young.

Elaine knew all about the sort of bitterness Marco carried inside him, only his was much worse. At least her father loved her—even if he did try to impose his medieval ideals on her. What Marco had endured was unspeakable, and she knew his scars ran much deeper than hers.

The elevator ride from the bottom floor of the apartment building to Marco's top-floor penthouse left her feeling nauseous. She barely made it into the marble bathroom before losing the measly amount of food she'd managed to choke down during the last leg of the flight.

A warm hand settled on her clammy forehead and she tried to move away, hating that Marco was seeing her huddled up against the toilet, sweating and shaking.

"Is this normal?" he asked, his accent thickened with concern. "It doesn't seem like this can possibly be normal."

"I'm afraid it is. At least, that's what I've heard from female co-workers over the years," she said weakly.

"You must see a doctor. This cannot be good for the baby. You are not getting enough nutrition."

Of course he was concerned for the baby, not for her. Still, pleasure curled at the edges of her heart. He cared about the baby, as she was beginning to. She had been so frightened at first, so unable to believe that she could actually be pregnant, that it had been easy to detach. But now that the symptoms were so pronounced, now that she truly felt different, it was easier to believe, easier to imagine the reality of a child—her child—growing inside of her. It was easier to truly love the small baby that was nestled in the protective embrace of her womb.

"I know." She stood on shaky knees, feeling like a newborn giraffe and certain she looked just as ungainly. "My normal gynecologist is also an OB. I'll give her a call."

"What is her name?" Marco asked, the request more of a demand, coming from his autocratic mouth.

"Dr. Alyssa Calvin."

As soon as she'd blurted out the name Marco had retrieved his phone from his pocket and hit the one on his speed dial.

"Cassie, I need you to phone Dr. Alyssa Calvin and make an appointment for one o' clock today for Mrs. Elaine De Luca." He snapped the phone shut and placed it back in his jacket pocket.

"Marco! What if she has appointments?"

He shrugged. "Not my concern. I happen to be free today, and I want to be present at the appointment."

"What if I don't want you to be there?" she asked, knowing already that the argument was a loss. It would take several fully armed guards to stop Marco when he was on a mission.

"You would have me miss the medical confirmation of

our little miracle?" He regarded her closely, his sexy mouth pressed into a grim line. "Is there a reason for that?"

"Are you implying that I've lied to you about being pregnant?"

"It is not unheard of."

"You think I engineered *this?*" She gestured to the toilet.

"I've known a great many women who could empty their stomach contents on demand."

Rage vibrated through her. "I'm not going to spend the rest of this marriage trying to prove that I'm not plotting against you!"

Anger was replaced by a feeling of crushing defeat, and she swayed on her feet. Marco reached out an arm to steady her, bringing her close to the heat of his body. It was the first time she'd been so close to him since she'd found out about the baby and she melted into him, her body craving the heat from his.

Marco felt wetness from her tears penetrate the fabric of his shirt. Guilt assailed him. He was not a man who allowed uncertainties. He made decisions and he acted on them. He charted a course and he followed it. There was no room for doubt, no room for any sort of confusion. And yet with Elaine he wasn't certain of anything. She could be strong, yet she could also be achingly vulnerable. He wanted to lash out at her, condemn her for what she had done, and yet he also wanted to fold her into his embrace and promise her that everything would be all right.

"I'm sorry, Elaine."

She stiffened in his arms. "For?"

"For what I said a moment ago. I know you did not lie about being pregnant."

She pulled away from him and turned to face the vanity, trying to put her disheveled hair in order. "But you're not sorry for saying I orchestrated the whole thing in the first place?"

"It does seem rather convenient."

She laughed. "Oh, yes, so convenient. The vomiting combined with being married to a man who thinks me so mercenary that I would conceive his baby to get my hands on his cash is about the most *convenient* thing that has ever happened to me." Tears welled up in her blue eyes and spilled down her waxen cheeks.

His heart twisted, the pain from witnessing her anguish was like a physical blow.

He clenched his teeth and hardened himself against the unconscionable swell of emotion.

He turned away from her. "I cannot be manipulated, Elaine. Do not waste your time trying to appeal to my softer side with your tears."

It took every ounce of discipline to leave her standing there, looking shocked and injured, but he could not allow her to affect him. He'd never had trouble keeping his emotions separate from his affairs, and yet he had allowed Elaine to get closer, deeper inside of him, than he had ever allowed another woman to get.

It had been his mistake—trusting her, permitting her to mean something to him. He was not a fool. He had clawed his way up from the depths of poverty, he had built up a billion-dollar industry from nothing, and he would not allow himself to be taken down by a woman.

He would not make the mistake of trusting her again.

CHAPTER TEN

"Everything looks good, Mrs. De Luca," Dr. Calvin said as she wiped the ultrasound gel from Elaine's stomach. "I'll need to see you again in another month, but until then, unless you have any questions, I think you're free to go."

Elaine opened her mouth to say she didn't have any questions but Marco, who was standing next to the exam room bed, arms folded, looking like some Roman god of thunder, interrupted.

"You are certain that she can continue to work?"

Dr. Calvin gave Elaine an understanding smile before addressing Marco. "She should be able to continue all of her usual activities, within reason."

"But if her work is too stressful…"

"Then give her a foot-rub when she gets home. Really, Mr. De Luca, women have been having babies since the dawn of time. As much as it might feel that way, your wife isn't the first woman to experience pregnancy."

Elaine tried to hide the smile that crept slowly across her face. Marco was looking stormier than he had a moment ago.

It was easy to pretend that he was just like any other

concerned husband, even though she knew that was far from the truth. She was just the vessel to carry his child—the female figurehead who would play the role of mother to his heir. He hated her. He had made it abundantly clear that morning. If he'd experienced a moment of concern over her being sick it was simply because he was worried about the health of the baby.

Yet—silly, stupid woman that she was—she'd soaked in his attentiveness, craving his touch, the feel of his lips on hers. It was humiliating to love him so much when she knew that he would get rid of her if his conscience would allow it. Even more humiliating that she couldn't kill her love for him. And he couldn't kill the love she felt for him either, though he was doing a good job of trying.

When they left the doctor's office Marco's limo was already parked against the curb, waiting for them. Marco let her get in first, and when he sat down she noticed that he kept a long stretch of empty seat between them.

"I have to go to the office now," he said curtly.

"Then I'm going to work too," she said, daring him to disagree. "The doctor said it was fine."

He turned, his dark eyes flashing. "You need rest. You must be jet lagged, and you spent the entire flight being sick."

"I need to check in," she insisted.

"Absolutely not." He leaned forward and pressed the intercom, and spoke in rapid Italian to the driver. He leaned back heavily and pulled his BlackBerry out of his jacket pocket, intent on email and very purposefully ignoring her.

The car pulled up at the De Luca Corporation headquarters and Marco got out with barely a nod of farewell. The slam of the car door expressed the anger he had chosen not to voice.

She leaned back in the seat, fighting the uncharacteristic tears that were threatening to fall again. She *was* tired. She *did* just want to go home and curl up in a ball and sleep. But she was not going to be dictated to, and the sooner Marco realized that the easier life would be.

She pressed the button on the intercom. *"Scusi?"* She knew her Italian was pitiful, but she thought it would be best to at least try.

"Si?" Paolo's muffled voice came over the speaker.

"I've changed my mind. About going home, that is. I need to go to Burke and Black. It's on Sixth."

"Si."

She managed to make it through a half day without falling asleep at her desk, and took the rest of her work back to the penthouse to finish in the comfort of her own bed, with the aid of Chinese takeout.

Paolo, Marco's chauffeur, had made himself available to her when he wasn't shuttling Marco around, and he'd agreed to take her to her favorite Chinese restaurant and then back home.

She'd ordered three extra entrées with the feeble hope that Marco might be home in time for dinner, and that he might join her. Both desires seemed to be unlikely, but she was always painfully hopeful when it came to Marco.

Any normal person would be angry with him for the assumptions he'd jumped to, but it was becoming clear to her that when it came to Marco her emotions defied logic. There was some anger, but mostly she just ached for the boy who had grown up with no one to show him what true, unselfish love was, and for the man he had become—the man who couldn't trust anyone for fear of being hurt again.

She'd been hurt. Her own family had been a dismal example of suburban dysfunction, and she'd let that affect her. She'd also allowed what had happened with Daniel to halt her dating career. But none of those things mattered. Not now. She was making a new life with Marco, with their child. She was determined it would be a good life, better than the childhood either Marco or herself had experienced.

Finding out she was pregnant had been the single most terrifying thing that had ever happened to her, but after going to the doctor, after seeing the little barely formed shape on the ultrasound screen, she knew she wanted her baby. She knew she loved her baby.

She didn't know where the company would fit in yet. It still mattered—she'd worked her whole adult life at becoming qualified and finding a way to take over Chapman Electronics. But the baby had to come first. On that point both she and Marco were in total agreement.

Her stomach was begging for nourishment before she finally gave in and ate, abandoning the idea of a nice dinner together. She ate the Chinese food with none of the relish that she normally felt. It all just seemed bland without him.

She opted against working in her room, and spread all her documents out on the coffee table in her usual organized disaster. She tried to pretend she wasn't watching the clock and listening for the sound of the elevator moving between floors.

The overwhelming pull of exhaustion finally won out over her desire to be awake when Marco arrived home and she fell asleep on the couch, her work still spread over her lap.

The pinging of the lift doors jerked her out of her sleep. "Marco?"

He moved stiffly from the entry to the living area, his jaw tight, his eyes flat and unreadable. "You should be in bed."

"I was working and I fell asleep." She stretched, trying to get the kinks worked out of her joints.

"You need your rest," he said curtly. "This isn't good for the baby."

"There's leftover Chinese food in the fridge," she said, ignoring his autocratic statement.

"I already ate."

It hurt her that he'd had dinner without her, without even letting her know. It was a small, stupid thing, but in Hawaii, before she'd found out about the baby, they'd shared every meal together. Her face heated as she remembered the time they'd shared a mango at the private beach, and he'd let the juices of the sweet fruit drip down her chin before licking away the stickiness.

The face of the man standing before her and the face of the man in her memory were impossible to meld together. The man from the beach was a fantasy—her lover, her friend. This man was a cold, remote stranger.

She stood and took a step toward him. He turned away and began to move in the direction of his office. "I have more to do," he said by way of explanation. "I'll be leaving early for work, so I doubt we will see each other in the morning. Get some rest."

He left her standing there, her arms wrapped around herself, trying to hold in what body heat she had left, trying not to give in to the misery that was filling her entire being.

Marco managed to completely avoid her over the next week. He spent most of his time at the office, and when he wasn't there he was in the home office. She wanted nothing more than to close the ever-widening gap that had opened up between them, but he seemed determined to speak as few words to her as possible. He only ever talked to her to ask about her health, and that was out of concern for the baby.

She looked at the clock that hung on the wall of her cubicle. It was pushing nine o'clock and she was still at work. All of her co-workers had left hours ago, and she was still sitting, alternating between quadruple-checking that week's time card and adding up some data projections for Chapman Electronics. She didn't want to go home and face Marco's chilly silence. It was always painful, but she was even more aware of his rejection when they were both in the same space.

Finally, at ten, she knew that she couldn't avoid the penthouse any longer. Marco was likely to be cloistered in his office by now anyway, pretending she didn't exist. Her heart clenched.

By the time she made it back home she felt ready to fall asleep standing up. She'd had to take a cab home, which she didn't like to do, but she'd liked the prospect of walking home in the dark, almost overcome by exhaustion, even less. The lift doors swung open and she stumbled into the living room, fatigue slowing her movements.

Marco was standing by the bar in the living room, his expression dark. He brought the tumbler of Scotch in his hand down onto the marble bar with a crack. "Where have you been?"

"Work," she said, trying to sound flippant.

"Tell me, *cara mia*, how will you bleed me for child support if you drop dead from exhaustion before you are able to collect it?" He crossed the room in long strides.

Were it any other man he might have frightened her, but she knew that Marco would never harm her, no matter how angry he was.

"The doctor said going to work was fine. I don't have to take orders from you."

"No, but you might want to try and engage some common sense."

"It isn't as though I was out running the New York Marathon! Sitting behind a desk isn't likely to put me at any great risk!" Her tiredness began to ebb as adrenaline surged through her veins.

"Is that what you were doing? Because I've had hours to put together all the possible scenarios for how you were spending your time. You could have been injured. Something might have happened to the baby."

He was leaning close to her now, the spicy scent of his cologne teasing her nostrils, reminding her of forbidden pleasures. Pleasures that seemed as though they were from another lifetime.

"You could have been in the hospital, or worse, and you didn't even afford me a courtesy call to let me know you would be late. Your office phone rang straight to voicemail, and you didn't have your mobile on you either, so I had no way of reaching you." His dark eyes were blazing with more heat than she'd seen in over a week.

"I…I'm sorry. I didn't want to worry you." That much was true. She hadn't really imagined that Marco would care where she was. He seemed content to avoid and ignore her when they were in the same vicinity, and she certainly hadn't envisioned him pacing the floor in concern over finding her missing.

"Anything could have happened to you!" he said roughly. He stroked his thumb over her tender lower lip. "I pictured you lost. Hurt. I could not reach you. You cannot do that to me again."

He hooked an arm around her waist and leaned in,

claiming her mouth hungrily, desperately, his tongue plundering the depths of her mouth, his lips moving furiously over hers.

She was helpless to do anything but submit to his passion. She wrapped her arms around his neck, pouring every ounce of the frustration that had been building over the past few days into the kiss.

Marco drew Elaine hard against the length of his body and pressed his erection firmly against her. Let her feel what she did to him, what he was powerless to control.

Rage had reached boiling point, turning to passion, desperation. He forked his fingers through her mass of blond hair and began to press hot open-mouthed kisses to her neck, her collarbone, the faint shadow of cleavage that was just barely hinted at by her demure blouse.

When he'd returned home and found her gone he had imagined her leaving, returning to her old apartment, or simply disappearing. It had gutted him. Utterly. Completely. He had imagined never seeing his child, not being able to care for him, raise him. He had promised himself that if he were to ever have children their care would be his top priority. He had imagined losing that chance. Imagined having his child grow up believing his father did not care.

And he had imagined never seeing Elaine again. Never kissing her soft lips or sinking into her warm, willing body—never having her legs wrapped around him again as she cried out his name in ecstasy.

She would not leave. He knew she wouldn't. There would be no way for her to collect her precious company if she did that. And yet old fears had claimed him, images of being left, of feeling stranded and utterly, completely alone.

It's because of the child.

If not for the baby the gold-digger could go and latch

onto any other man she pleased. What he felt for her was all about sex and lust. He should not want her as he did—not knowing what she was. And yet he was a slave to his passion for her. At this moment he could no more deny himself her body than he could deprive himself of oxygen.

"I need you," she whispered, her voice broken, her body trembling.

"I need you too, *bella. Amore mia.*" He deftly unbuttoned her shirt and parted the fabric, revealing her pearly skin. Her perfect breasts were shielded from him by only the sheerest whisper of lace. "So beautiful."

He swept her up off the floor and carried her down the hall. Her eyes were wide, her kiss-swollen mouth parted in surprise. "I cannot wait," he said. He could hear the torture evident in his own voice.

He laid her down on his bed and knew that he had never seen a lovelier sight than this woman, spread out before him, offering herself to him with total trust, total desire.

He knelt down on the bed and leaned over her, kissing her softly on the lips. She squirmed beneath him. She was hot for him, ready for the next step. But he would make her wait. He would make her feel the desperation that consumed him, make her ache as he did.

His pulse pounded in his head as he undid the front clasp of her bra and pushed the flimsy cups aside, leaving her bare for his inspection. Her rosy pink nipples were puckered, begging for the attention of his mouth.

He swirled his tongue around one tightened bud, careful to avoid the pouting tip. She arched beneath him, her breathing ragged. A low moan escaped her lips as he laved the swollen flesh that surrounded her taut nipple. She bowed off the bed when the tip of his tongue brushed the dusky skin of her areola.

"Marco, I can't wait."

He lifted his head and cupped her chin in his hand. "But the waiting makes it so much sweeter, *cara mia*. I want you to burn for me."

"I do," she whispered, her blue eyes unveiled, the honesty of her words beyond question.

"For me. Only for me."

"Yes, Marco, my love. Please."

He removed his clothing as quickly as his unsteady fingers would allow. He joined her on the bed, bare skin to bare skin. He flicked open the closure on her pants and slid them down her shapely legs, taking her filmy panties with them and consigning them to the floor with the rest of their clothes.

He ran a finger up the inside of her thigh and her muscles quivered. "Elaine, *bella*, I would spend all night exploring your lovely body, but I cannot wait to have you."

He parted her thighs and moved between them, placing the tip of his erection at the opening of her slick channel. She gripped his shoulders, her dainty fingernails digging into his skin, the light pain making the blinding pleasure of easing into her tight, wet body almost bearable.

Her short cry of ecstasy and the gentle pulse of her internal muscles as he filled her to the hilt nearly sent him over the edge. He bit back a groan and tensed every muscle in his body, using every ounce of his self-control to keep himself from coming then and there.

Her sweet feminine sighs worked against the last vestiges of his control, shredding it, leaving him exposed. He pumped into her wildly, no longer able to think about making it last, no longer able to think about anything but the roar of ecstasy pounding through his blood, bringing him closer to completion with each stroke.

He felt her muscles clench around him, the rhythmic pulsing signaling her impending orgasm. He thrust into her hard, emptying himself into her, giving himself up to the blinding heat of his climax. She wrapped her legs tightly around his waist and gripped his shoulders, her petite body arching stiffly beneath him as she rode out the wave of her orgasm.

They lay entwined together, their breathing harsh and broken.

She'd called him her love.

He rolled away from her and sat up. His chest suddenly felt too full. He stood and walked into the bathroom, closing the door behind him. He turned the shower on cold and stepped under the harsh spray, trying to numb the conflicting feelings that had invaded his body.

Elaine brought her knees to her chest and tried to still her thundering heartbeat. She closed her eyes and attempted to block out the sound of the shower. The sound of Marco washing her off his skin.

Nausea rolled through her. There was no excuse for the way she'd behaved, for what she'd allowed herself to do. Marco had made his feelings for her plain, and yet she'd still fallen into bed with him at a speed that left her feeling a deep sense of shame.

It hadn't been this way before. She'd known that he hadn't loved her, but he hadn't hated her either. Tonight she had been nothing more than a body to him. Nothing more than a means of finding physical release. He had taken her to bed, joined himself to her in the most intimate way, and he'd hated her the whole time.

She climbed out of his bed and scrambled to collect her clothes. She clenched her hands into fists and tried to stop the uncontrollable shaking that had taken over her limbs. Tears blinded her vision. She hated what she'd allowed herself to do. That she'd let him use her like that—that she'd wanted him to do that to her even knowing how he felt about her.

It would be so easy to blame Marco, but the blame lay with her. She'd let herself become that weak-willed woman she'd hated all of her life.

She didn't know when it had started, but everything in her life now depended on Marco. The fate of the company, her happiness, her self-worth. Everything. She had despised her mother growing up, never understood how she had allowed her father's indifference to destroy her the way it had. She knew how it could happen now. She had been letting it happen to *her*.

Marco didn't love her. He never would. In her pig-headedness she'd imagined making him see her love, making him understand what love was, making him love her in return. It had never occurred to her that it wouldn't work out—not deep down. She, who should have lost every ounce of idealism at the hands of her awful childhood and her initiation into the real world as an adult, had not really believed that her ending would be unhappy.

In a blinding moment of clarity she saw herself in the future as a bitter, unhappy woman, unable to give her child the love and support it needed because she was so wrapped up in contriving ways to gain her husband's affection. An affection she would never be able to earn.

She covered her mouth with her hand to keep a sob from escaping.

She dressed quickly and went back to her own bedroom. She locked the door behind her and slid down the smooth wood, finally letting misery overtake her.

CHAPTER ELEVEN

AT FIVE-THIRTY the next morning she heard Marco's bedroom door open. She hadn't slept at all. She'd been packing. She'd only packed the essentials—nothing that had been purchased with Marco's money. Child support she would accept, but she wasn't going to take anything for herself.

She opened the door and walked slowly out into the kitchen, her shoes loud on the hard floor in the quiet of the morning.

Marco turned, his expression flat, no indication of what had passed between them the night before evident in his dark eyes. "You're up early. Are you feeling well?"

She swallowed, hoping he wouldn't hear the lump in her throat when she spoke. "I'm fine."

He turned away from her and poured a cup of coffee. She couldn't stop herself from drinking in his appearance—his broad shoulders encased in the tailored black suit jacket, his lean waist and hips. She took a breath and winced at the sharp pain that hit her heart. She might never have a chance to just look at him again, to take in all that masculine beauty that would never really be hers.

She took a shuddering breath. "Marco, I want a

divorce." Her words were amplified in the silence of the kitchen.

Marco stilled, his shoulders tightening. He turned toward her, the coffee mug gripped tightly in his fist. *"Che cosa?"* He spat out a tirade of violent Italian. She'd never heard Marco's English desert him before, but at that moment he seemed incapable of using his second language.

"I don't speak Italian," she said quietly.

"And I must not speak English very well," he said, his accent thick, "because I heard you asking for a divorce."

"I did," she said, striving for calm, trying to keep the wobble out of her voice.

"You will not get the company if you leave me. You know that, don't you?"

She blinked furiously. "I understand that. We had a deal, and I'm backing out of it. The terms of the contract are very clear."

She knew she was losing her chance at having the company and, far more painful than that, she was losing Marco, but she had to do it. She couldn't face waking up one day and discovering that she'd lost the essence of who she was, trying to gain the love and affection of a man who would prefer it if she'd never entered his life. The pain, the cost, were simply too great.

"And what about the baby?"

"I'm having the baby. A lot of people share custody of their children, Marco. We can make it work."

His lips went white around the edges and a deadly calm came over him. He turned away from her, as if suddenly he was uninterested in her. "If that is what you want, then of course I will not fight you. I did not want to be married to you any more than you desired to be married to me. I only suggested that we try to make it work for the sake of the baby, and for your own sake. It would have made your life much easier. I will have my lawyer contact yours, and we can discuss a custody arrangement that pleases both of us."

Numbness settled over her. Marco didn't care if she left. Maybe he didn't hate her. Maybe hate was an emotion that was far too passionate for him to bother feeling for her.

"I packed my essentials," she said quietly. "I was going to leave the rest."

"As you wish." He didn't turn to face her again.

"My lawyer will be in touch, then."

Marco made no effort to look at the lying witch's face. *"Si,"* he bit out.

He heard her timid footsteps as she crossed the wood floor and listened for the final click of the elevator doors. Then he threw his mug of coffee at the wall and watched it shatter, the dark liquid staining the pristine white of the wall. He clenched his fists, trying to control the driving need to tear the apartment apart, to make it as broken as everything else in his life. She had been in his bed last night. She had clung to him, dug her nails into his skin, cried out his name in ecstasy as he joined his body to hers. And this morning she had walked out the door without hesitation.

Why would she leave now? Why when she knew she would not get the company? He clenched his jaw. It didn't matter why. It was better that she was gone. Better that she leave now than in ten years. And he had never honestly thought that she would stay. A slow ache grew inside of him and he placed his hand on his chest to try and stanch the flow, shocked at the intensity of the real physical pain that he was feeling.

Yes. It was much better that she was gone now. He had already let her mean too much—had already let her get too far beneath his skin.

At least he had let her go without betraying his pain. He had clung to his mother, begged her not to go. It had made no difference. He would not debase himself like again— least of all for a faithless harlot.

He looked over at his tidy living room; the mess of paperwork that normally cluttered his coffee table was gone. Elaine was gone. He steeled himself against the onslaught of fresh pain that tore at the bloody hole in his chest where his heart used to be.

Elaine sat at her desk, ensconced in the privacy of her cubicle, and stared blankly at the gray walls while her fingers moved over her ten-key on autopilot.

Sometimes a smell or a sound would trigger a memory of her time with Marco, and a pain would assail her that was so swift, so acute, that it nearly made her knees give way.

She blinked. Her eyes felt like sandpaper. She had no more tears left in her after a week of constant crying jags. All that was left now was a deep-seated ache that pervaded her entire being.

"Mrs. De Luca?"

Fresh pain wrenched through her at the sound of her married name. She turned and saw one of the interns standing in her cubicle doorway, a manila envelope in her hand.

"Yes?" Elaine dug her nails into her palms, trying to offset the shooting pain that was racing through her body.

"This came for you just a minute ago."

The girl thrust the envelope into her hand. When Elaine saw the name of Marco's lawyer emblazoned across the top she started to feel dizzy.

The intern bent down in front of her. "Are you all right? You look sick."

Elaine nodded, trying to swallow. "I'm fine."

The girl nodded and left, giving Elaine a concerned, lingering look.

Elaine tore into the package, her fingers trembling. Inside was a very official-looking letter, obviously drafted by Marco. Elaine skimmed it, looking for mentions of the word "divorce".

When she'd finished the missive, her heart was pounding. He had given her the company. No strings. A *gift*. Which was perfectly in keeping with her father's contract. There was nothing that said she couldn't inherit the company, and nothing that said she couldn't receive it as a free gift.

A soft curse escaped her lips and she let the paper in her hand fall to the floor. He'd given her everything but what she wanted most. She just wanted him. It was a bitter moment to discover that the company, her life's ambition, meant absolutely nothing without Marco by her side to share in it with her.

Early Saturday morning Elaine walked through the dimly lit halls of Chapman Electronics and took the elevator to the top floor—to her new office. She still had two weeks left at Burke and Black, and she wasn't about to leave her co-workers in the lurch by leaving without notice.

Her father's former secretary, Lynne, had agreed to come in later that morning and help her get familiarized with the layout of things. Elaine would have to remember to get the older woman a gift for being so nice.

She opened the door to the office and grimaced. It was exactly as she remembered it: stuffed duck mounts frozen in eternal flight on the wall, a dark wooden desk and forest-green carpet. She would change everything about it as soon as possible.

She positioned herself in the wingback chair and laid her head down on the desk, hoping the cold surface would cool her heated skin. She was suddenly very aware that she had no one to share this moment with.

She cradled her flat stomach with her hand. "Well, little one, I made it. Funny thing is it doesn't seem so important anymore." A fat tear slid down her cheek and splashed onto the desk.

She ached for Marco's touch, for the sound of his husky, faintly accented voice, for his presence. She clenched her fist and sat up straight. This was why she'd left in the first place. It wasn't healthy, this obsessive unreturned love. The pain would fade; her feelings would fade. They had to.

She spent the rest of the morning getting to know her father's antiquated filing system with the aid of the ever-helpful Lynne. By lunchtime her stomach was shouting at her to get nourishment quickly, and she'd learned since becoming pregnant that she couldn't ignore hunger pangs when they started gnawing at her.

"I think I'm going to order some Chinese food. Lynne, do you want anything?"

The other woman flushed a bit. "No, I brown bagged. Actually, you have a lunch appointment."

"I do?" Her stomach protested the idea of anything coming between her and her sweet and sour chicken.

"Yes. It's an old appointment, and it couldn't be re-scheduled. You can handle it though. You're a sharp girl."

"Thanks, Lynne. I'd still like to order some Chinese, though."

"I'll take care of it for you," Lynne said, backing out of the office with a smile.

"Sweet and sour chicken, please!" she shouted through the closed door.

For the first time in more than a week the pain her chest had ebbed, replaced by a teeming fleet of butterflies in her stomach that were threatening to demolish her critical thinking skills. She didn't even know what the meeting was about, much less if she was ready for it!

Of course you are! You've been training for this day all of your adult life!

She leaned back in her chair and smoothed her hair down, trying to look cool and professional. She straightened a line of pencils on the desk four different times in an effort to keep her hands busy.

Only five minutes later the door to her office cracked open and the smell of crispy chicken wafted into the room. She pulled her head up sharply and blinked. She'd finally started hallucinating. Because there was no way that Marco was standing in the doorway holding takeout boxes. She had fantasized about him too many times. Had dreamt that he was with her again, in bed, holding her tightly against his body, his heartbeat pounding rhythmically against her back.

"I assume that your craving is still sweet and sour?" He moved into the room, bringing the tantalizing smell of food and the musky, unique scent that was all Marco with him.

She nodded dumbly. "You're my lunch appointment?" She still didn't fully believe that the man standing in front of her was really there.

"Yes. I'm sorry. I asked Lynne to tell a white lie for me." Which explained why Lynne had looked so sheepish!

"What…what are you doing here?"

"I'm here to see you." He spread his hands apart in a helpless gesture.

"Did you bring your lawyer?"

"I thought it might be best if we talked without legal counsel present." Marco sat heavily in the chair that was placed in front of her desk.

She'd been so bowled over by his presence that she hadn't noticed until just then how worn out he looked, how tired. His lean face looked almost sunken; his golden pallor had an ashen overtone. His normally immaculate hair looked as though he'd run his fingers through it too many times, and the brackets around his mouth looked as if they'd deepened. He looked exactly as she felt. Older. Tired.

Marco looked up, his dark eyes holding a depth of emotion she couldn't fathom. "I want you to come back."

She put a hand to her breast to try and keep her heart from leaping out of her chest. It was her every fantasy come true. Except she had left him, and her reasons for leaving were still sound. She loved him, body and soul, but having that love unreturned would ultimately destroy her.

"I can't, Marco." She formed the words slowly, her mouth rebelling against the order to speak them.

"What is it you need? An allowance? A different home? I can give you whatever you need."

"No. I don't think you can."

He swore violently and stood from the chair. "Do you need me to beg? Because I promised myself I would never lay down my pride like that again. But if that is what it takes to get you to come home to me I will do it and condemn my pride to hell. Please, Elaine. Come home to me."

"Marco…"

"I love you. And I will do whatever it takes to make you love me in return."

Her mouth went completely dry, and it seemed as if the walls of the office, the desk, the chair, everything holding her to the earth had fallen away, leaving only the two of them. "You're just saying that because of the baby," she said hoarsely.

"No. I love our unborn child, but you're the one who has left a gaping hole in my life. I miss your laughter. I miss your wit, your beauty, your body—the mess you leave on my coffee table," he ground out. "I miss your smell, your touch, arguing with you. I miss everything about you, Elaine, and I need you to come home to me. I need you to be my wife in every sense of the word."

Fresh tears welled up in her eyes and she fought to speak around the lump that had formed in her throat. "But you seemed so…indifferent when I left."

"I was an idiot. I was clinging to my pride. I didn't want you to know. I didn't want to face what you had come to mean to me. But I'm done having pride. It means nothing if I cannot have you. I would rather lose everything I have than lose you. I know I said unforgivable things to you when you told me about the baby and I cannot make excuses." He rounded the desk and knelt before her, taking her hands in his. "I can only explain to you what I felt. I felt too much for you—more than I ever had for any woman. It was much easier to tell myself that you had tricked me, that you were not who I believed you to be. Anything to lessen my attachment for you. But nothing worked. I had already begun to love you, though I was too much of a fool to see it. When you said you were leaving I told myself it was best—that you, like everyone else in my life, would leave eventually, and it was better if you did it sooner than later. I knew the moment you'd gone, the moment you forfeited the company, that I was the only liar among the two of us. I had lied to myself. I know you don't feel the same way, but I can make you happy. We can be a family."

"Marco." She threw her arms around his neck and kissed his face—the face that she loved so painfully. "I love you too—so much!"

"But you left."

"I know. I was an even bigger idiot than you were," she said, laughing through her tears. "I was afraid that by staying, by loving you, I would become my mother—that I would lose myself in an effort to gain your affection. I was arrogant enough to think that I was not at all affected by my childhood, that you were the one who needed to learn about love. But I was just as guilty of bringing the past in, of returning to old hurts and using them to shield myself from hurt. I was a big coward."

"No bigger than I was. When you left I lost myself. I had never felt such pain—not even after losing my mother. I knew I had made a mistake—the biggest of my life—driving you away. I wanted to beg you to stay then, but I knew I wouldn't be able to face it if I threw myself on the ground before you and you left anyway. Like my mother did."

Her heart clenched. "Oh, Marco. I'm so sorry." She cradled his head against her breast. A momentary surge of rage at the woman who had hurt Marco so badly nearly stole her joy. "The past has a lot to make up for."

"I think we can start now. We're building a strong future." He put his hand on her stomach.

"Why did you give me the company, Marco?"

"Because it was what you wanted. And I wanted you to be happy, even if your happiness did not lie with me. At least that's what I told myself. But today…I couldn't stay away any longer." He leaned in from his position on the floor and kissed her gently on the lips—a kiss of barely leashed passion, a kiss of love. "I'd like it if we could work at rebuilding Chapman Electronics together. I love how your mind works. I'd love a chance to see you in action."

"What about when the baby comes?"

"We'll do whatever you think is best. We can put a daycare facility in the building, or we could alternate days so that one of us is always with him."

Her eyes widened. "Well, that's very progressive of you. I think you might be getting enlightened."

"Don't let it get around."

"I would never try to damage your formidable reputation." She slid out of her chair and knelt with him on the floor, wrapping her arms tightly around him. "I don't know exactly what I want to do after I have the baby. I'm sure I'll want to stay home for a few months at least. But I am also sure that I love you, and that I want to spend the rest of my life with you. So what do you think?"

"I think—" he pressed a kiss to her neck "—that marriage is the only logical course of action."

She laughed. "Oh, is that right?"

"Mmm." He trailed kisses from just beneath her ear down to her collarbone, swirling his tongue in the hollow at the base of her neck. "I've done my research." He flicked the buttons of her blouse open.

She sucked in a breath as he feathered kisses over the swell of her breasts. "Have you?"

"Yes. And according to my research you and I are destined to be together forever and ever."

"Is that so?" she gasped.

"It's an indisputable fact. My figures are always accurate." He nipped her neck and she melted into him.

"And how did you arrive at your conclusion?"

"It's very simple. I love you. And I will love you, and honor you, and cherish you, for all of my days."

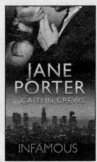
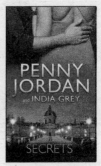
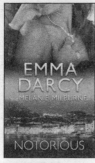

Happy ever after is only the beginning!

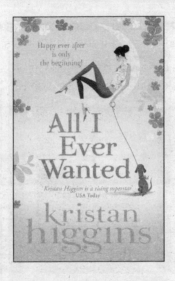

Callie Grey has got a great job, a great man and, fingers crossed, a whopping great diamond—then her boss/boyfriend gives her dream and her sparkly ring to someone else…

She's spent her life reaching for the moon. Now Callie's let go and, falling among the stars, who will be there to catch her?

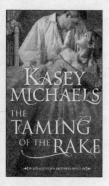

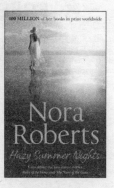

Have Your Say

You've just finished your book.
So what did you think?

We'd love to hear your thoughts on our
'Have your say' online panel
www.millsandboon.co.uk/haveyoursay

- 🌹 Easy to use
- 🌹 Short questionnaire
- 🌹 Chance to win Mills & Boon® goodies

The World of Mills & Boon®

There's a Mills & Boon® series that's perfect for you. We publish ten series and with new titles every month, you never have to wait long for your favourite to come along.

Blaze® — Scorching hot, sexy reads

By Request — Relive the romance with the best of the best

Cherish™ — Romance to melt the heart every time

Desire™ — Passionate and dramatic love stories